GLITCH

SARAH GRALEY

PLAYBOX
DUNGEON CITY
DUNGEON CITY

graphix
An Imprint of
SCHOLASTIC

All rights reserved. Published by Graphix, an imprint of Scholastic Inc.,
Publishers since 1920. SCHOLASTIC, GRAPHIX, and associated logos are
trademarks and/or registered trademarks of Scholastic Inc.

The publisher does not have any control over and does not assume
any responsibility for author or third-party websites or their content.

Library of Congress Control Number: 2018948934

ISBN 978-1-338-17452-6 (hardcover)
ISBN 978-1-338-17451-9 (paperback)

10 9 8 7 6 5 4 3 2 1   19 20 21 22 23

Printed in China   62
First edition, May 2019
Edited by Cassandra Pelham Fulton
Book design by Shivana Sookdeo
Lettering and color flatting by Stef Purenins
Creative Director: Phil Falco
Publisher: David Saylor

J
FIC
GRA

For my parents.
Thank you for believing in me
and for getting me into
video games at an early age.

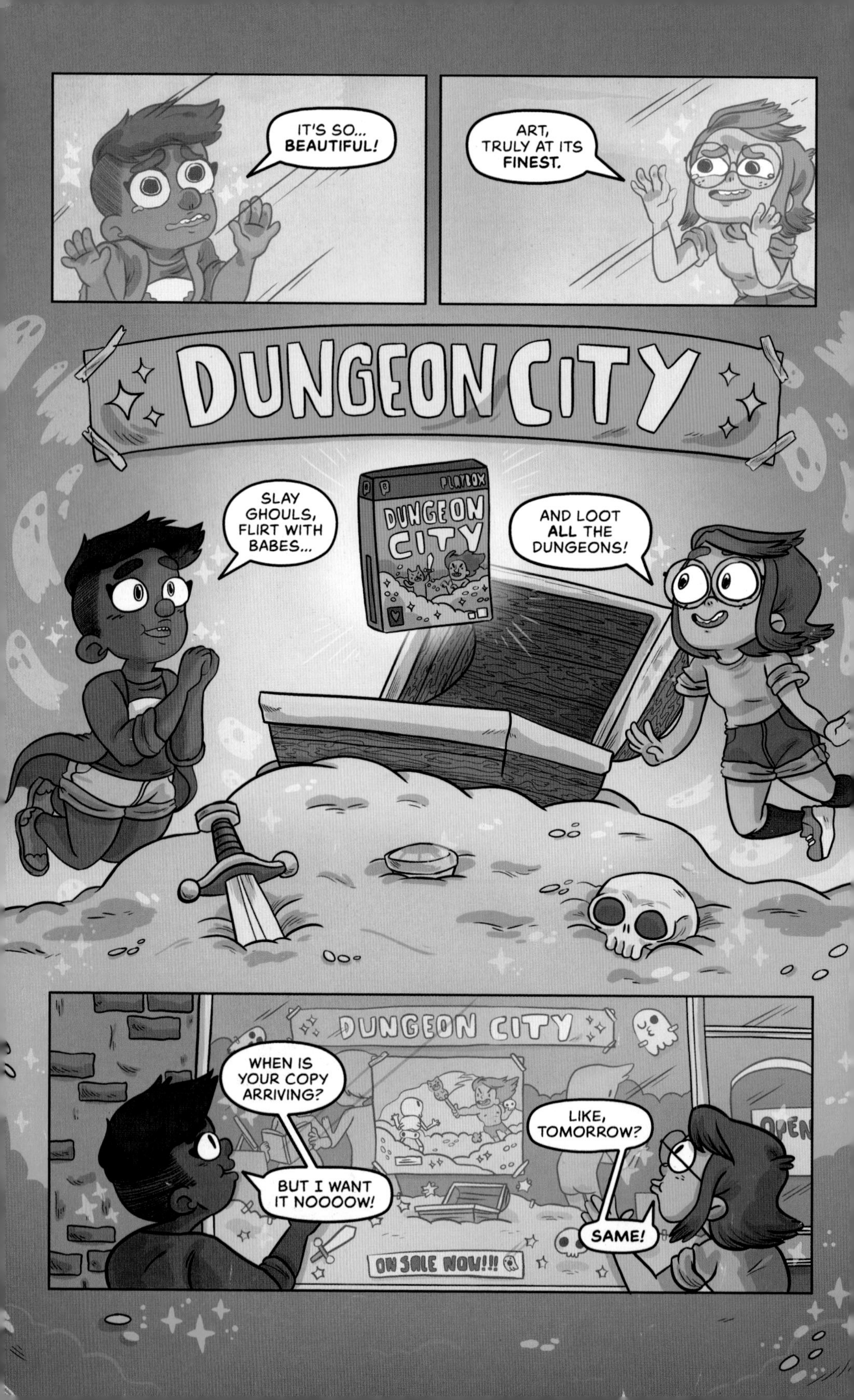
IT'S SO... BEAUTIFUL!
ART, TRULY AT ITS FINEST.
DUNGEON CITY
PLAYBOX
DUNGEON CITY
SLAY GHOULS, FLIRT WITH BABES...
AND LOOT ALL THE DUNGEONS!
DUNGEON CITY
WHEN IS YOUR COPY ARRIVING?
LIKE, TOMORROW?
BUT I WANT IT NOOOOW!
SAME!
ON SALE NOW!!!

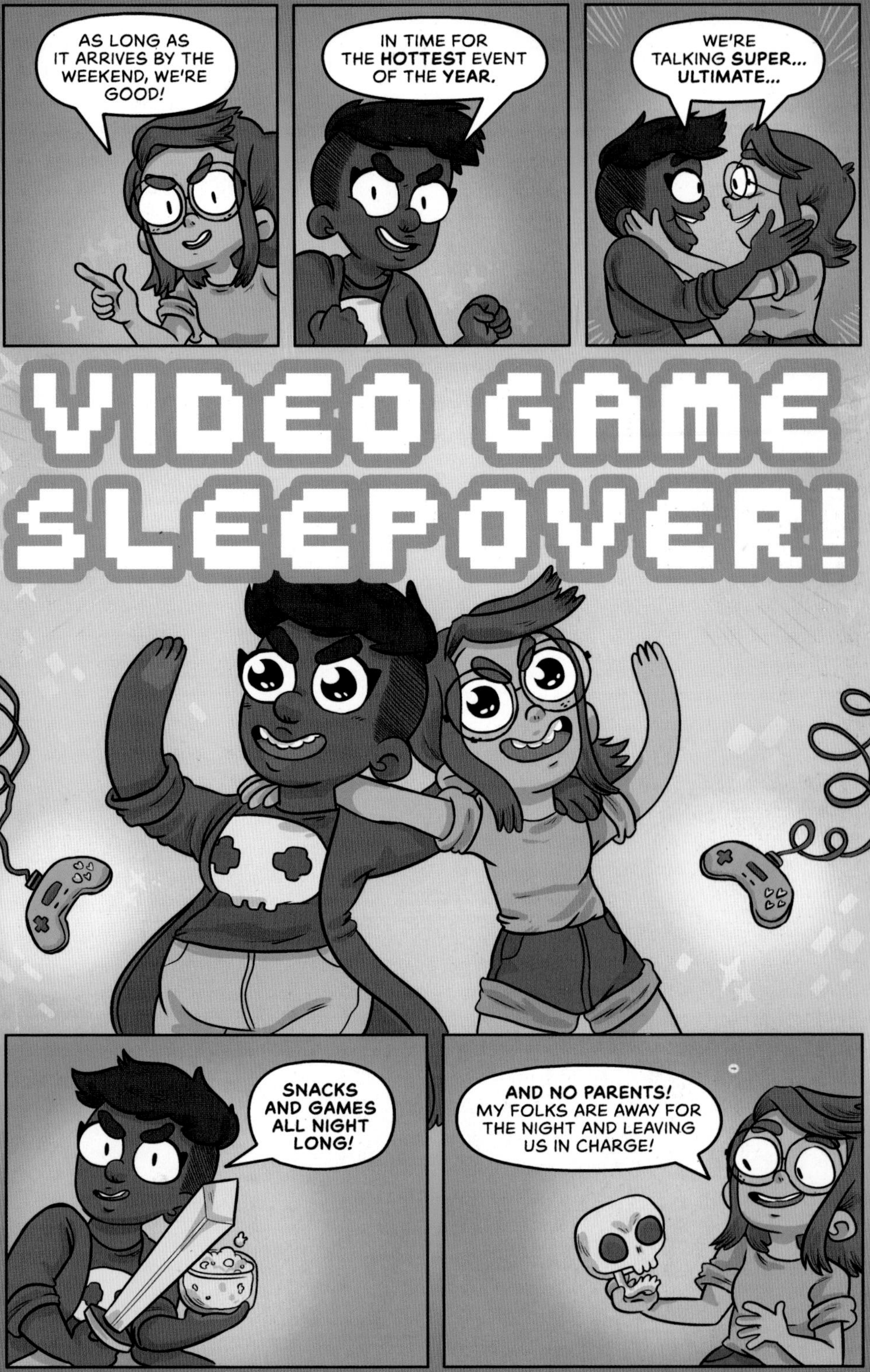

AS LONG AS IT ARRIVES BY THE WEEKEND, WE'RE GOOD!
IN TIME FOR THE HOTTEST EVENT OF THE YEAR.
WE'RE TALKING SUPER... ULTIMATE...
VIDEO GAME SLEEPOVER!
SNACKS AND GAMES ALL NIGHT LONG!
AND NO PARENTS! MY FOLKS ARE AWAY FOR THE NIGHT AND LEAVING US IN CHARGE!

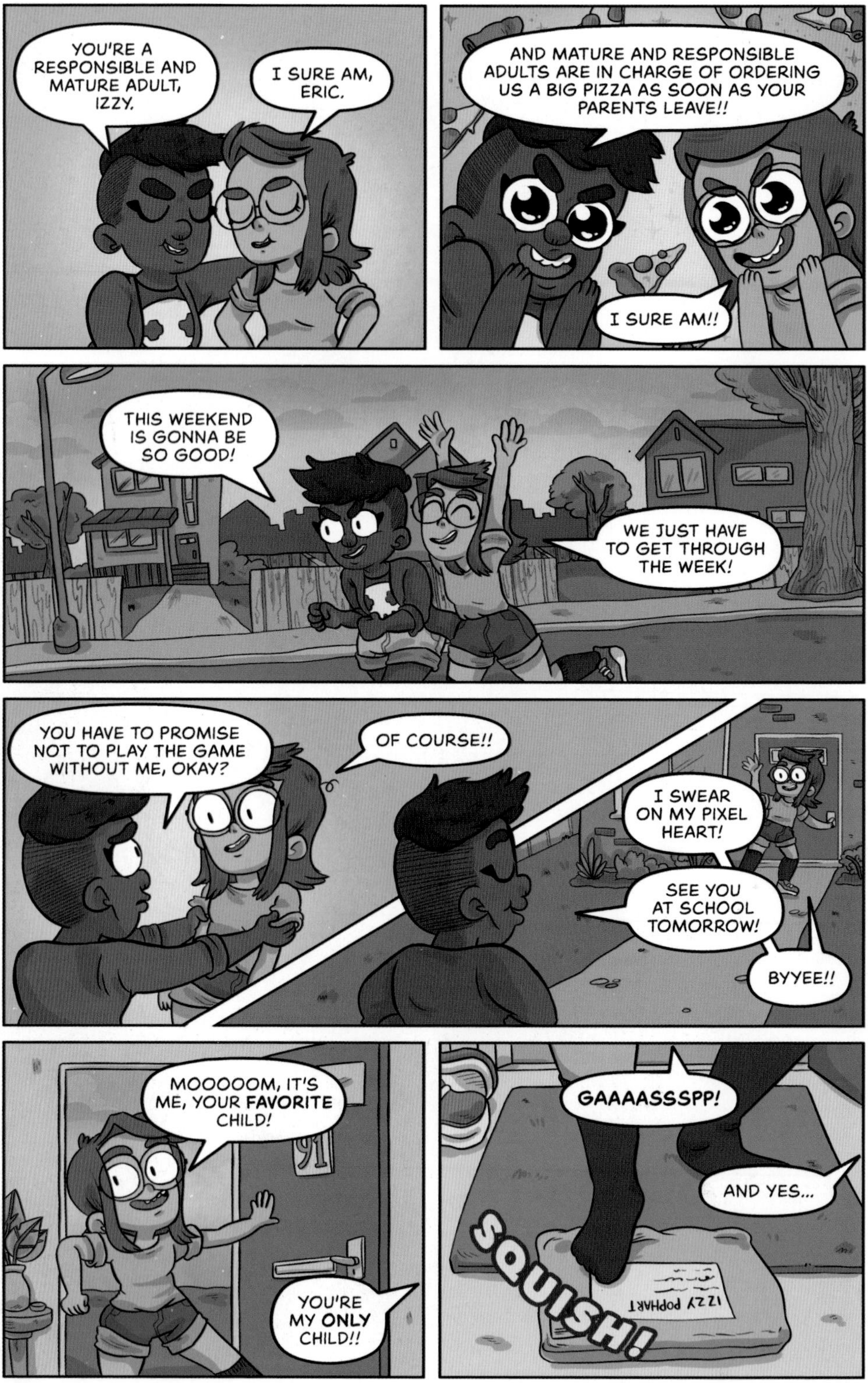
YOU'RE A RESPONSIBLE AND MATURE ADULT, IZZY.
I SURE AM, ERIC.
AND MATURE AND RESPONSIBLE ADULTS ARE IN CHARGE OF ORDERING US A BIG PIZZA AS SOON AS YOUR PARENTS LEAVE!!
I SURE AM!!
THIS WEEKEND IS GONNA BE SO GOOD!
WE JUST HAVE TO GET THROUGH THE WEEK!
YOU HAVE TO PROMISE NOT TO PLAY THE GAME WITHOUT ME, OKAY?
OF COURSE!!
I SWEAR ON MY PIXEL HEART!
SEE YOU AT SCHOOL TOMORROW!
BYYEE!!
MOOOOOM, IT'S ME, YOUR **FAVORITE** CHILD!
91
YOU'RE MY **ONLY** CHILD!!
GAAAASSSPP!
AND YES...
SQUISH!
IZZY POPHART

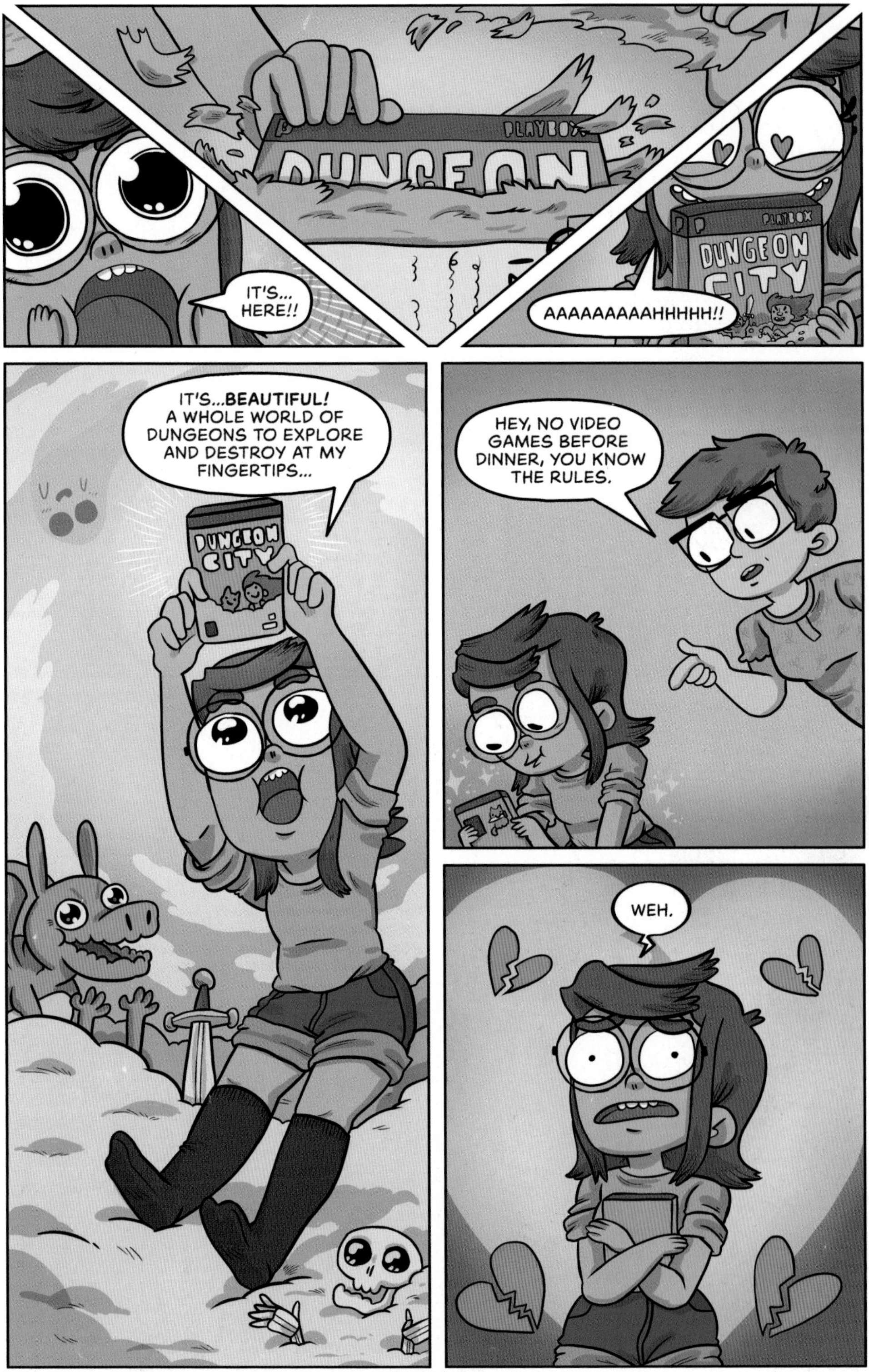
PLAYBOX
DUNGEON
IT'S...
HERE!!
PLAYBOX
DUNGEON
CITY
AAAAAAAAAHHHHH!!
IT'S...BEAUTIFUL!
A WHOLE WORLD OF
DUNGEONS TO EXPLORE
AND DESTROY AT MY
FINGERTIPS...
DUNGEON
CITY
HEY, NO VIDEO
GAMES BEFORE
DINNER, YOU KNOW
THE RULES.
WEH.

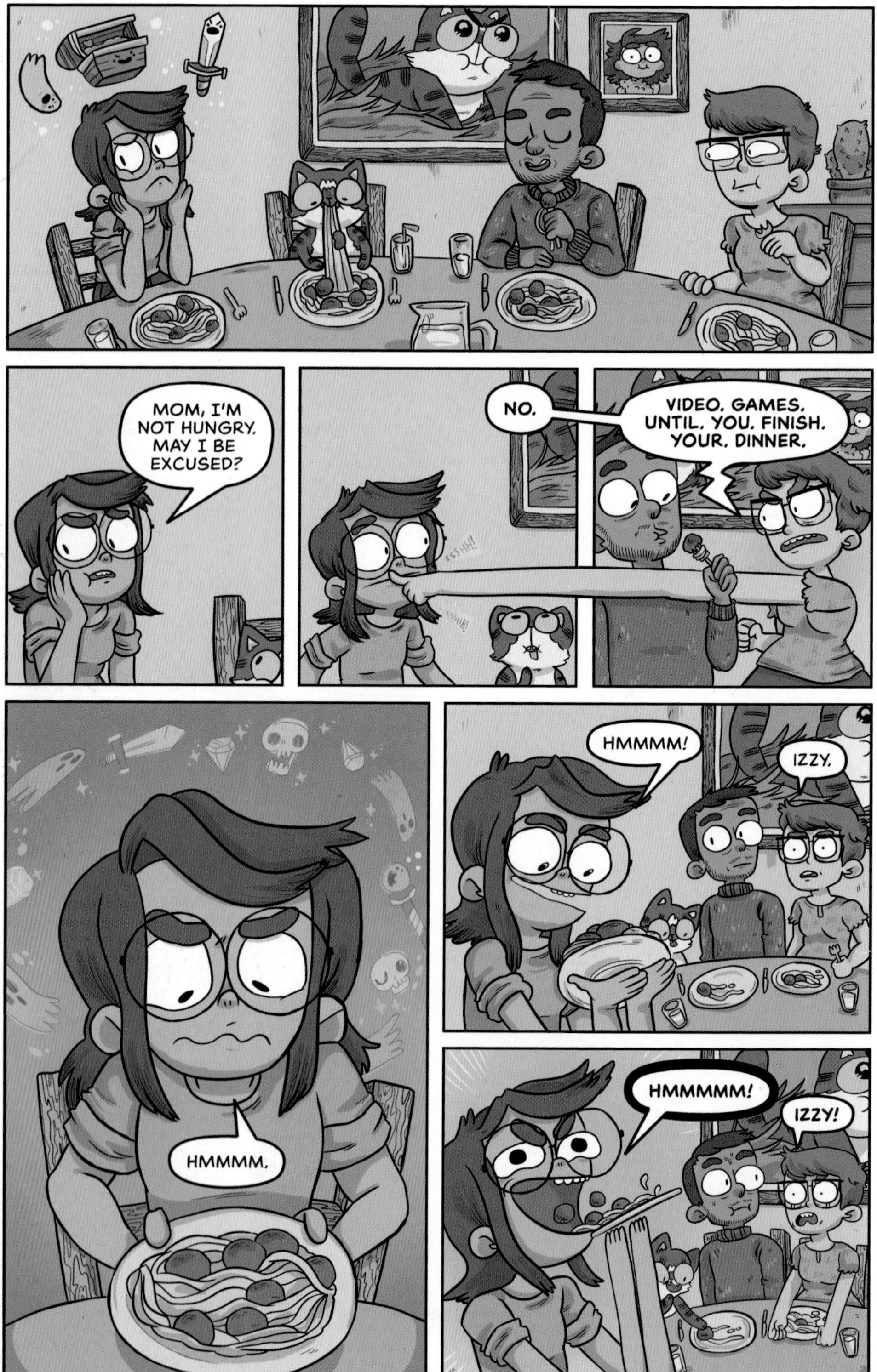
MOM, I'M NOT HUNGRY. MAY I BE EXCUSED?
NO.
VIDEO. GAMES. UNTIL. YOU. FINISH. YOUR. DINNER.
HMMMM.
HMMMM!
IZZY.
HMMMMM!
IZZY!

HA HA HA

FINALLY! I'VE BEEN WAITING FOREVER TO PLAY THIS GAME!!

I DID PROMISE ERIC I WOULDN'T PLAY IT WITHOUT HER...

BUT I **SHOULD** CHECK THAT THE DISK WORKS!

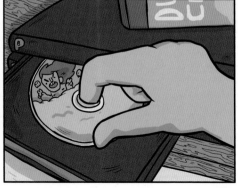

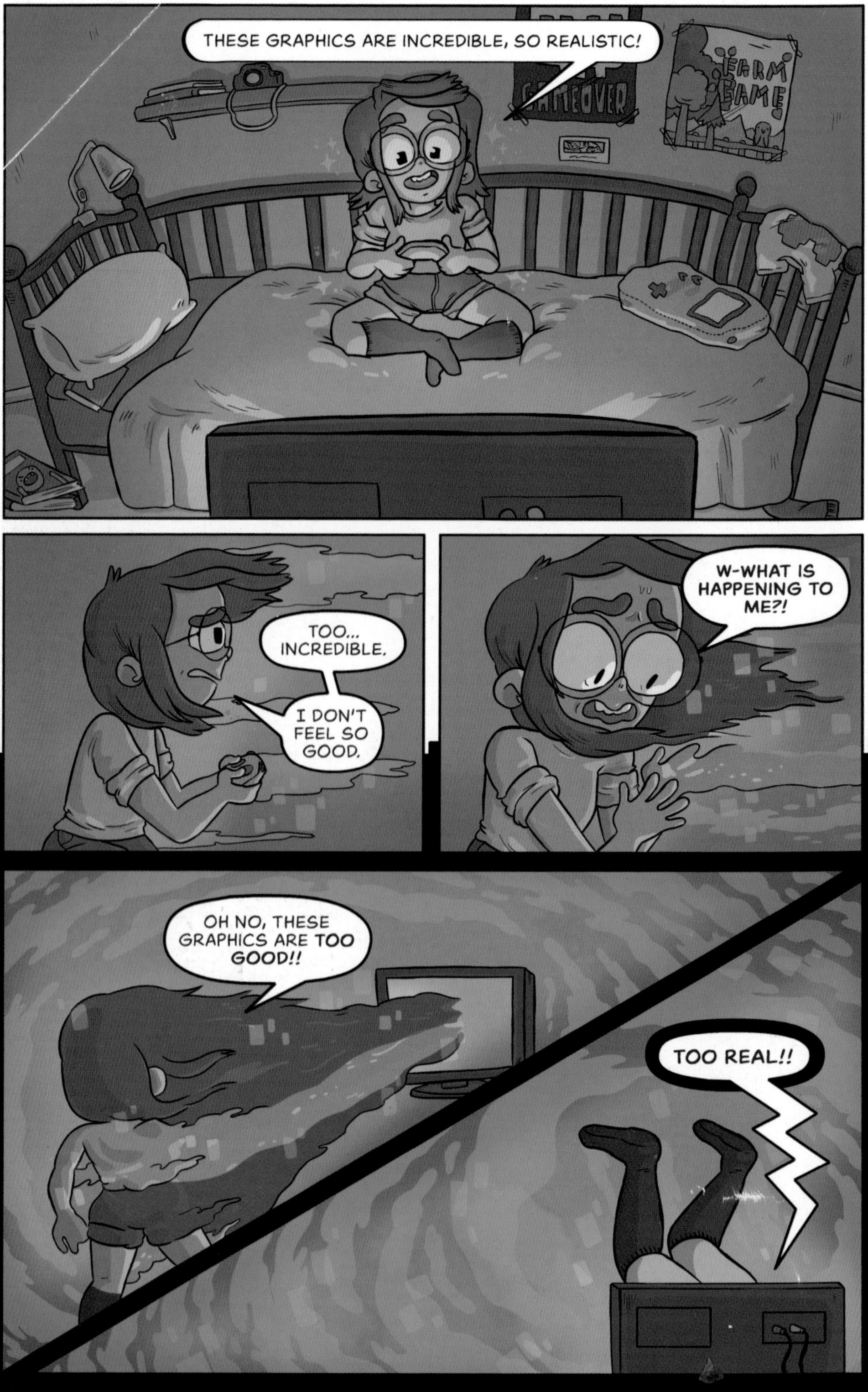
THESE GRAPHICS ARE INCREDIBLE, SO REALISTIC!
GAMEOVER
FARM GAME
TOO... INCREDIBLE.
I DON'T FEEL SO GOOD.
W-WHAT IS HAPPENING TO ME?!
OH NO, THESE GRAPHICS ARE **TOO GOOD!!**
TOO REAL!!

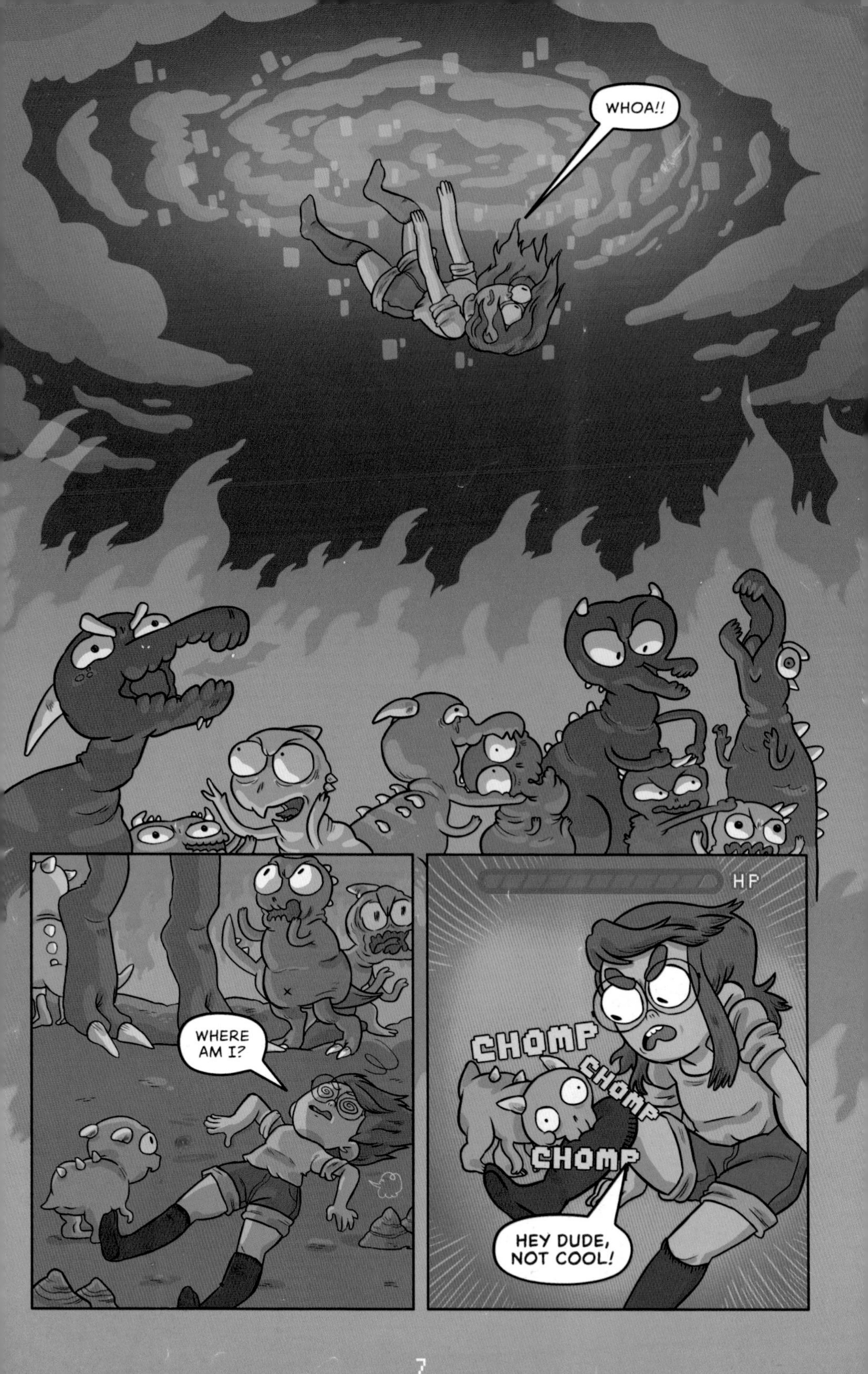
WHOA!!
WHERE AM I?
HP
CHOMP
CHOMP
CHOMP
CHOMP
HEY DUDE, NOT COOL!

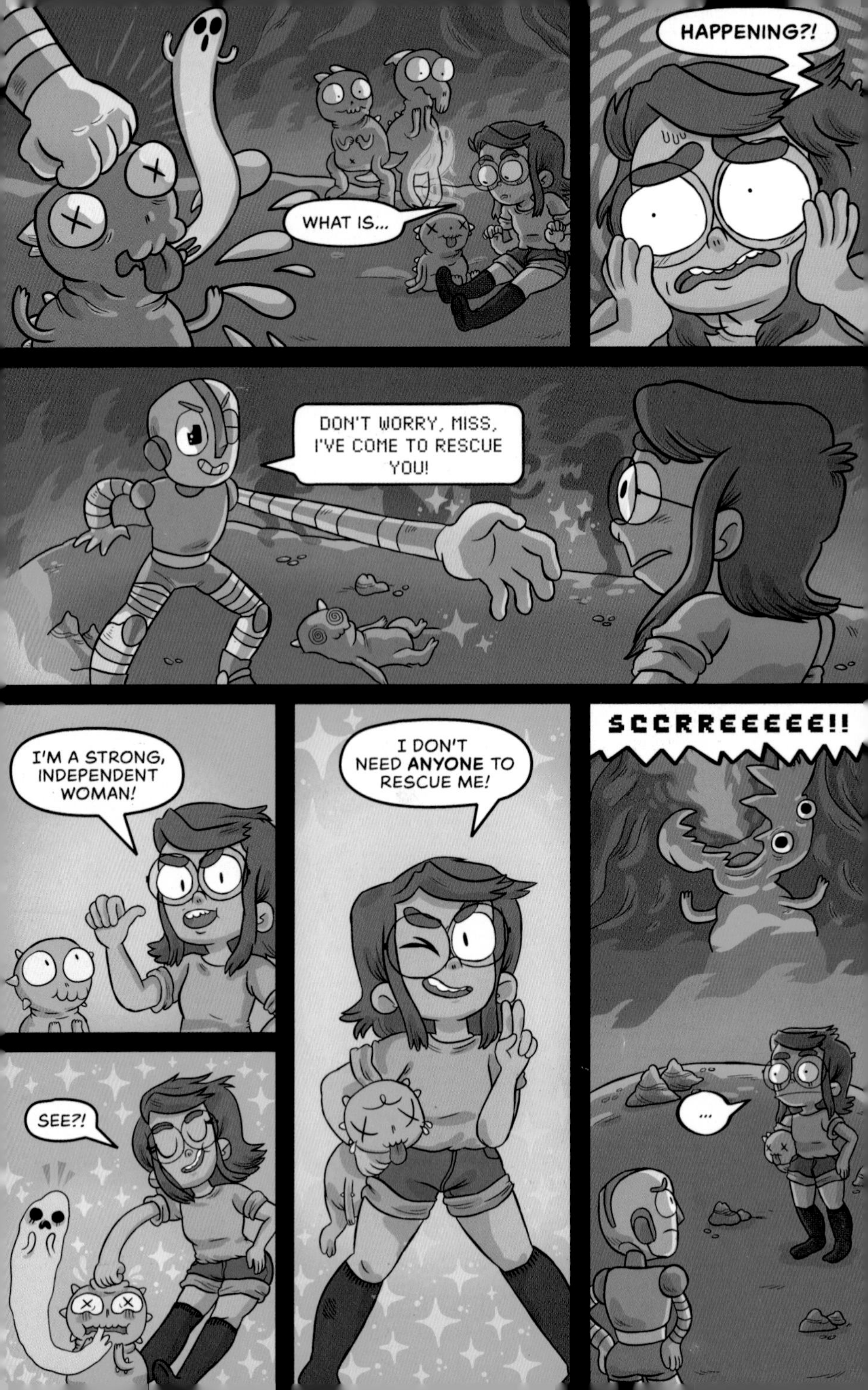
WHAT IS...
HAPPENING?!
DON'T WORRY, MISS, I'VE COME TO RESCUE YOU!
I'M A STRONG, INDEPENDENT WOMAN!
SEE?!
I DON'T NEED **ANYONE** TO RESCUE ME!
SCCRREEEEEE!!
...

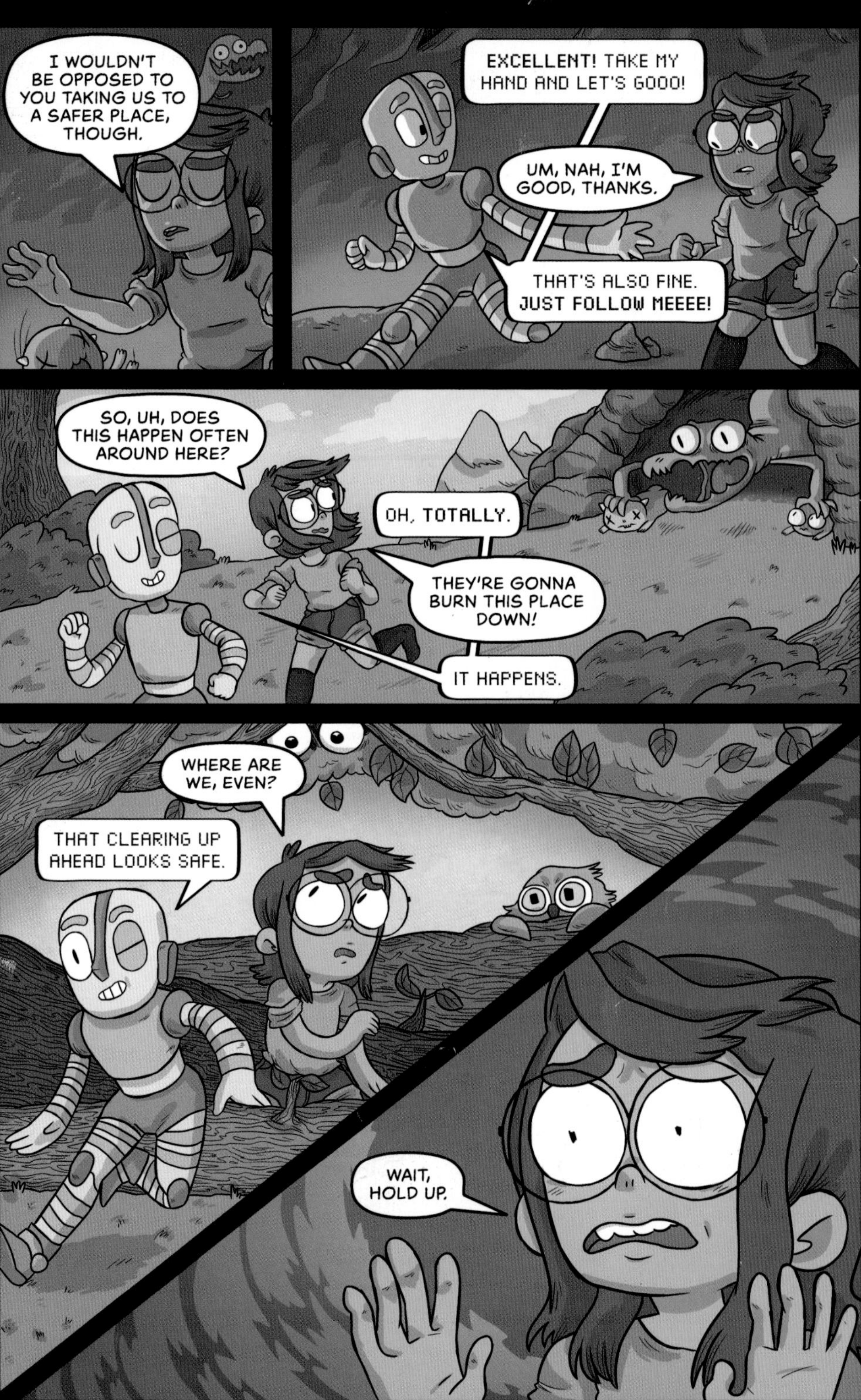
I WOULDN'T BE OPPOSED TO YOU TAKING US TO A SAFER PLACE, THOUGH.
EXCELLENT! TAKE MY HAND AND LET'S GOOO!
UM, NAH, I'M GOOD, THANKS.
THAT'S ALSO FINE. JUST FOLLOW MEEEE!
SO, UH, DOES THIS HAPPEN OFTEN AROUND HERE?
OH, TOTALLY.
THEY'RE GONNA BURN THIS PLACE DOWN!
IT HAPPENS.
WHERE ARE WE, EVEN?
THAT CLEARING UP AHEAD LOOKS SAFE.
WAIT, HOLD UP.

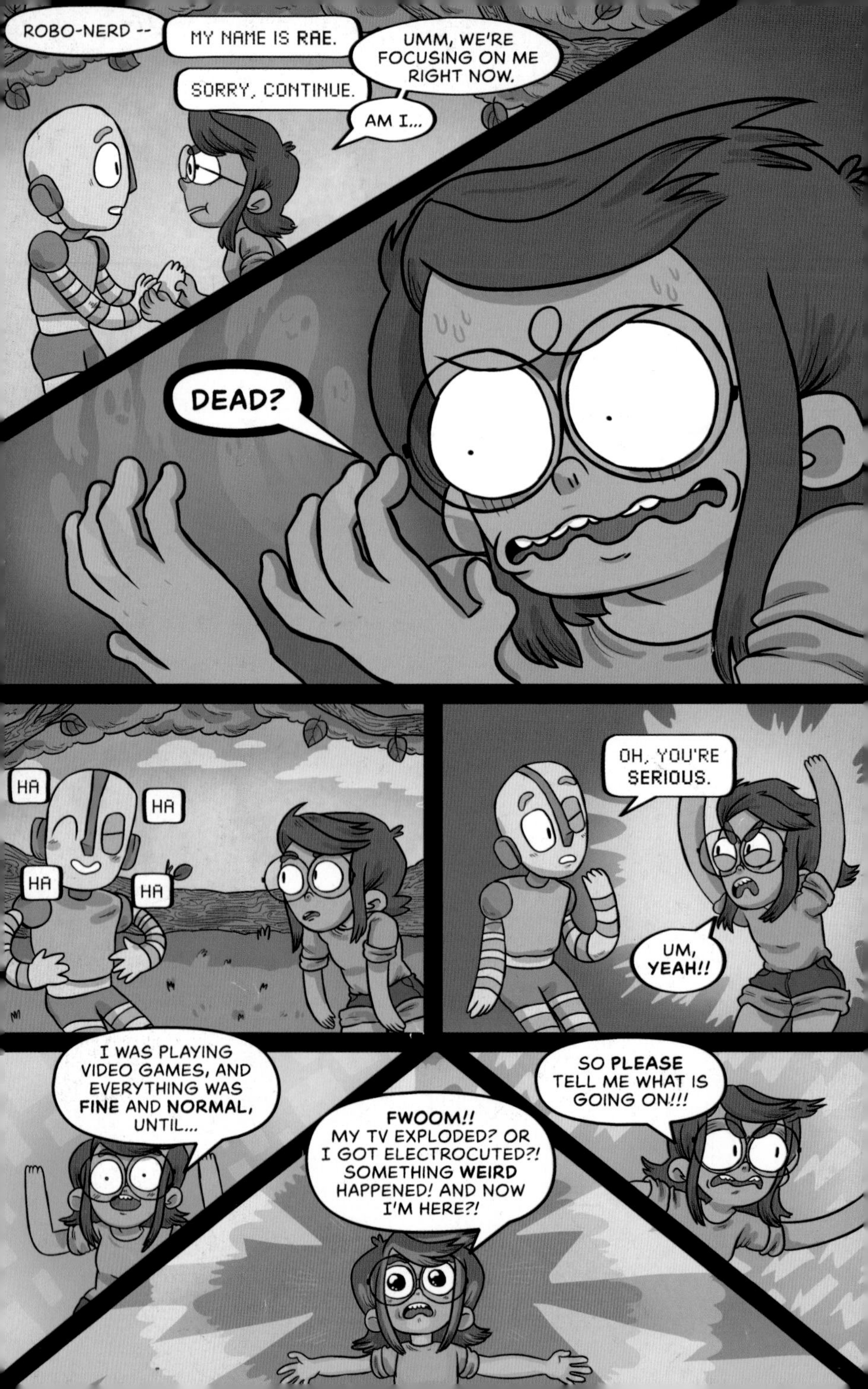
ROBO-NERD --
MY NAME IS RAE.
UMM, WE'RE FOCUSING ON ME RIGHT NOW.
SORRY, CONTINUE.
AM I...
DEAD?
HA
HA
HA
HA
OH, YOU'RE SERIOUS.
UM, YEAH!!
I WAS PLAYING VIDEO GAMES, AND EVERYTHING WAS FINE AND NORMAL, UNTIL...
FWOOM!! MY TV EXPLODED? OR I GOT ELECTROCUTED?! SOMETHING WEIRD HAPPENED! AND NOW I'M HERE?!
SO PLEASE TELL ME WHAT IS GOING ON!!!

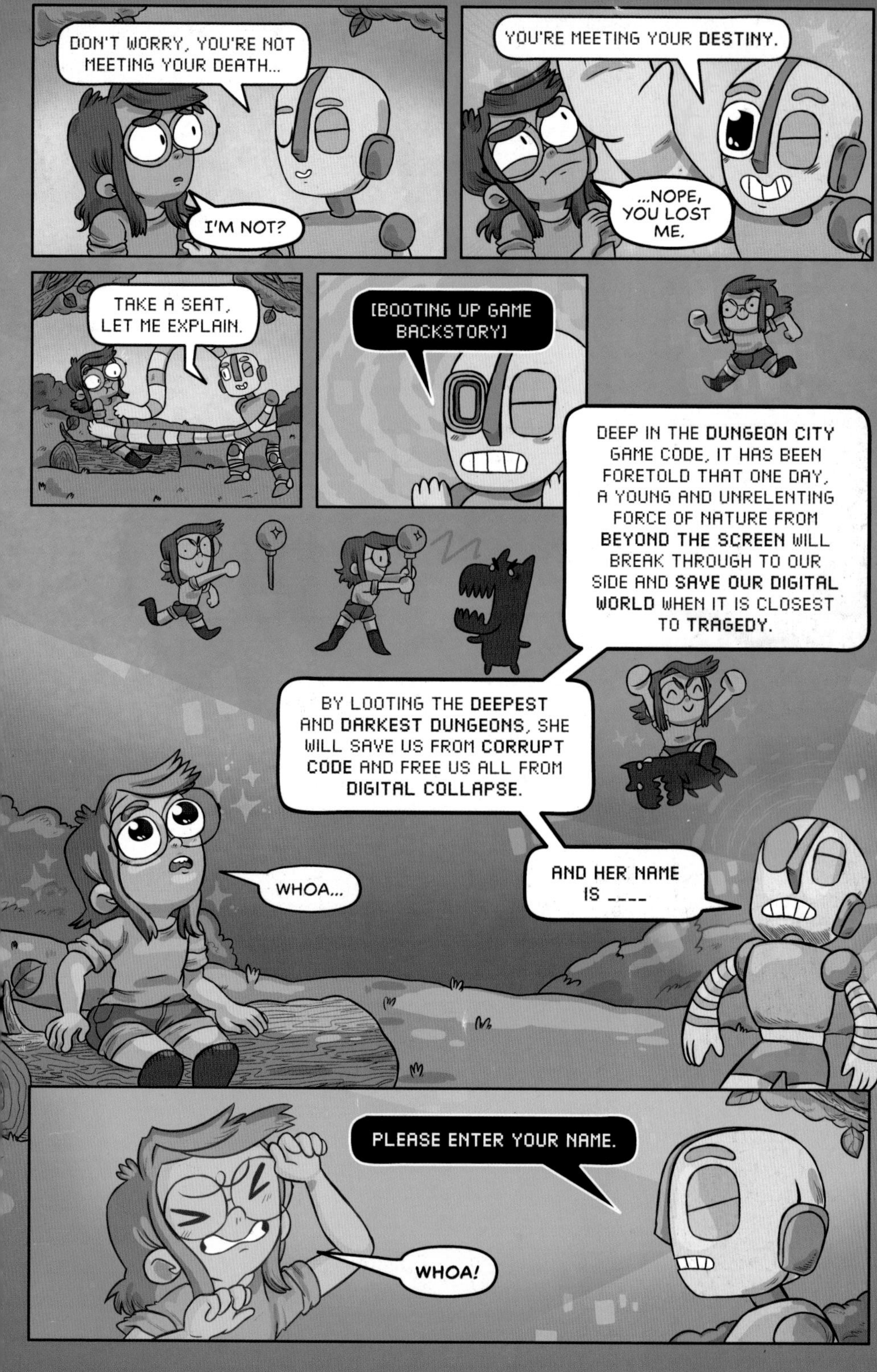
DON'T WORRY, YOU'RE NOT MEETING YOUR DEATH...
I'M NOT?
YOU'RE MEETING YOUR DESTINY.
...NOPE, YOU LOST ME.
TAKE A SEAT, LET ME EXPLAIN.
[BOOTING UP GAME BACKSTORY]
DEEP IN THE DUNGEON CITY GAME CODE, IT HAS BEEN FORETOLD THAT ONE DAY, A YOUNG AND UNRELENTING FORCE OF NATURE FROM BEYOND THE SCREEN WILL BREAK THROUGH TO OUR SIDE AND SAVE OUR DIGITAL WORLD WHEN IT IS CLOSEST TO TRAGEDY.
BY LOOTING THE DEEPEST AND DARKEST DUNGEONS, SHE WILL SAVE US FROM CORRUPT CODE AND FREE US ALL FROM DIGITAL COLLAPSE.
WHOA...
AND HER NAME IS ____
PLEASE ENTER YOUR NAME.
WHOA!

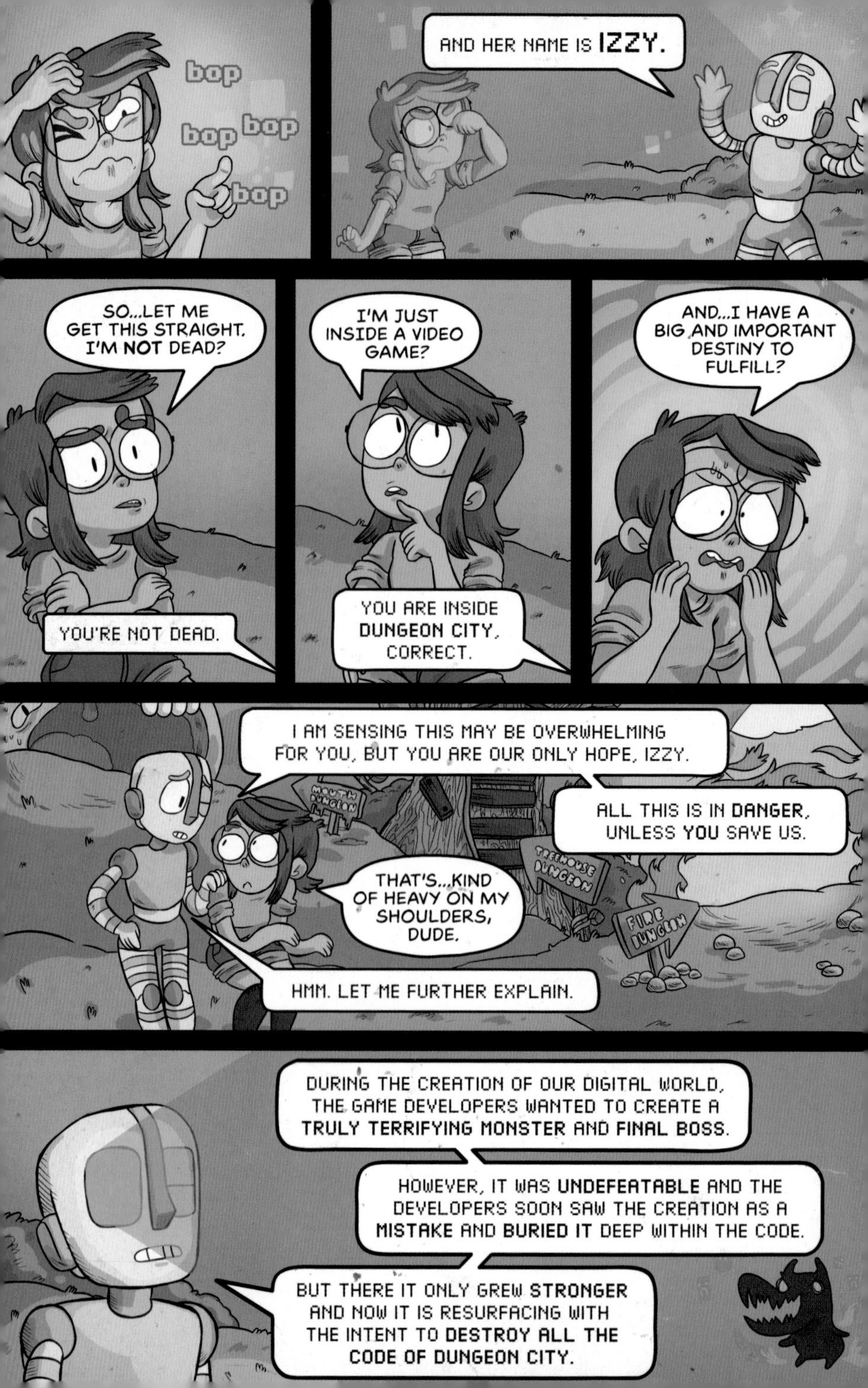
bop
bop
bop
bop
AND HER NAME IS IZZY.
SO...LET ME GET THIS STRAIGHT. I'M NOT DEAD?
YOU'RE NOT DEAD.
I'M JUST INSIDE A VIDEO GAME?
YOU ARE INSIDE DUNGEON CITY, CORRECT.
AND...I HAVE A BIG AND IMPORTANT DESTINY TO FULFILL?
I AM SENSING THIS MAY BE OVERWHELMING FOR YOU, BUT YOU ARE OUR ONLY HOPE, IZZY.
ALL THIS IS IN DANGER, UNLESS YOU SAVE US.
MOUTH DUNGEON
TREEHOUSE DUNGEON
FIRE DUNGEON
THAT'S...KIND OF HEAVY ON MY SHOULDERS, DUDE.
HMM. LET ME FURTHER EXPLAIN.
DURING THE CREATION OF OUR DIGITAL WORLD, THE GAME DEVELOPERS WANTED TO CREATE A TRULY TERRIFYING MONSTER AND FINAL BOSS.
HOWEVER, IT WAS UNDEFEATABLE AND THE DEVELOPERS SOON SAW THE CREATION AS A MISTAKE AND BURIED IT DEEP WITHIN THE CODE.
BUT THERE IT ONLY GREW STRONGER AND NOW IT IS RESURFACING WITH THE INTENT TO DESTROY ALL THE CODE OF DUNGEON CITY.

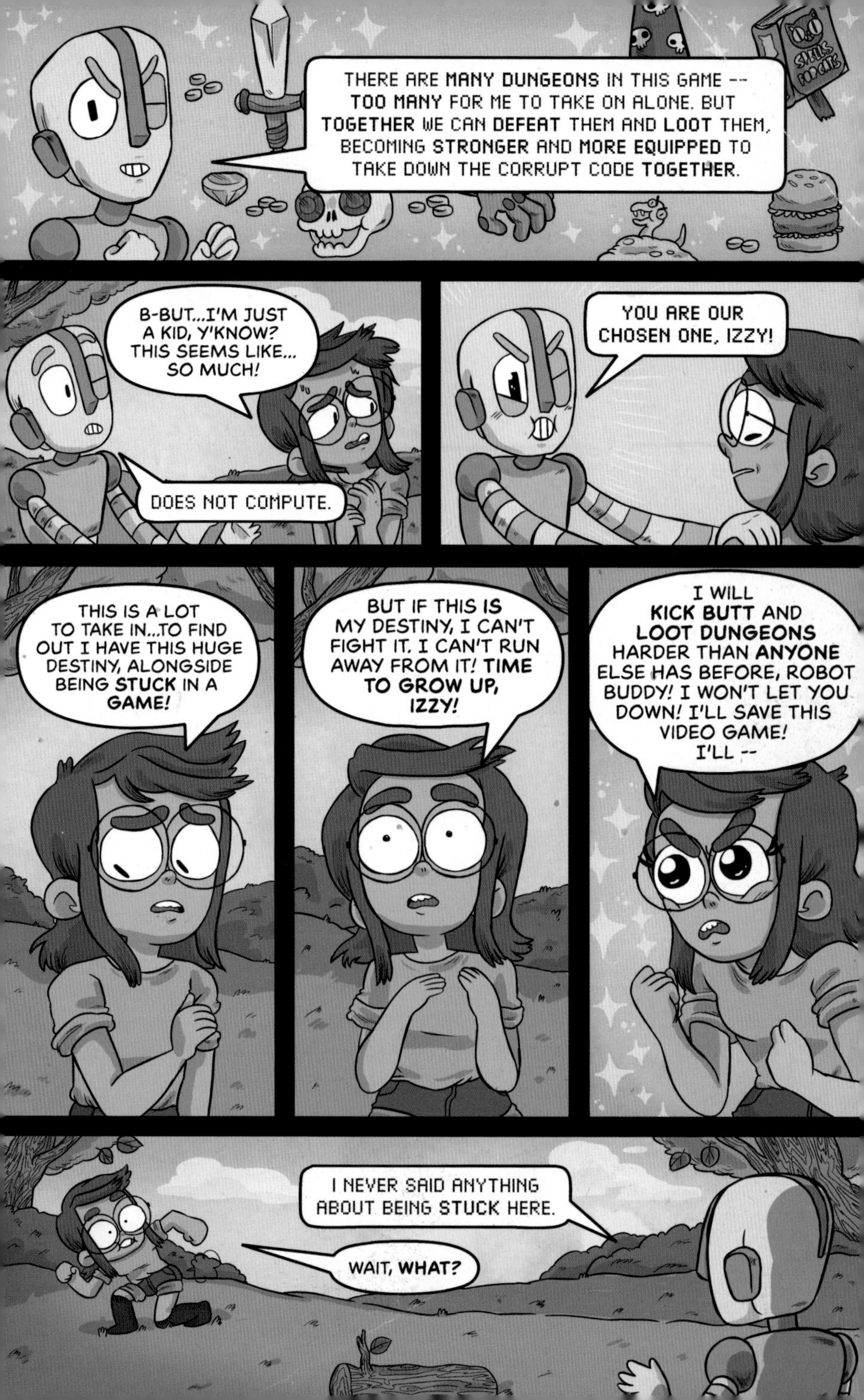
THERE ARE MANY DUNGEONS IN THIS GAME -- TOO MANY FOR ME TO TAKE ON ALONE. BUT TOGETHER WE CAN DEFEAT THEM AND LOOT THEM, BECOMING STRONGER AND MORE EQUIPPED TO TAKE DOWN THE CORRUPT CODE TOGETHER.
SPELLS FOR CATS
B-BUT...I'M JUST A KID, Y'KNOW? THIS SEEMS LIKE... SO MUCH!
DOES NOT COMPUTE.
YOU ARE OUR CHOSEN ONE, IZZY!
THIS IS A LOT TO TAKE IN...TO FIND OUT I HAVE THIS HUGE DESTINY, ALONGSIDE BEING STUCK IN A GAME!
BUT IF THIS IS MY DESTINY, I CAN'T FIGHT IT. I CAN'T RUN AWAY FROM IT! TIME TO GROW UP, IZZY!
I WILL KICK BUTT AND LOOT DUNGEONS HARDER THAN ANYONE ELSE HAS BEFORE, ROBOT BUDDY! I WON'T LET YOU DOWN! I'LL SAVE THIS VIDEO GAME! I'LL --
I NEVER SAID ANYTHING ABOUT BEING STUCK HERE.
WAIT, WHAT?

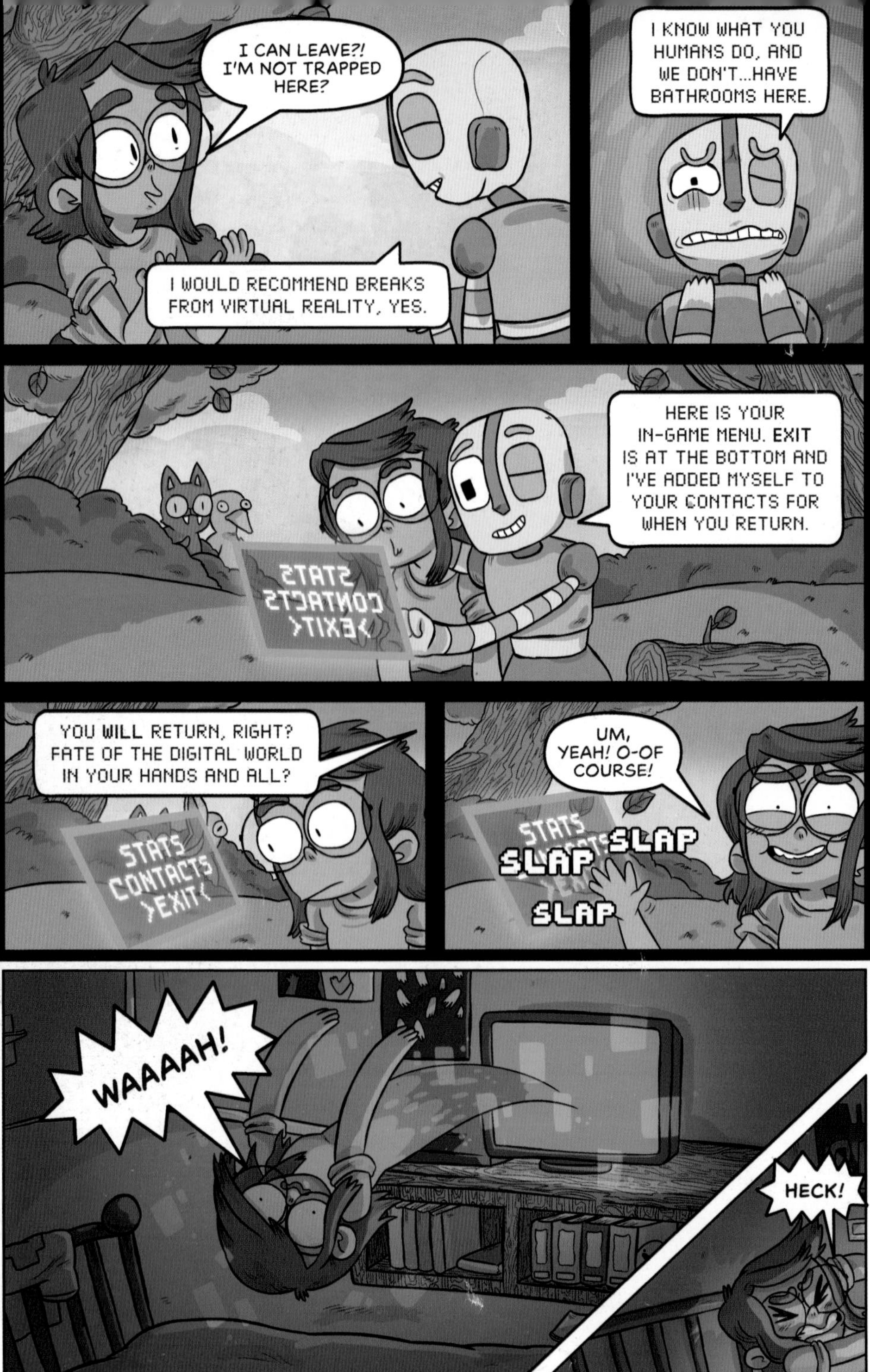
I CAN LEAVE?! I'M NOT TRAPPED HERE?
I WOULD RECOMMEND BREAKS FROM VIRTUAL REALITY, YES.
I KNOW WHAT YOU HUMANS DO, AND WE DON'T...HAVE BATHROOMS HERE.
HERE IS YOUR IN-GAME MENU. EXIT IS AT THE BOTTOM AND I'VE ADDED MYSELF TO YOUR CONTACTS FOR WHEN YOU RETURN.
STATS
CONTACTS
>EXIT<
YOU WILL RETURN, RIGHT? FATE OF THE DIGITAL WORLD IN YOUR HANDS AND ALL?
STATS
CONTACTS
>EXIT<
UM, YEAH! O-OF COURSE!
SLAP
SLAP
SLAP
WAAAAH!
HECK!

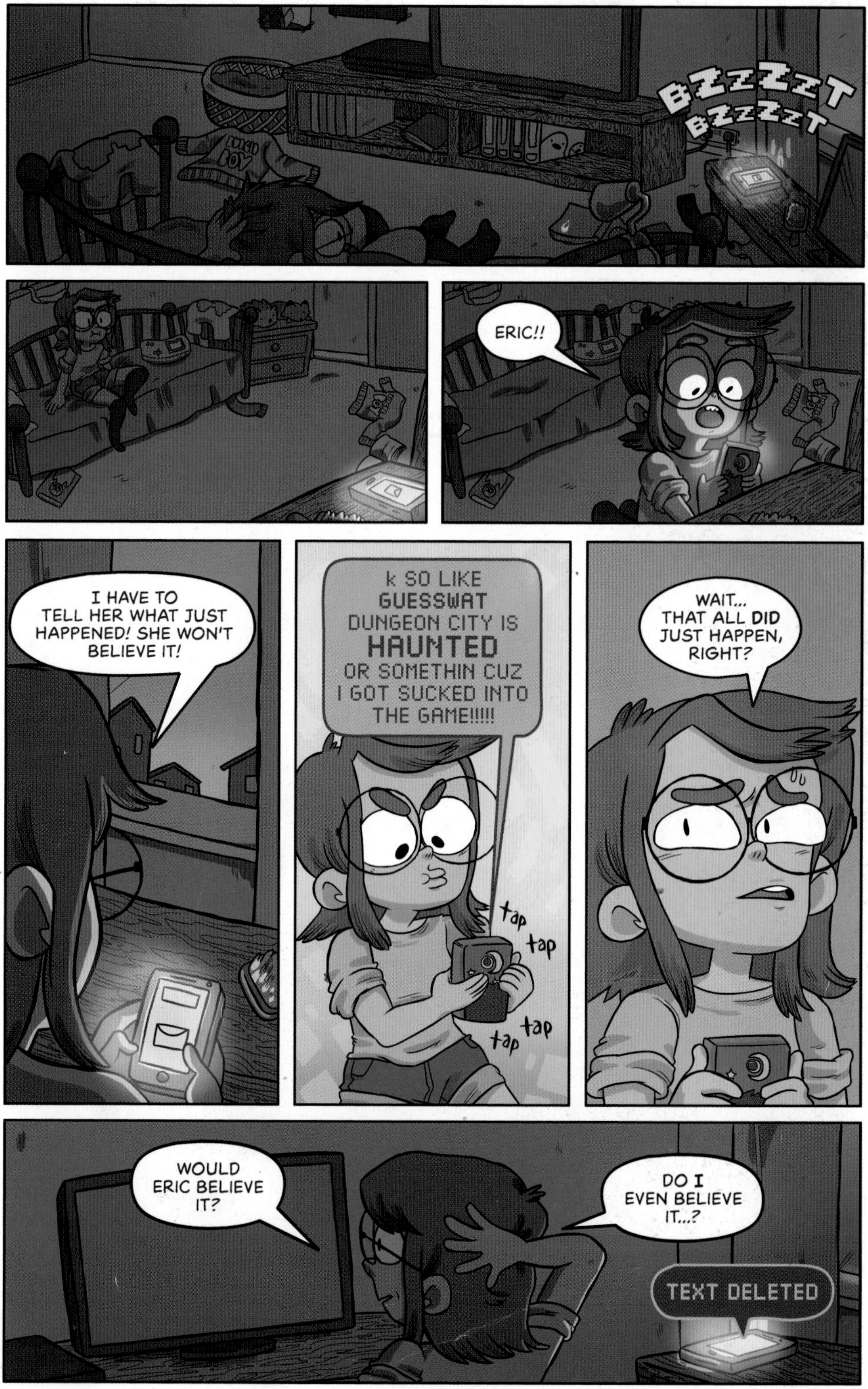
BZZZZZT
BZZZZZT
ERIC!!
I HAVE TO TELL HER WHAT JUST HAPPENED! SHE WON'T BELIEVE IT!
k SO LIKE GUESSWAT DUNGEON CITY IS HAUNTED OR SOMETHIN CUZ I GOT SUCKED INTO THE GAME!!!!!
tap tap
tap tap
WAIT... THAT ALL DID JUST HAPPEN, RIGHT?
WOULD ERIC BELIEVE IT?
DO I EVEN BELIEVE IT...?
TEXT DELETED

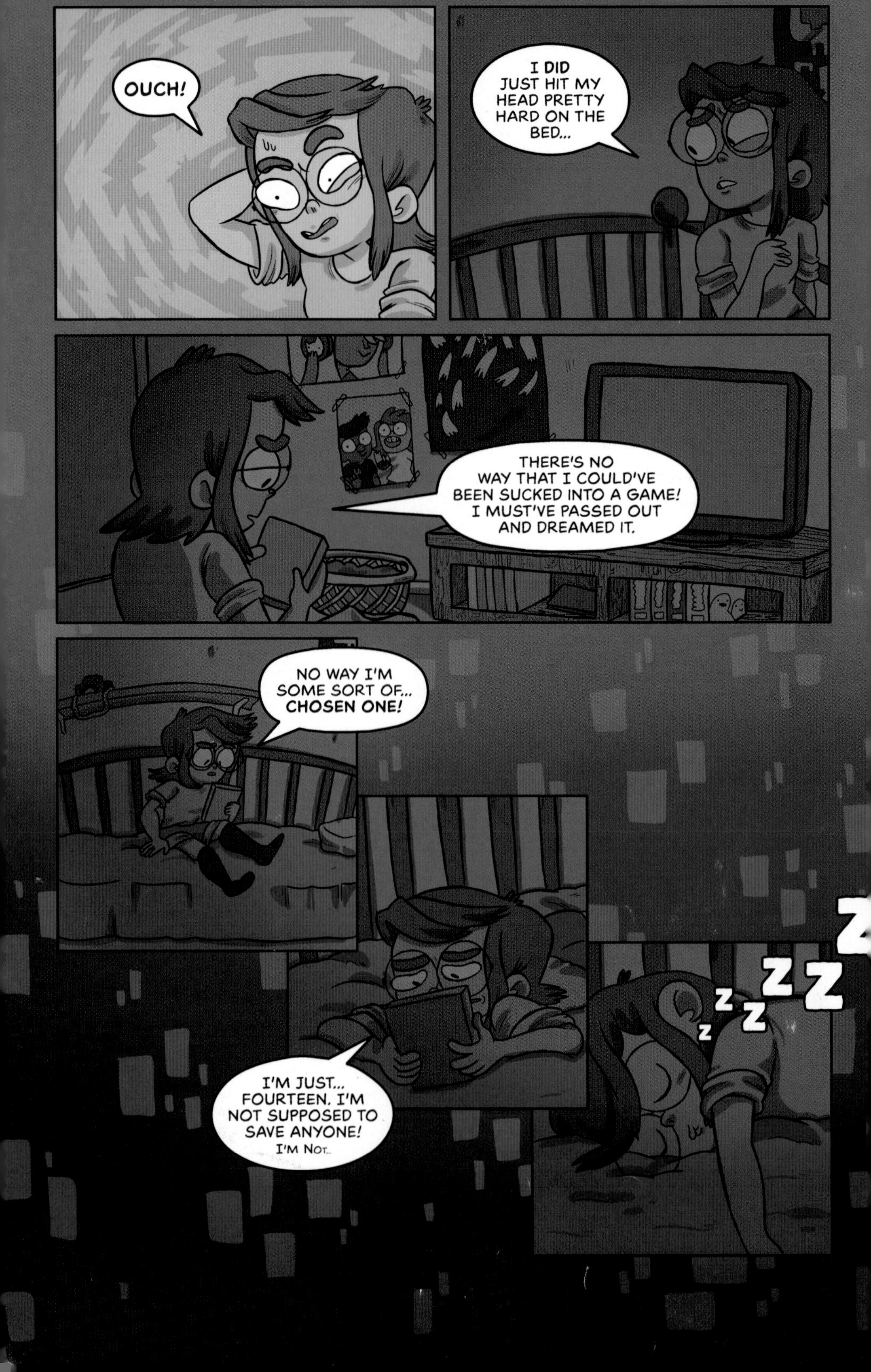
OUCH!
I DID JUST HIT MY HEAD PRETTY HARD ON THE BED...
THERE'S NO WAY THAT I COULD'VE BEEN SUCKED INTO A GAME! I MUST'VE PASSED OUT AND DREAMED IT.
NO WAY I'M SOME SORT OF... CHOSEN ONE!
I'M JUST... FOURTEEN. I'M NOT SUPPOSED TO SAVE ANYONE! I'M NOT...
Z Z Z Z Z Z

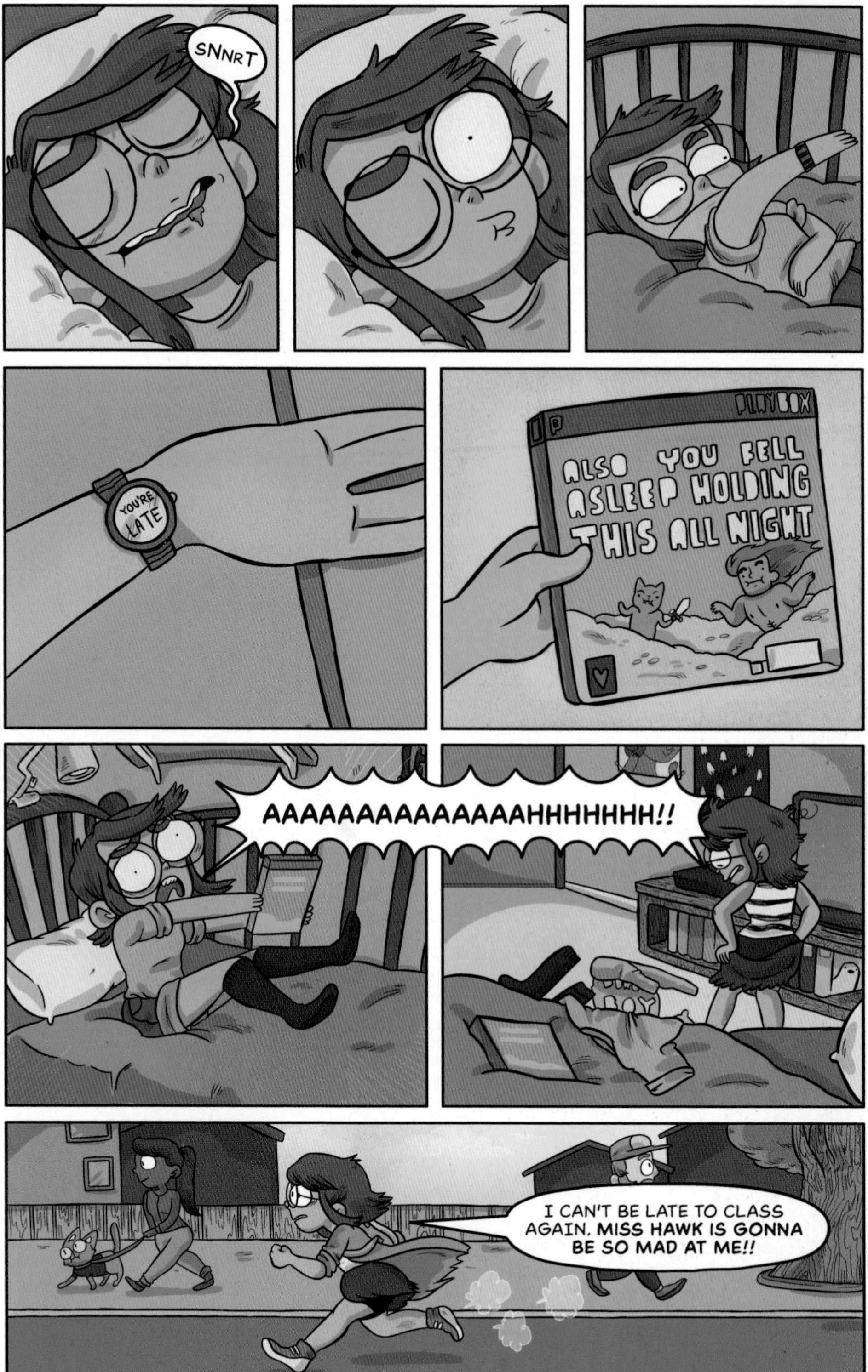
SNNRT
YOU'RE LATE
PLAYBOX
ALSO YOU FELL ASLEEP HOLDING THIS ALL NIGHT
AAAAAAAAAAAAAAHHHHHHH!!
I CAN'T BE LATE TO CLASS AGAIN. MISS HAWK IS GONNA BE SO MAD AT ME!!

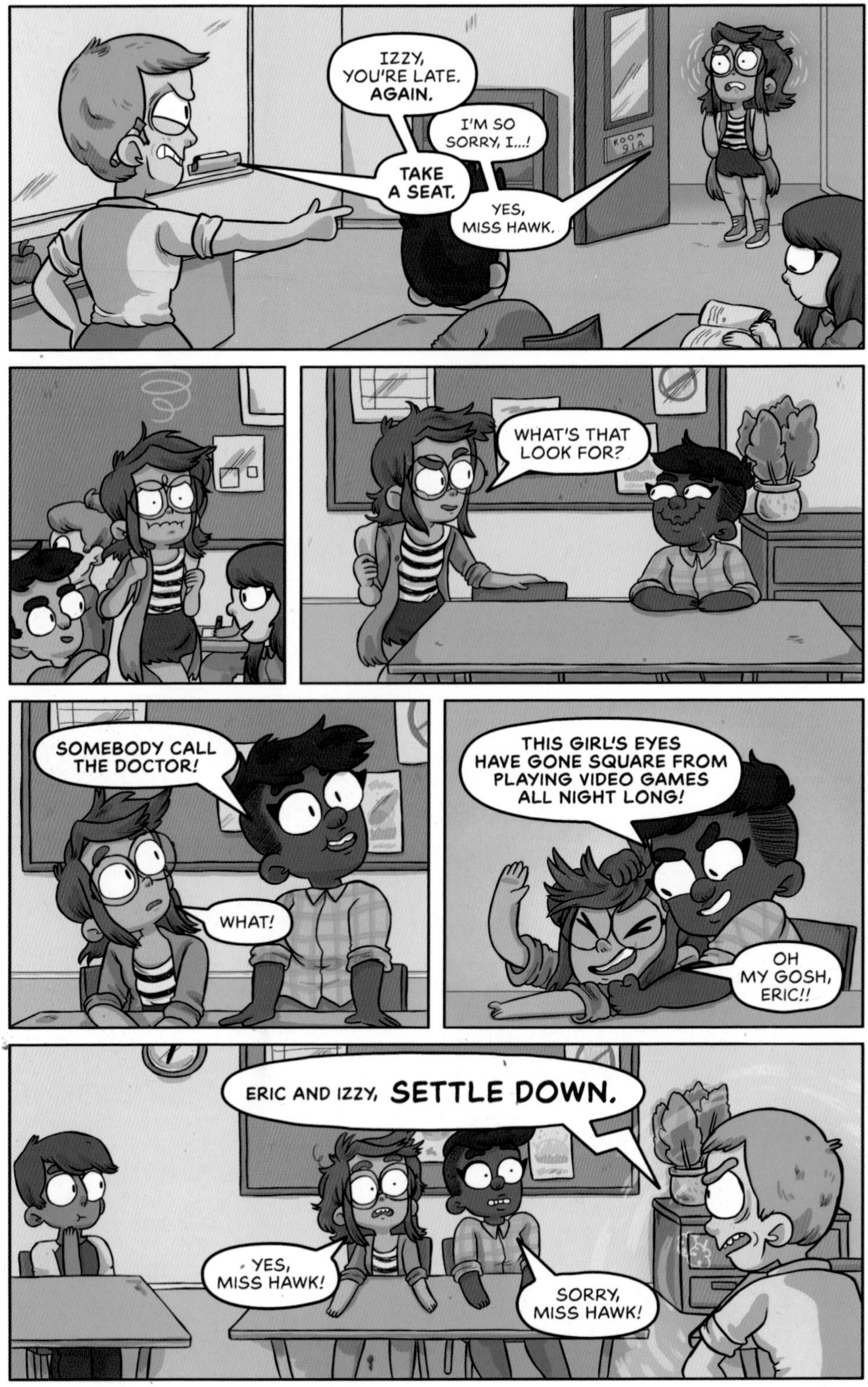
IZZY, YOU'RE LATE. AGAIN.
I'M SO SORRY, I...!
TAKE A SEAT.
YES, MISS HAWK.
ROOM 91A
WHAT'S THAT LOOK FOR?
SOMEBODY CALL THE DOCTOR!
WHAT!
THIS GIRL'S EYES HAVE GONE SQUARE FROM PLAYING VIDEO GAMES ALL NIGHT LONG!
OH MY GOSH, ERIC!!
ERIC AND IZZY, SETTLE DOWN.
YES, MISS HAWK!
SORRY, MISS HAWK!

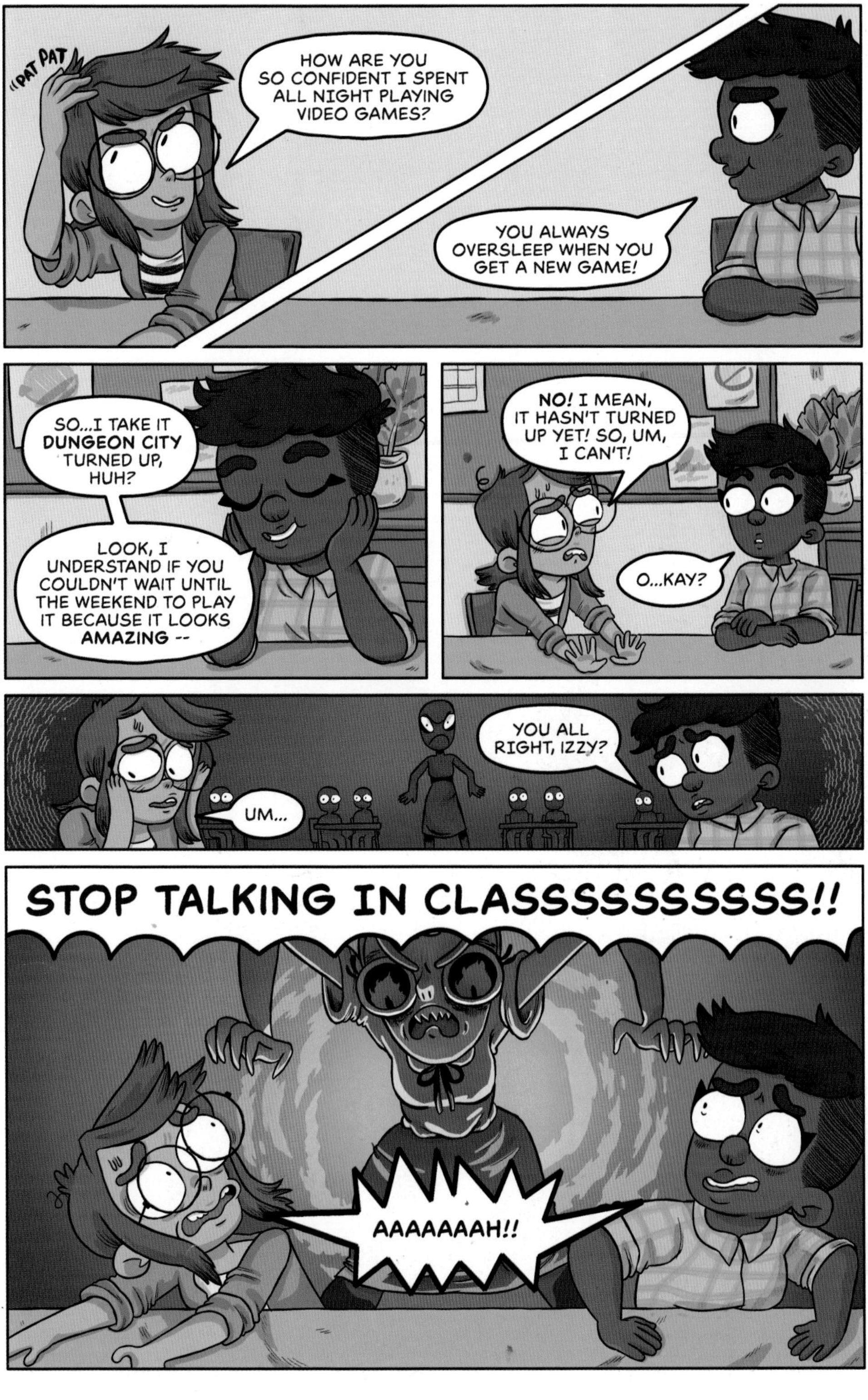
PAT PAT
HOW ARE YOU SO CONFIDENT I SPENT ALL NIGHT PLAYING VIDEO GAMES?
YOU ALWAYS OVERSLEEP WHEN YOU GET A NEW GAME!
SO...I TAKE IT DUNGEON CITY TURNED UP, HUH?
LOOK, I UNDERSTAND IF YOU COULDN'T WAIT UNTIL THE WEEKEND TO PLAY IT BECAUSE IT LOOKS AMAZING --
NO! I MEAN, IT HASN'T TURNED UP YET! SO, UM, I CAN'T!
O...KAY?
UM...
YOU ALL RIGHT, IZZY?
STOP TALKING IN CLASSSSSSSSSS!!
AAAAAAAH!!

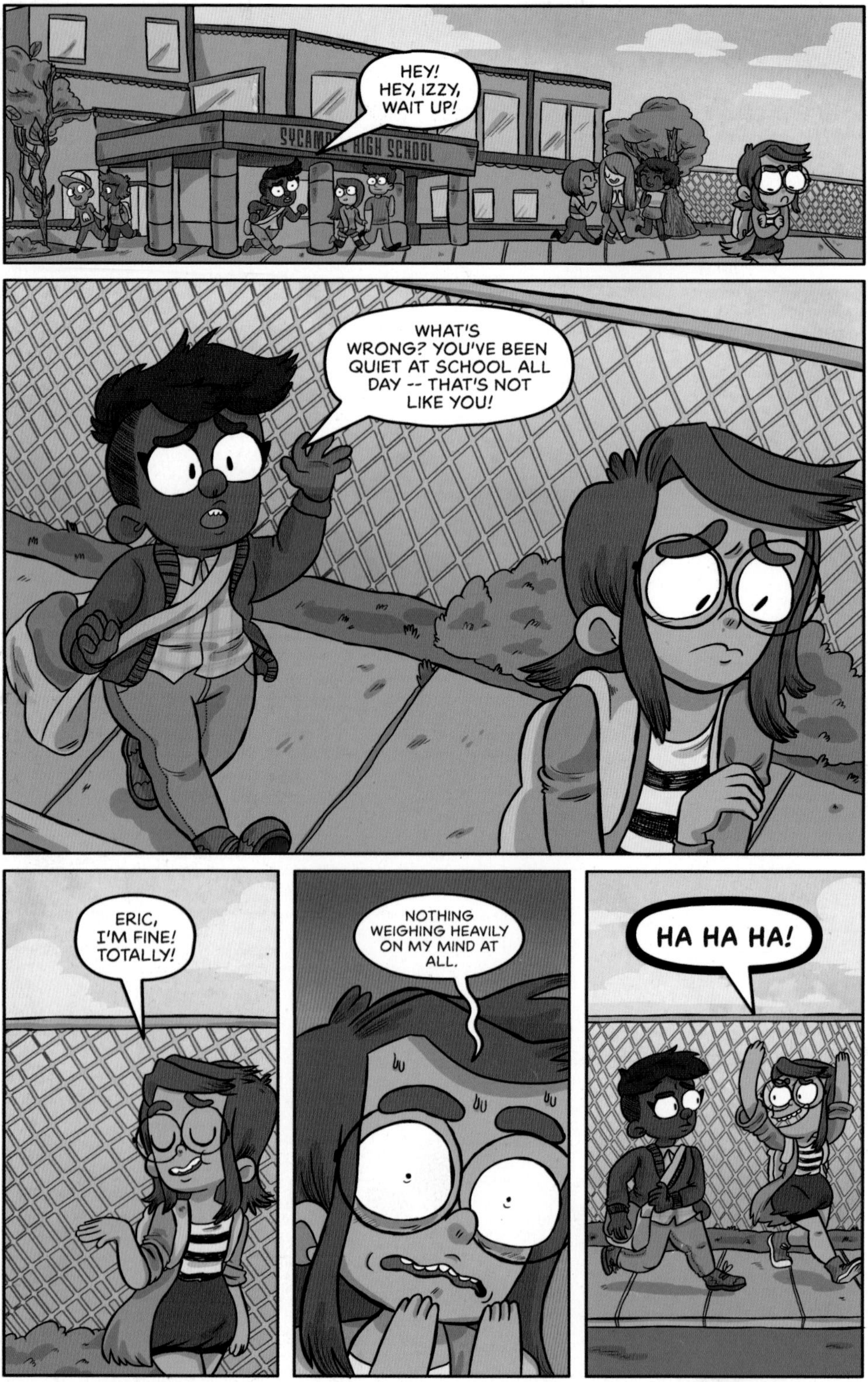
SYCAMORE HIGH SCHOOL
HEY! HEY, IZZY, WAIT UP!
WHAT'S WRONG? YOU'VE BEEN QUIET AT SCHOOL ALL DAY -- THAT'S NOT LIKE YOU!
ERIC, I'M FINE! TOTALLY!
NOTHING WEIGHING HEAVILY ON MY MIND AT ALL.
HA HA HA!

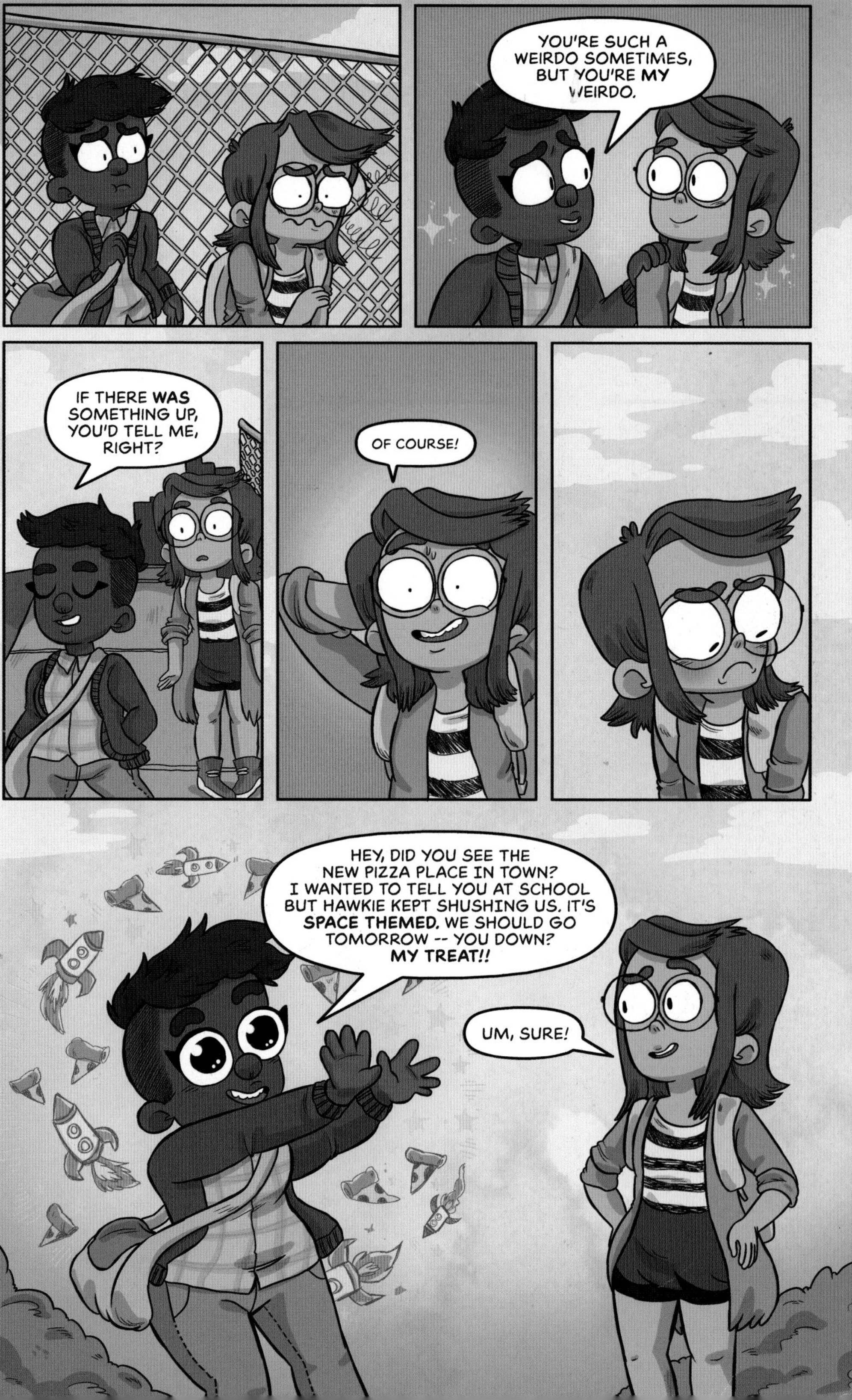
YOU'RE SUCH A WEIRDO SOMETIMES, BUT YOU'RE MY WEIRDO.
IF THERE WAS SOMETHING UP, YOU'D TELL ME, RIGHT?
OF COURSE!
HEY, DID YOU SEE THE NEW PIZZA PLACE IN TOWN? I WANTED TO TELL YOU AT SCHOOL BUT HAWKIE KEPT SHUSHING US. IT'S SPACE THEMED. WE SHOULD GO TOMORROW -- YOU DOWN? MY TREAT!!
UM, SURE!

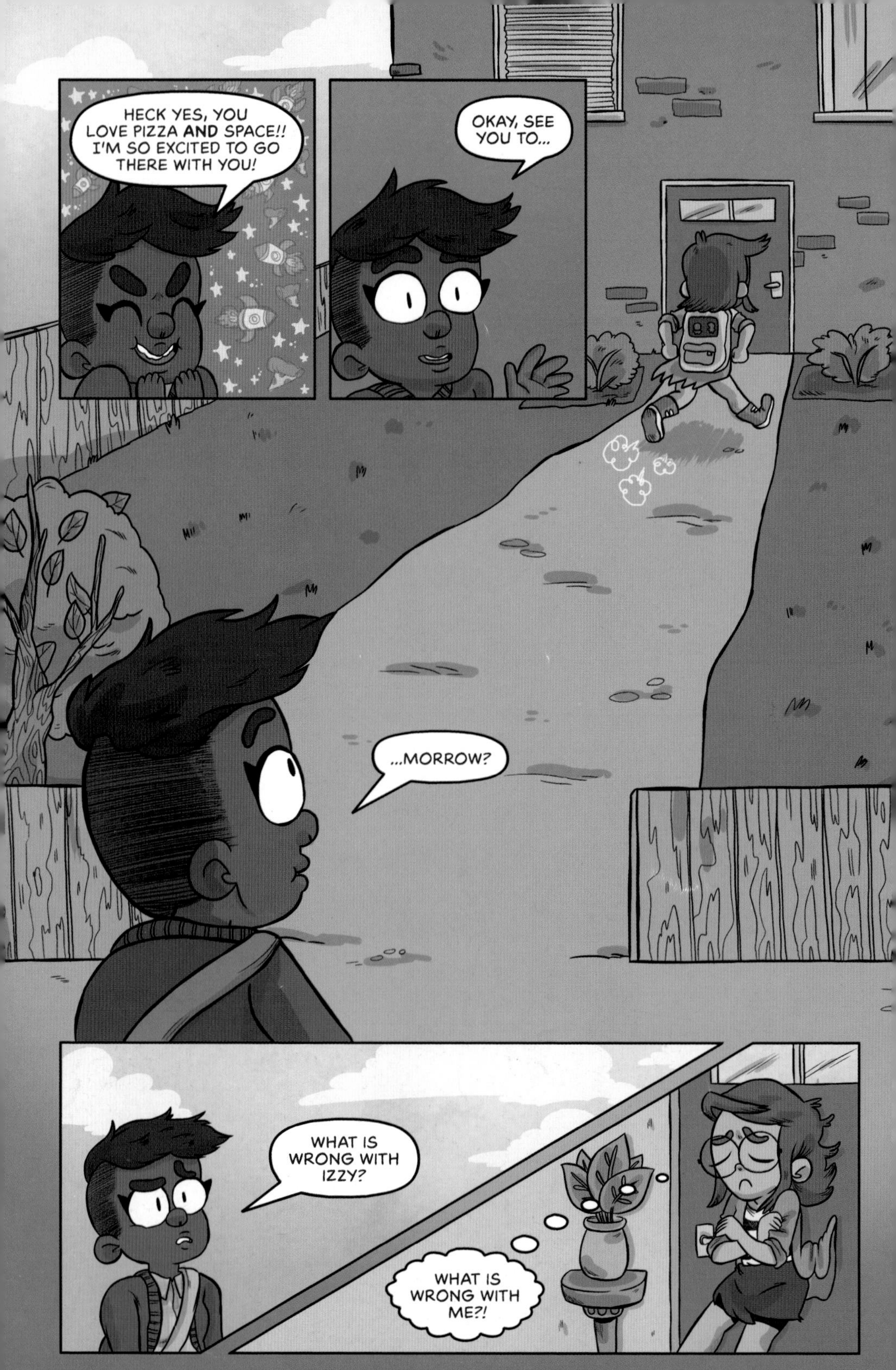
HECK YES, YOU LOVE PIZZA AND SPACE!! I'M SO EXCITED TO GO THERE WITH YOU!
OKAY, SEE YOU TO...
...MORROW?
WHAT IS WRONG WITH IZZY?
WHAT IS WRONG WITH ME?!

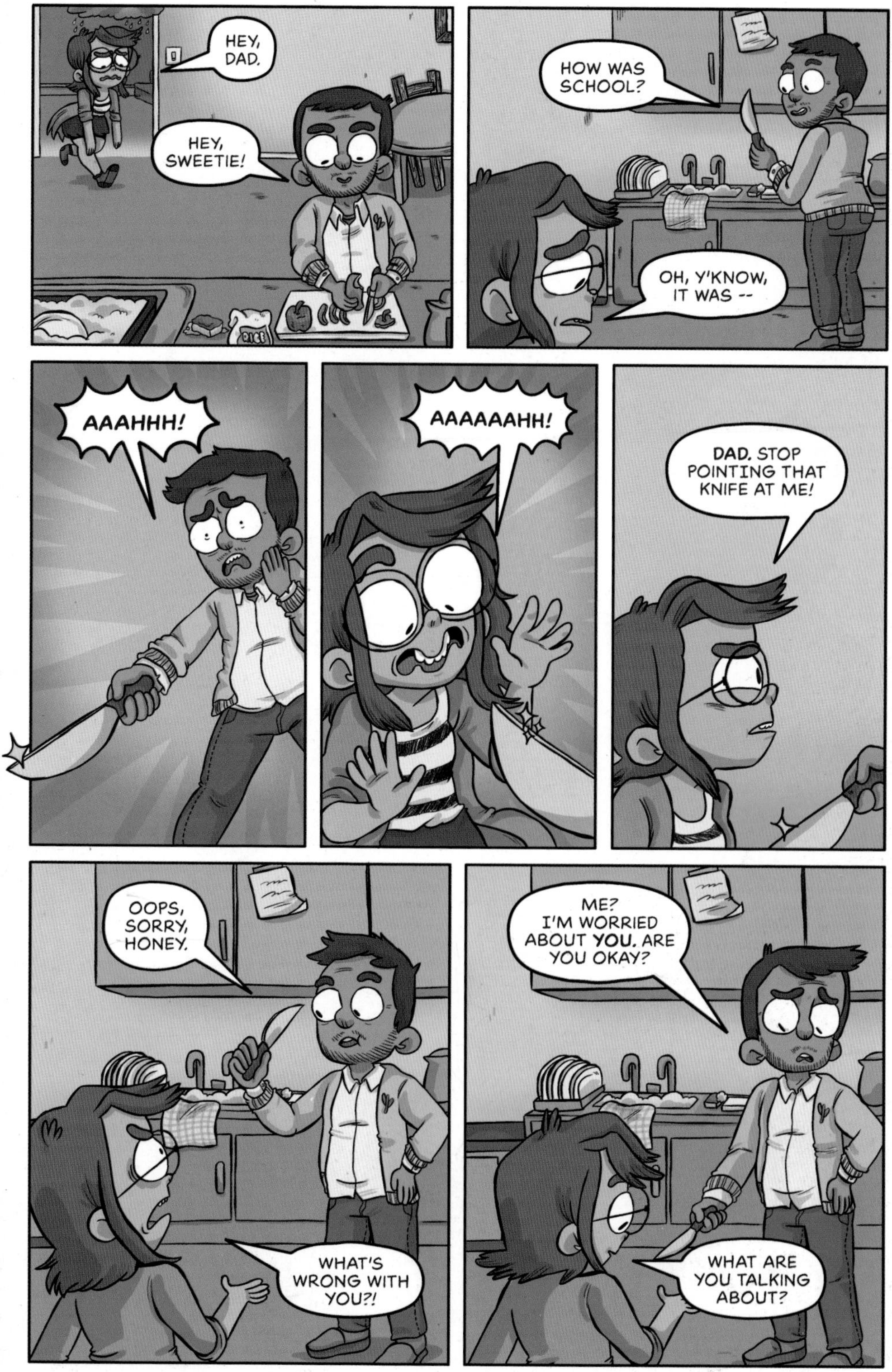
HEY, DAD.
HEY, SWEETIE!
HOW WAS SCHOOL?
OH, Y'KNOW, IT WAS --
RICE
AAAHHH!
AAAAAAHH!
DAD. STOP POINTING THAT KNIFE AT ME!
OOPS, SORRY, HONEY.
WHAT'S WRONG WITH YOU?!
ME? I'M WORRIED ABOUT YOU. ARE YOU OKAY?
WHAT ARE YOU TALKING ABOUT?

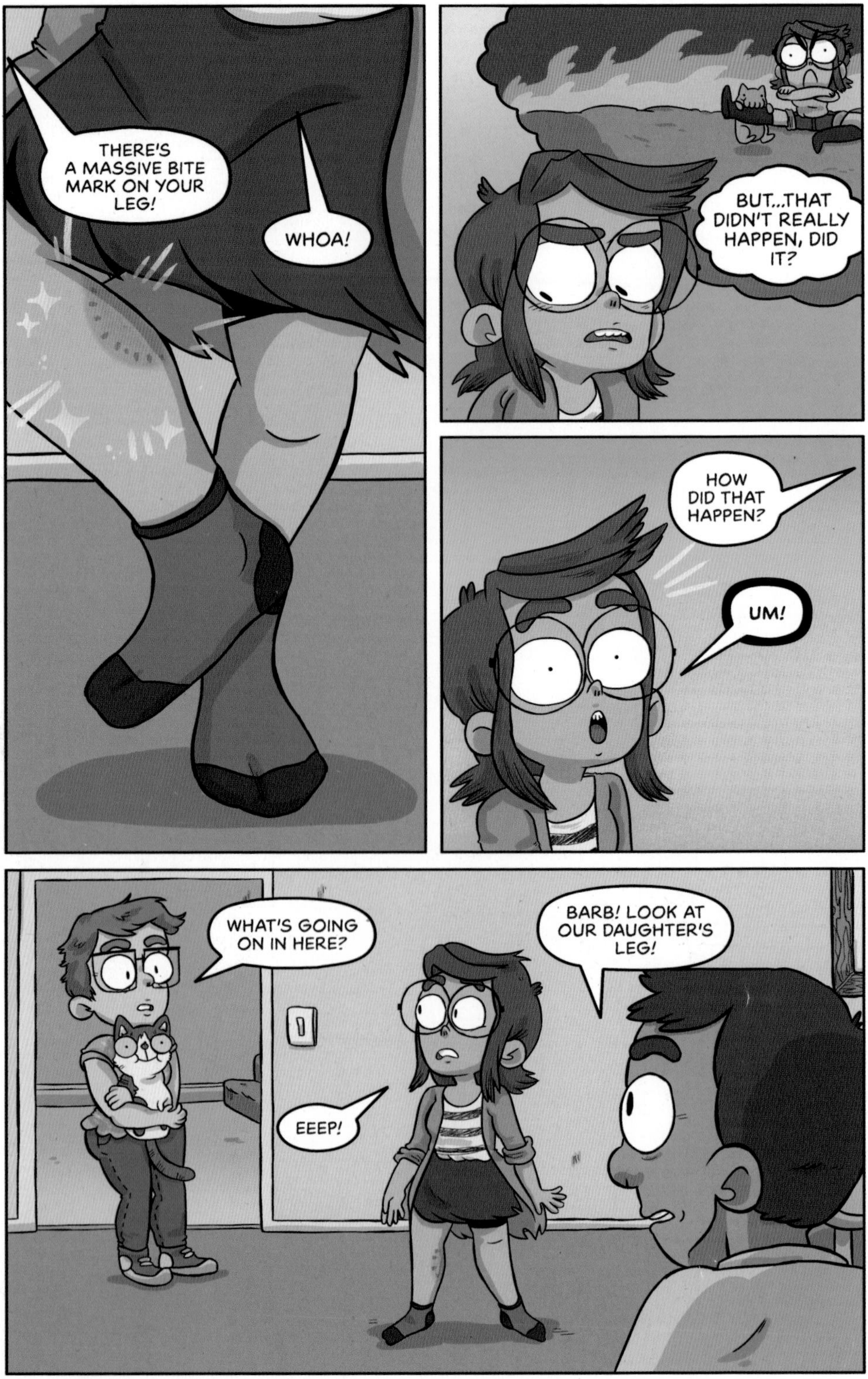
THERE'S A MASSIVE BITE MARK ON YOUR LEG!
WHOA!
BUT...THAT DIDN'T REALLY HAPPEN, DID IT?
HOW DID THAT HAPPEN?
UM!
WHAT'S GOING ON IN HERE?
BARB! LOOK AT OUR DAUGHTER'S LEG!
EEEP!

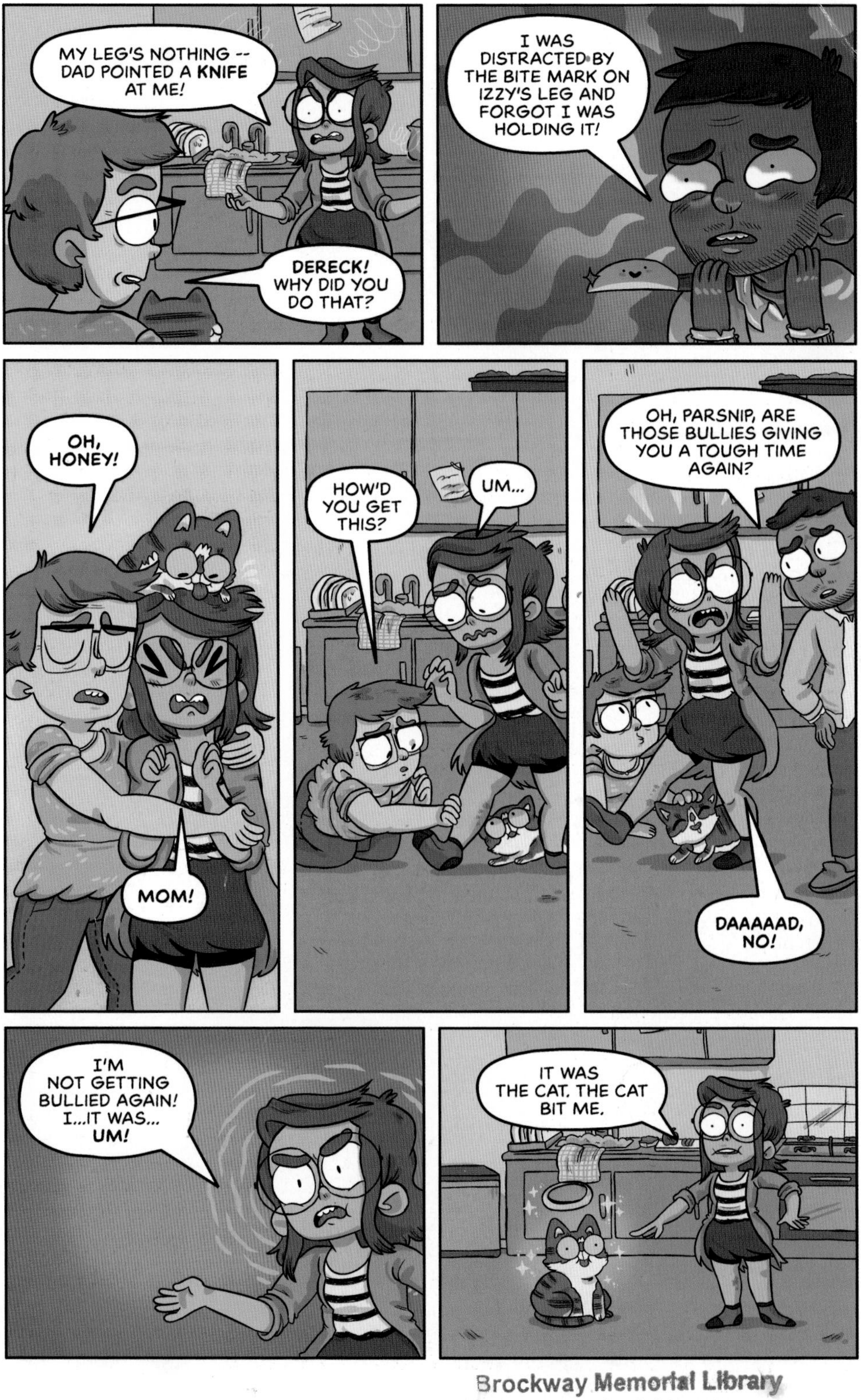

MY LEG'S NOTHING -- DAD POINTED A **KNIFE** AT ME!
DERECK! WHY DID YOU DO THAT?
I WAS DISTRACTED BY THE BITE MARK ON IZZY'S LEG AND FORGOT I WAS HOLDING IT!
OH, HONEY!
MOM!
HOW'D YOU GET THIS?
UM...
OH, PARSNIP, ARE THOSE BULLIES GIVING YOU A TOUGH TIME AGAIN?
DAAAAAD, NO!
I'M NOT GETTING BULLIED AGAIN! I...IT WAS... **UM!**
IT WAS THE CAT. THE CAT BIT ME.

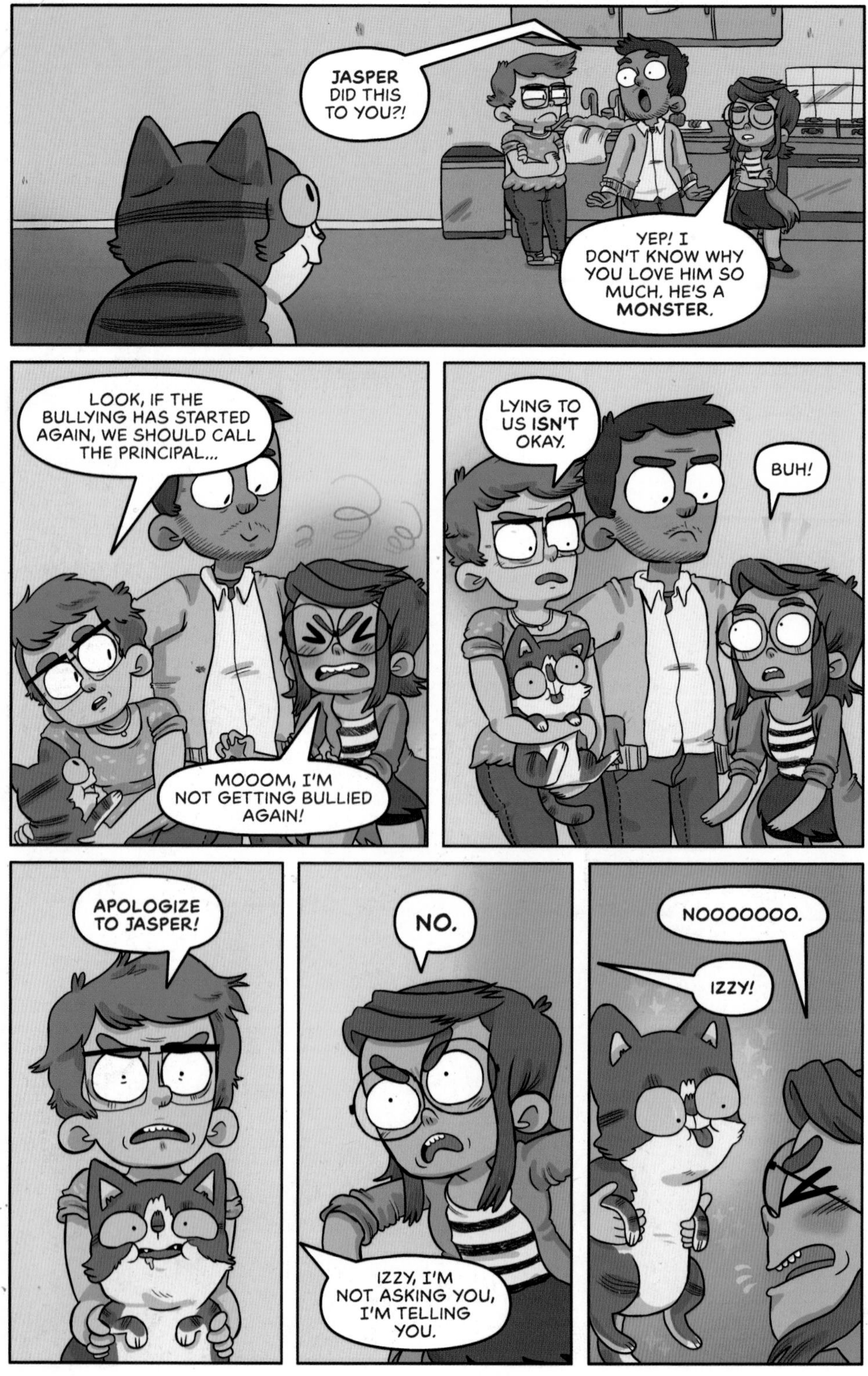
JASPER DID THIS TO YOU?!
YEP! I DON'T KNOW WHY YOU LOVE HIM SO MUCH. HE'S A MONSTER.
LOOK, IF THE BULLYING HAS STARTED AGAIN, WE SHOULD CALL THE PRINCIPAL...
MOOOM, I'M NOT GETTING BULLIED AGAIN!
LYING TO US ISN'T OKAY.
BUH!
APOLOGIZE TO JASPER!
NO.
IZZY, I'M NOT ASKING YOU, I'M TELLING YOU.
NOOOOOOO.
IZZY!

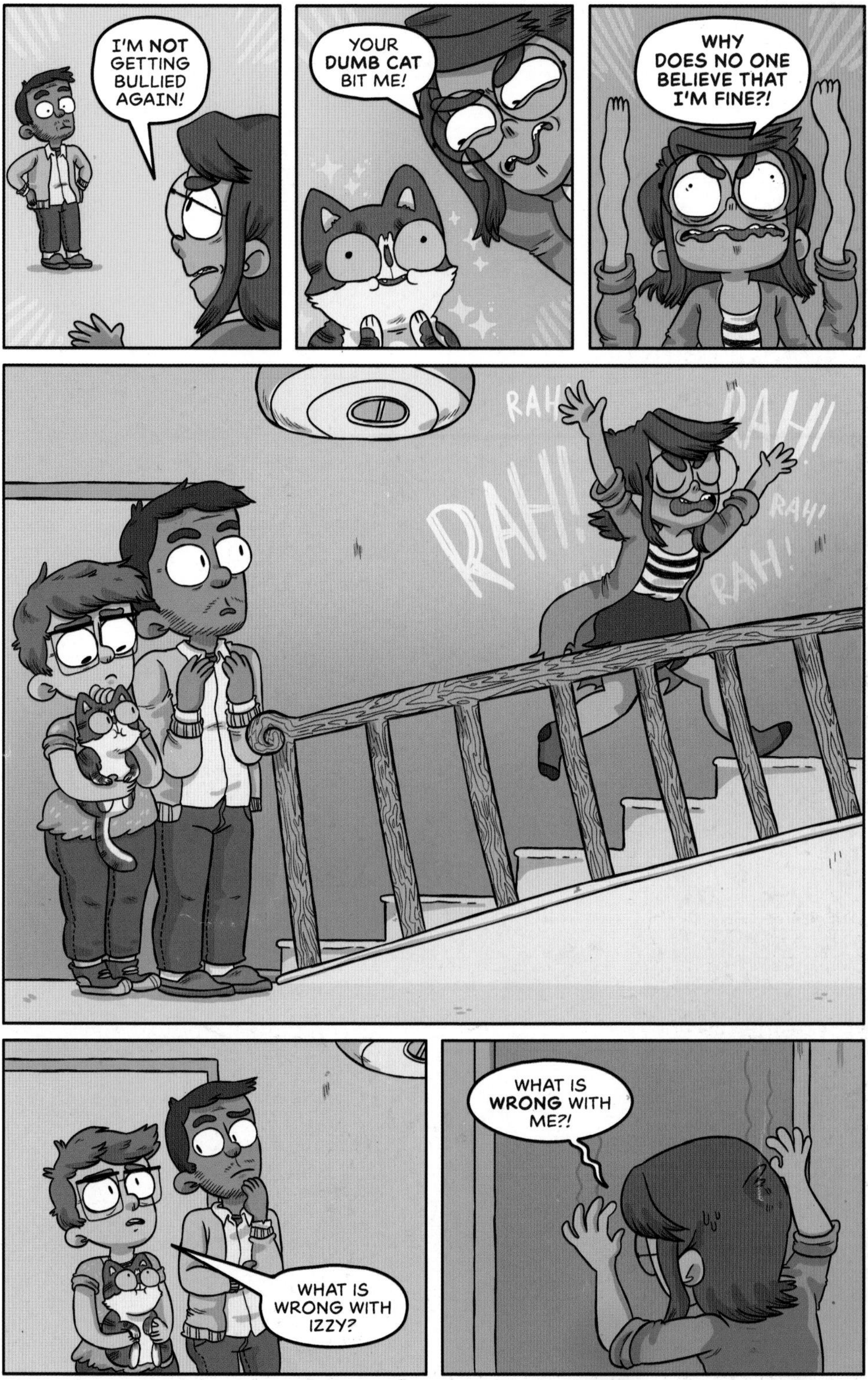
I'M NOT GETTING BULLIED AGAIN!
YOUR DUMB CAT BIT ME!
WHY DOES NO ONE BELIEVE THAT I'M FINE?!
RAH RAH! RAH! RAH! RAH! RAH!
WHAT IS WRONG WITH IZZY?
WHAT IS WRONG WITH ME?!

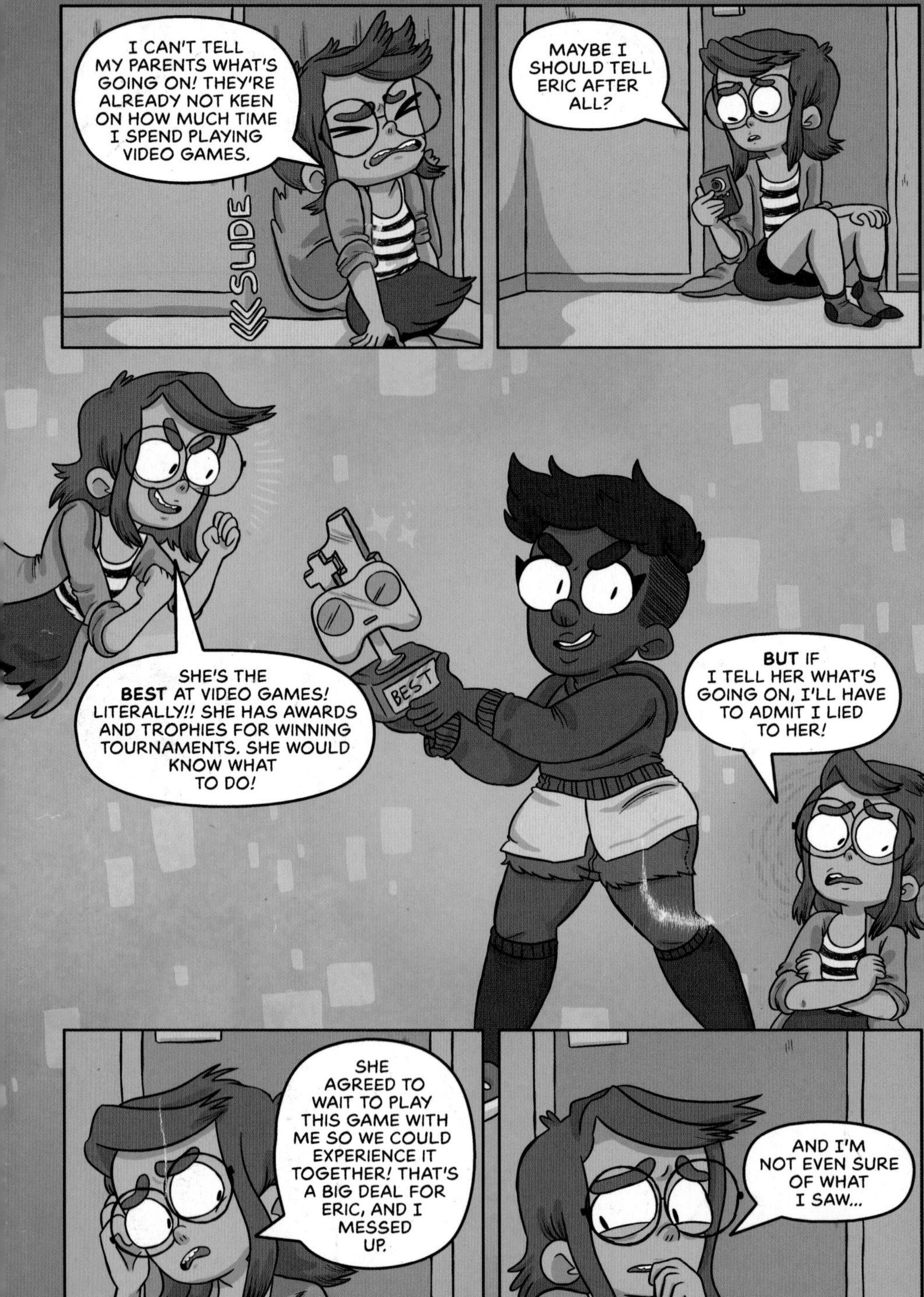
I CAN'T TELL MY PARENTS WHAT'S GOING ON! THEY'RE ALREADY NOT KEEN ON HOW MUCH TIME I SPEND PLAYING VIDEO GAMES.
SLIDE
MAYBE I SHOULD TELL ERIC AFTER ALL?
SHE'S THE **BEST** AT VIDEO GAMES! LITERALLY!! SHE HAS AWARDS AND TROPHIES FOR WINNING TOURNAMENTS. SHE WOULD KNOW WHAT TO DO!
BEST
BUT IF I TELL HER WHAT'S GOING ON, I'LL HAVE TO ADMIT I LIED TO HER!
SHE AGREED TO WAIT TO PLAY THIS GAME WITH ME SO WE COULD EXPERIENCE IT TOGETHER! THAT'S A BIG DEAL FOR ERIC, AND I MESSED UP.
AND I'M NOT EVEN SURE OF WHAT I SAW...

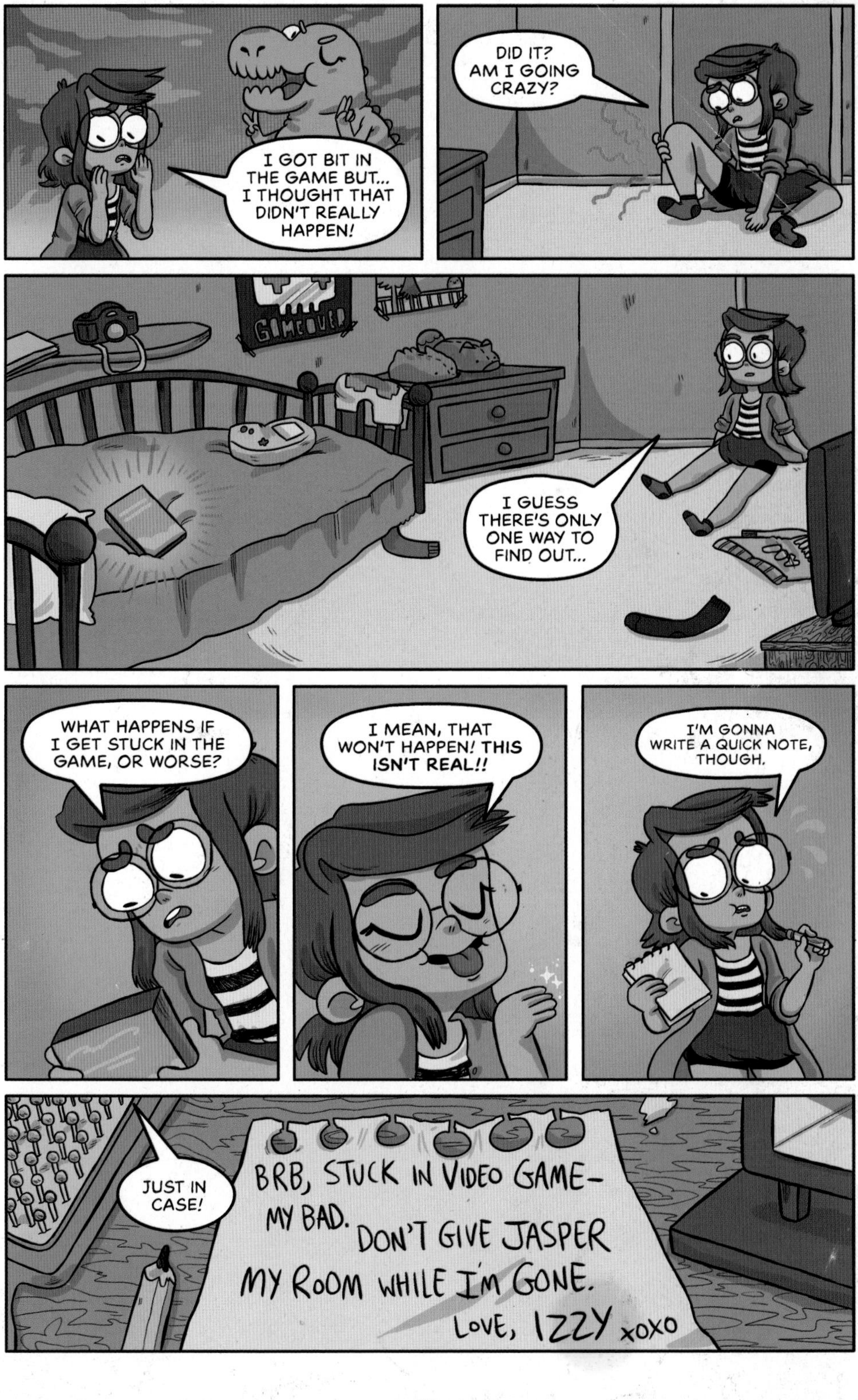
I GOT BIT IN THE GAME BUT... I THOUGHT THAT DIDN'T REALLY HAPPEN!
DID IT? AM I GOING CRAZY?
GAMEOVER
I GUESS THERE'S ONLY ONE WAY TO FIND OUT...
WHAT HAPPENS IF I GET STUCK IN THE GAME, OR WORSE?
I MEAN, THAT WON'T HAPPEN! THIS ISN'T REAL!!
I'M GONNA WRITE A QUICK NOTE, THOUGH.
JUST IN CASE!
BRB, STUCK IN VIDEO GAME- MY BAD. DON'T GIVE JASPER MY ROOM WHILE I'M GONE.
LOVE, IZZY xoxo

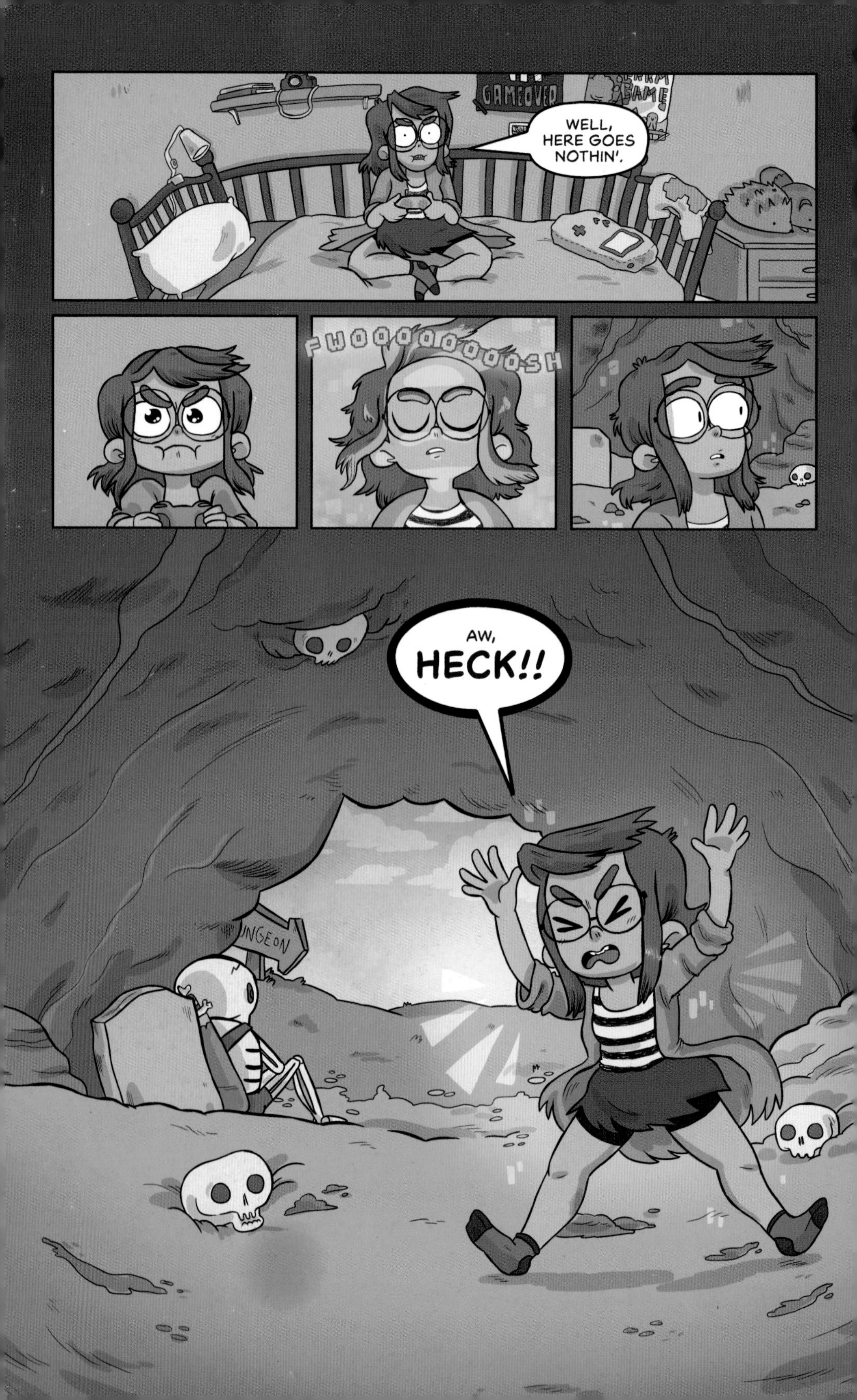
GAMEOVER
WELL, HERE GOES NOTHIN'.
FWOOOOOOOOSH
AW, HECK!!

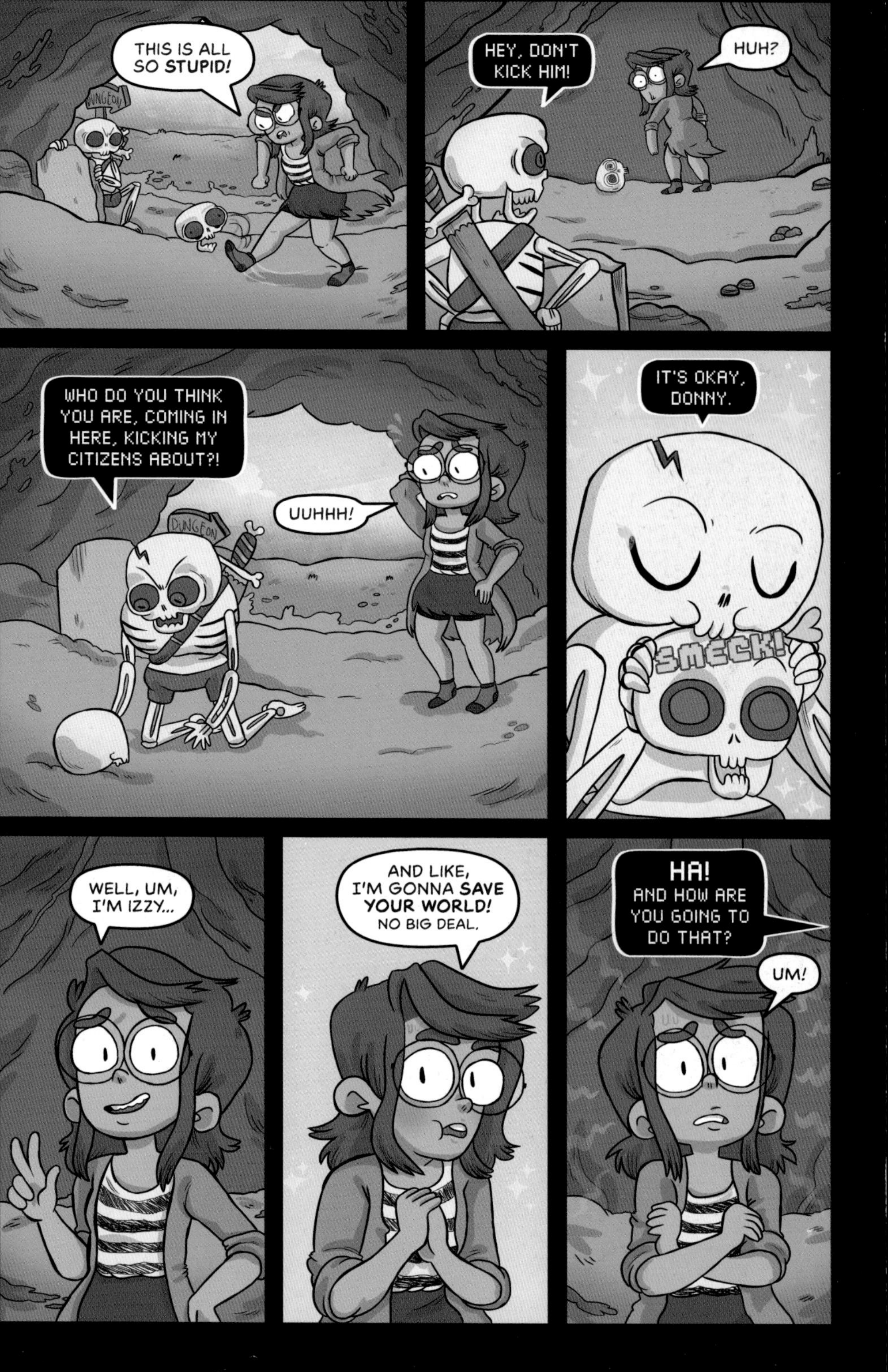

DUNGEON
THIS IS ALL SO STUPID!
HEY, DON'T KICK HIM!
HUH?
WHO DO YOU THINK YOU ARE, COMING IN HERE, KICKING MY CITIZENS ABOUT?!
DUNGEON
UUHHH!
IT'S OKAY, DONNY.
SMECK!
WELL, UM, I'M IZZY...
AND LIKE, I'M GONNA SAVE YOUR WORLD! NO BIG DEAL.
HA! AND HOW ARE YOU GOING TO DO THAT?
UM!

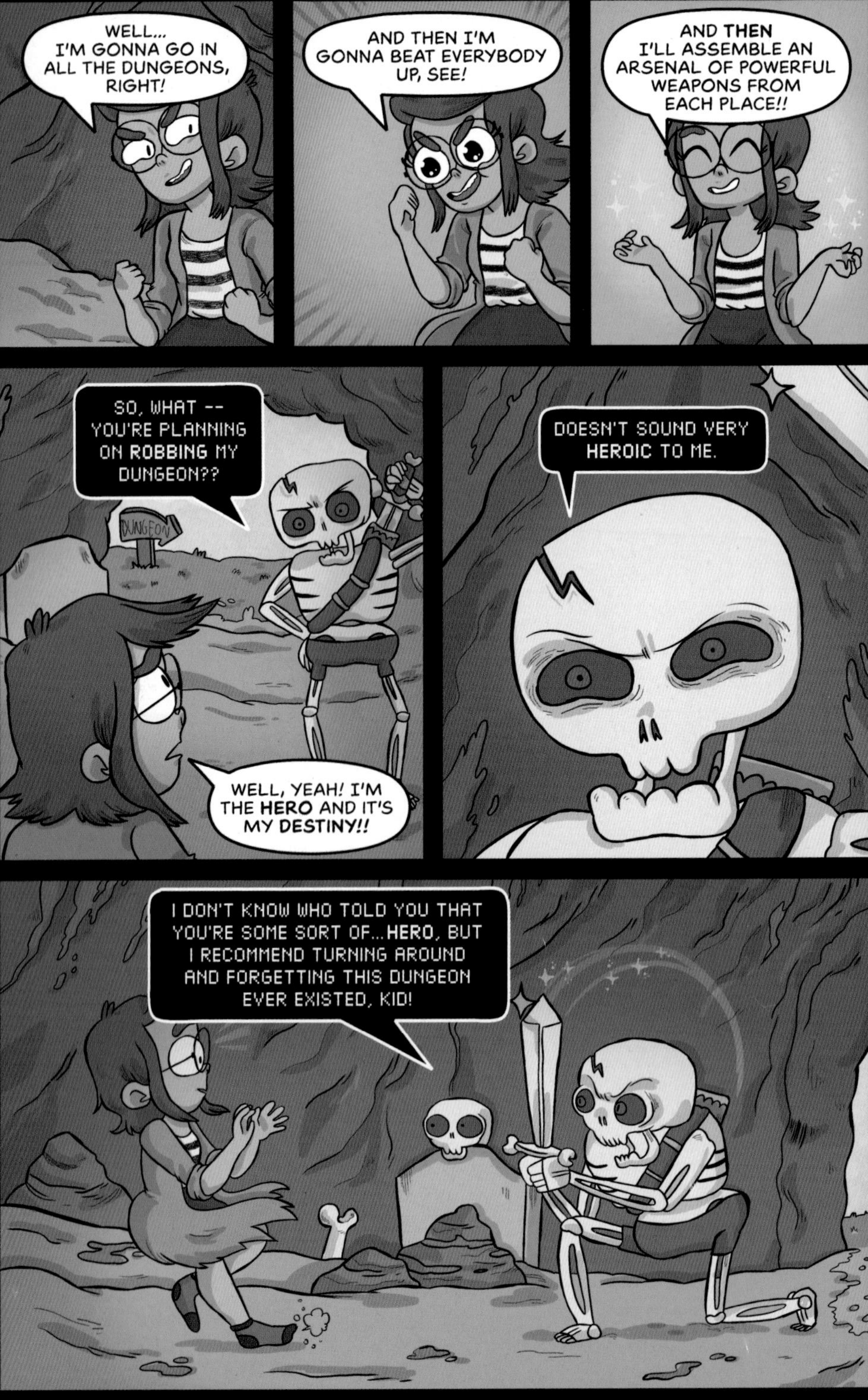
WELL... I'M GONNA GO IN ALL THE DUNGEONS, RIGHT!
AND THEN I'M GONNA BEAT EVERYBODY UP, SEE!
AND THEN I'LL ASSEMBLE AN ARSENAL OF POWERFUL WEAPONS FROM EACH PLACE!!
SO, WHAT -- YOU'RE PLANNING ON ROBBING MY DUNGEON??
DUNGEON
WELL, YEAH! I'M THE HERO AND IT'S MY DESTINY!!
DOESN'T SOUND VERY HEROIC TO ME.
I DON'T KNOW WHO TOLD YOU THAT YOU'RE SOME SORT OF...HERO, BUT I RECOMMEND TURNING AROUND AND FORGETTING THIS DUNGEON EVER EXISTED, KID!

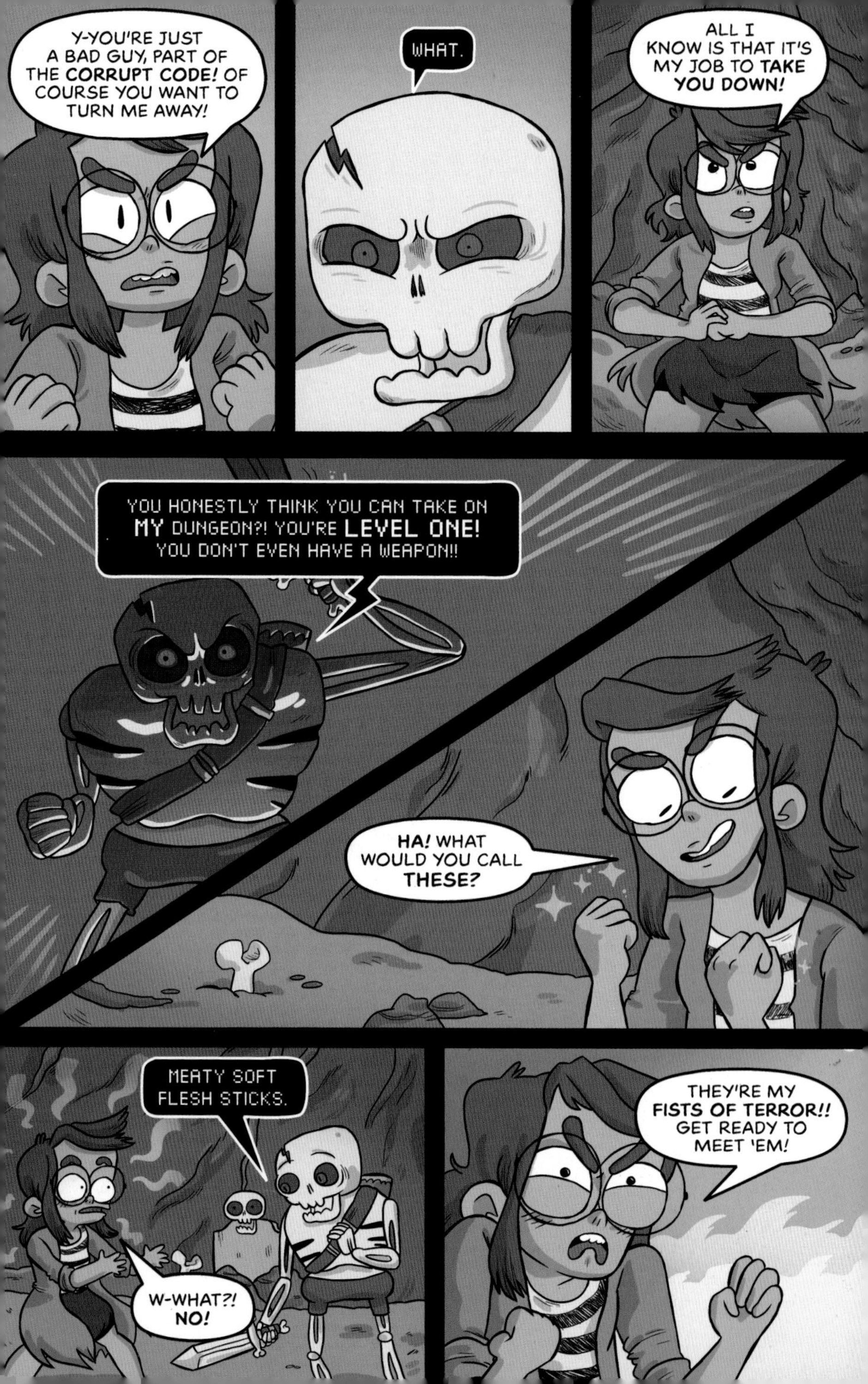
Y-YOU'RE JUST A BAD GUY, PART OF THE CORRUPT CODE! OF COURSE YOU WANT TO TURN ME AWAY!
WHAT.
ALL I KNOW IS THAT IT'S MY JOB TO TAKE YOU DOWN!
YOU HONESTLY THINK YOU CAN TAKE ON MY DUNGEON?! YOU'RE LEVEL ONE! YOU DON'T EVEN HAVE A WEAPON!!
HA! WHAT WOULD YOU CALL THESE?
MEATY SOFT FLESH STICKS.
W-WHAT?! NO!
THEY'RE MY FISTS OF TERROR!! GET READY TO MEET 'EM!

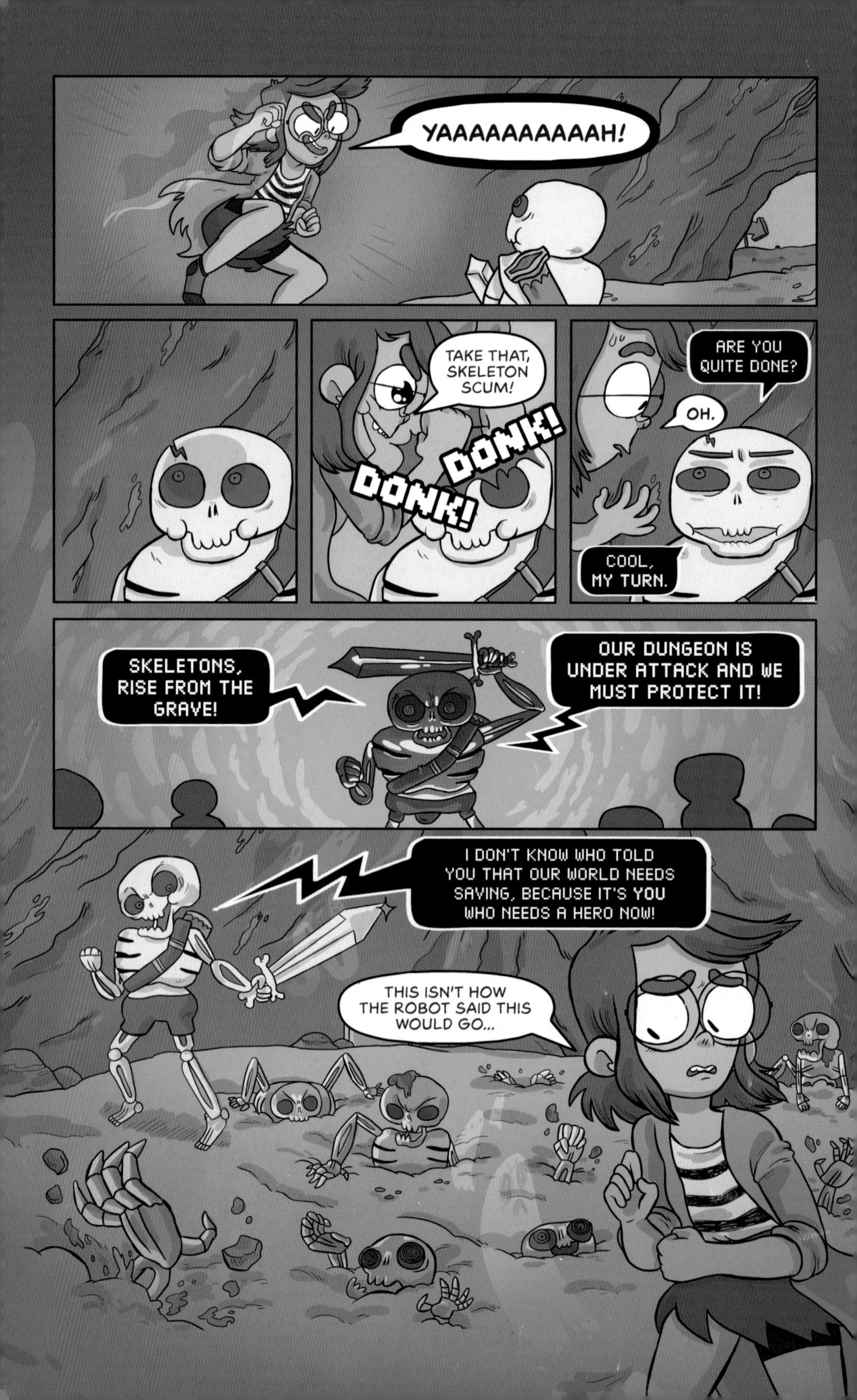
YAAAAAAAAAAH!
TAKE THAT, SKELETON SCUM!
DONK!
DONK!
ARE YOU QUITE DONE?
OH.
COOL, MY TURN.
SKELETONS, RISE FROM THE GRAVE!
OUR DUNGEON IS UNDER ATTACK AND WE MUST PROTECT IT!
I DON'T KNOW WHO TOLD YOU THAT OUR WORLD NEEDS SAVING, BECAUSE IT'S YOU WHO NEEDS A HERO NOW!
THIS ISN'T HOW THE ROBOT SAID THIS WOULD GO...

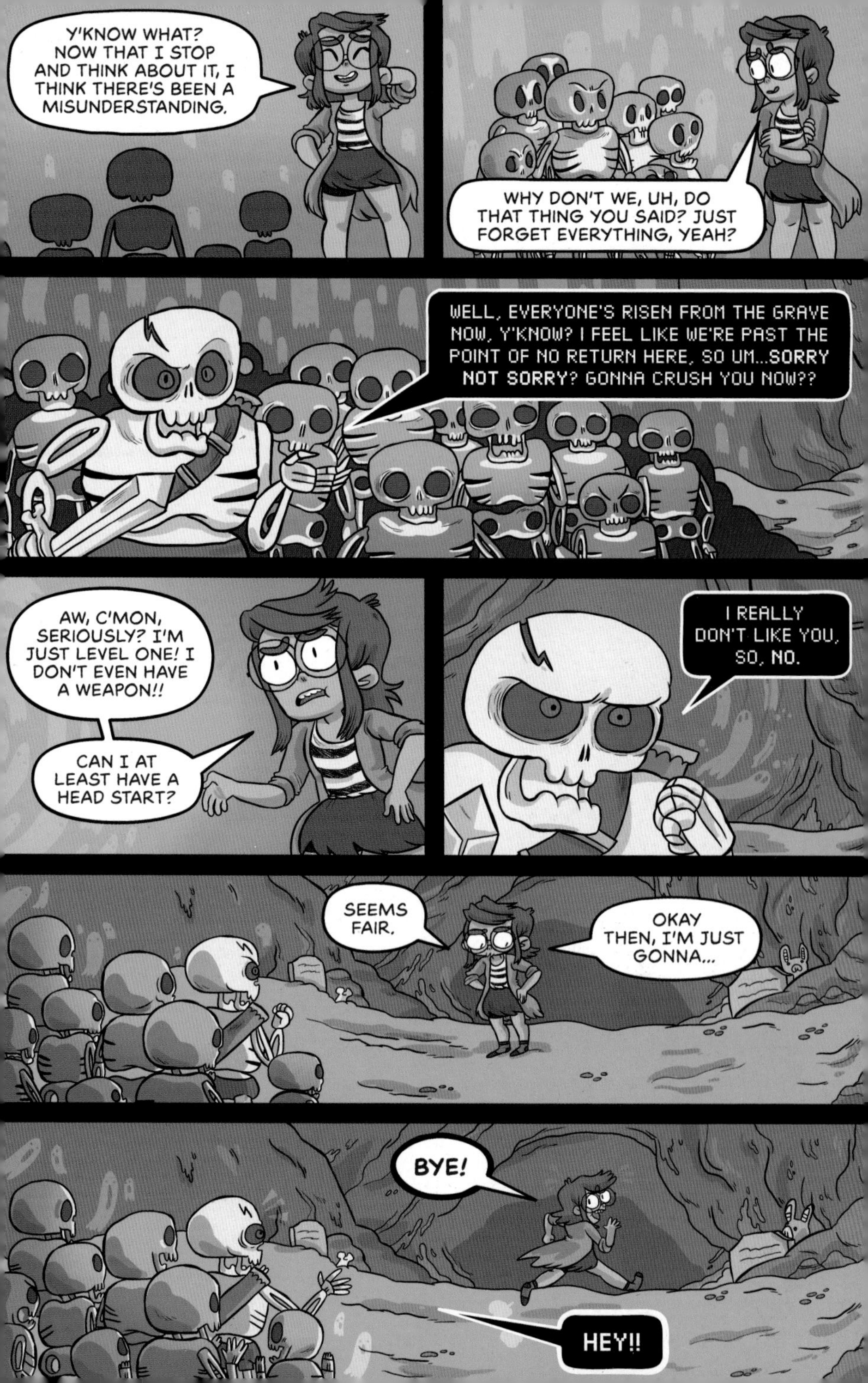
Y'KNOW WHAT? NOW THAT I STOP AND THINK ABOUT IT, I THINK THERE'S BEEN A MISUNDERSTANDING.
WHY DON'T WE, UH, DO THAT THING YOU SAID? JUST FORGET EVERYTHING, YEAH?
WELL, EVERYONE'S RISEN FROM THE GRAVE NOW, Y'KNOW? I FEEL LIKE WE'RE PAST THE POINT OF NO RETURN HERE, SO UM...SORRY NOT SORRY? GONNA CRUSH YOU NOW??
AW, C'MON, SERIOUSLY? I'M JUST LEVEL ONE! I DON'T EVEN HAVE A WEAPON!!
CAN I AT LEAST HAVE A HEAD START?
I REALLY DON'T LIKE YOU, SO, NO.
SEEMS FAIR.
OKAY THEN, I'M JUST GONNA...
BYE!
HEY!!

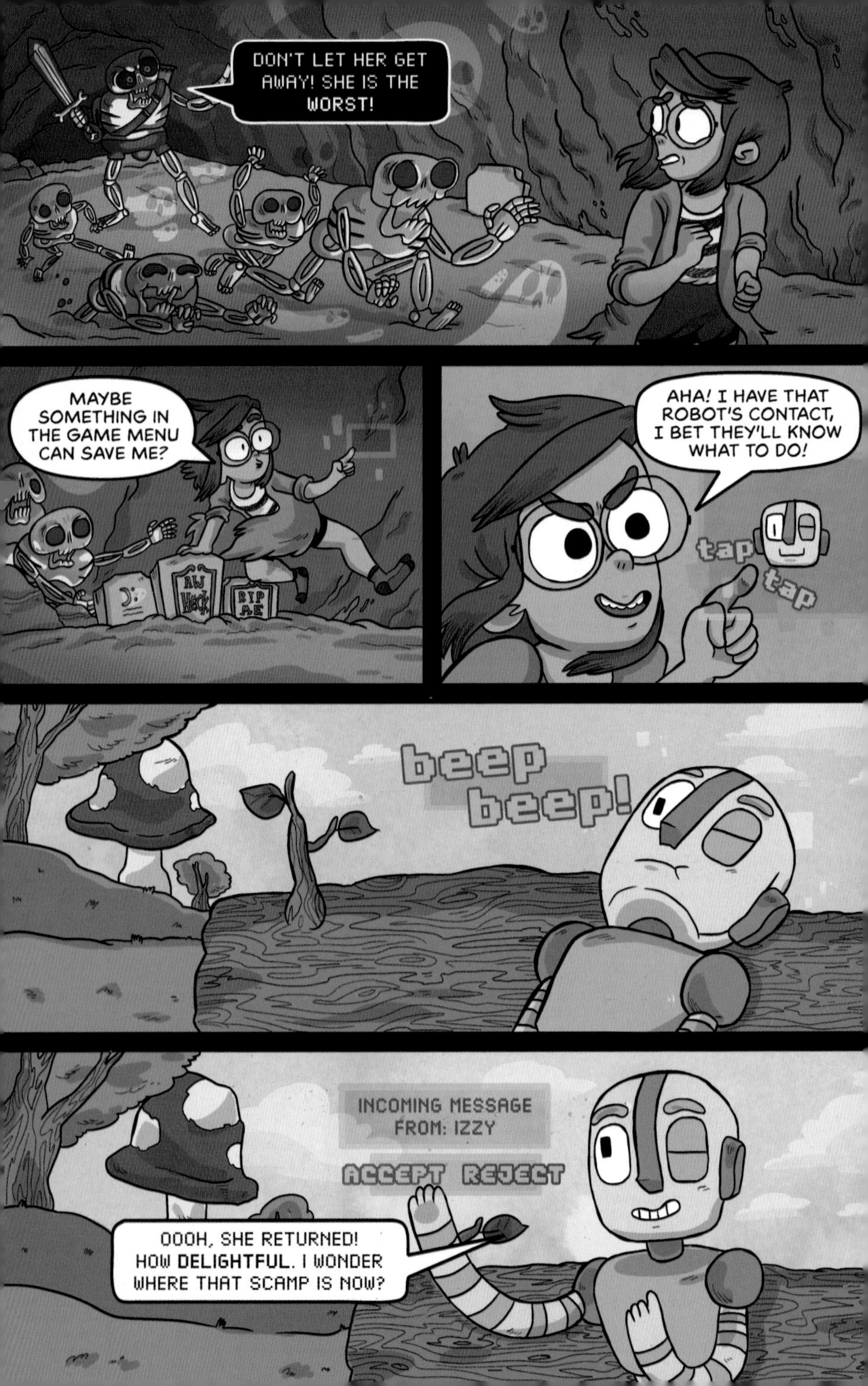
DON'T LET HER GET AWAY! SHE IS THE WORST!
AW Heck
RIP ME
MAYBE SOMETHING IN THE GAME MENU CAN SAVE ME?
AHA! I HAVE THAT ROBOT'S CONTACT, I BET THEY'LL KNOW WHAT TO DO!
tap tap
beep beep!
INCOMING MESSAGE FROM: IZZY
ACCEPT REJECT
OOOH, SHE RETURNED! HOW **DELIGHTFUL**. I WONDER WHERE THAT SCAMP IS NOW?

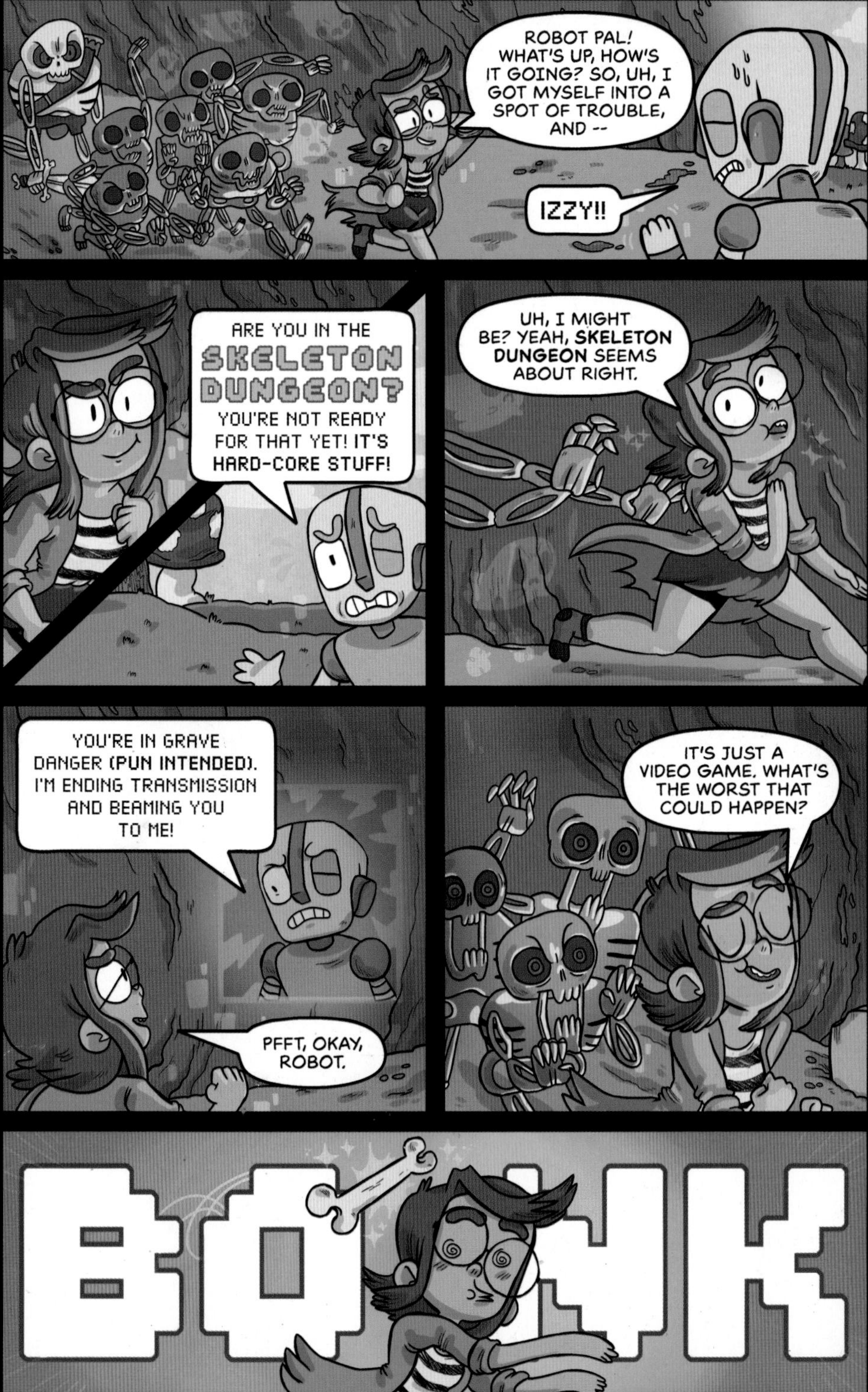
ROBOT PAL! WHAT'S UP, HOW'S IT GOING? SO, UH, I GOT MYSELF INTO A SPOT OF TROUBLE, AND --
IZZY!!
ARE YOU IN THE SKELETON DUNGEON? YOU'RE NOT READY FOR THAT YET! IT'S HARD-CORE STUFF!
UH, I MIGHT BE? YEAH, SKELETON DUNGEON SEEMS ABOUT RIGHT.
YOU'RE IN GRAVE DANGER (PUN INTENDED). I'M ENDING TRANSMISSION AND BEAMING YOU TO ME!
PFFT, OKAY, ROBOT.
IT'S JUST A VIDEO GAME. WHAT'S THE WORST THAT COULD HAPPEN?
BONK

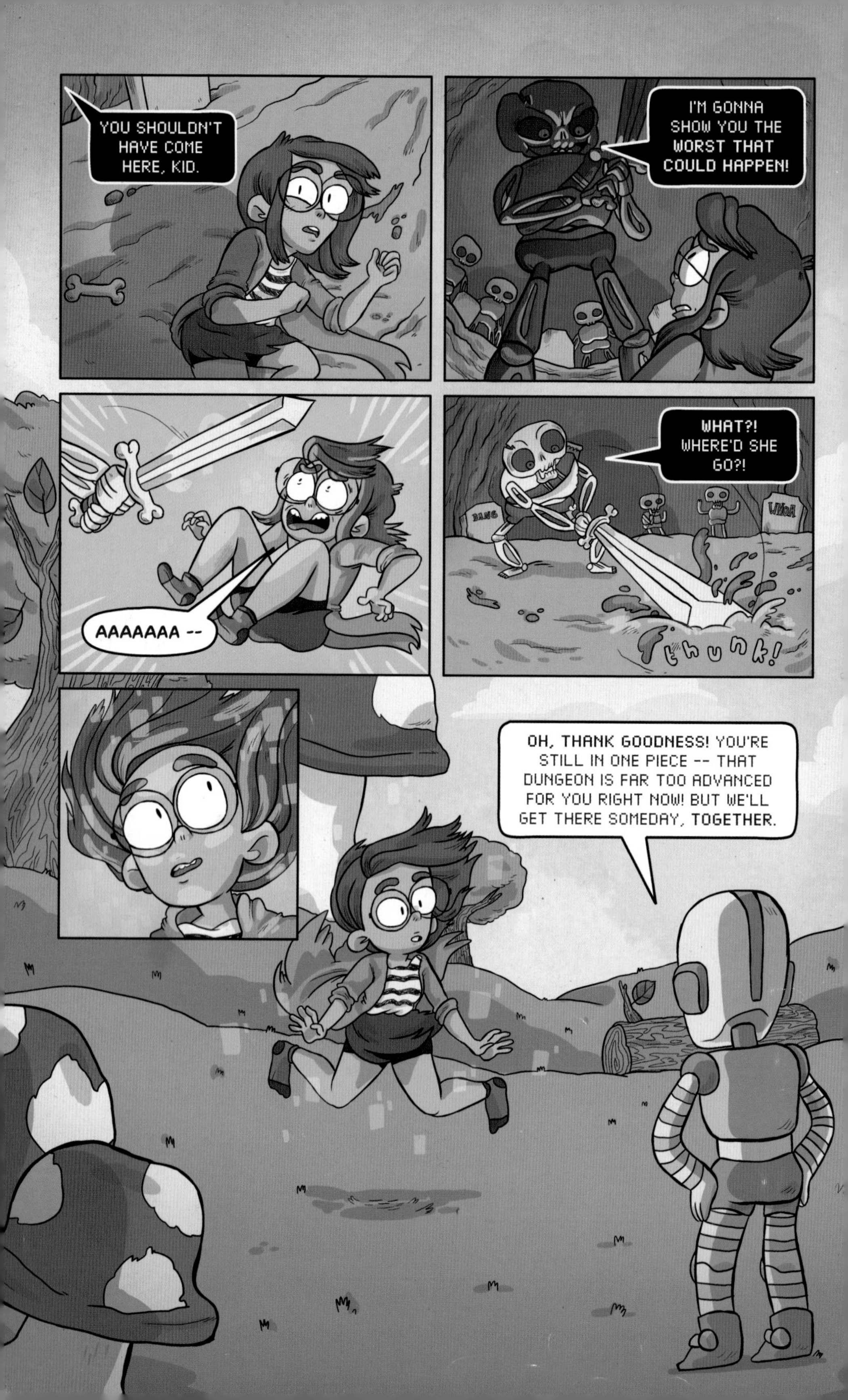
YOU SHOULDN'T HAVE COME HERE, KID.
I'M GONNA SHOW YOU THE WORST THAT COULD HAPPEN!
AAAAAAA --
WHAT?! WHERE'D SHE GO?!
BANG
WHOA
thunk!
OH, THANK GOODNESS! YOU'RE STILL IN ONE PIECE -- THAT DUNGEON IS FAR TOO ADVANCED FOR YOU RIGHT NOW! BUT WE'LL GET THERE SOMEDAY, TOGETHER.

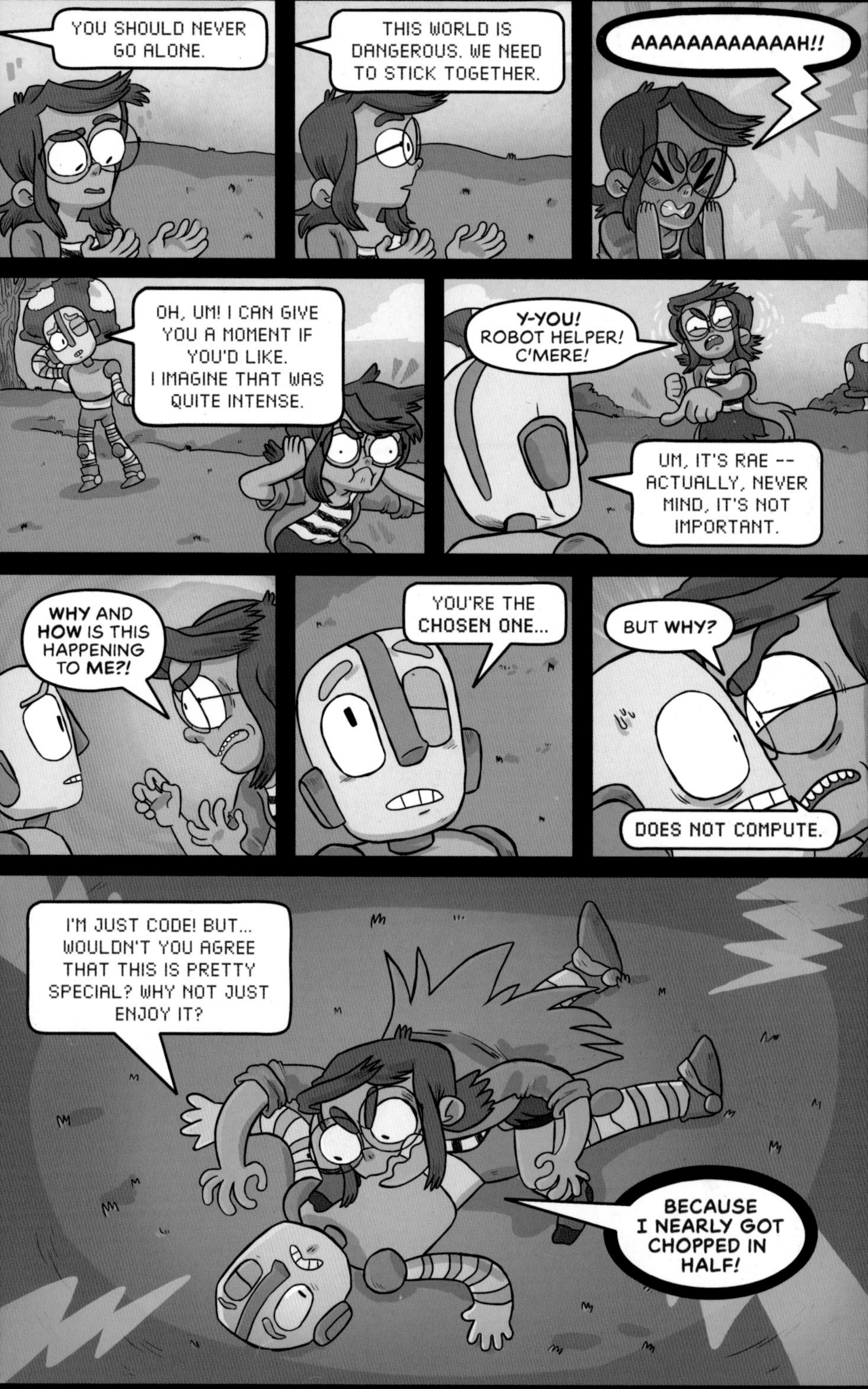
YOU SHOULD NEVER GO ALONE.
THIS WORLD IS DANGEROUS. WE NEED TO STICK TOGETHER.
AAAAAAAAAAAAH!!
OH, UM! I CAN GIVE YOU A MOMENT IF YOU'D LIKE. I IMAGINE THAT WAS QUITE INTENSE.
Y-YOU! ROBOT HELPER! C'MERE!
UM, IT'S RAE -- ACTUALLY, NEVER MIND, IT'S NOT IMPORTANT.
WHY AND HOW IS THIS HAPPENING TO ME?!
YOU'RE THE CHOSEN ONE...
BUT WHY?
DOES NOT COMPUTE.
I'M JUST CODE! BUT... WOULDN'T YOU AGREE THAT THIS IS PRETTY SPECIAL? WHY NOT JUST ENJOY IT?
BECAUSE I NEARLY GOT CHOPPED IN HALF!

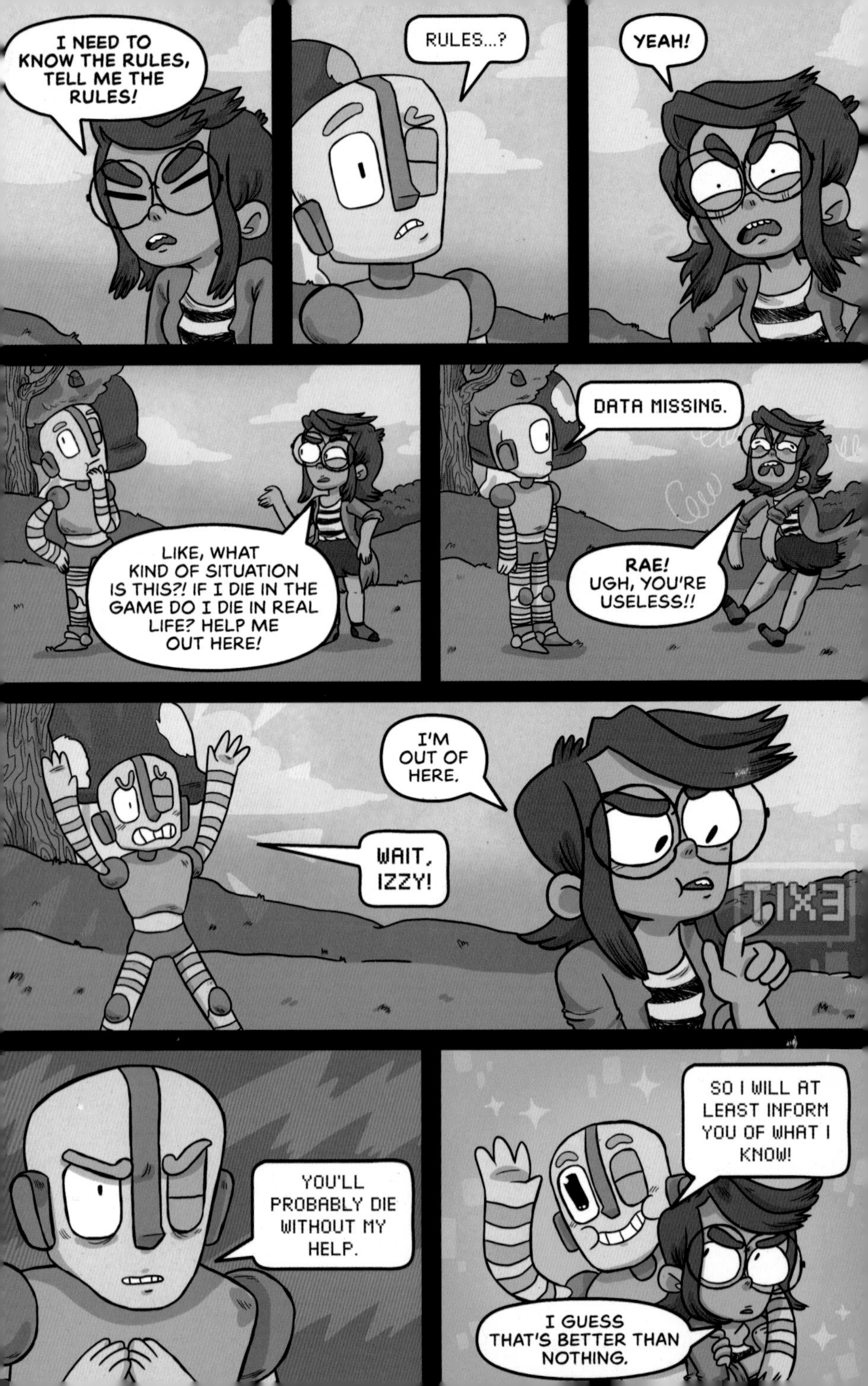
I NEED TO KNOW THE RULES, TELL ME THE RULES!
RULES...?
YEAH!
LIKE, WHAT KIND OF SITUATION IS THIS?! IF I DIE IN THE GAME DO I DIE IN REAL LIFE? HELP ME OUT HERE!
DATA MISSING.
RAE! UGH, YOU'RE USELESS!!
I'M OUT OF HERE.
WAIT, IZZY!
EXIT
YOU'LL PROBABLY DIE WITHOUT MY HELP.
SO I WILL AT LEAST INFORM YOU OF WHAT I KNOW!
I GUESS THAT'S BETTER THAN NOTHING.

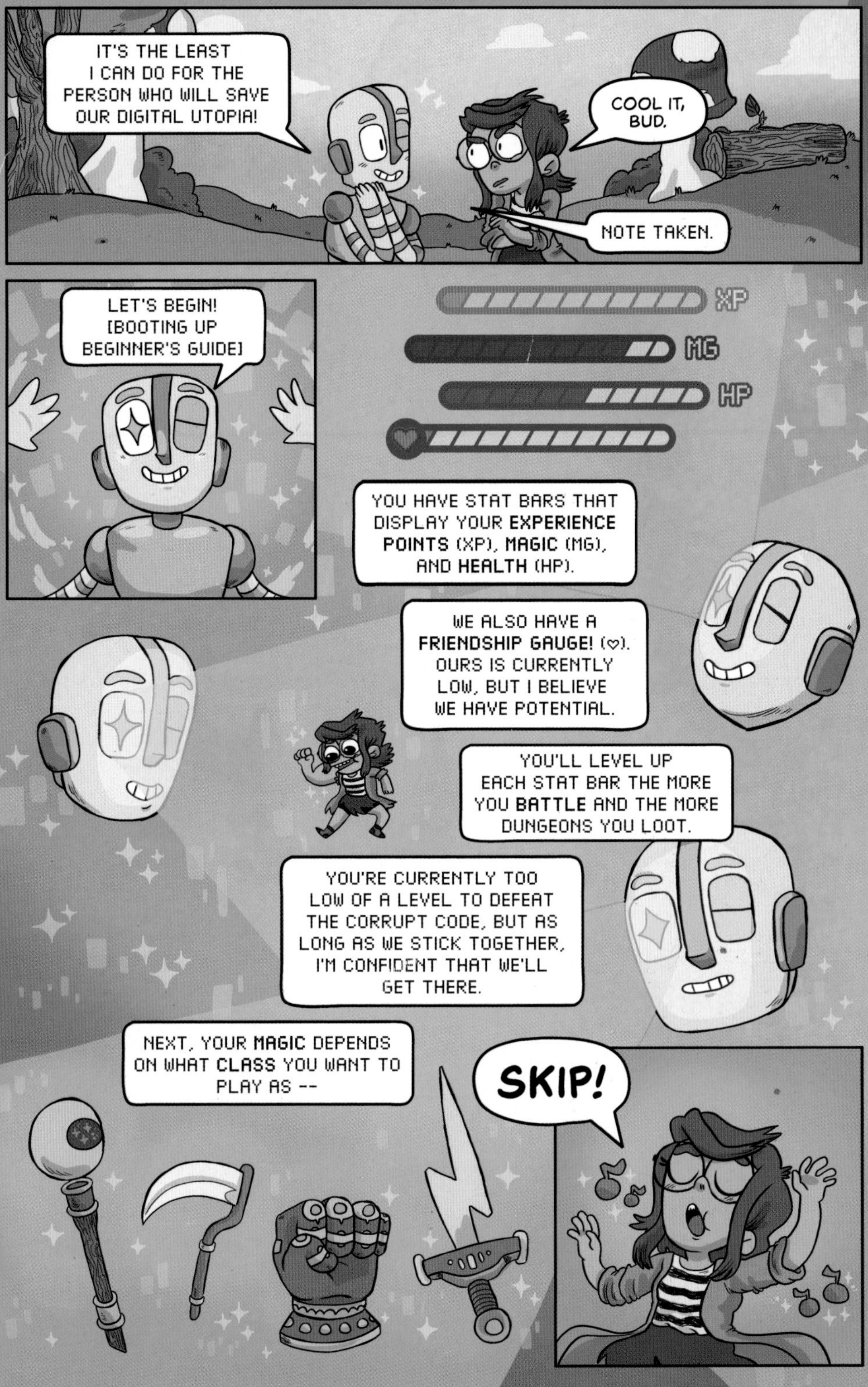
IT'S THE LEAST I CAN DO FOR THE PERSON WHO WILL SAVE OUR DIGITAL UTOPIA!
COOL IT, BUD.
NOTE TAKEN.
LET'S BEGIN! [BOOTING UP BEGINNER'S GUIDE]
XP
MG
HP
YOU HAVE STAT BARS THAT DISPLAY YOUR EXPERIENCE POINTS (XP), MAGIC (MG), AND HEALTH (HP).
WE ALSO HAVE A FRIENDSHIP GAUGE! (♡). OURS IS CURRENTLY LOW, BUT I BELIEVE WE HAVE POTENTIAL.
YOU'LL LEVEL UP EACH STAT BAR THE MORE YOU BATTLE AND THE MORE DUNGEONS YOU LOOT.
YOU'RE CURRENTLY TOO LOW OF A LEVEL TO DEFEAT THE CORRUPT CODE, BUT AS LONG AS WE STICK TOGETHER, I'M CONFIDENT THAT WE'LL GET THERE.
NEXT, YOUR MAGIC DEPENDS ON WHAT CLASS YOU WANT TO PLAY AS --
SKIP!

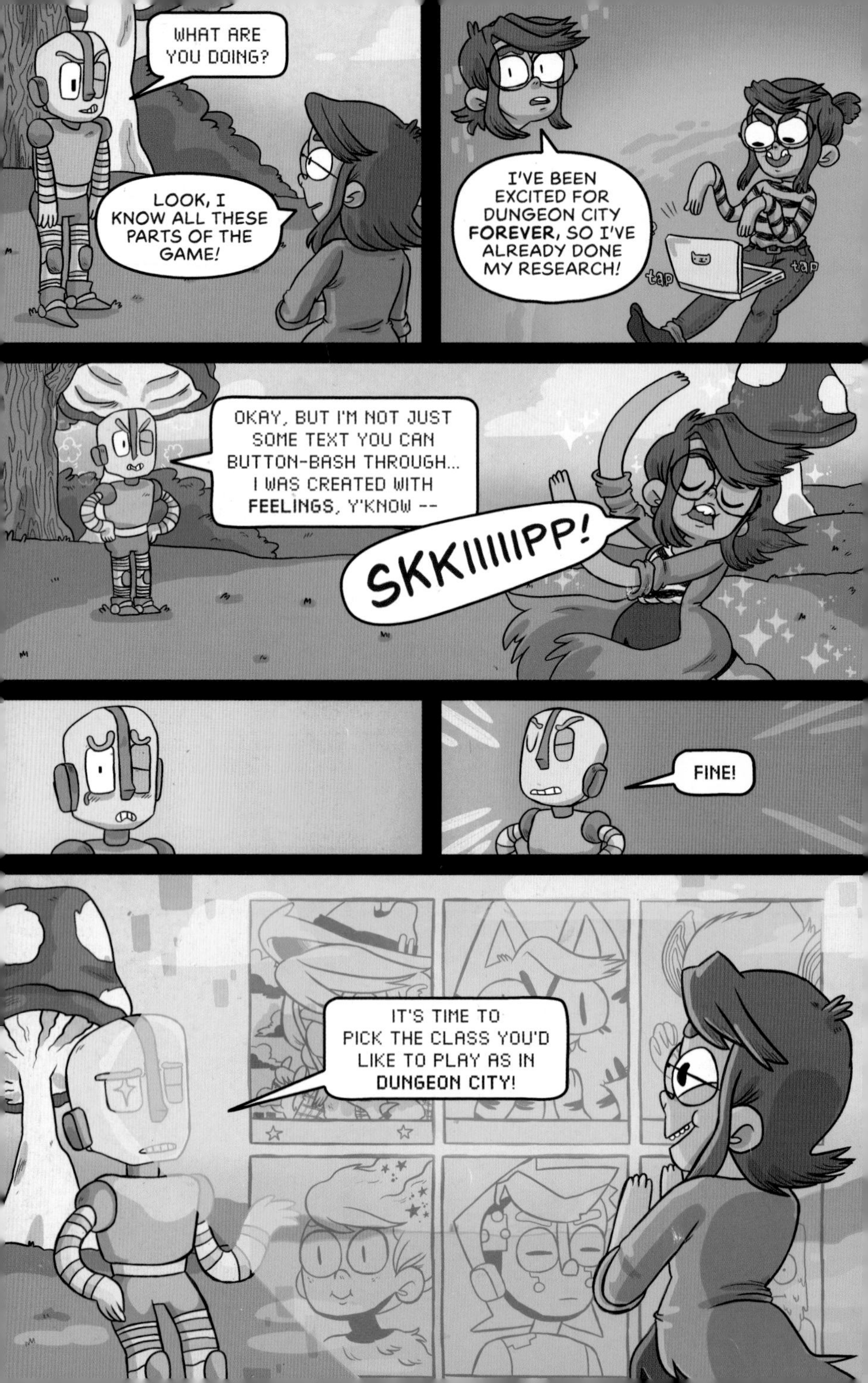
WHAT ARE YOU DOING?
LOOK, I KNOW ALL THESE PARTS OF THE GAME!
I'VE BEEN EXCITED FOR DUNGEON CITY FOREVER, SO I'VE ALREADY DONE MY RESEARCH!
tap
tap
OKAY, BUT I'M NOT JUST SOME TEXT YOU CAN BUTTON-BASH THROUGH... I WAS CREATED WITH FEELINGS, Y'KNOW --
SKKIIIIIPP!
FINE!
IT'S TIME TO PICK THE CLASS YOU'D LIKE TO PLAY AS IN DUNGEON CITY!

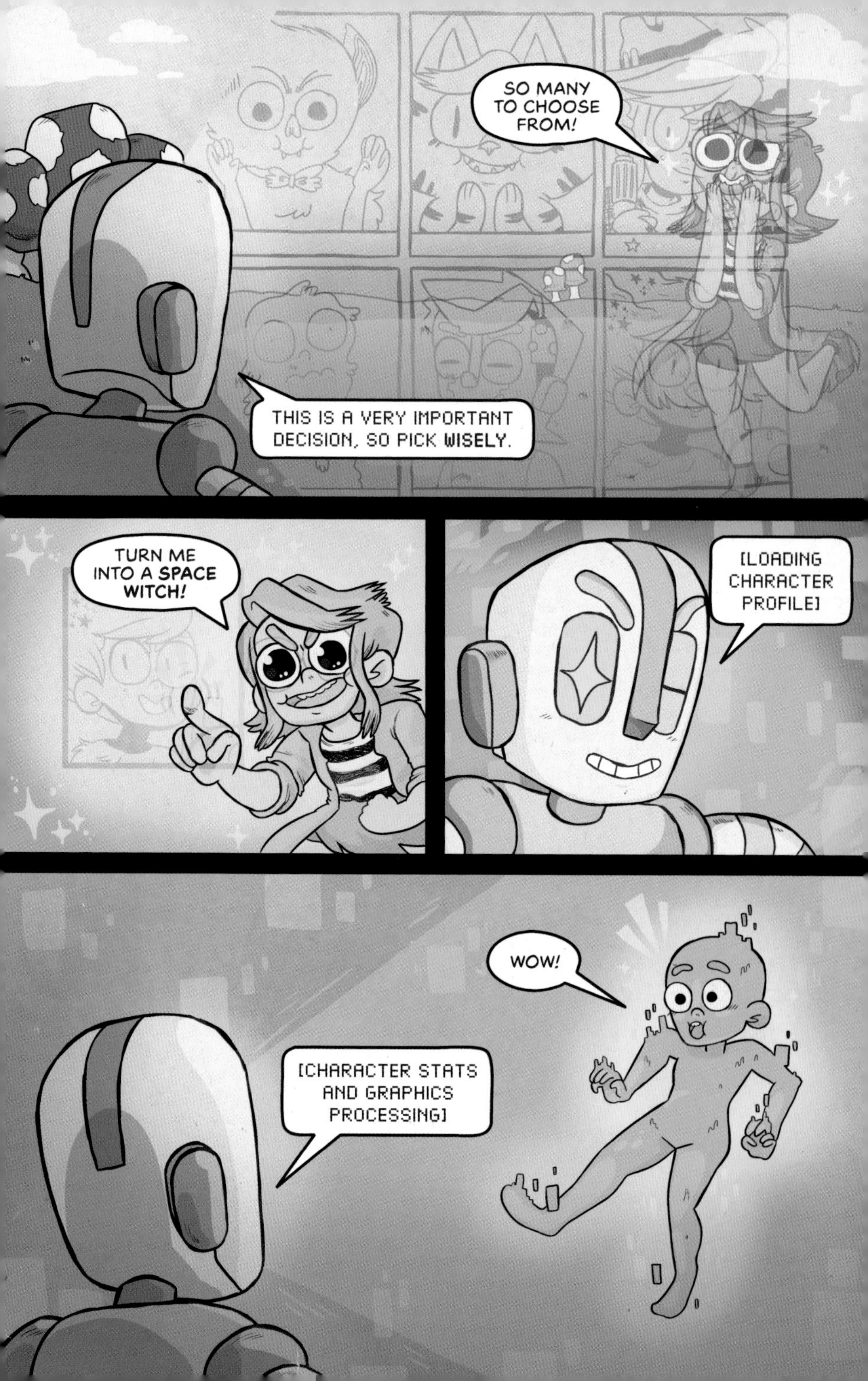
SO MANY TO CHOOSE FROM!
THIS IS A VERY IMPORTANT DECISION, SO PICK WISELY.
TURN ME INTO A SPACE WITCH!
[LOADING CHARACTER PROFILE]
WOW!
[CHARACTER STATS AND GRAPHICS PROCESSING]

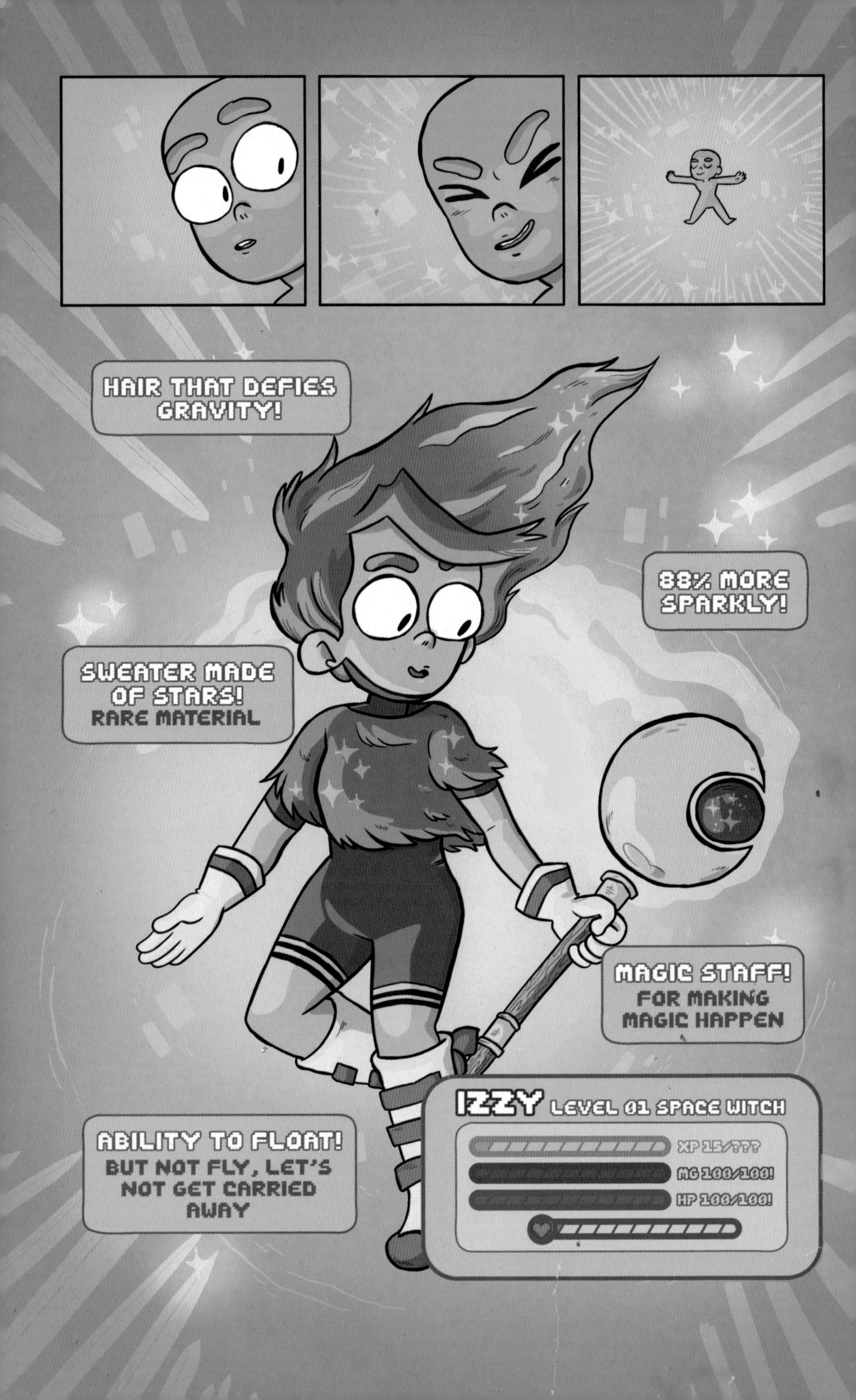

HAIR THAT DEFIES GRAVITY!
88% MORE SPARKLY!
SWEATER MADE OF STARS!
RARE MATERIAL
MAGIC STAFF!
FOR MAKING MAGIC HAPPEN
ABILITY TO FLOAT!
BUT NOT FLY, LET'S NOT GET CARRIED AWAY
IZZY LEVEL 01 SPACE WITCH
XP 15/???
MG 100/100!
HP 100/100!

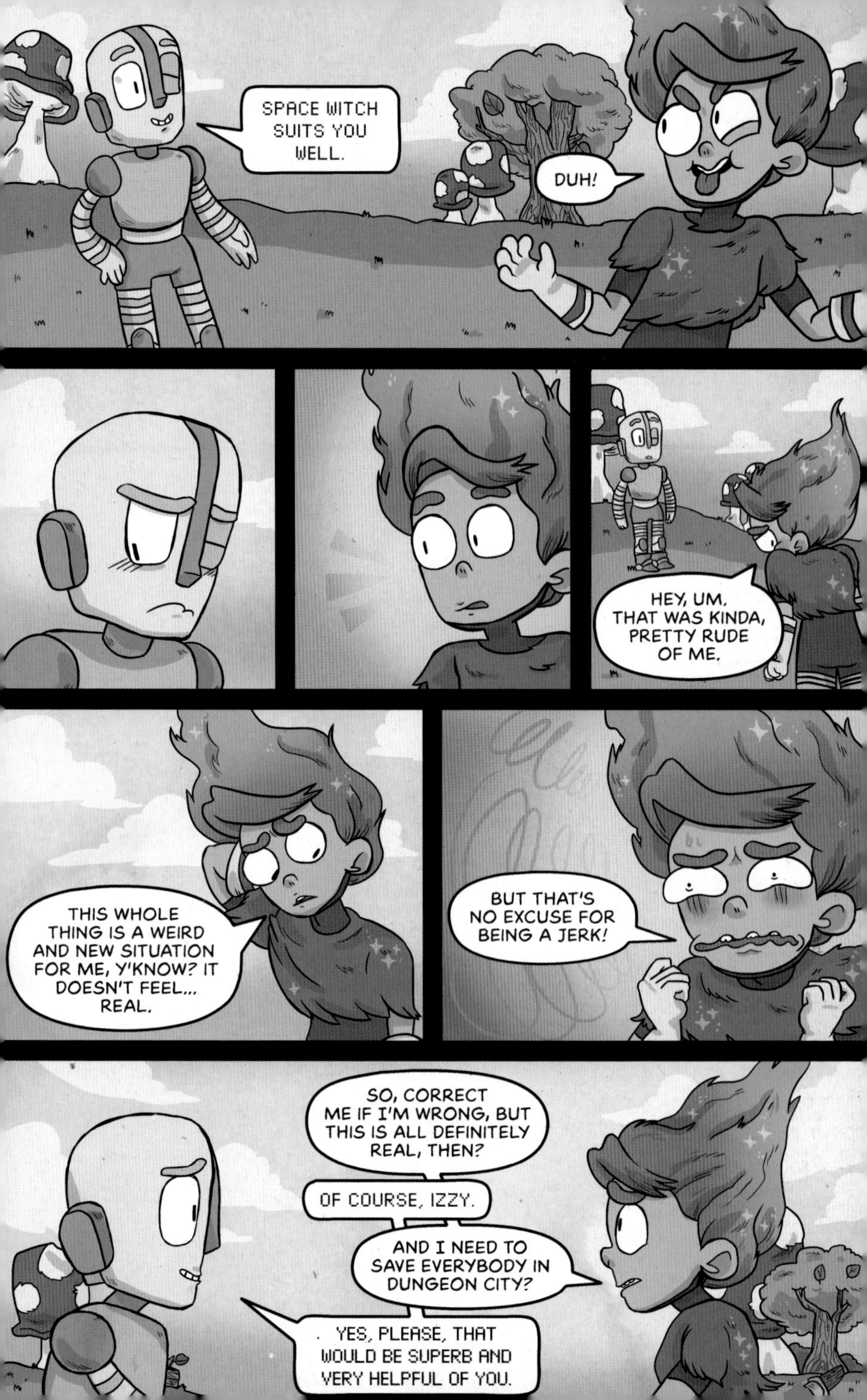
SPACE WITCH SUITS YOU WELL.
DUH!
HEY, UM, THAT WAS KINDA, PRETTY RUDE OF ME.
THIS WHOLE THING IS A WEIRD AND NEW SITUATION FOR ME, Y'KNOW? IT DOESN'T FEEL... REAL.
BUT THAT'S NO EXCUSE FOR BEING A JERK!
SO, CORRECT ME IF I'M WRONG, BUT THIS IS ALL DEFINITELY REAL, THEN?
OF COURSE, IZZY.
AND I NEED TO SAVE EVERYBODY IN DUNGEON CITY?
YES, PLEASE, THAT WOULD BE SUPERB AND VERY HELPFUL OF YOU.

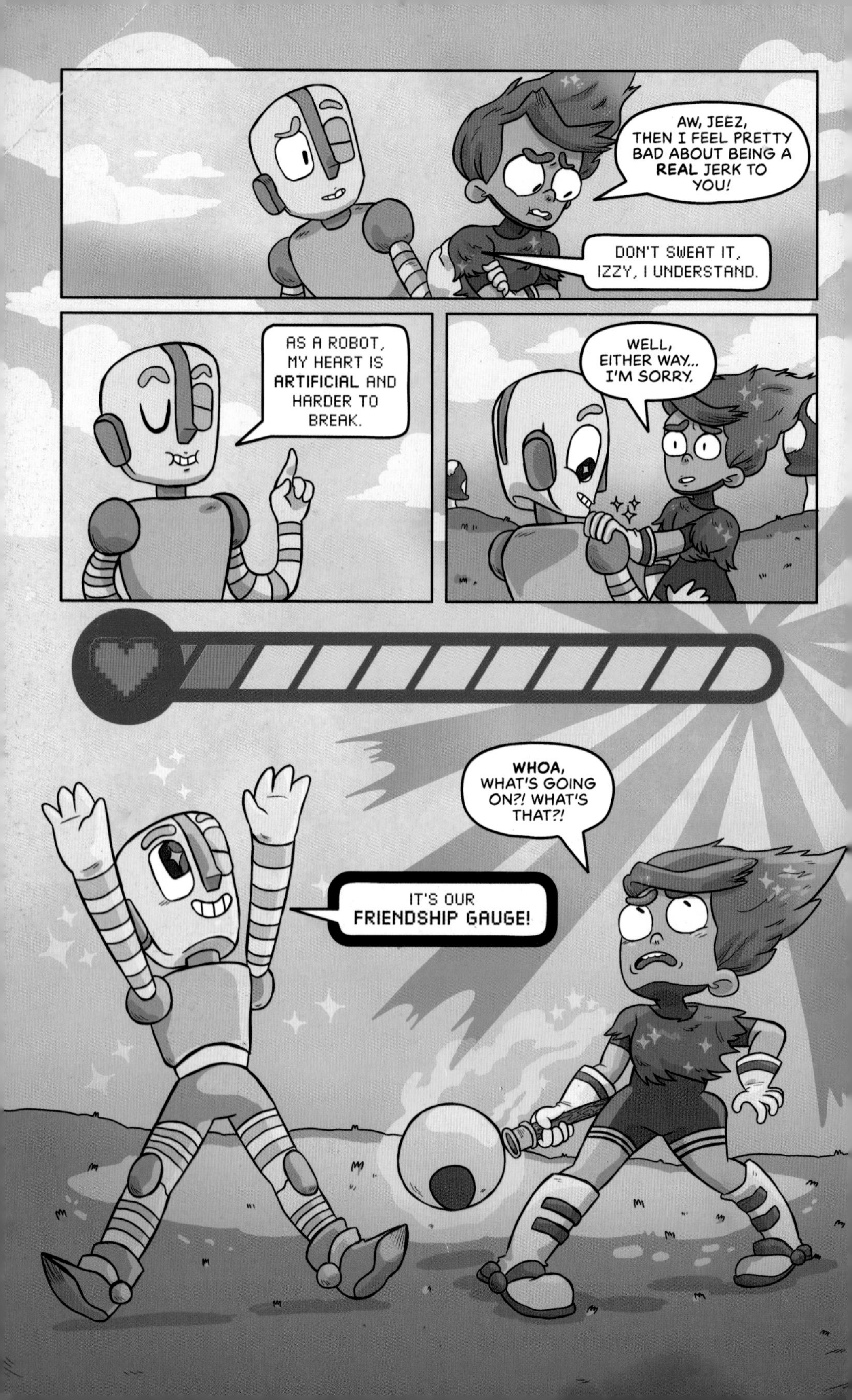
AW, JEEZ, THEN I FEEL PRETTY BAD ABOUT BEING A **REAL** JERK TO YOU!
DON'T SWEAT IT, IZZY, I UNDERSTAND.
AS A ROBOT, MY HEART IS **ARTIFICIAL** AND HARDER TO BREAK.
WELL, EITHER WAY... I'M SORRY.
WHOA, WHAT'S GOING ON?! WHAT'S THAT?!
IT'S OUR **FRIENDSHIP GAUGE!**

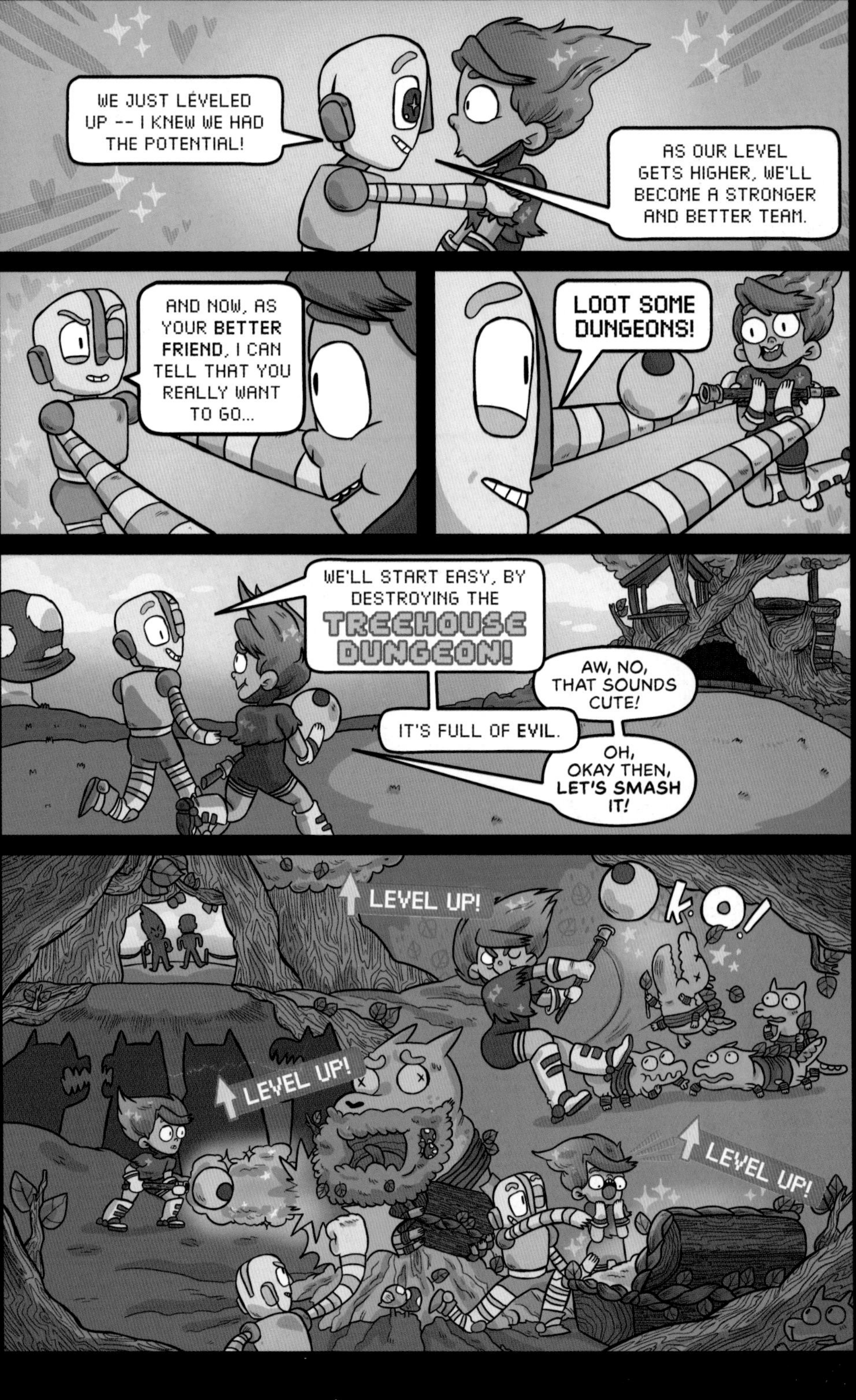
WE JUST LEVELED UP -- I KNEW WE HAD THE POTENTIAL!
AS OUR LEVEL GETS HIGHER, WE'LL BECOME A STRONGER AND BETTER TEAM.
AND NOW, AS YOUR BETTER FRIEND, I CAN TELL THAT YOU REALLY WANT TO GO...
LOOT SOME DUNGEONS!
WE'LL START EASY, BY DESTROYING THE TREEHOUSE DUNGEON!
AW, NO, THAT SOUNDS CUTE!
IT'S FULL OF EVIL.
OH, OKAY THEN, LET'S SMASH IT!
LEVEL UP!
K.O!
LEVEL UP!
LEVEL UP!

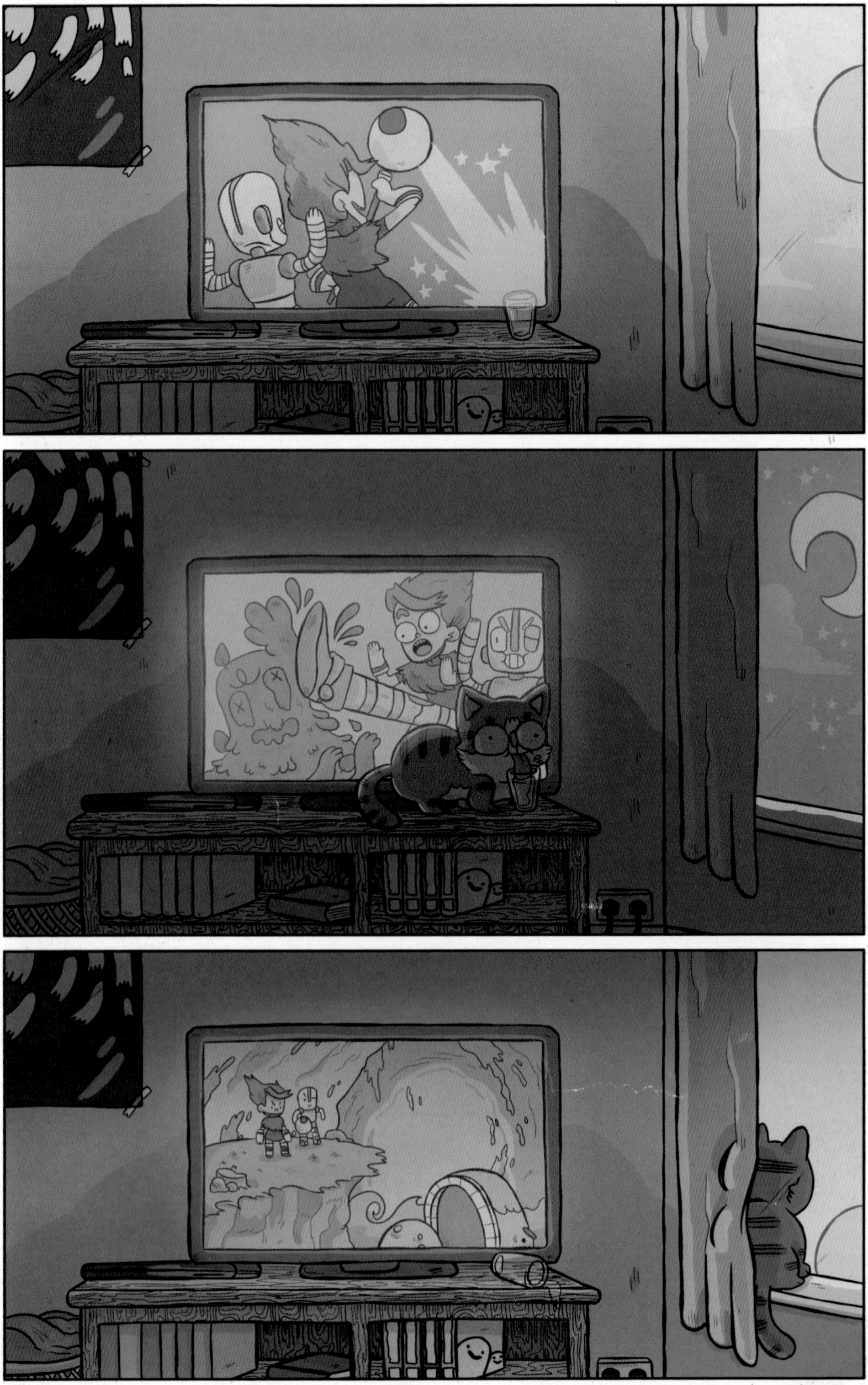

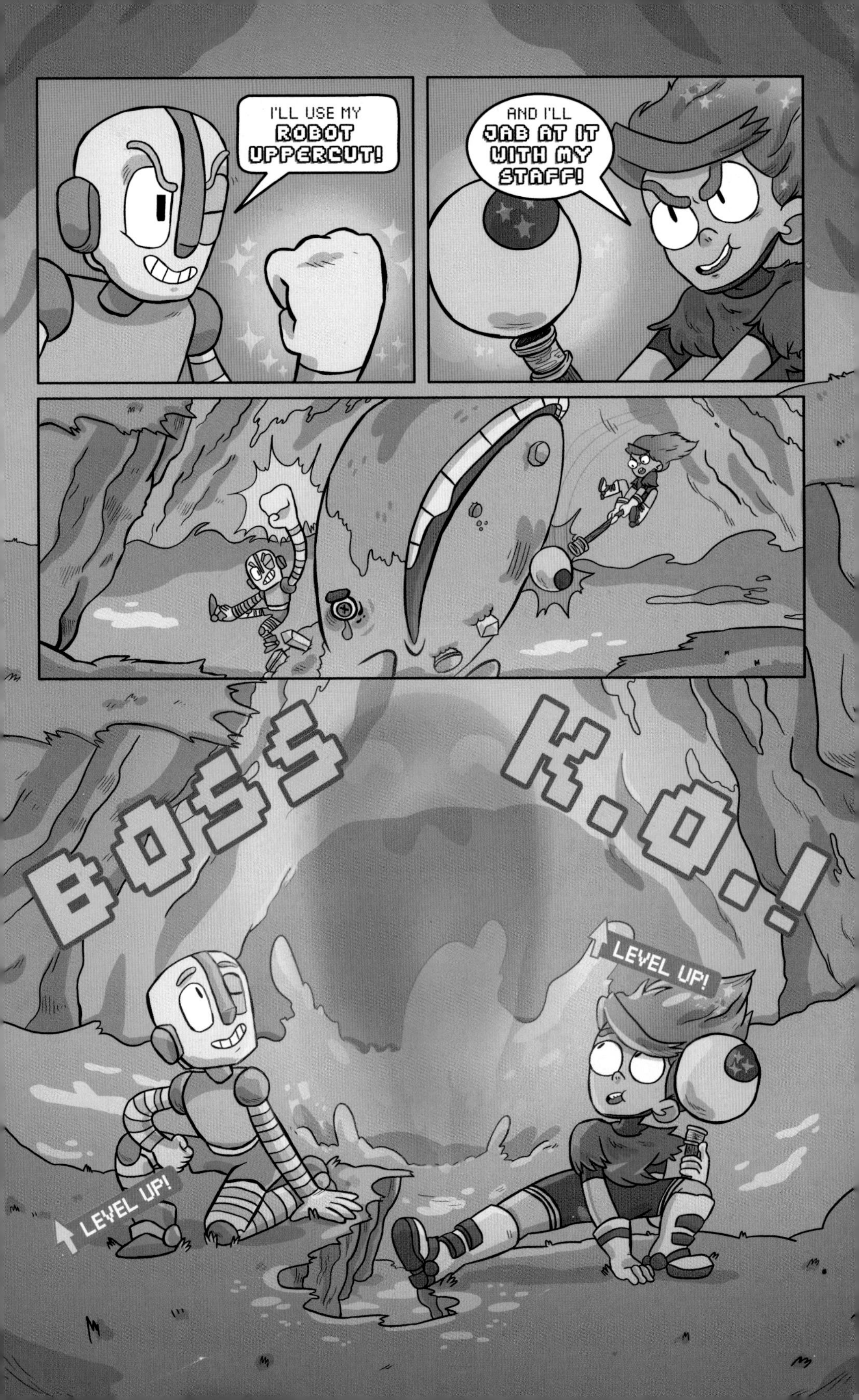
I'LL USE MY ROBOT UPPERCUT!
AND I'LL JAB AT IT WITH MY STAFF!
BOSS K.O.!
LEVEL UP!
LEVEL UP!

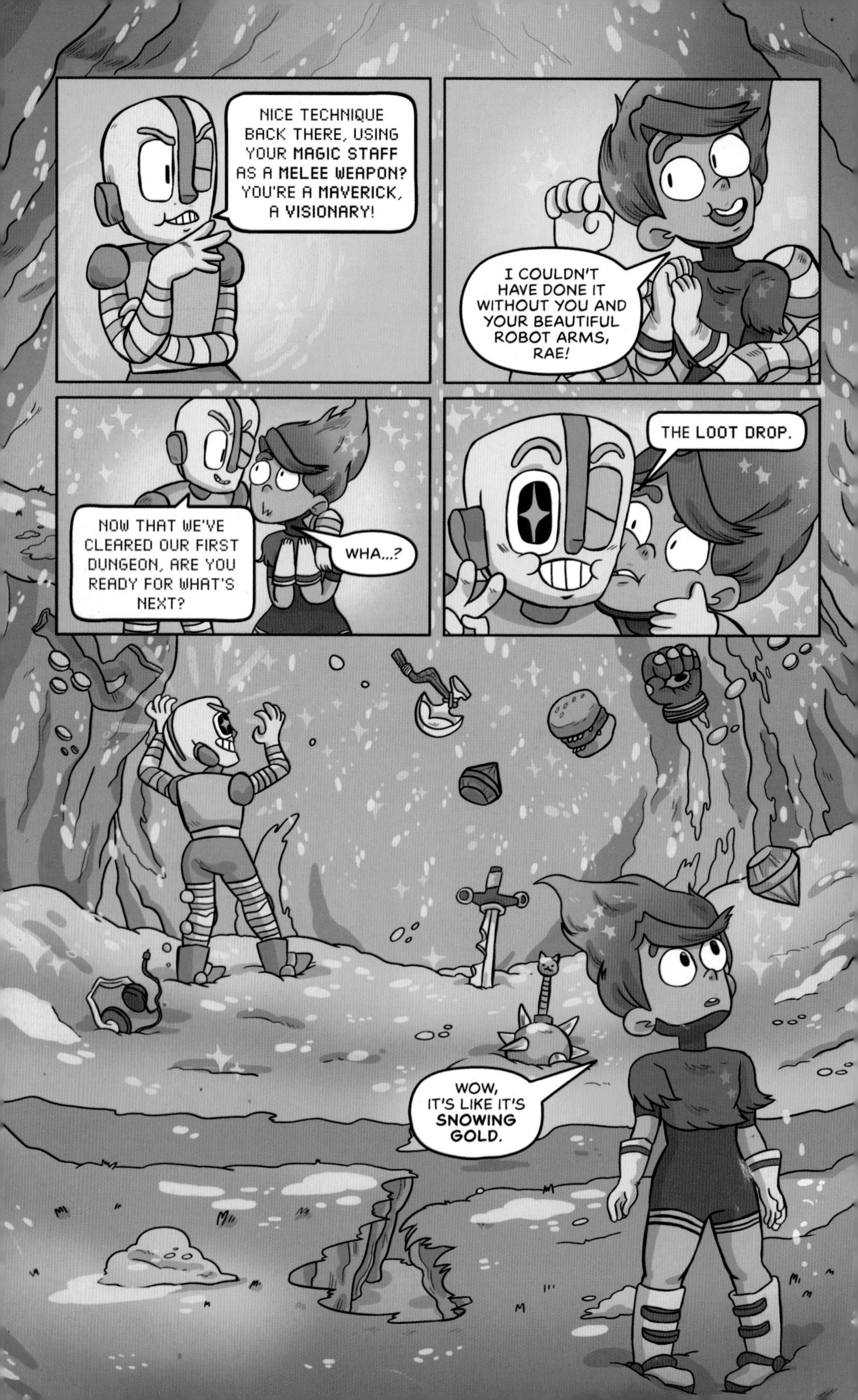

NICE TECHNIQUE BACK THERE, USING YOUR MAGIC STAFF AS A MELEE WEAPON? YOU'RE A MAVERICK, A VISIONARY!
I COULDN'T HAVE DONE IT WITHOUT YOU AND YOUR BEAUTIFUL ROBOT ARMS, RAE!
NOW THAT WE'VE CLEARED OUR FIRST DUNGEON, ARE YOU READY FOR WHAT'S NEXT?
WHA...?
THE LOOT DROP.
WOW, IT'S LIKE IT'S SNOWING GOLD.

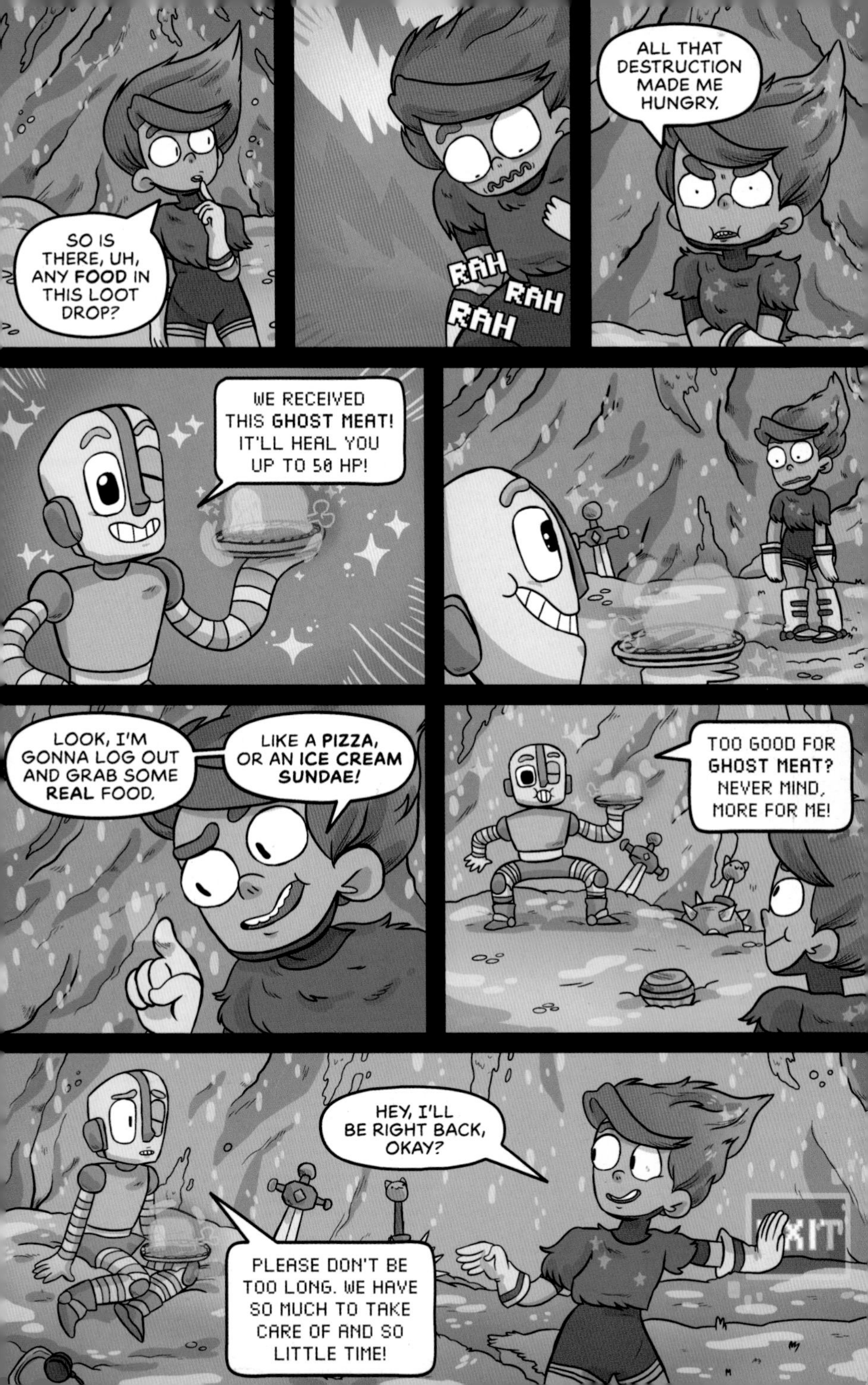
SO IS THERE, UH, ANY FOOD IN THIS LOOT DROP?
RAH RAH RAH
ALL THAT DESTRUCTION MADE ME HUNGRY.
WE RECEIVED THIS GHOST MEAT! IT'LL HEAL YOU UP TO 50 HP!
LOOK, I'M GONNA LOG OUT AND GRAB SOME REAL FOOD.
LIKE A PIZZA, OR AN ICE CREAM SUNDAE!
TOO GOOD FOR GHOST MEAT? NEVER MIND, MORE FOR ME!
HEY, I'LL BE RIGHT BACK, OKAY?
PLEASE DON'T BE TOO LONG. WE HAVE SO MUCH TO TAKE CARE OF AND SO LITTLE TIME!

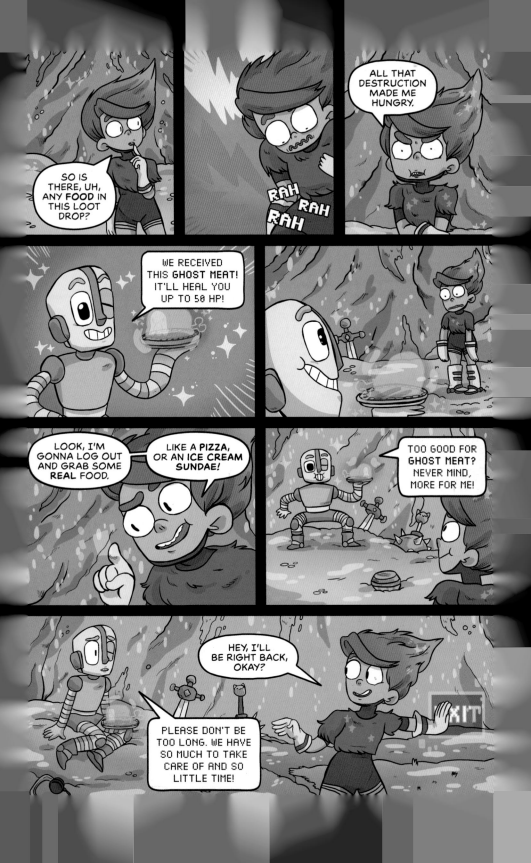

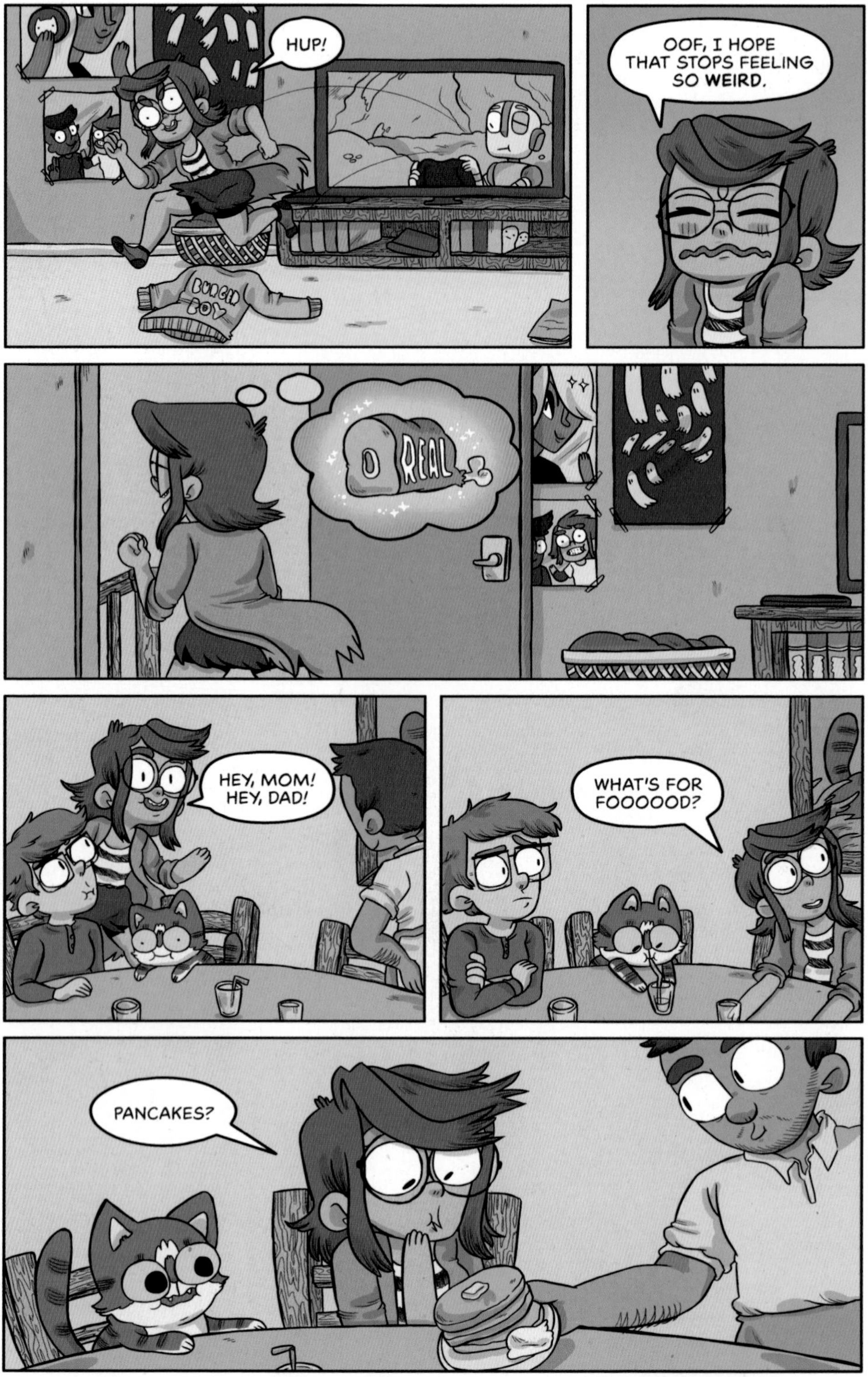
HUP!
BURGER BOY
OOF, I HOPE THAT STOPS FEELING SO **WEIRD**.
O REAL
HEY, MOM! HEY, DAD!
WHAT'S FOR FOOOOOD?
PANCAKES?

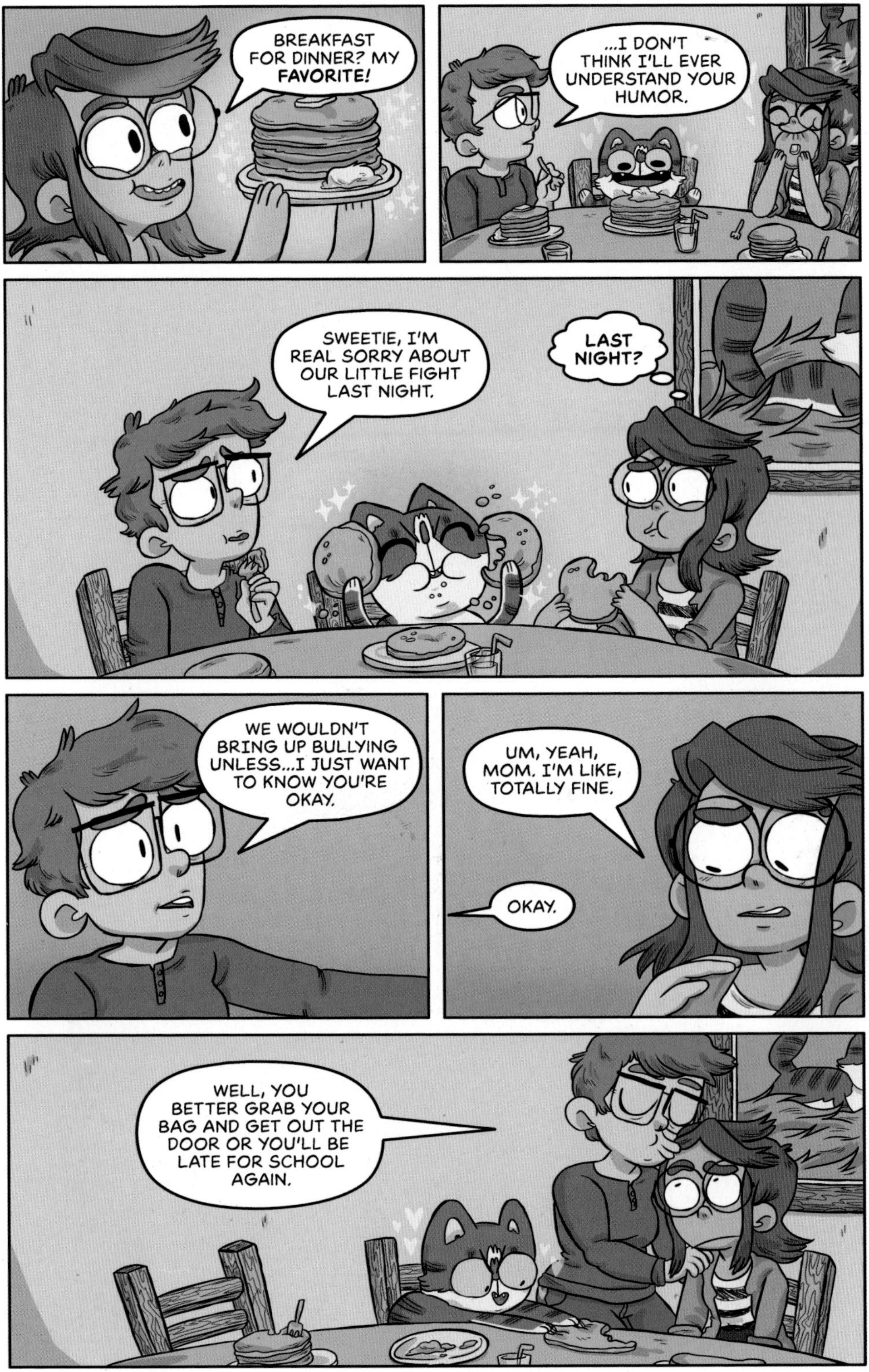
BREAKFAST FOR DINNER? MY FAVORITE!
...I DON'T THINK I'LL EVER UNDERSTAND YOUR HUMOR.
SWEETIE, I'M REAL SORRY ABOUT OUR LITTLE FIGHT LAST NIGHT.
LAST NIGHT?
WE WOULDN'T BRING UP BULLYING UNLESS...I JUST WANT TO KNOW YOU'RE OKAY.
UM, YEAH, MOM. I'M LIKE, TOTALLY FINE.
OKAY.
WELL, YOU BETTER GRAB YOUR BAG AND GET OUT THE DOOR OR YOU'LL BE LATE FOR SCHOOL AGAIN.

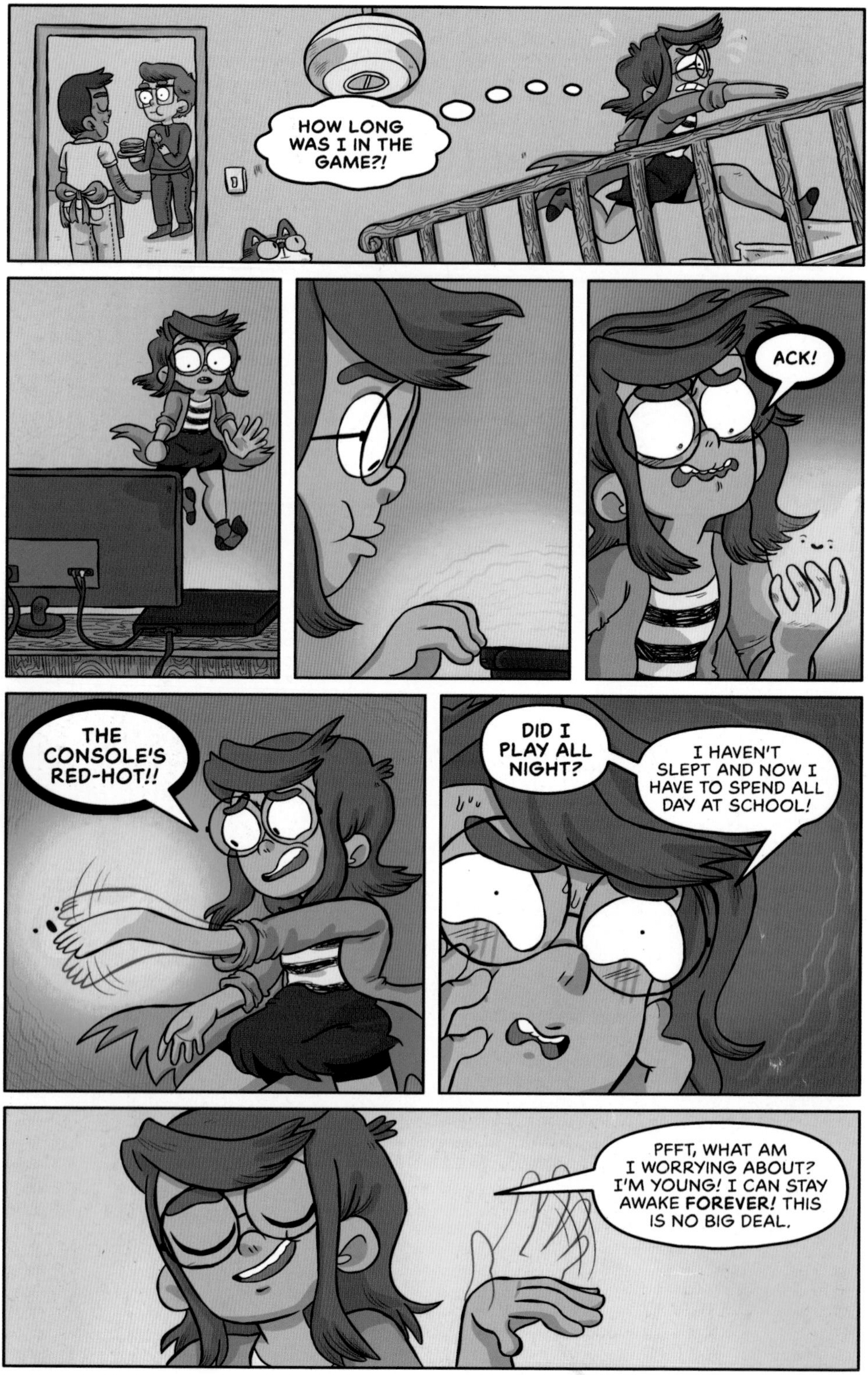
HOW LONG WAS I IN THE GAME?!
ACK!
THE CONSOLE'S RED-HOT!!
DID I PLAY ALL NIGHT?
I HAVEN'T SLEPT AND NOW I HAVE TO SPEND ALL DAY AT SCHOOL!
PFFT, WHAT AM I WORRYING ABOUT? I'M YOUNG! I CAN STAY AWAKE FOREVER! THIS IS NO BIG DEAL.

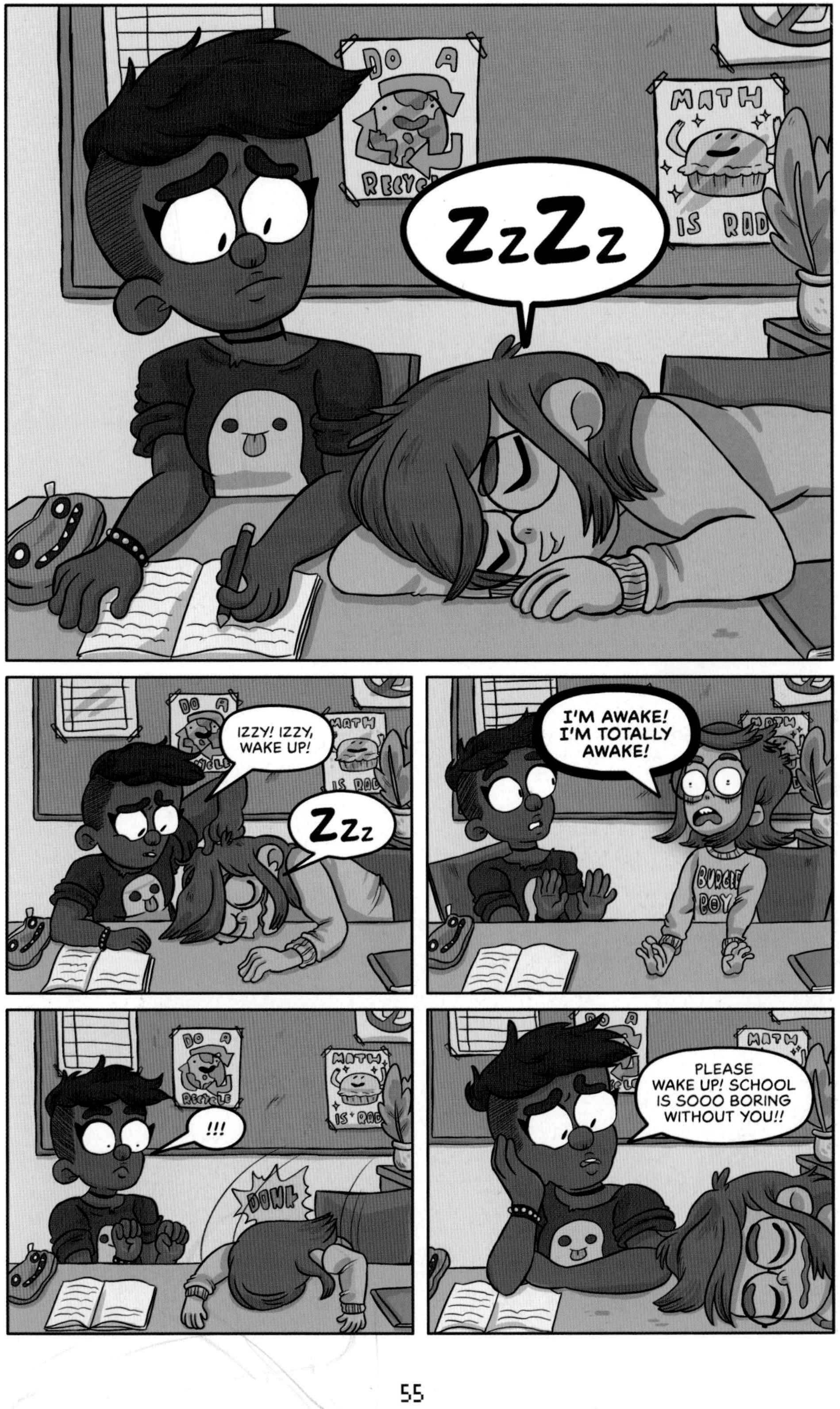
DO A RECYCLE
MATH IS RAD
ZzZz
IZZY! IZZY, WAKE UP!
Zzz
I'M AWAKE! I'M TOTALLY AWAKE!
BURGER BOY
!!!
DONK
PLEASE WAKE UP! SCHOOL IS SOOO BORING WITHOUT YOU!!

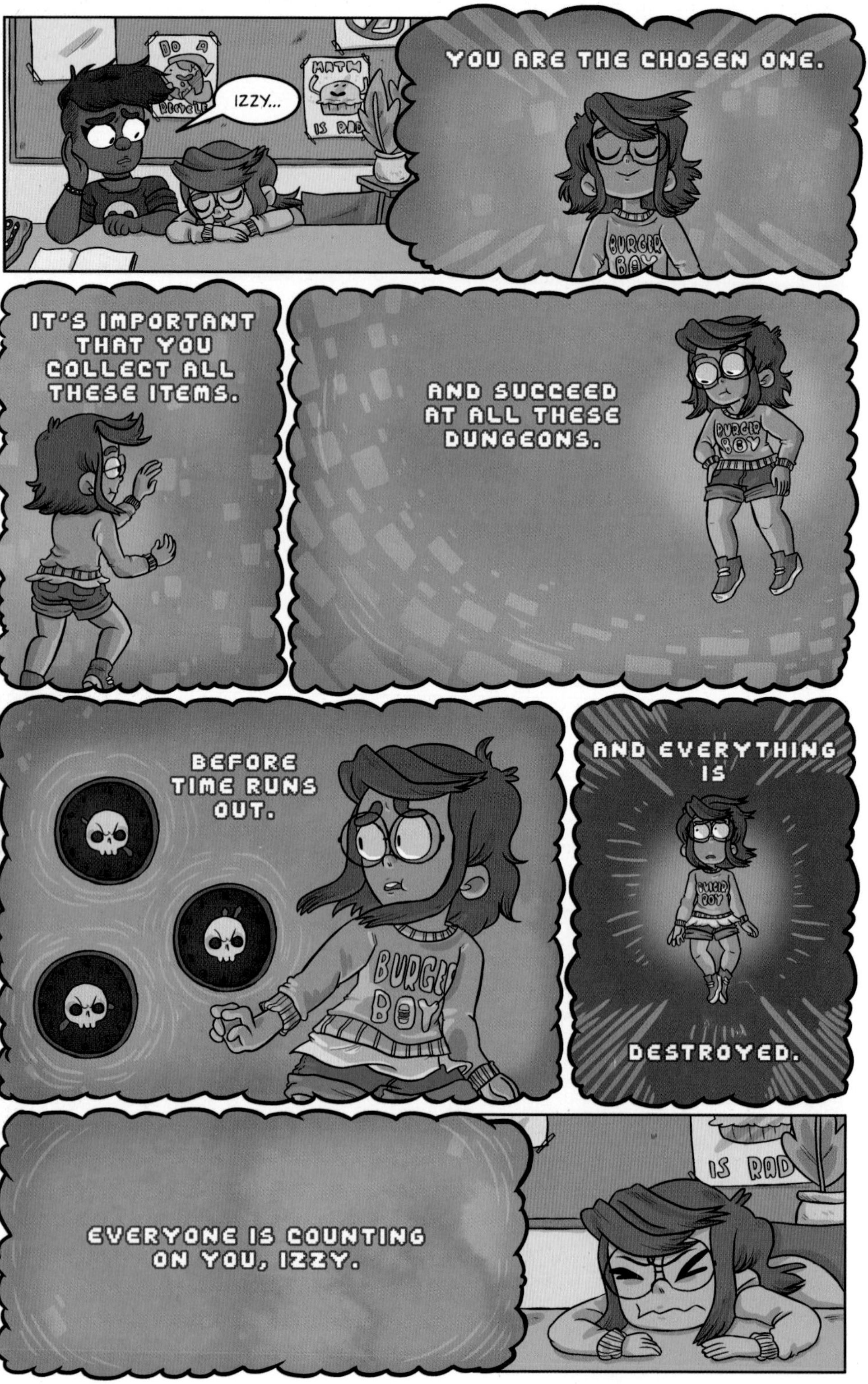
IZZY...
YOU ARE THE CHOSEN ONE.
IT'S IMPORTANT THAT YOU COLLECT ALL THESE ITEMS.
AND SUCCEED AT ALL THESE DUNGEONS.
BEFORE TIME RUNS OUT.
AND EVERYTHING IS
DESTROYED.
EVERYONE IS COUNTING ON YOU, IZZY.

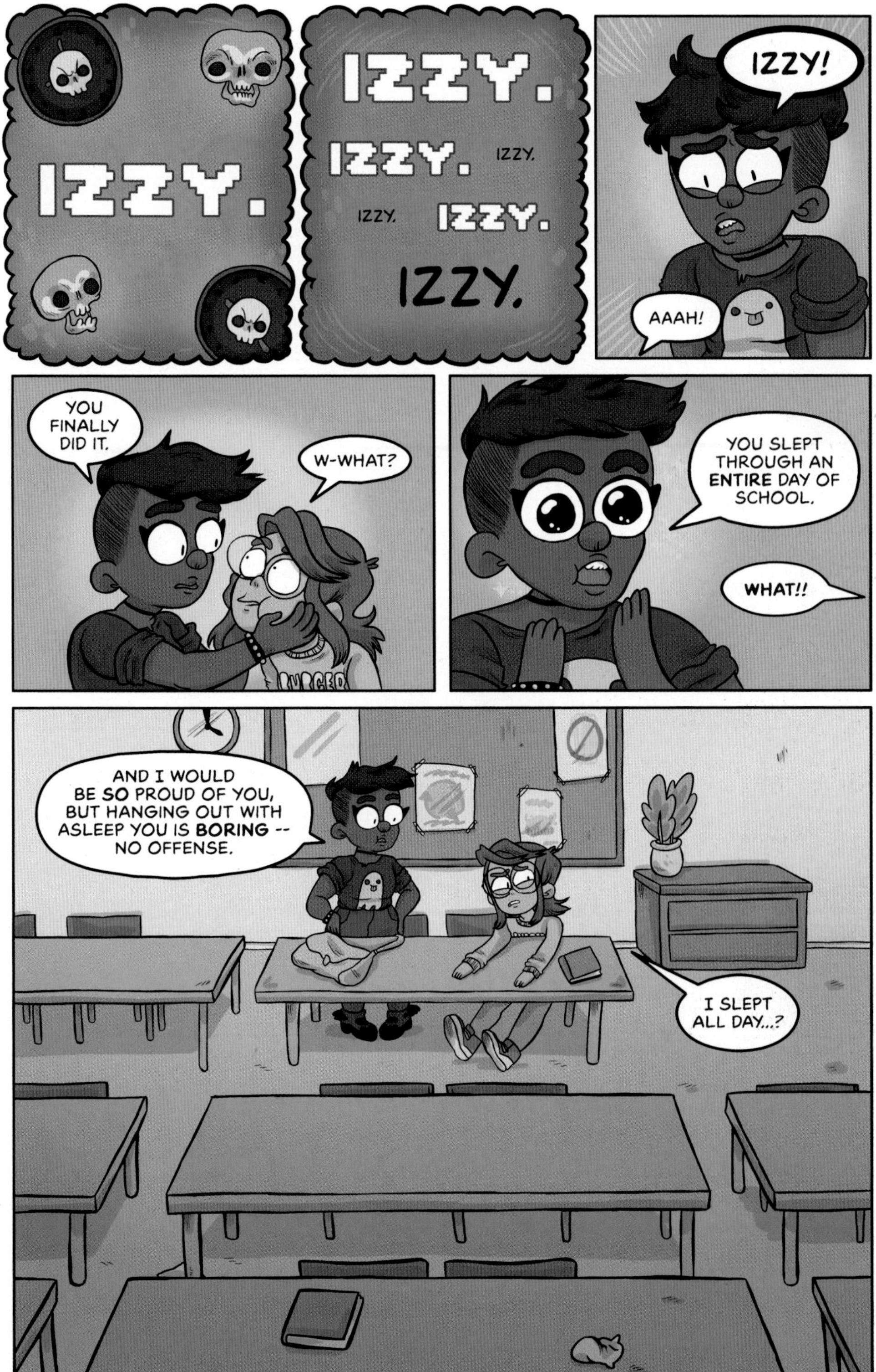
IZZY.
IZZY.
IZZY.
IZZY.
IZZY.
IZZY.
IZZY.
IZZY!
AAAH!
YOU FINALLY DID IT.
W-WHAT?
YOU SLEPT THROUGH AN ENTIRE DAY OF SCHOOL.
WHAT!!
AND I WOULD BE SO PROUD OF YOU, BUT HANGING OUT WITH ASLEEP YOU IS BORING -- NO OFFENSE.
I SLEPT ALL DAY...?

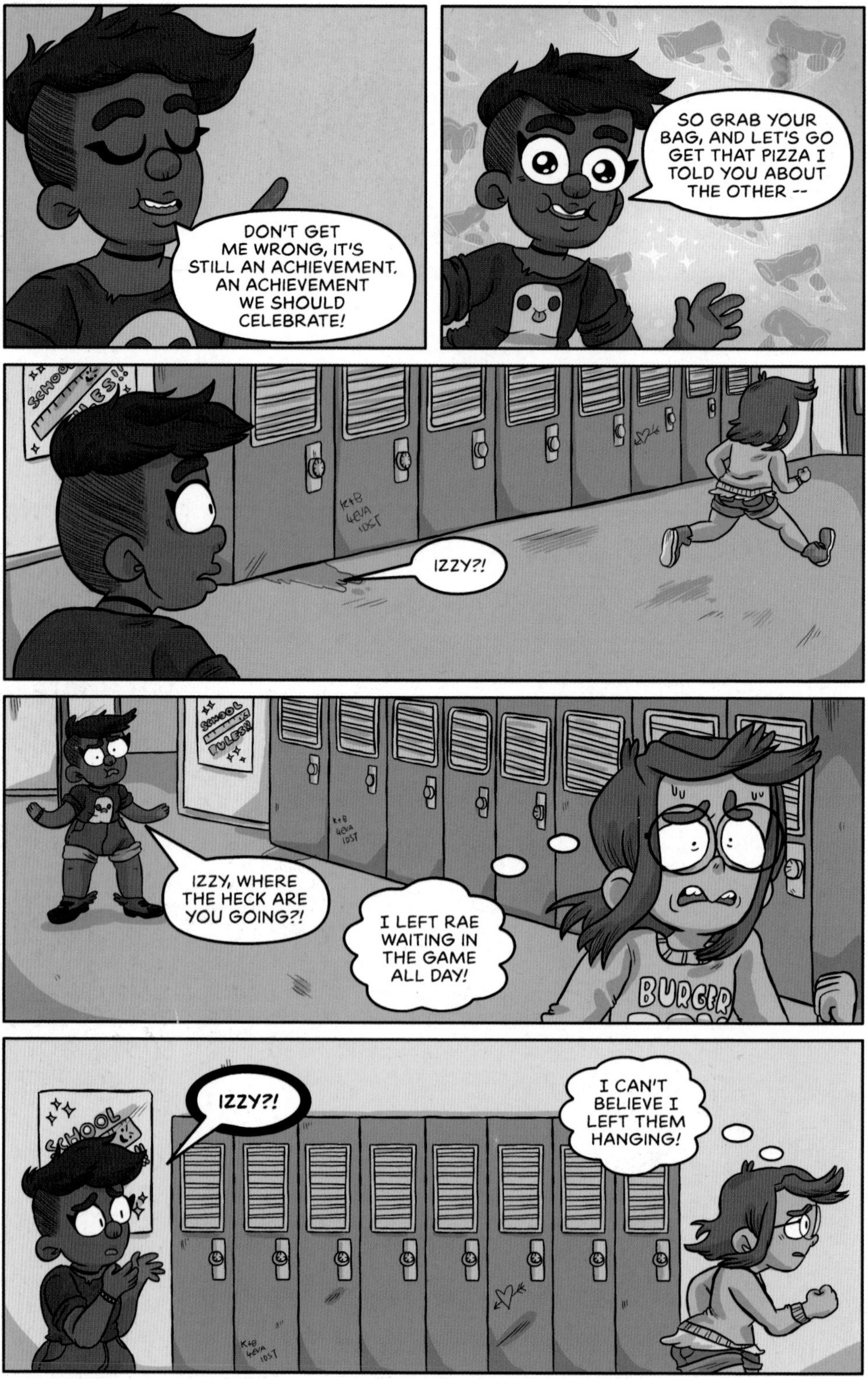
DON'T GET ME WRONG, IT'S STILL AN ACHIEVEMENT. AN ACHIEVEMENT WE SHOULD CELEBRATE!
SO GRAB YOUR BAG, AND LET'S GO GET THAT PIZZA I TOLD YOU ABOUT THE OTHER --
SCHOOL RULES!!
IZZY?!
IZZY, WHERE THE HECK ARE YOU GOING?!
I LEFT RAE WAITING IN THE GAME ALL DAY!
BURGER
IZZY?!
I CAN'T BELIEVE I LEFT THEM HANGING!

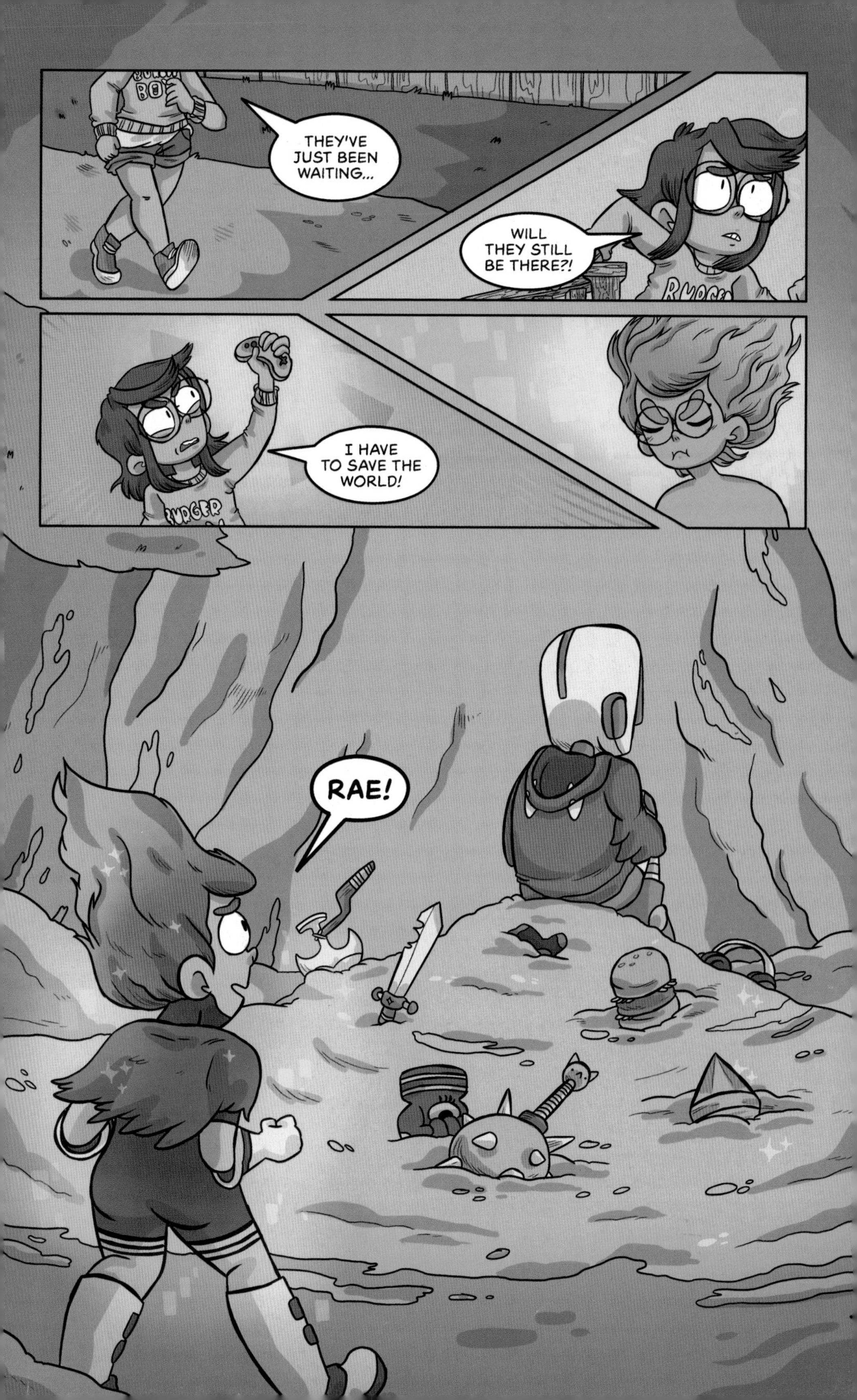
THEY'VE JUST BEEN WAITING...
WILL THEY STILL BE THERE?!
I HAVE TO SAVE THE WORLD!
RAE!

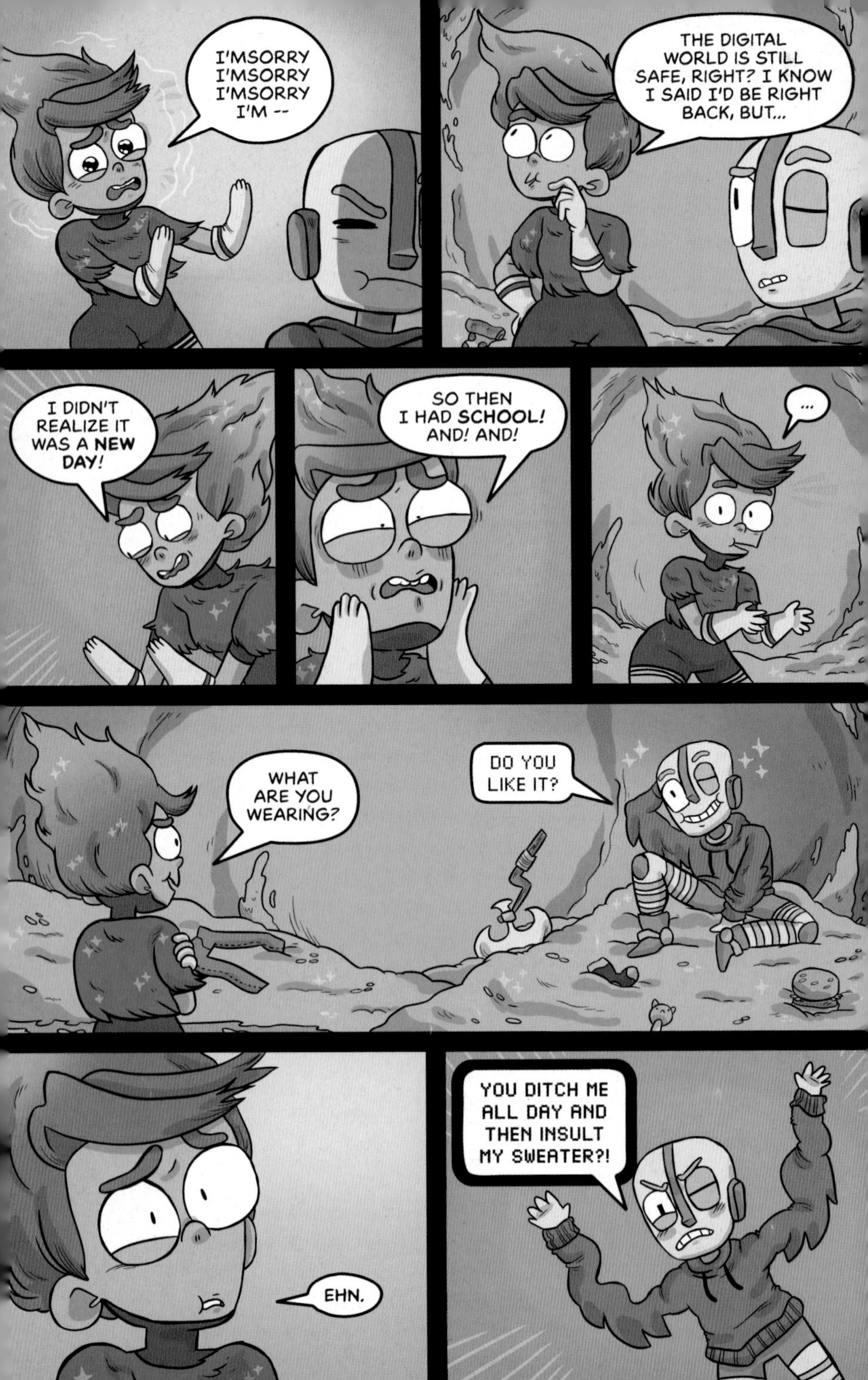
I'MSORRY I'MSORRY I'MSORRY I'M --
THE DIGITAL WORLD IS STILL SAFE, RIGHT? I KNOW I SAID I'D BE RIGHT BACK, BUT...
I DIDN'T REALIZE IT WAS A NEW DAY!
SO THEN I HAD SCHOOL! AND! AND!
...
WHAT ARE YOU WEARING?
DO YOU LIKE IT?
EHN.
YOU DITCH ME ALL DAY AND THEN INSULT MY SWEATER?!

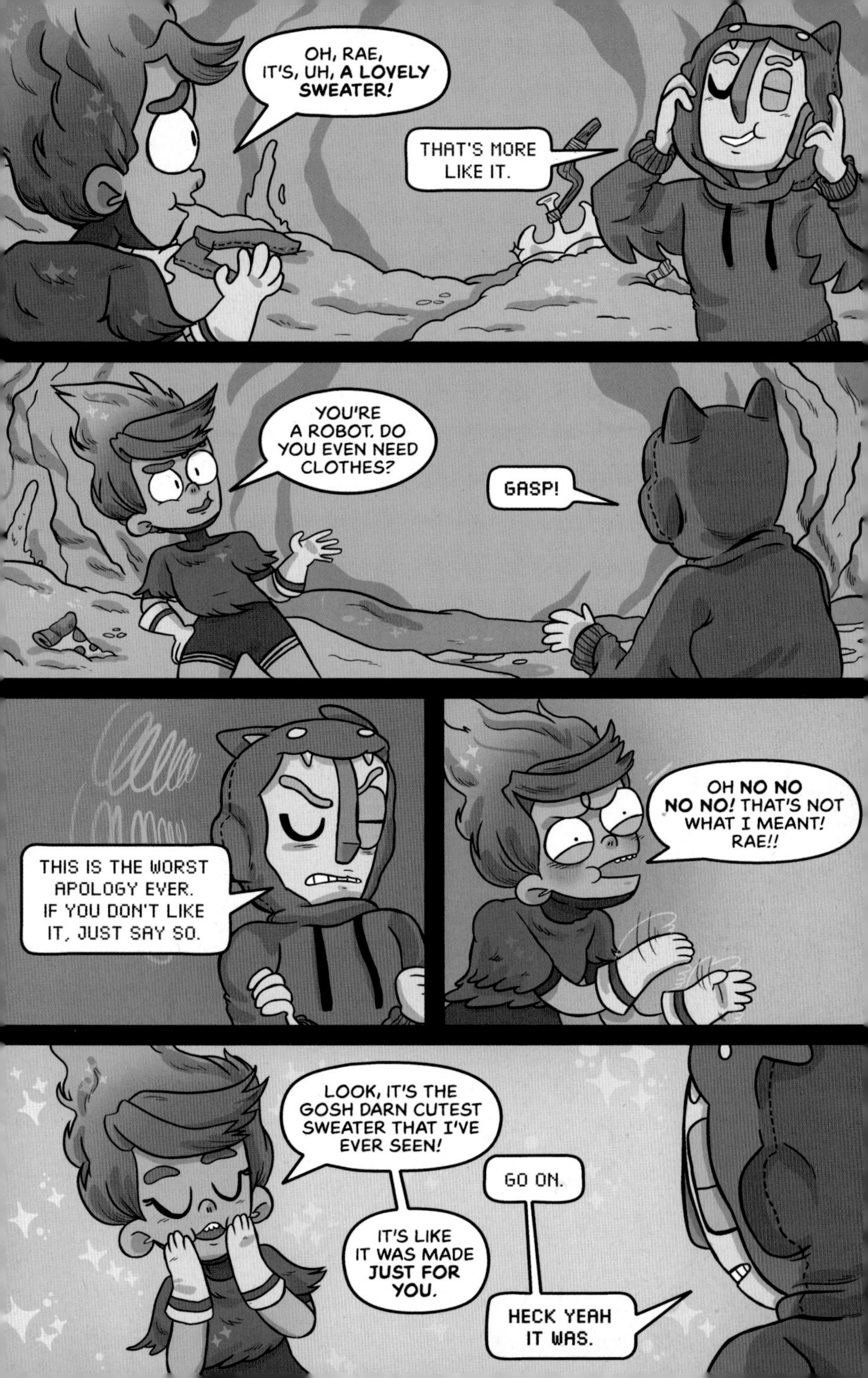
OH, RAE, IT'S, UH, A LOVELY SWEATER!
THAT'S MORE LIKE IT.
YOU'RE A ROBOT. DO YOU EVEN NEED CLOTHES?
GASP!
THIS IS THE WORST APOLOGY EVER. IF YOU DON'T LIKE IT, JUST SAY SO.
OH NO NO NO NO! THAT'S NOT WHAT I MEANT! RAE!!
LOOK, IT'S THE GOSH DARN CUTEST SWEATER THAT I'VE EVER SEEN!
GO ON.
IT'S LIKE IT WAS MADE JUST FOR YOU.
HECK YEAH IT WAS.

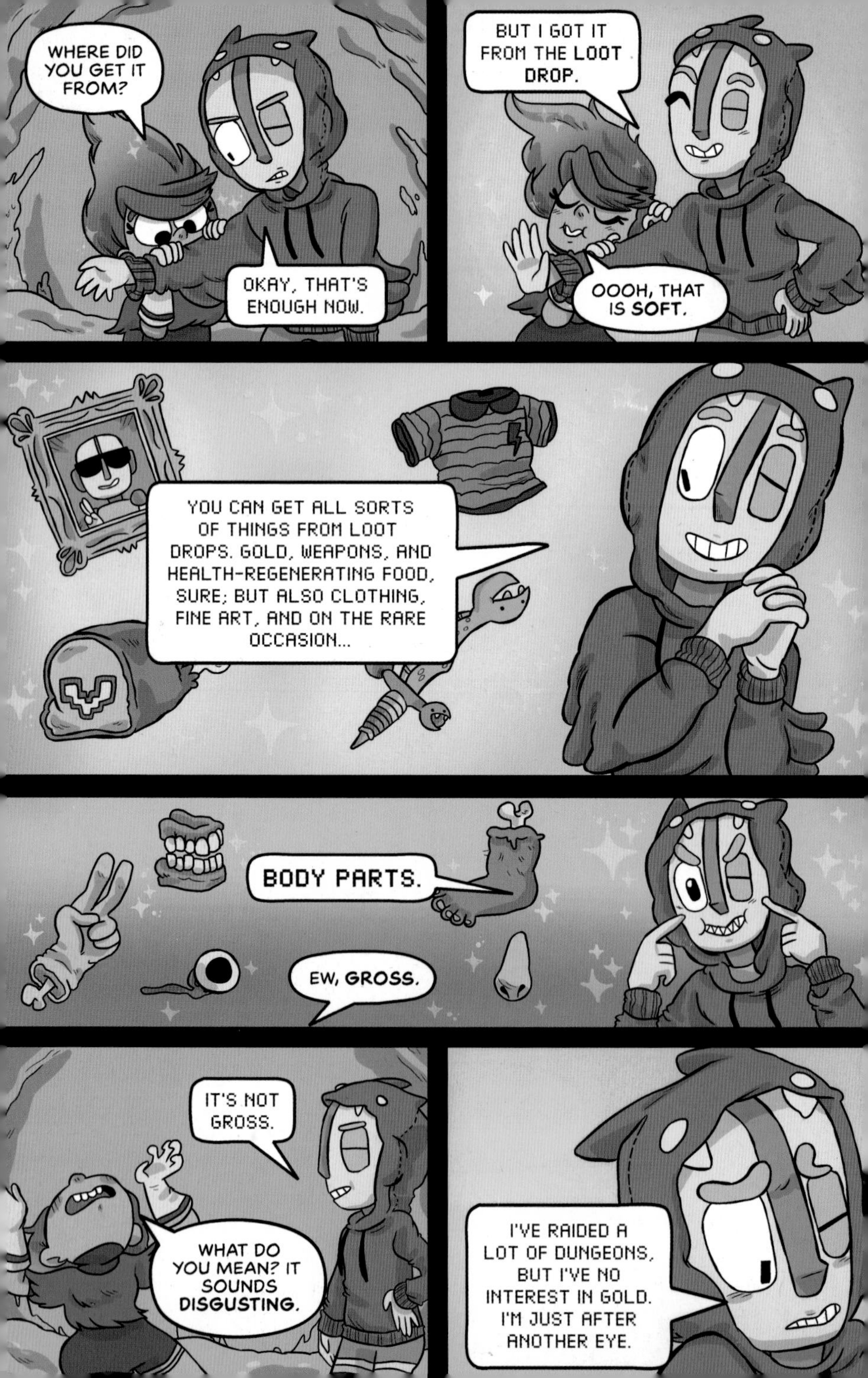
WHERE DID YOU GET IT FROM?
OKAY, THAT'S ENOUGH NOW.
BUT I GOT IT FROM THE LOOT DROP.
OOOH, THAT IS SOFT.
YOU CAN GET ALL SORTS OF THINGS FROM LOOT DROPS. GOLD, WEAPONS, AND HEALTH-REGENERATING FOOD, SURE; BUT ALSO CLOTHING, FINE ART, AND ON THE RARE OCCASION...
BODY PARTS.
EW, GROSS.
IT'S NOT GROSS.
WHAT DO YOU MEAN? IT SOUNDS DISGUSTING.
I'VE RAIDED A LOT OF DUNGEONS, BUT I'VE NO INTEREST IN GOLD. I'M JUST AFTER ANOTHER EYE.

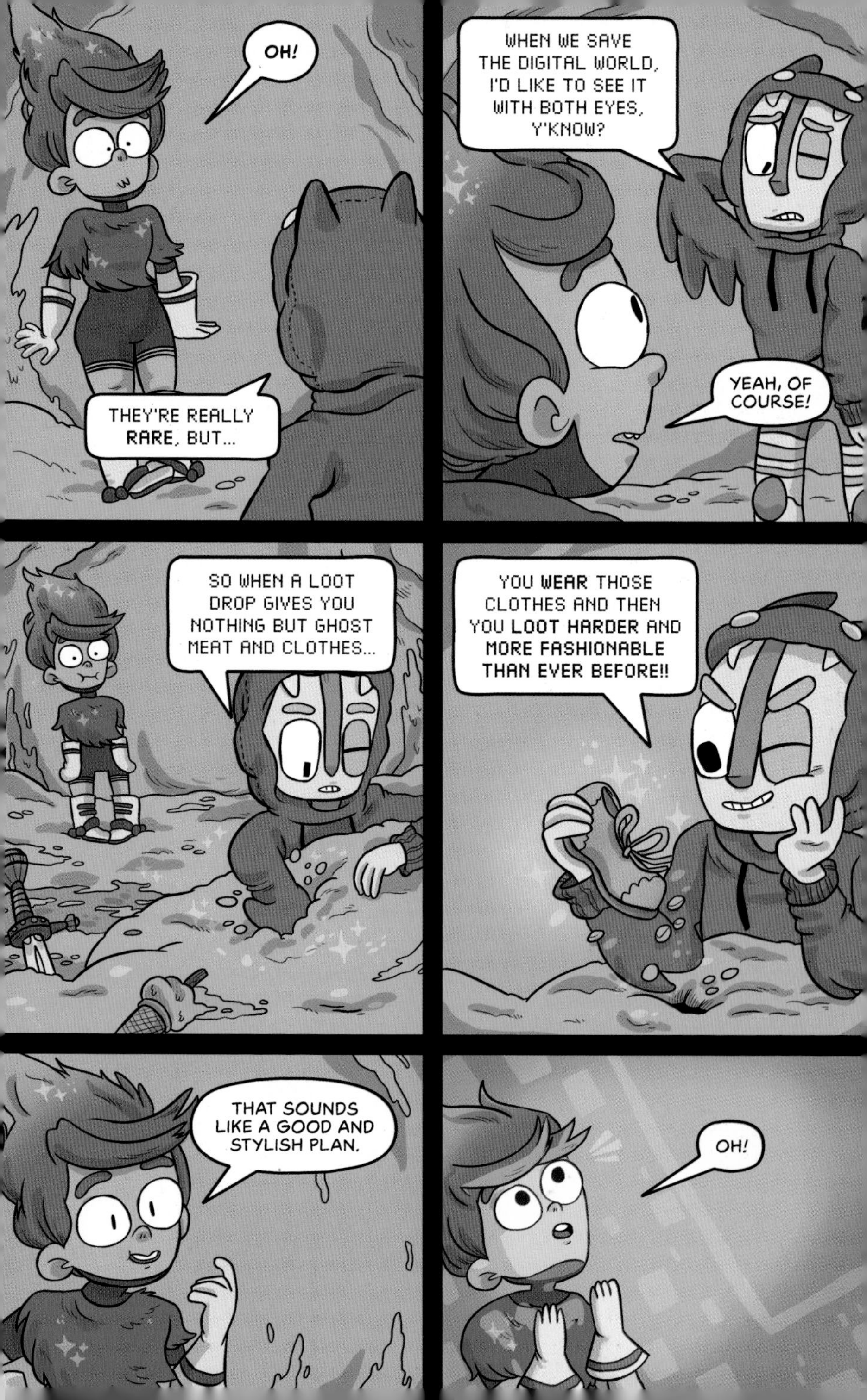
OH!
THEY'RE REALLY RARE, BUT...
WHEN WE SAVE THE DIGITAL WORLD, I'D LIKE TO SEE IT WITH BOTH EYES, Y'KNOW?
YEAH, OF COURSE!
SO WHEN A LOOT DROP GIVES YOU NOTHING BUT GHOST MEAT AND CLOTHES...
YOU WEAR THOSE CLOTHES AND THEN YOU LOOT HARDER AND MORE FASHIONABLE THAN EVER BEFORE!!
THAT SOUNDS LIKE A GOOD AND STYLISH PLAN.
OH!

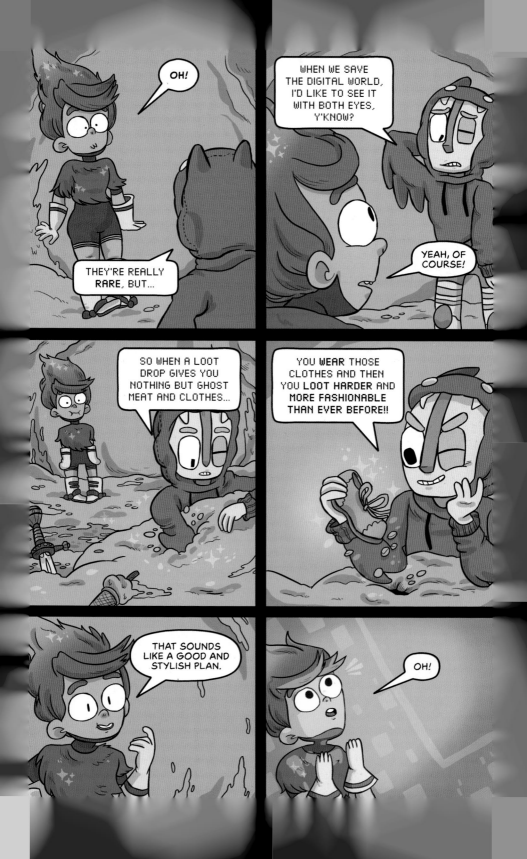

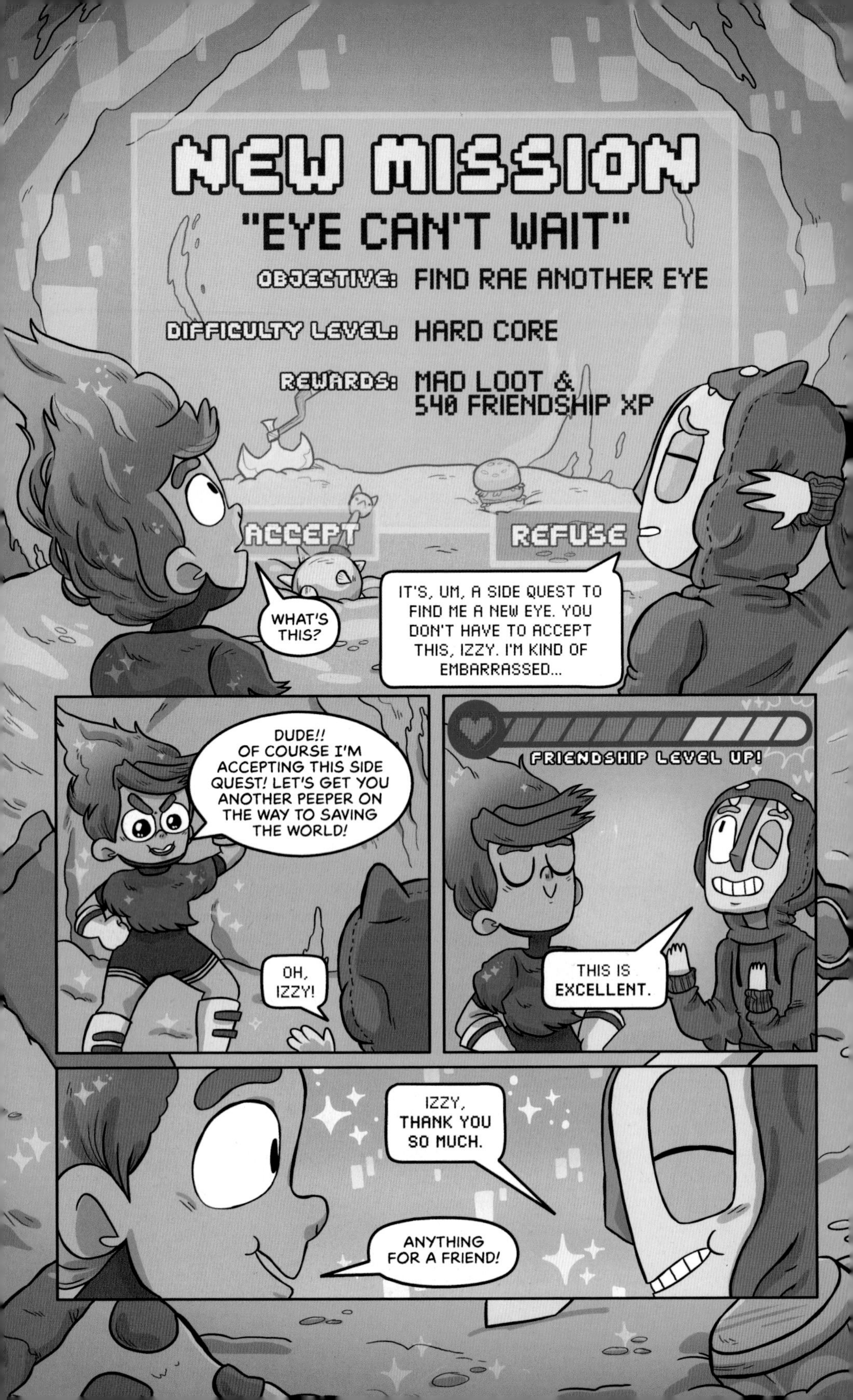
NEW MISSION
"EYE CAN'T WAIT"
OBJECTIVE: FIND RAE ANOTHER EYE
DIFFICULTY LEVEL: HARD CORE
REWARDS: MAD LOOT & 540 FRIENDSHIP XP
ACCEPT
REFUSE
WHAT'S THIS?
IT'S, UM, A SIDE QUEST TO FIND ME A NEW EYE. YOU DON'T HAVE TO ACCEPT THIS, IZZY. I'M KIND OF EMBARRASSED...
DUDE!! OF COURSE I'M ACCEPTING THIS SIDE QUEST! LET'S GET YOU ANOTHER PEEPER ON THE WAY TO SAVING THE WORLD!
OH, IZZY!
FRIENDSHIP LEVEL UP!
THIS IS EXCELLENT.
IZZY, THANK YOU SO MUCH.
ANYTHING FOR A FRIEND!

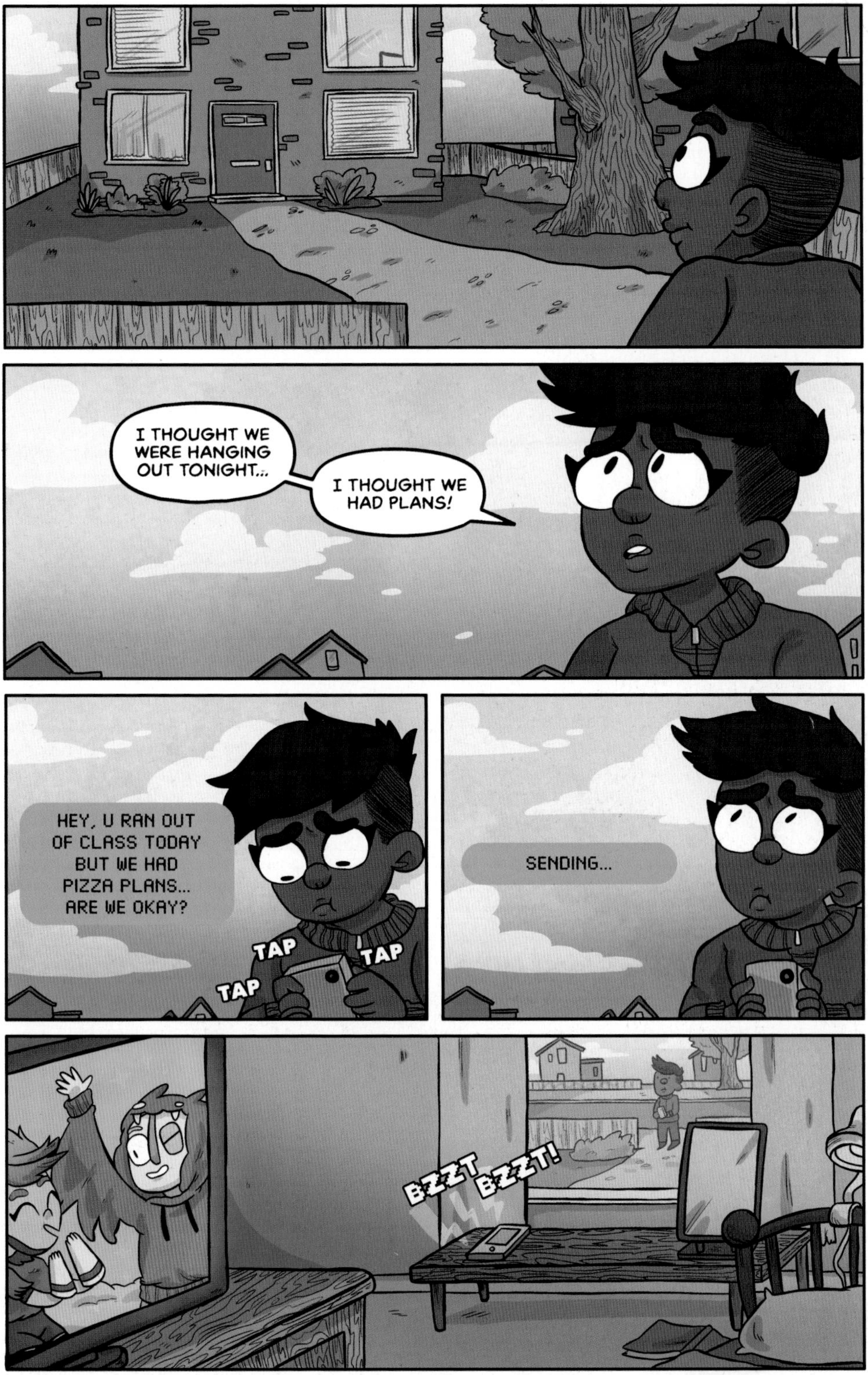

I THOUGHT WE WERE HANGING OUT TONIGHT...
I THOUGHT WE HAD PLANS!
HEY, U RAN OUT OF CLASS TODAY BUT WE HAD PIZZA PLANS... ARE WE OKAY?
TAP
TAP
TAP
SENDING...
BZZT BZZT!

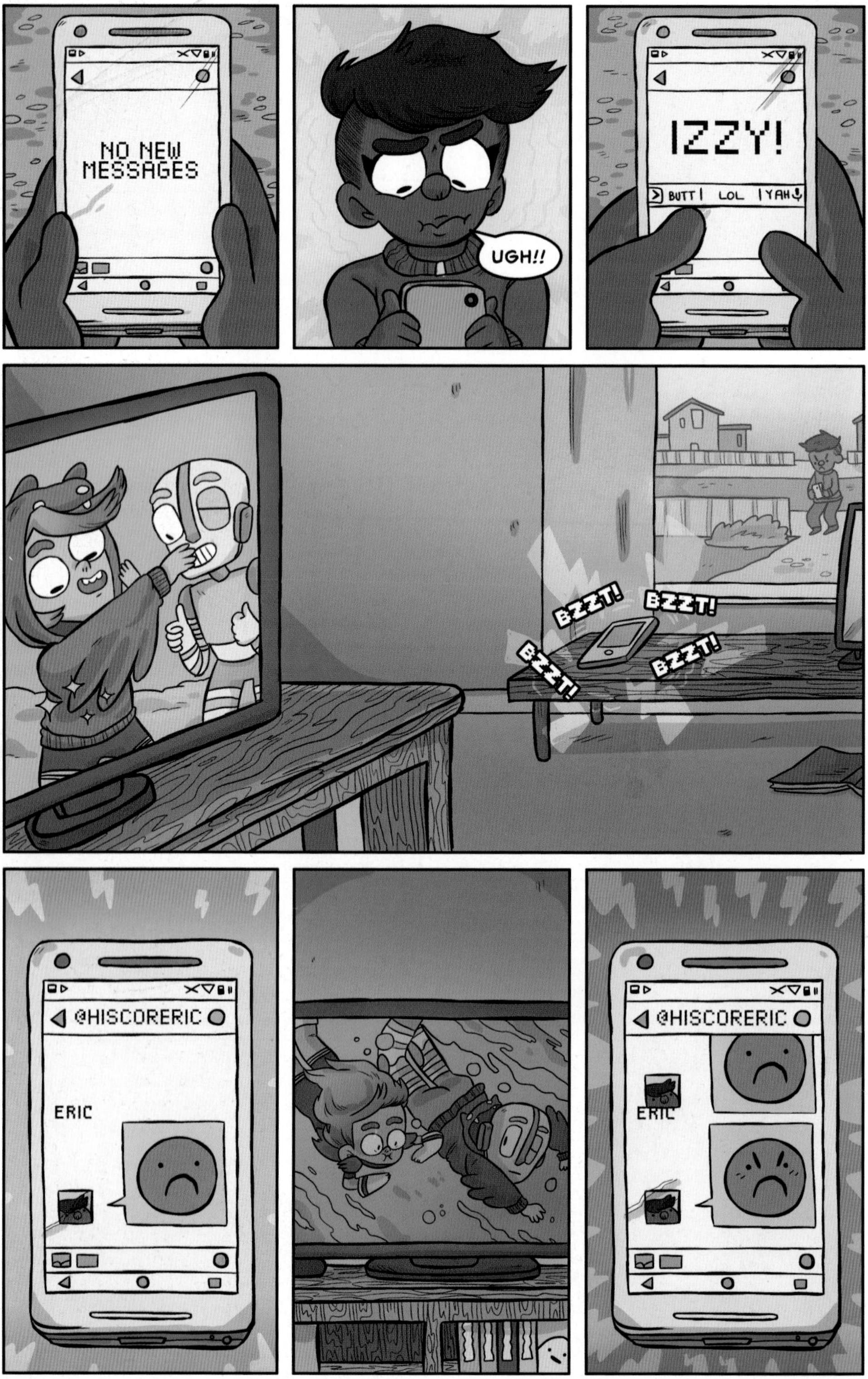
NO NEW MESSAGES
UGH!!
IZZY!
BUTT | LOL | YAH
BZZT!
BZZT!
BZZT!
BZZT!
@HISCORERIC
ERIC
@HISCORERIC
ERIC

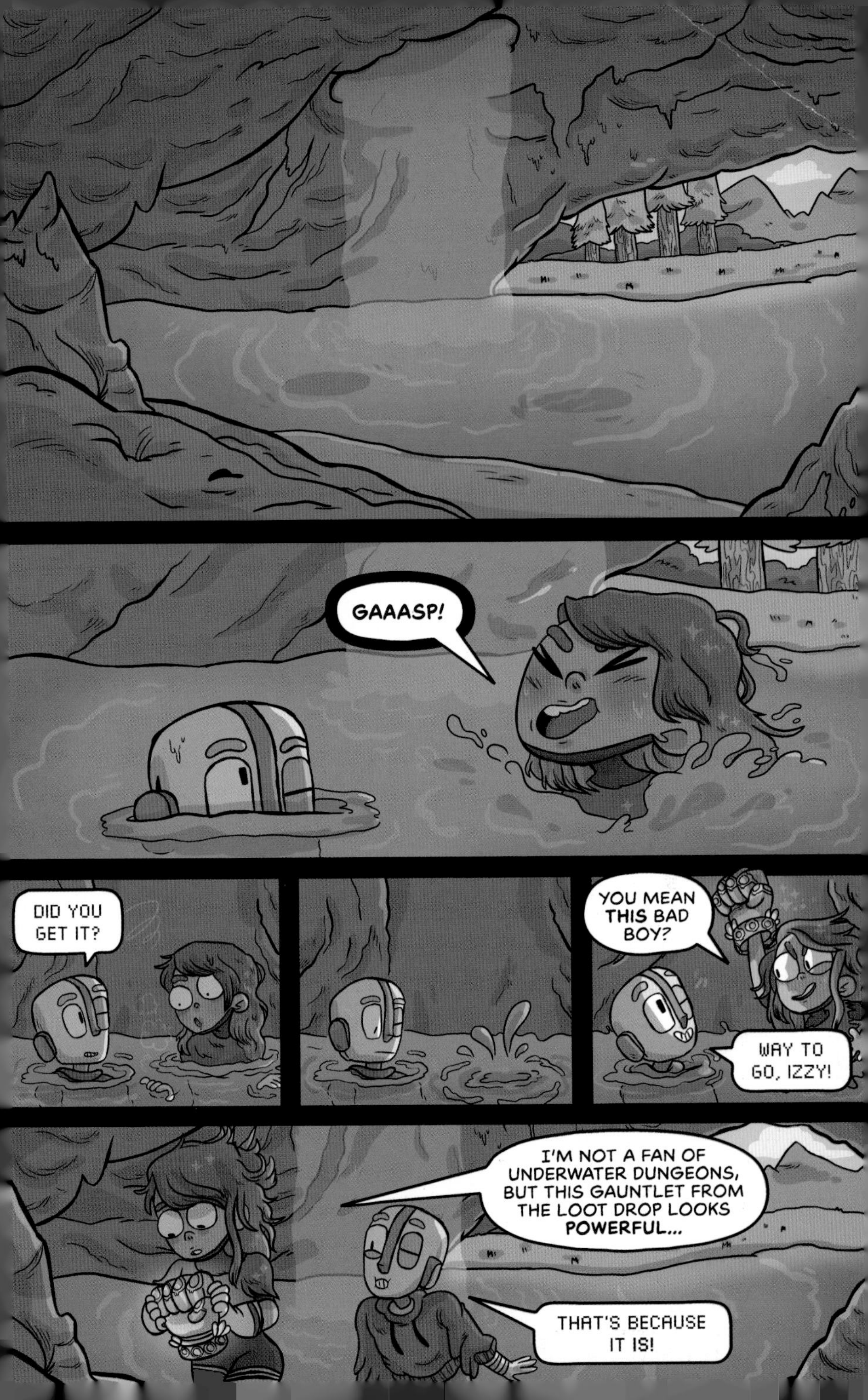
GAAASP!
DID YOU GET IT?
YOU MEAN THIS BAD BOY?
WAY TO GO, IZZY!
I'M NOT A FAN OF UNDERWATER DUNGEONS, BUT THIS GAUNTLET FROM THE LOOT DROP LOOKS POWERFUL...
THAT'S BECAUSE IT IS!

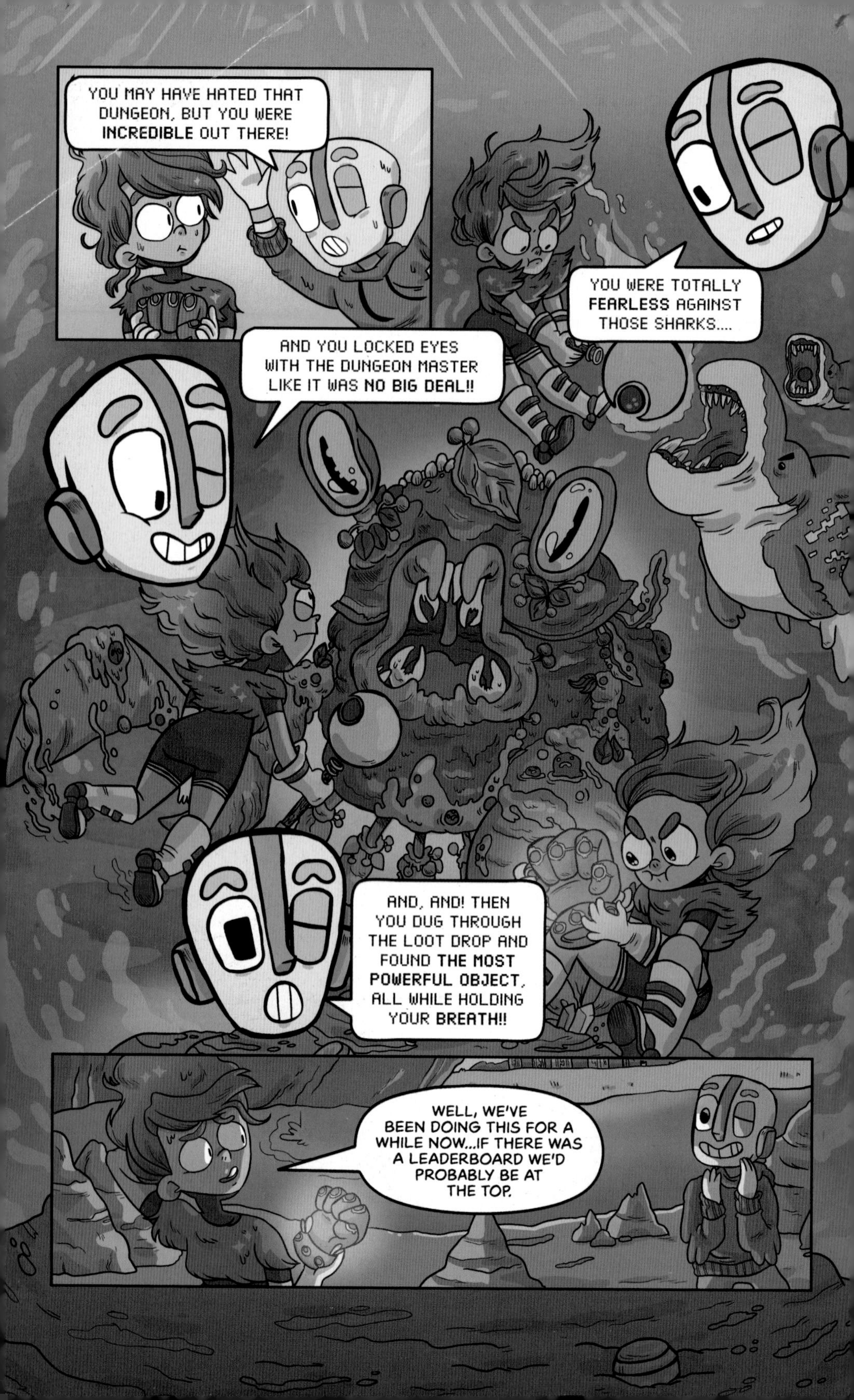
YOU MAY HAVE HATED THAT DUNGEON, BUT YOU WERE **INCREDIBLE** OUT THERE!
YOU WERE TOTALLY **FEARLESS** AGAINST THOSE SHARKS....
AND YOU LOCKED EYES WITH THE DUNGEON MASTER LIKE IT WAS **NO BIG DEAL**!!
AND, AND! THEN YOU DUG THROUGH THE LOOT DROP AND FOUND **THE MOST POWERFUL OBJECT**, ALL WHILE HOLDING YOUR **BREATH**!!
WELL, WE'VE BEEN DOING THIS FOR A WHILE NOW...IF THERE WAS A LEADERBOARD WE'D PROBABLY BE AT THE TOP.

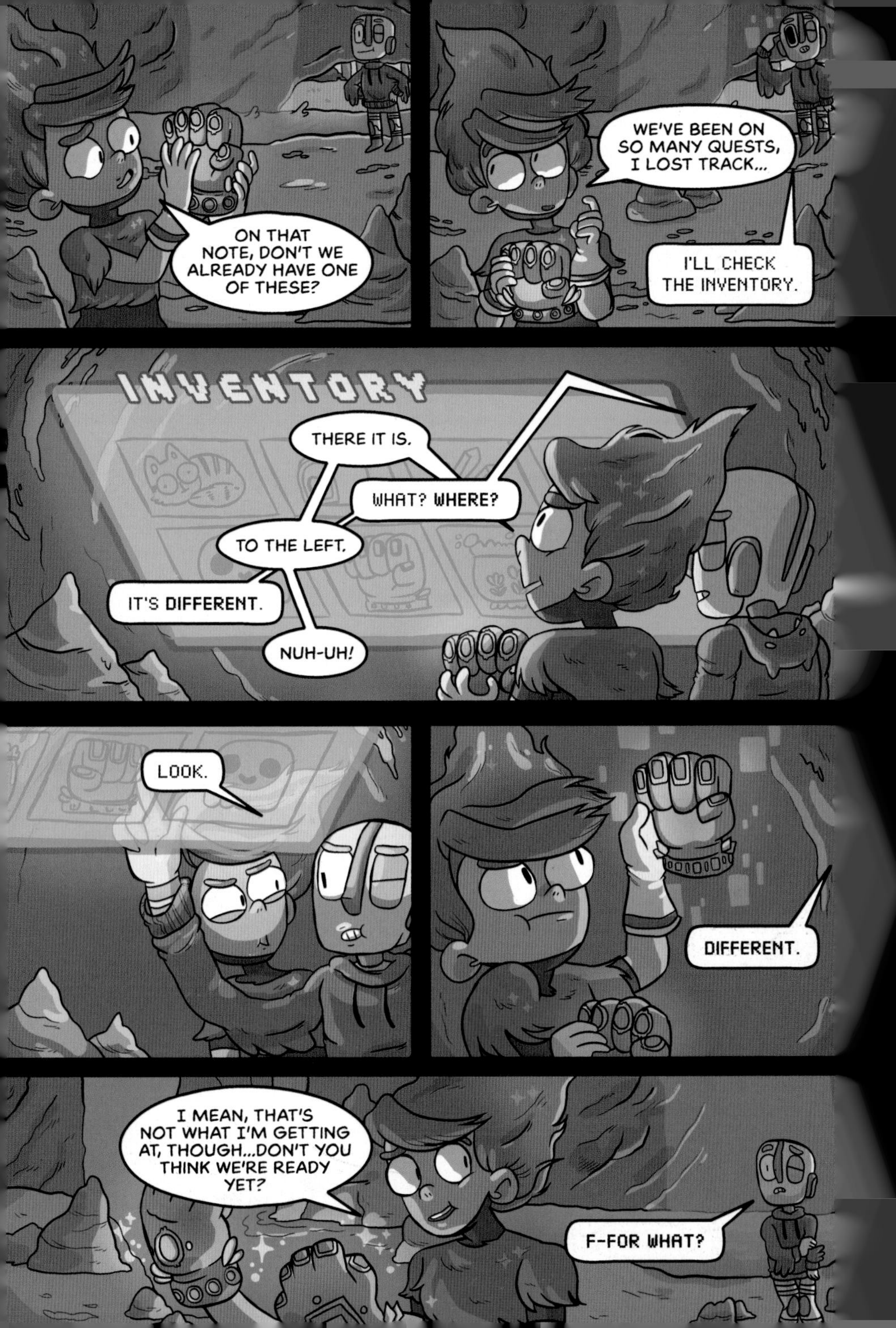
ON THAT NOTE, DON'T WE ALREADY HAVE ONE OF THESE?
WE'VE BEEN ON SO MANY QUESTS, I LOST TRACK...
I'LL CHECK THE INVENTORY.
INVENTORY
THERE IT IS.
WHAT? WHERE?
TO THE LEFT.
IT'S DIFFERENT.
NUH-UH!
LOOK.
DIFFERENT.
I MEAN, THAT'S NOT WHAT I'M GETTING AT, THOUGH...DON'T YOU THINK WE'RE READY YET?
F-FOR WHAT?

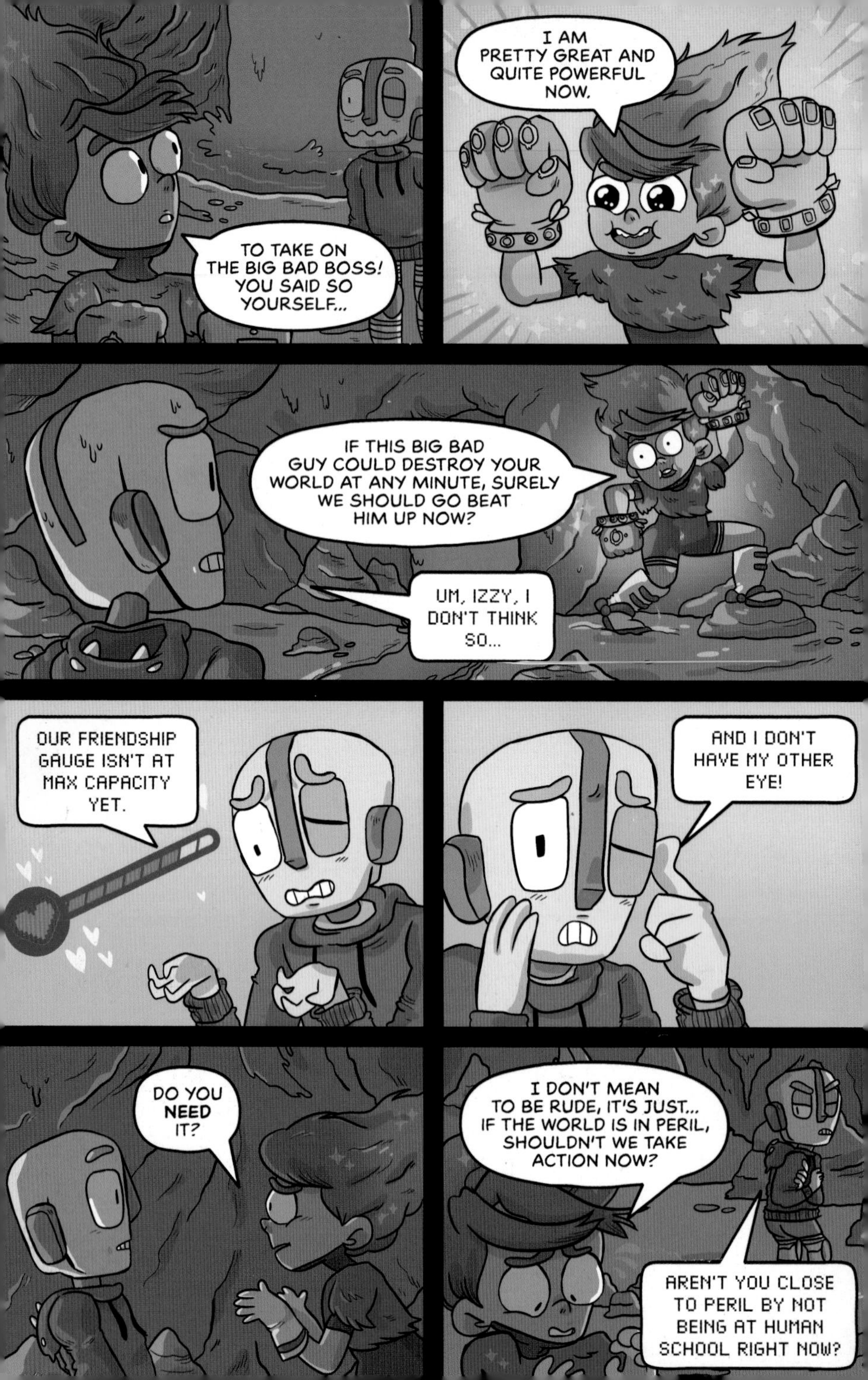
TO TAKE ON THE BIG BAD BOSS! YOU SAID SO YOURSELF...
I AM PRETTY GREAT AND QUITE POWERFUL NOW.
IF THIS BIG BAD GUY COULD DESTROY YOUR WORLD AT ANY MINUTE, SURELY WE SHOULD GO BEAT HIM UP NOW?
UM, IZZY, I DON'T THINK SO...
OUR FRIENDSHIP GAUGE ISN'T AT MAX CAPACITY YET.
AND I DON'T HAVE MY OTHER EYE!
DO YOU **NEED** IT?
I DON'T MEAN TO BE RUDE, IT'S JUST... IF THE WORLD IS IN PERIL, SHOULDN'T WE TAKE ACTION NOW?
AREN'T YOU CLOSE TO PERIL BY NOT BEING AT HUMAN SCHOOL RIGHT NOW?

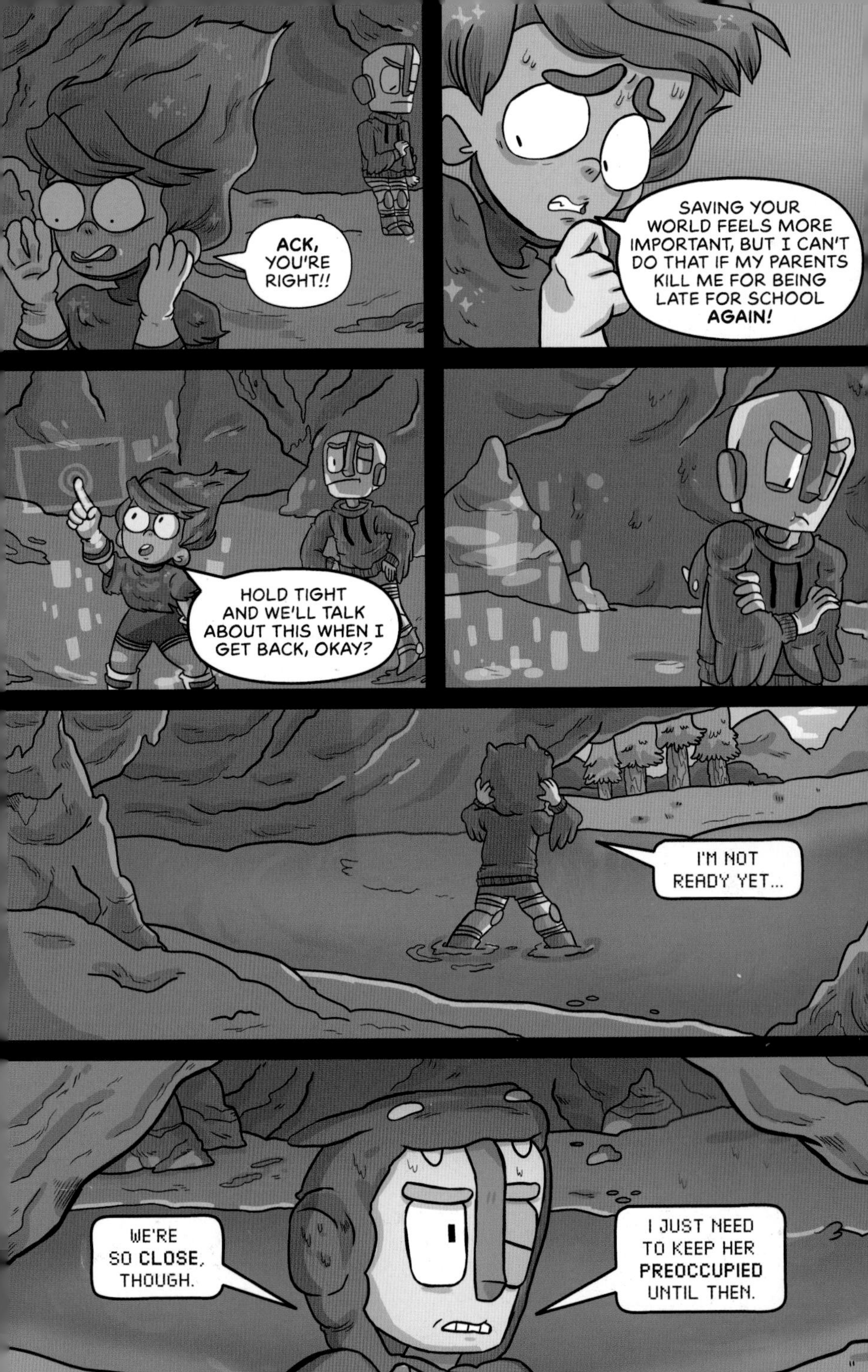

ACK, YOU'RE RIGHT!!
SAVING YOUR WORLD FEELS MORE IMPORTANT, BUT I CAN'T DO THAT IF MY PARENTS KILL ME FOR BEING LATE FOR SCHOOL **AGAIN!**
HOLD TIGHT AND WE'LL TALK ABOUT THIS WHEN I GET BACK, OKAY?
I'M NOT READY YET...
WE'RE SO **CLOSE,** THOUGH.
I JUST NEED TO KEEP HER **PREOCCUPIED** UNTIL THEN.

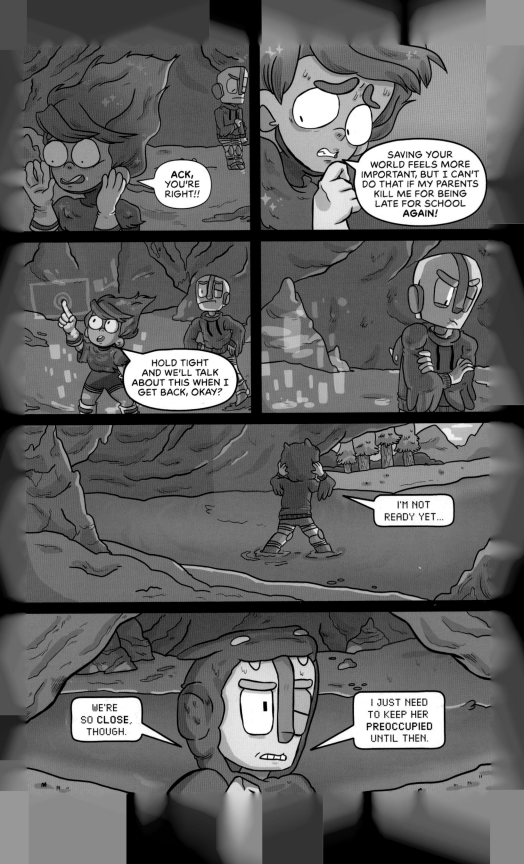

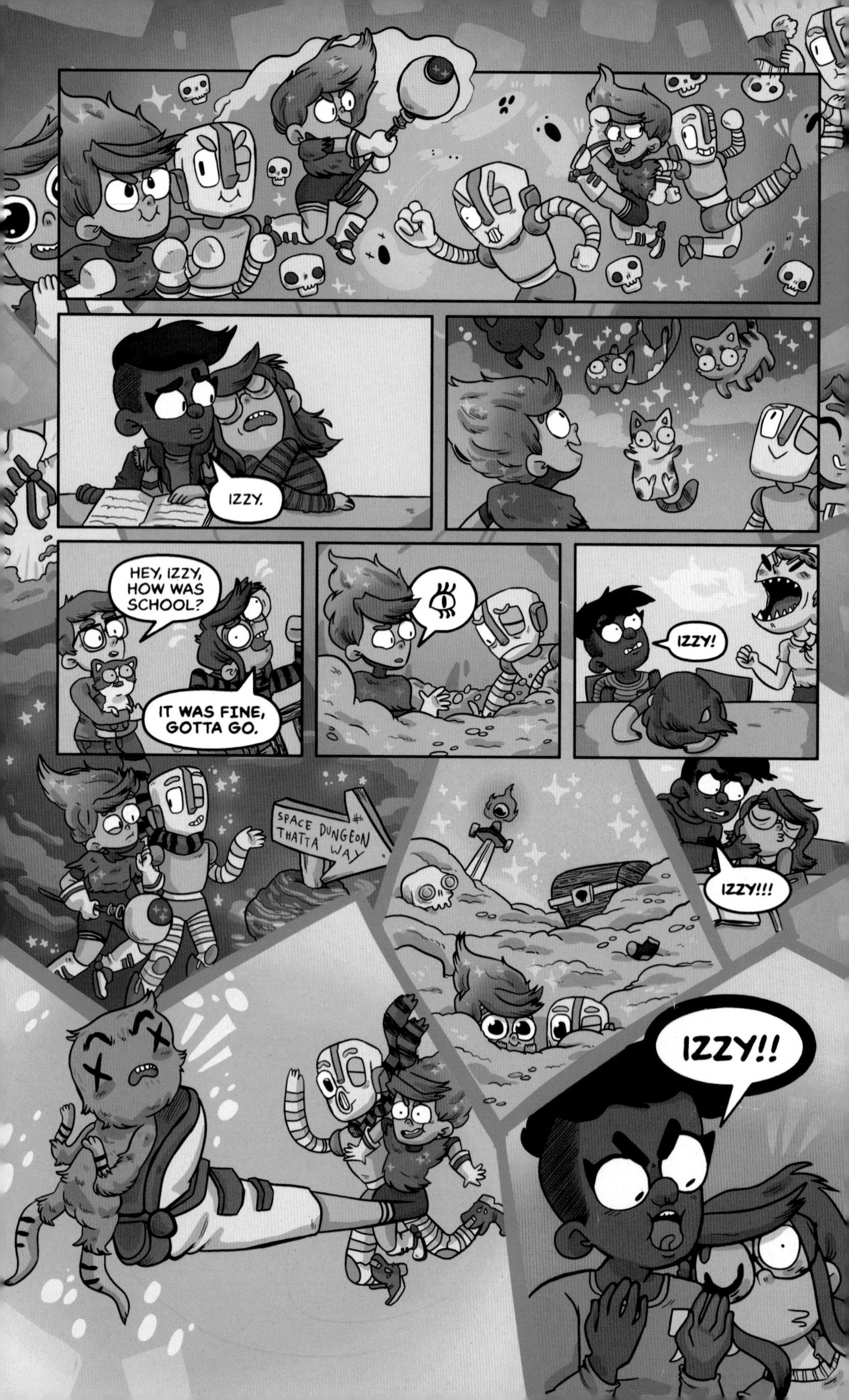
IZZY.
HEY, IZZY, HOW WAS SCHOOL?
IT WAS FINE, GOTTA GO.
IZZY!
SPACE DUNGEON THATTA WAY
IZZY!!!
IZZY!!

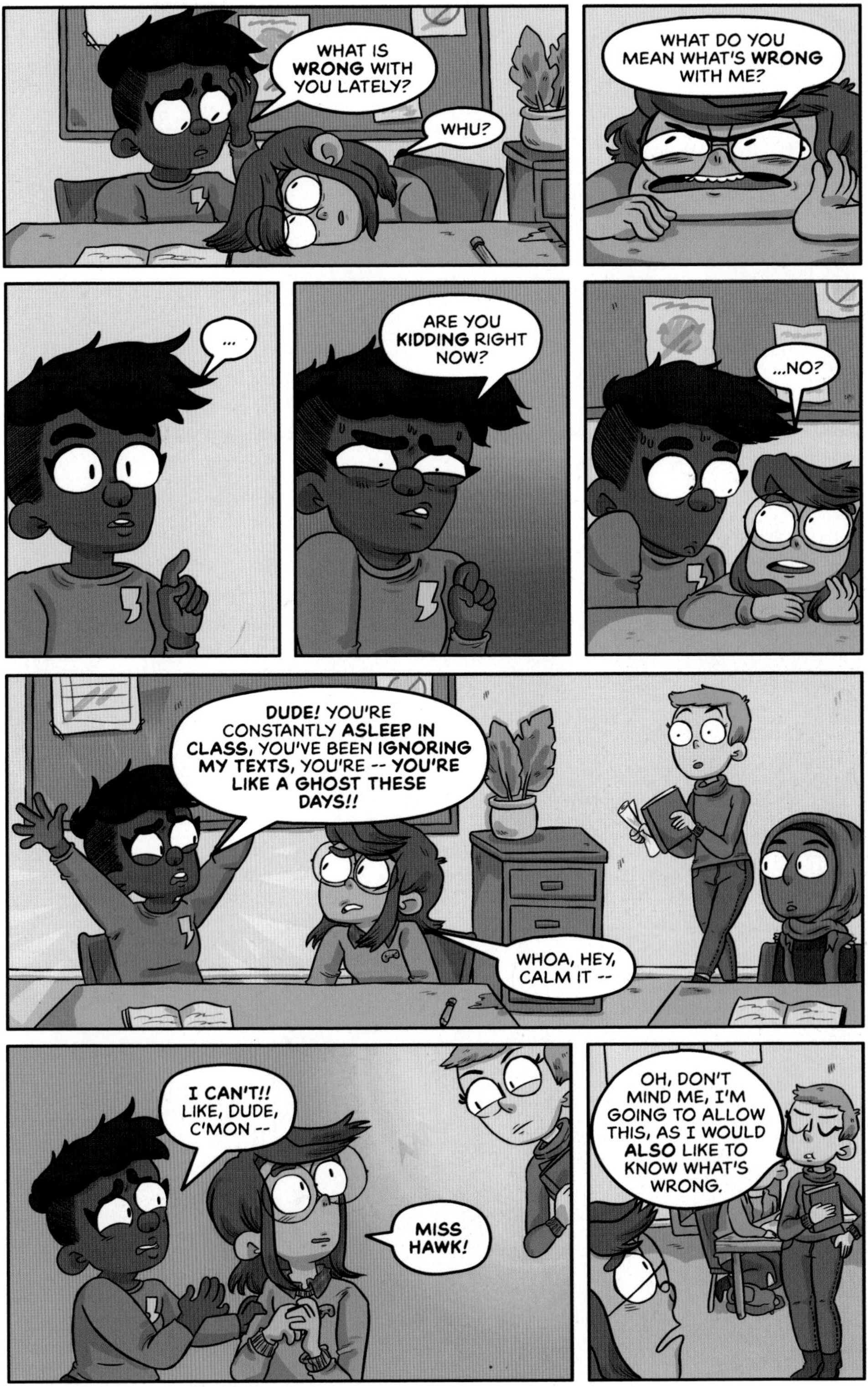
WHAT IS WRONG WITH YOU LATELY?
WHU?
WHAT DO YOU MEAN WHAT'S WRONG WITH ME?
...
ARE YOU KIDDING RIGHT NOW?
...NO?
DUDE! YOU'RE CONSTANTLY ASLEEP IN CLASS, YOU'VE BEEN IGNORING MY TEXTS, YOU'RE -- YOU'RE LIKE A GHOST THESE DAYS!!
WHOA, HEY, CALM IT --
I CAN'T!! LIKE, DUDE, C'MON --
MISS HAWK!
OH, DON'T MIND ME, I'M GOING TO ALLOW THIS, AS I WOULD ALSO LIKE TO KNOW WHAT'S WRONG.

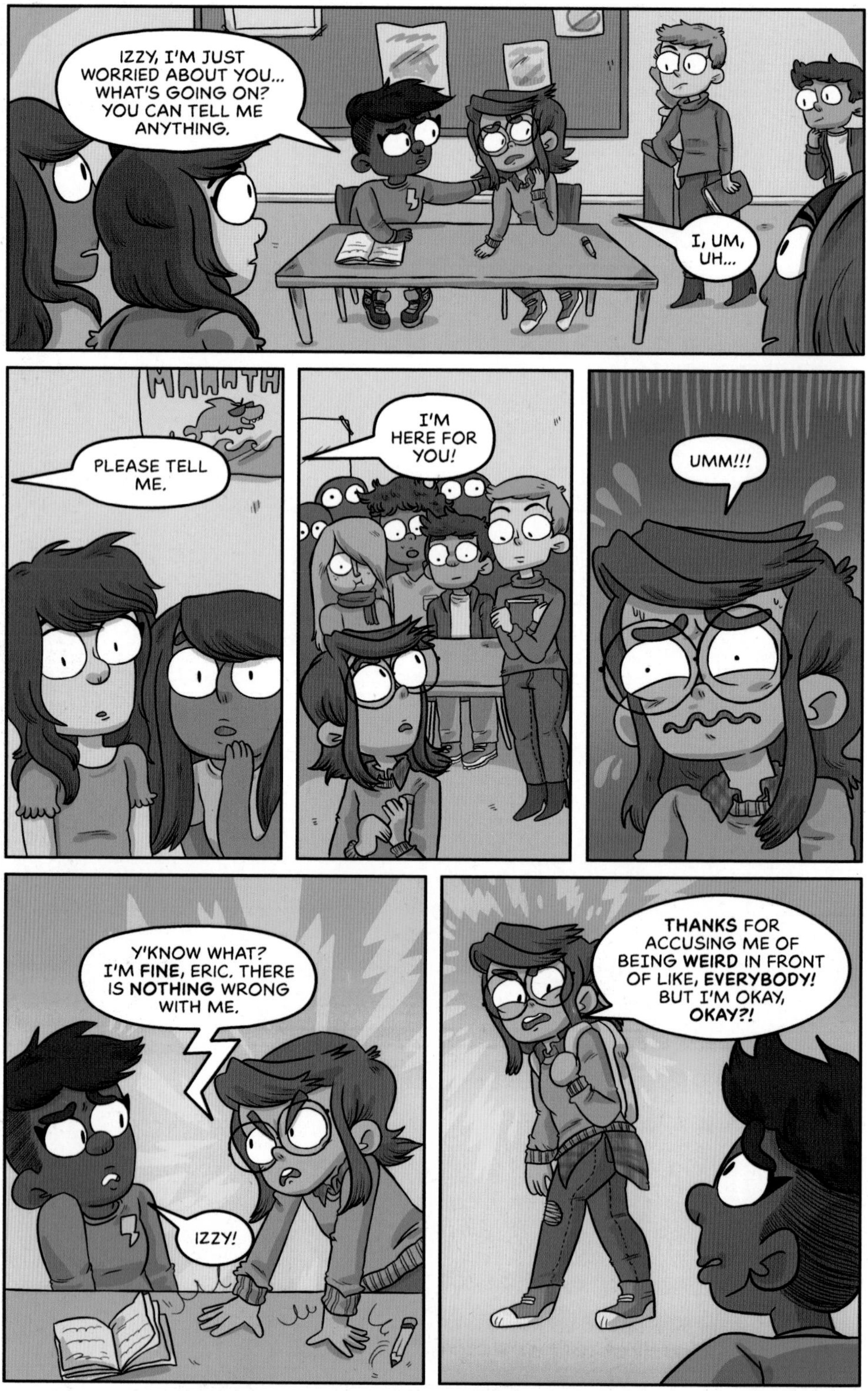
IZZY, I'M JUST WORRIED ABOUT YOU... WHAT'S GOING ON? YOU CAN TELL ME ANYTHING.
I, UM, UH...
PLEASE TELL ME.
I'M HERE FOR YOU!
UMM!!!
Y'KNOW WHAT? I'M **FINE**, ERIC. THERE IS **NOTHING** WRONG WITH ME.
IZZY!
THANKS FOR ACCUSING ME OF BEING **WEIRD** IN FRONT OF LIKE, **EVERYBODY!** BUT I'M OKAY, **OKAY?!**
MAAATH

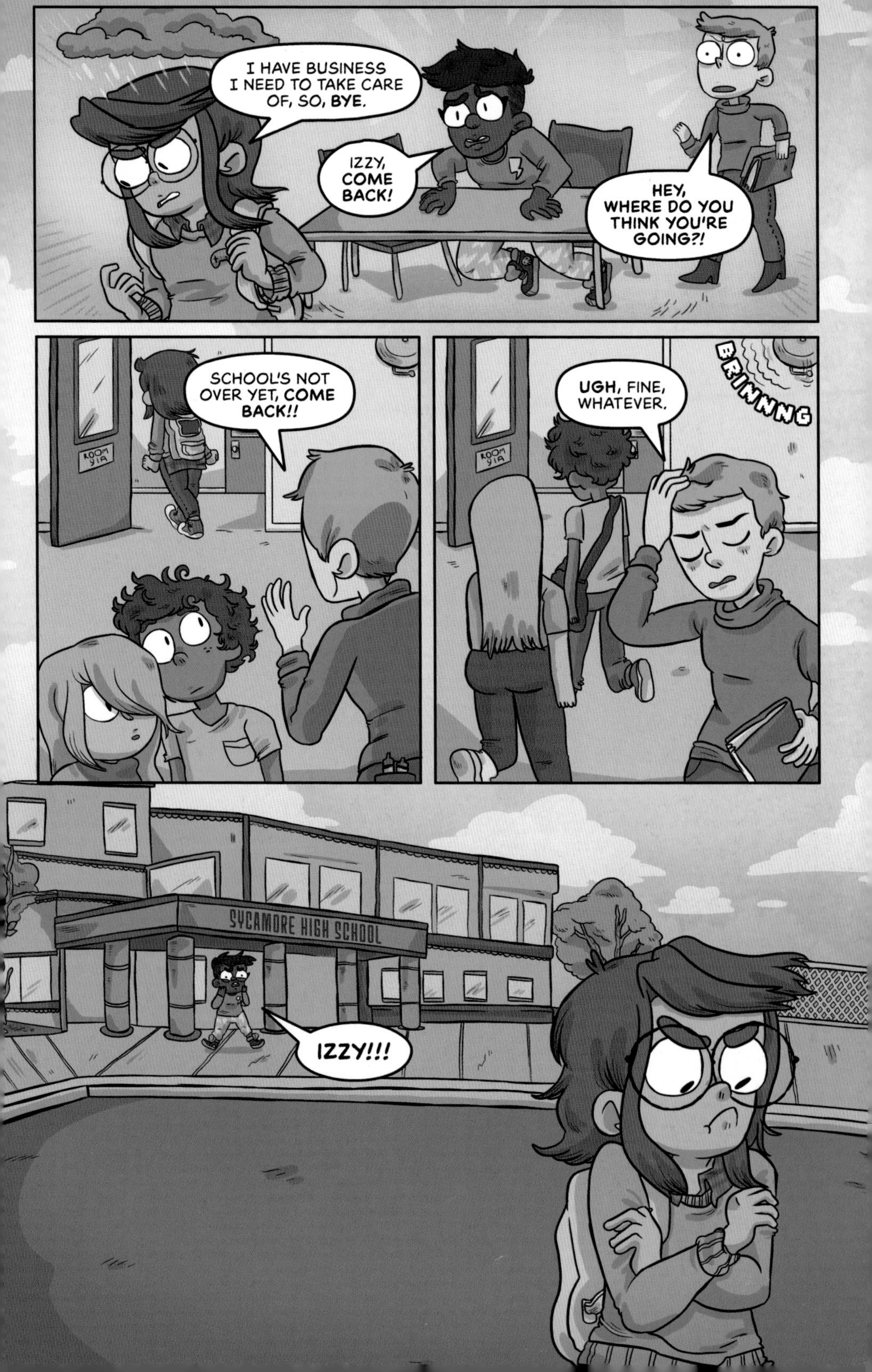

I HAVE BUSINESS I NEED TO TAKE CARE OF, SO, BYE.
IZZY, COME BACK!
HEY, WHERE DO YOU THINK YOU'RE GOING?!
SCHOOL'S NOT OVER YET, COME BACK!!
ROOM 91A
UGH, FINE, WHATEVER.
BRINNNG
SYCAMORE HIGH SCHOOL
IZZY!!!

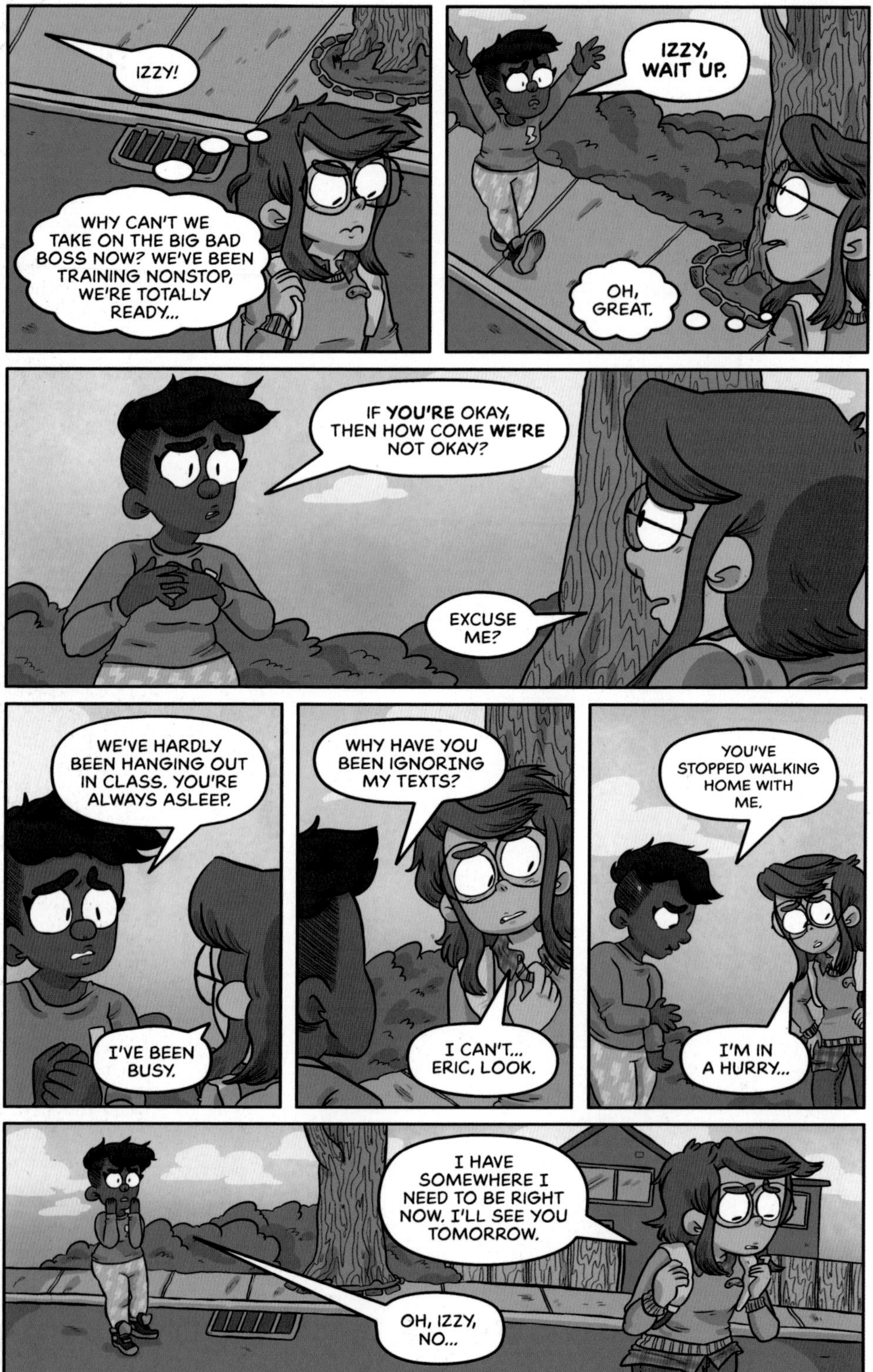
IZZY!
WHY CAN'T WE TAKE ON THE BIG BAD BOSS NOW? WE'VE BEEN TRAINING NONSTOP, WE'RE TOTALLY READY...
IZZY, WAIT UP.
OH, GREAT.
IF YOU'RE OKAY, THEN HOW COME WE'RE NOT OKAY?
EXCUSE ME?
WE'VE HARDLY BEEN HANGING OUT IN CLASS. YOU'RE ALWAYS ASLEEP.
I'VE BEEN BUSY.
WHY HAVE YOU BEEN IGNORING MY TEXTS?
I CAN'T... ERIC, LOOK.
YOU'VE STOPPED WALKING HOME WITH ME.
I'M IN A HURRY...
I HAVE SOMEWHERE I NEED TO BE RIGHT NOW. I'LL SEE YOU TOMORROW.
OH, IZZY, NO...

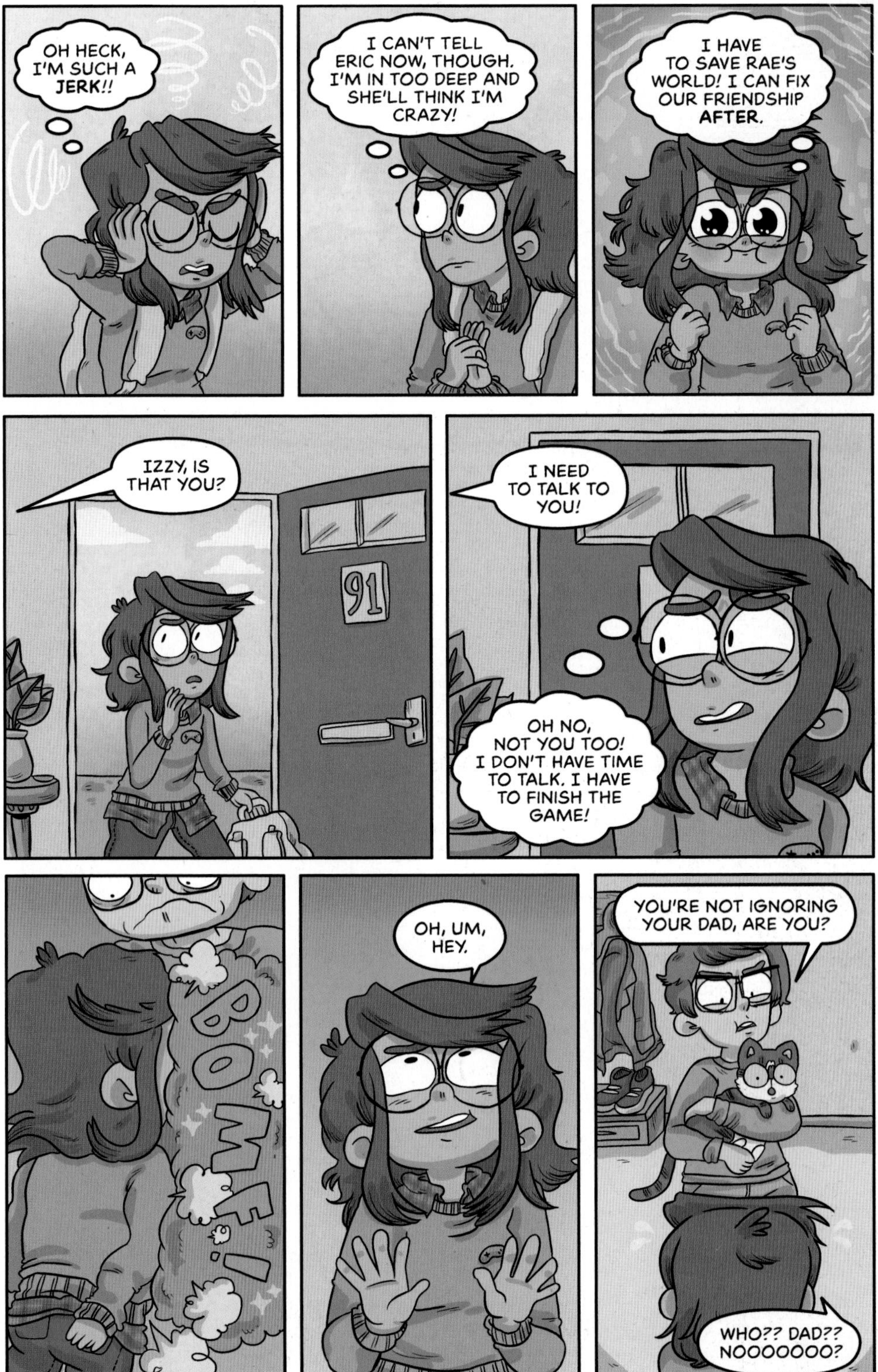
OH HECK, I'M SUCH A **JERK**!!
I CAN'T TELL ERIC NOW, THOUGH. I'M IN TOO DEEP AND SHE'LL THINK I'M CRAZY!
I HAVE TO SAVE RAE'S WORLD! I CAN FIX OUR FRIENDSHIP **AFTER**.
IZZY, IS THAT YOU?
91
I NEED TO TALK TO YOU!
OH NO, NOT YOU TOO! I DON'T HAVE TIME TO TALK. I HAVE TO FINISH THE GAME!
BOOM!
OH, UM, HEY.
YOU'RE NOT IGNORING YOUR DAD, ARE YOU?
WHO?? DAD?? NOOOOOOO?

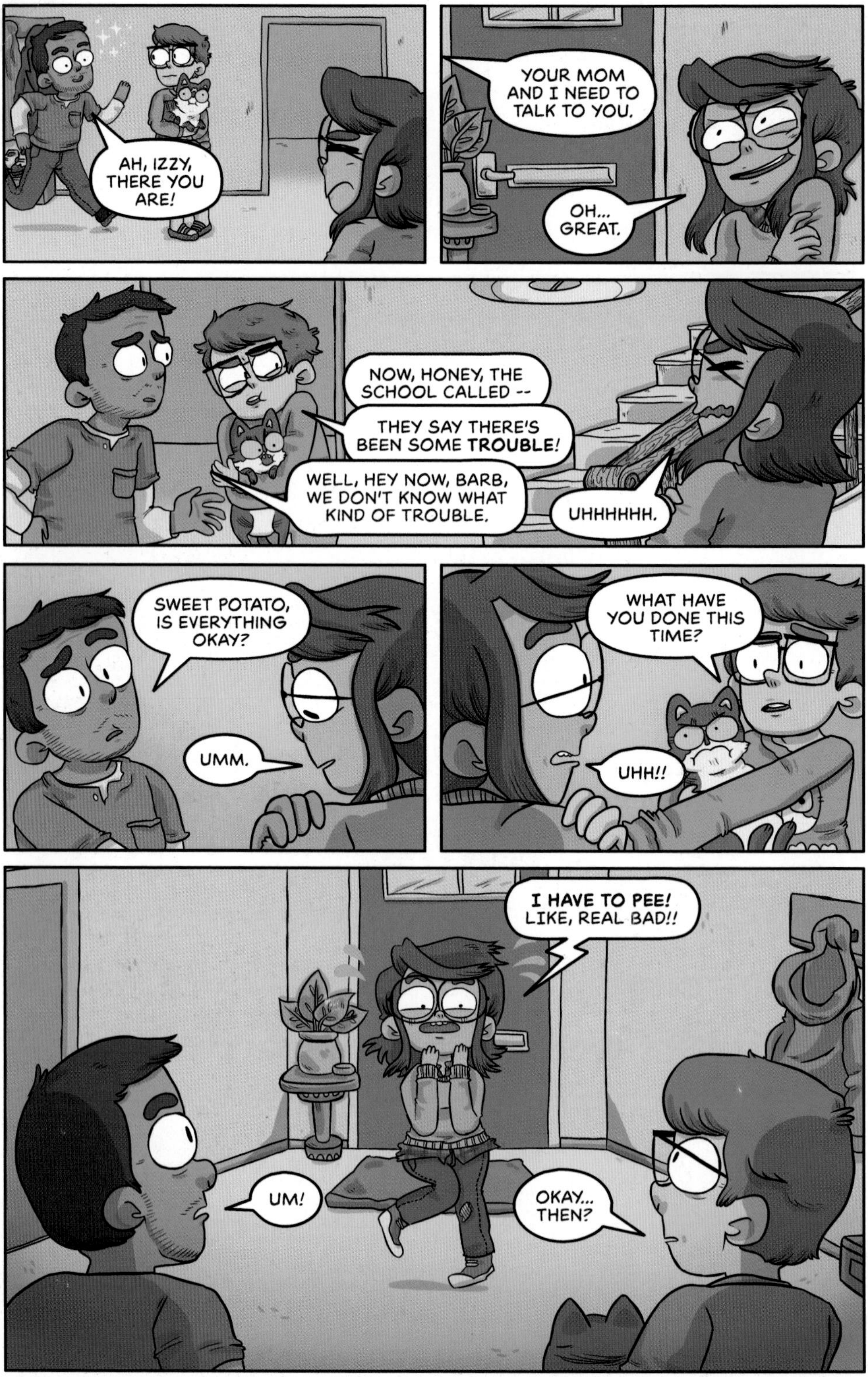
AH, IZZY, THERE YOU ARE!
YOUR MOM AND I NEED TO TALK TO YOU.
OH... GREAT.
NOW, HONEY, THE SCHOOL CALLED --
THEY SAY THERE'S BEEN SOME TROUBLE!
WELL, HEY NOW, BARB, WE DON'T KNOW WHAT KIND OF TROUBLE.
UHHHHHH.
SWEET POTATO, IS EVERYTHING OKAY?
UMM.
WHAT HAVE YOU DONE THIS TIME?
UHH!!
I HAVE TO PEE! LIKE, REAL BAD!!
UM!
OKAY... THEN?

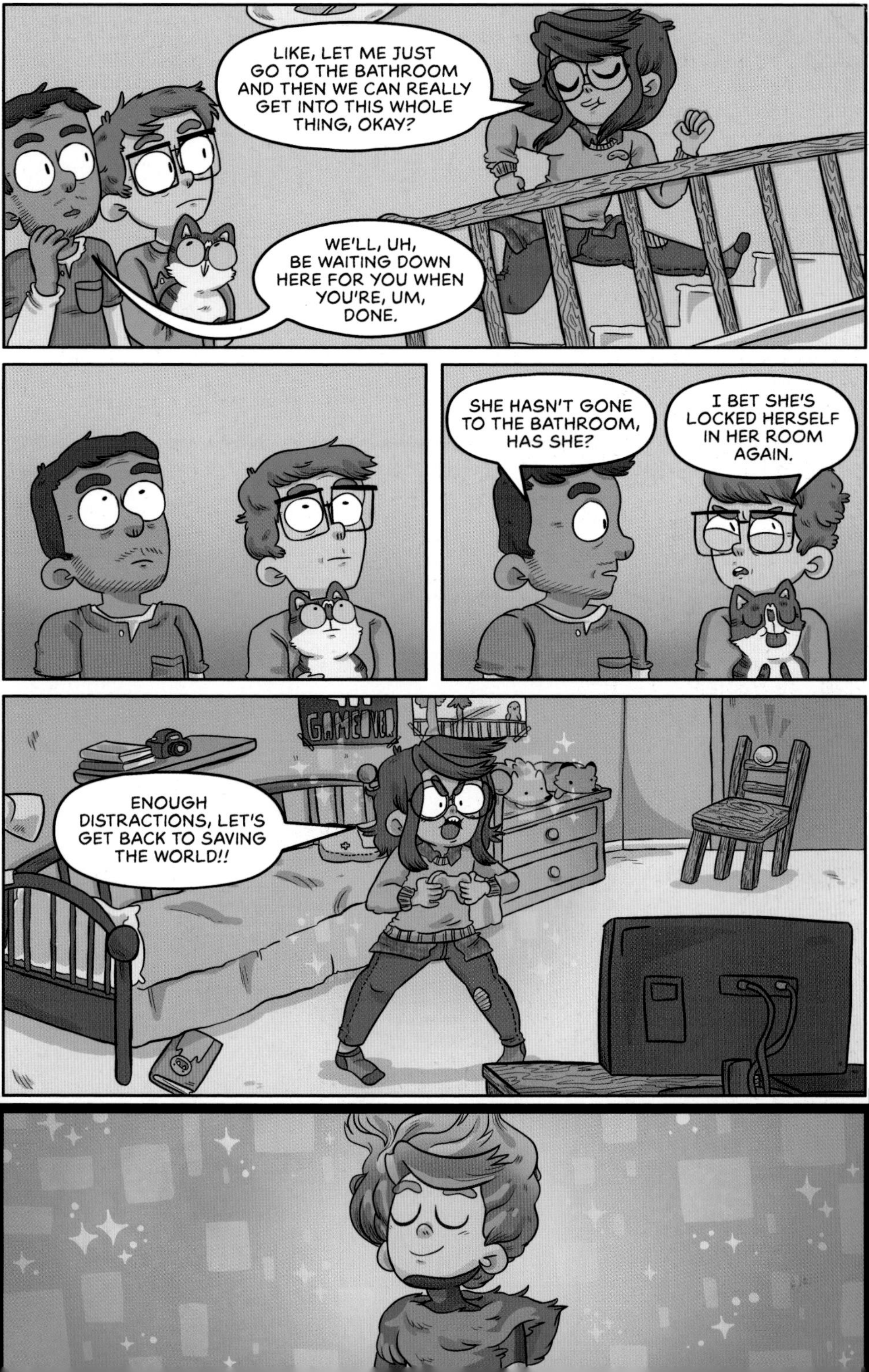
LIKE, LET ME JUST GO TO THE BATHROOM AND THEN WE CAN REALLY GET INTO THIS WHOLE THING, OKAY?
WE'LL, UH, BE WAITING DOWN HERE FOR YOU WHEN YOU'RE, UM, DONE.
SHE HASN'T GONE TO THE BATHROOM, HAS SHE?
I BET SHE'S LOCKED HERSELF IN HER ROOM AGAIN.
GAME OVER
ENOUGH DISTRACTIONS, LET'S GET BACK TO SAVING THE WORLD!!

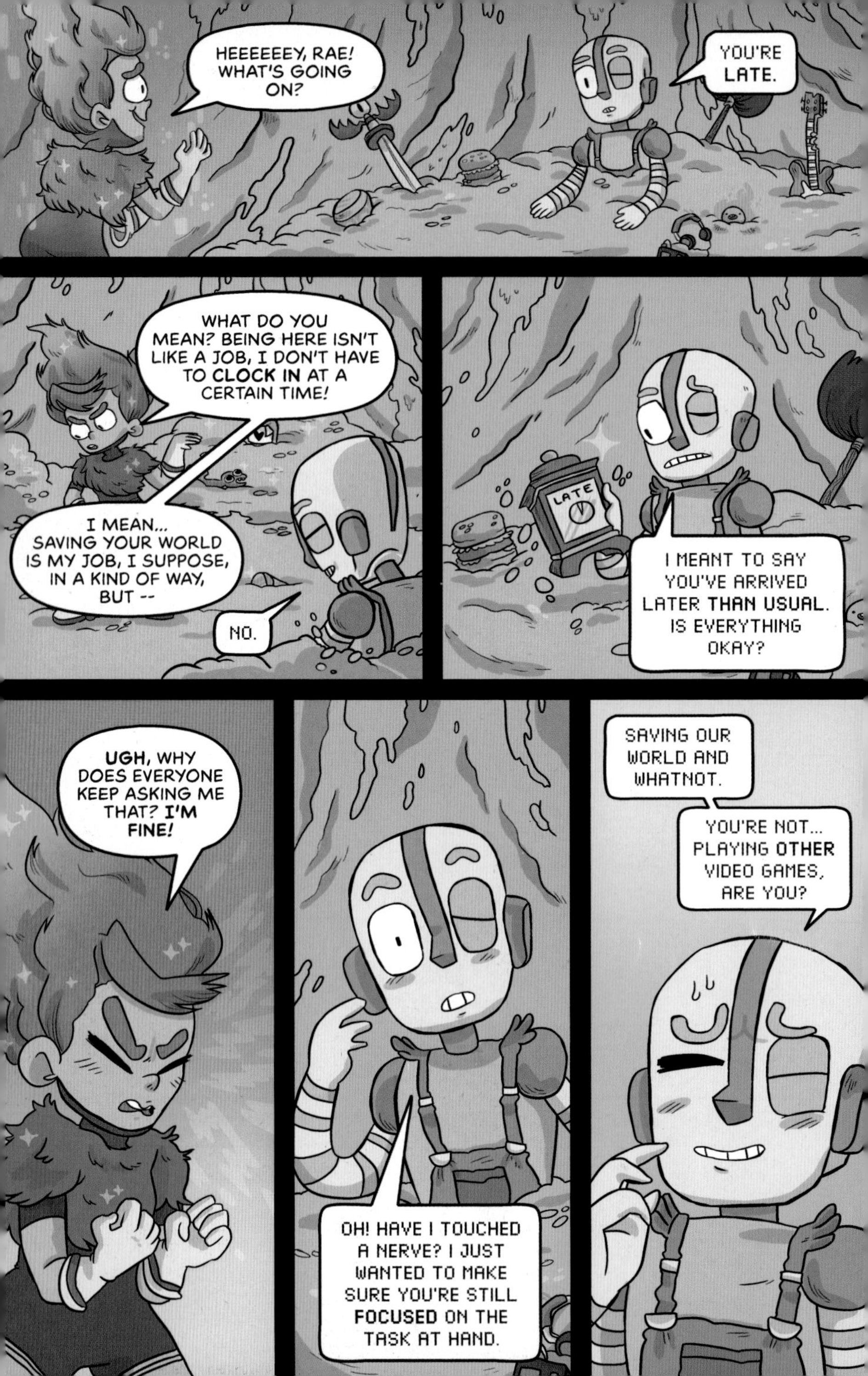
HEEEEEEY, RAE! WHAT'S GOING ON?
YOU'RE LATE.
WHAT DO YOU MEAN? BEING HERE ISN'T LIKE A JOB, I DON'T HAVE TO **CLOCK IN** AT A CERTAIN TIME!
I MEAN... SAVING YOUR WORLD IS MY JOB, I SUPPOSE, IN A KIND OF WAY, BUT --
NO.
LATE
I MEANT TO SAY YOU'VE ARRIVED LATER **THAN USUAL.** IS EVERYTHING OKAY?
UGH, WHY DOES EVERYONE KEEP ASKING ME THAT? **I'M FINE!**
OH! HAVE I TOUCHED A NERVE? I JUST WANTED TO MAKE SURE YOU'RE STILL **FOCUSED** ON THE TASK AT HAND.
SAVING OUR WORLD AND WHATNOT.
YOU'RE NOT... PLAYING **OTHER** VIDEO GAMES, ARE YOU?

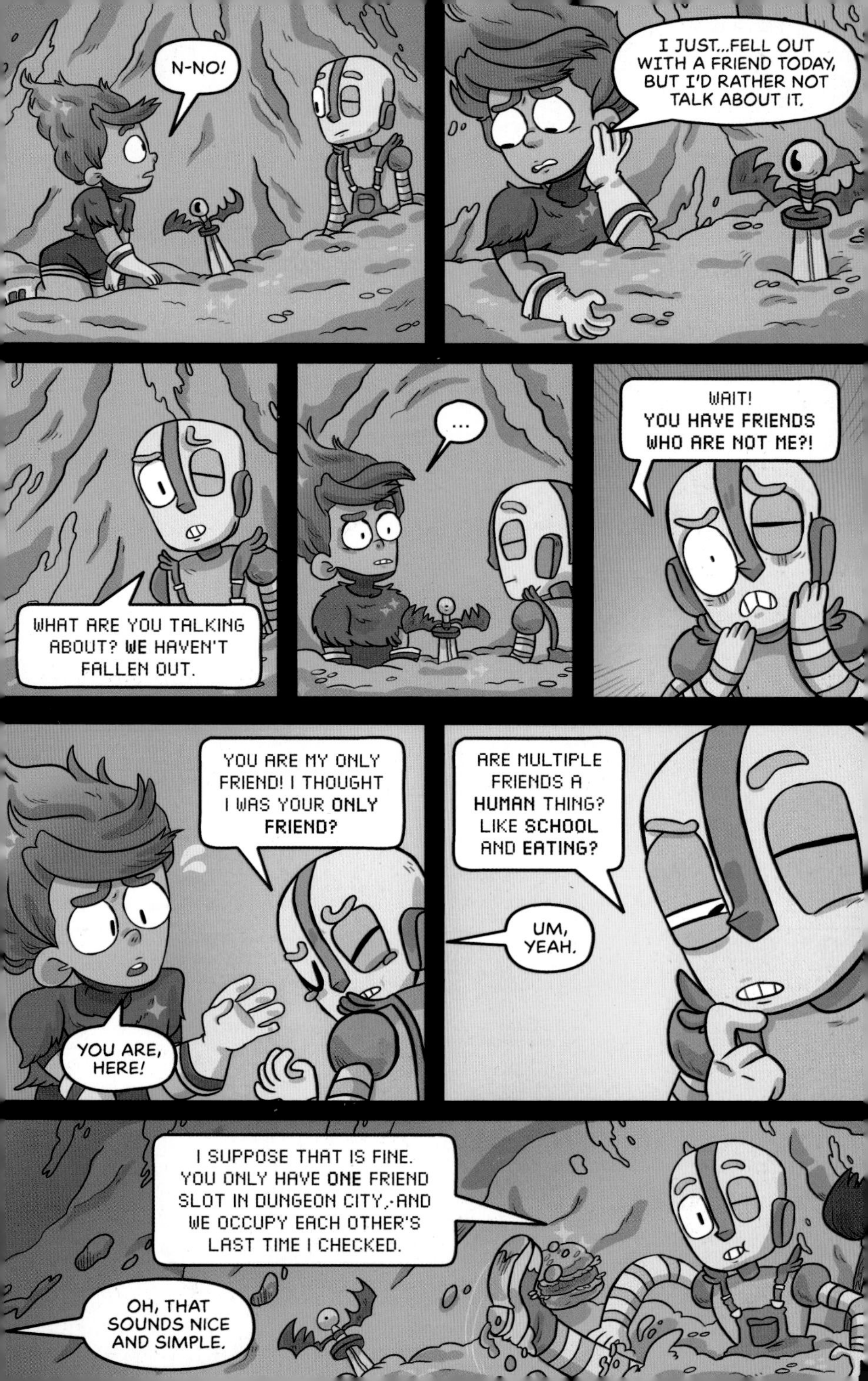
N-NO!
I JUST...FELL OUT WITH A FRIEND TODAY, BUT I'D RATHER NOT TALK ABOUT IT.
WHAT ARE YOU TALKING ABOUT? WE HAVEN'T FALLEN OUT.
...
WAIT! YOU HAVE FRIENDS WHO ARE NOT ME?!
YOU ARE MY ONLY FRIEND! I THOUGHT I WAS YOUR ONLY FRIEND?
YOU ARE, HERE!
ARE MULTIPLE FRIENDS A HUMAN THING? LIKE SCHOOL AND EATING?
UM, YEAH.
I SUPPOSE THAT IS FINE. YOU ONLY HAVE ONE FRIEND SLOT IN DUNGEON CITY, AND WE OCCUPY EACH OTHER'S LAST TIME I CHECKED.
OH, THAT SOUNDS NICE AND SIMPLE.

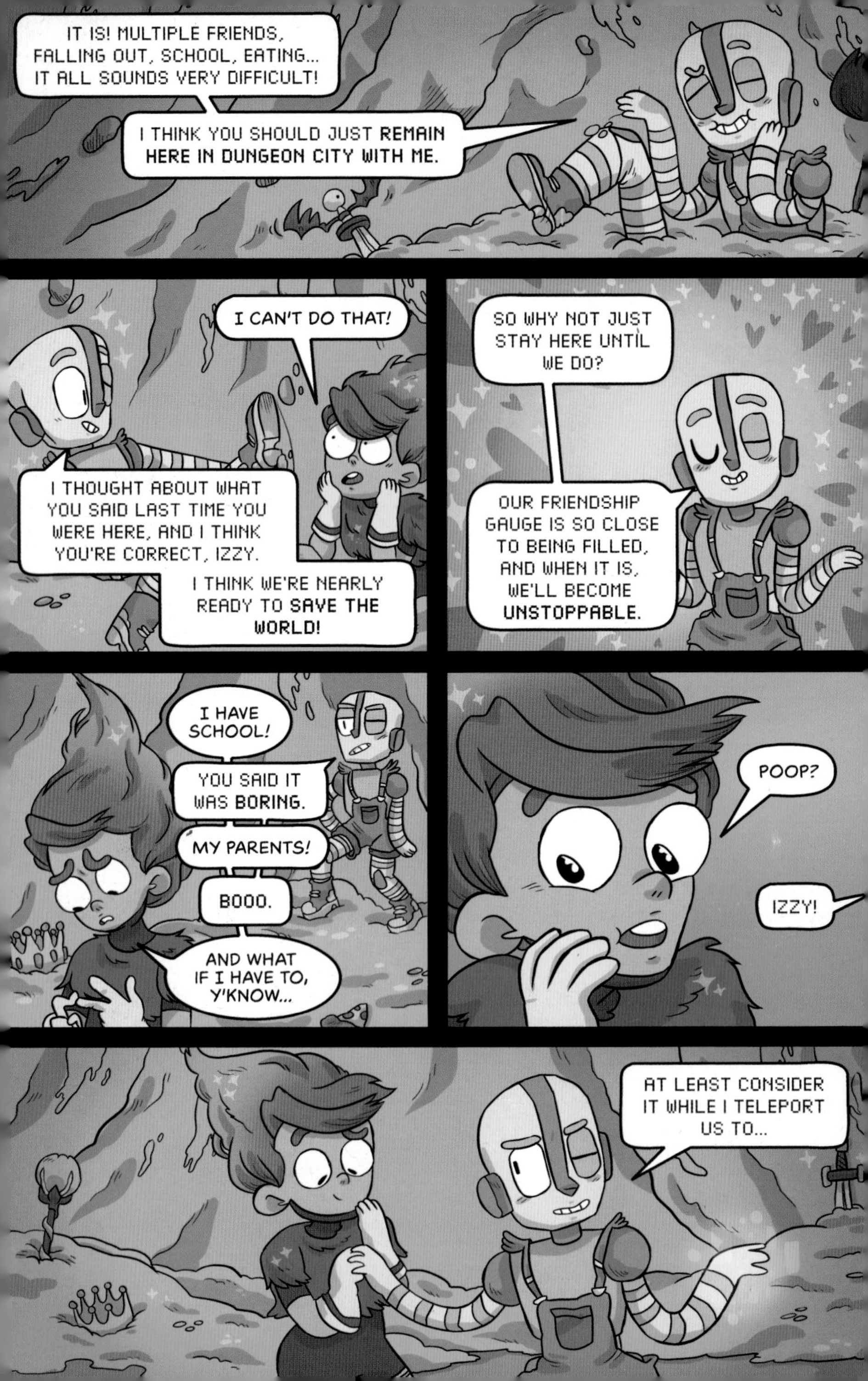
IT IS! MULTIPLE FRIENDS, FALLING OUT, SCHOOL, EATING... IT ALL SOUNDS VERY DIFFICULT!
I THINK YOU SHOULD JUST REMAIN HERE IN DUNGEON CITY WITH ME.
I CAN'T DO THAT!
I THOUGHT ABOUT WHAT YOU SAID LAST TIME YOU WERE HERE, AND I THINK YOU'RE CORRECT, IZZY.
I THINK WE'RE NEARLY READY TO SAVE THE WORLD!
SO WHY NOT JUST STAY HERE UNTIL WE DO?
OUR FRIENDSHIP GAUGE IS SO CLOSE TO BEING FILLED, AND WHEN IT IS, WE'LL BECOME UNSTOPPABLE.
I HAVE SCHOOL!
YOU SAID IT WAS BORING.
MY PARENTS!
BOOO.
AND WHAT IF I HAVE TO, Y'KNOW...
POOP?
IZZY!
AT LEAST CONSIDER IT WHILE I TELEPORT US TO...

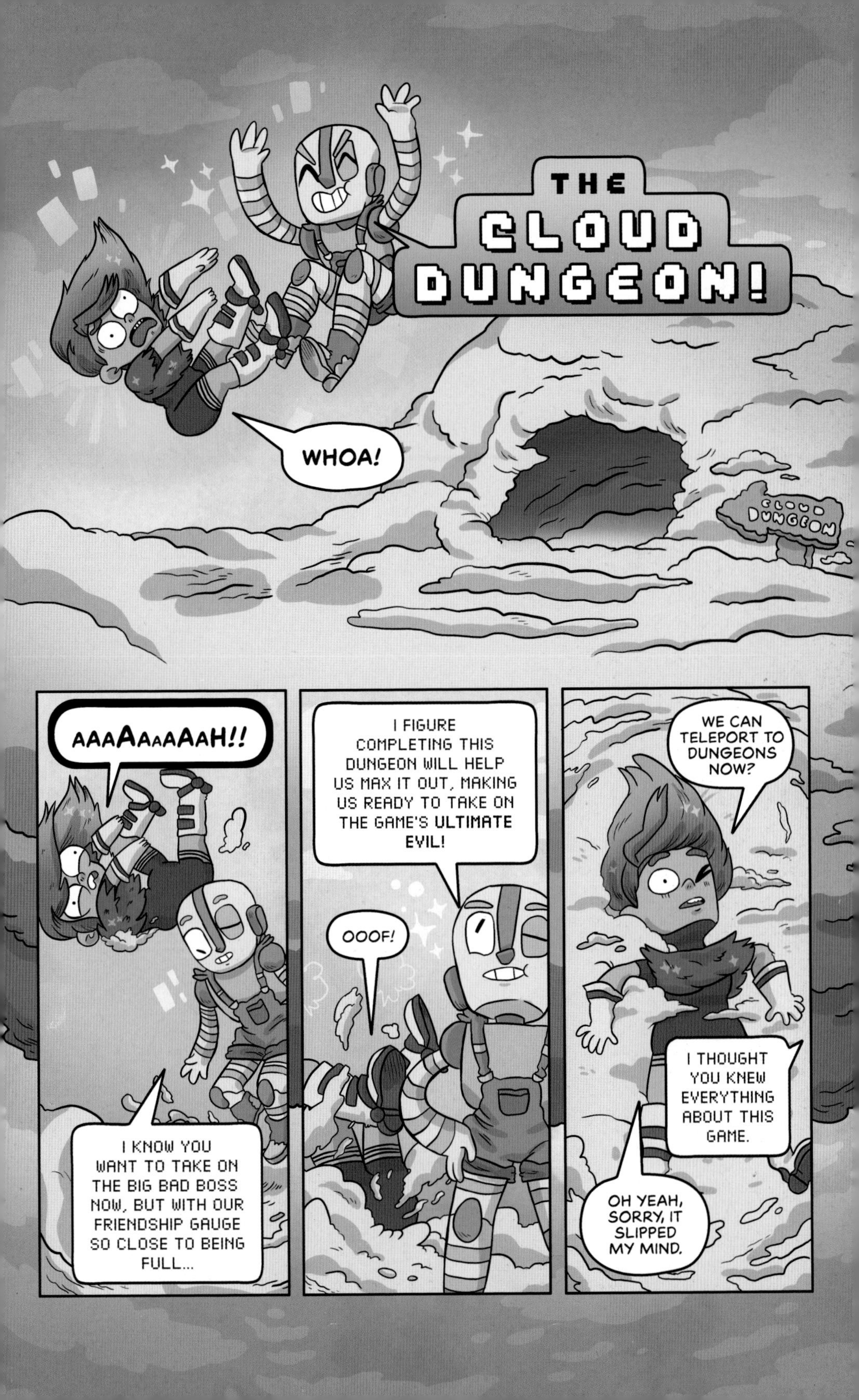
THE CLOUD DUNGEON!
WHOA!
CLOUD DUNGEON
AAAAAAAAAH!!
I KNOW YOU WANT TO TAKE ON THE BIG BAD BOSS NOW, BUT WITH OUR FRIENDSHIP GAUGE SO CLOSE TO BEING FULL...
I FIGURE COMPLETING THIS DUNGEON WILL HELP US MAX IT OUT, MAKING US READY TO TAKE ON THE GAME'S ULTIMATE EVIL!
OOOF!
WE CAN TELEPORT TO DUNGEONS NOW?
I THOUGHT YOU KNEW EVERYTHING ABOUT THIS GAME.
OH YEAH, SORRY, IT SLIPPED MY MIND.

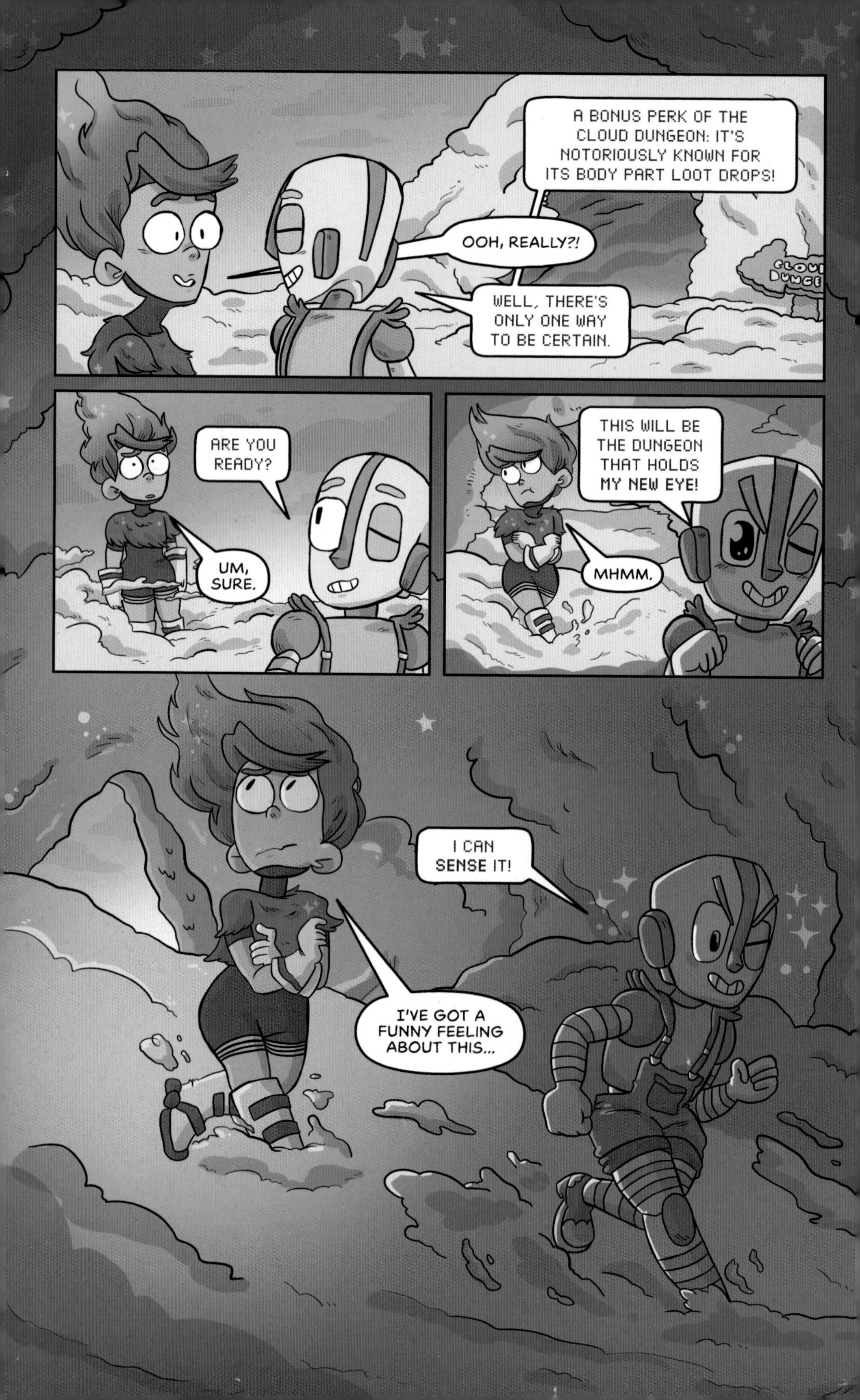
A BONUS PERK OF THE CLOUD DUNGEON: IT'S NOTORIOUSLY KNOWN FOR ITS BODY PART LOOT DROPS!
OOH, REALLY?!
WELL, THERE'S ONLY ONE WAY TO BE CERTAIN.
ARE YOU READY?
UM, SURE.
THIS WILL BE THE DUNGEON THAT HOLDS MY NEW EYE!
MHMM.
I CAN SENSE IT!
I'VE GOT A FUNNY FEELING ABOUT THIS...

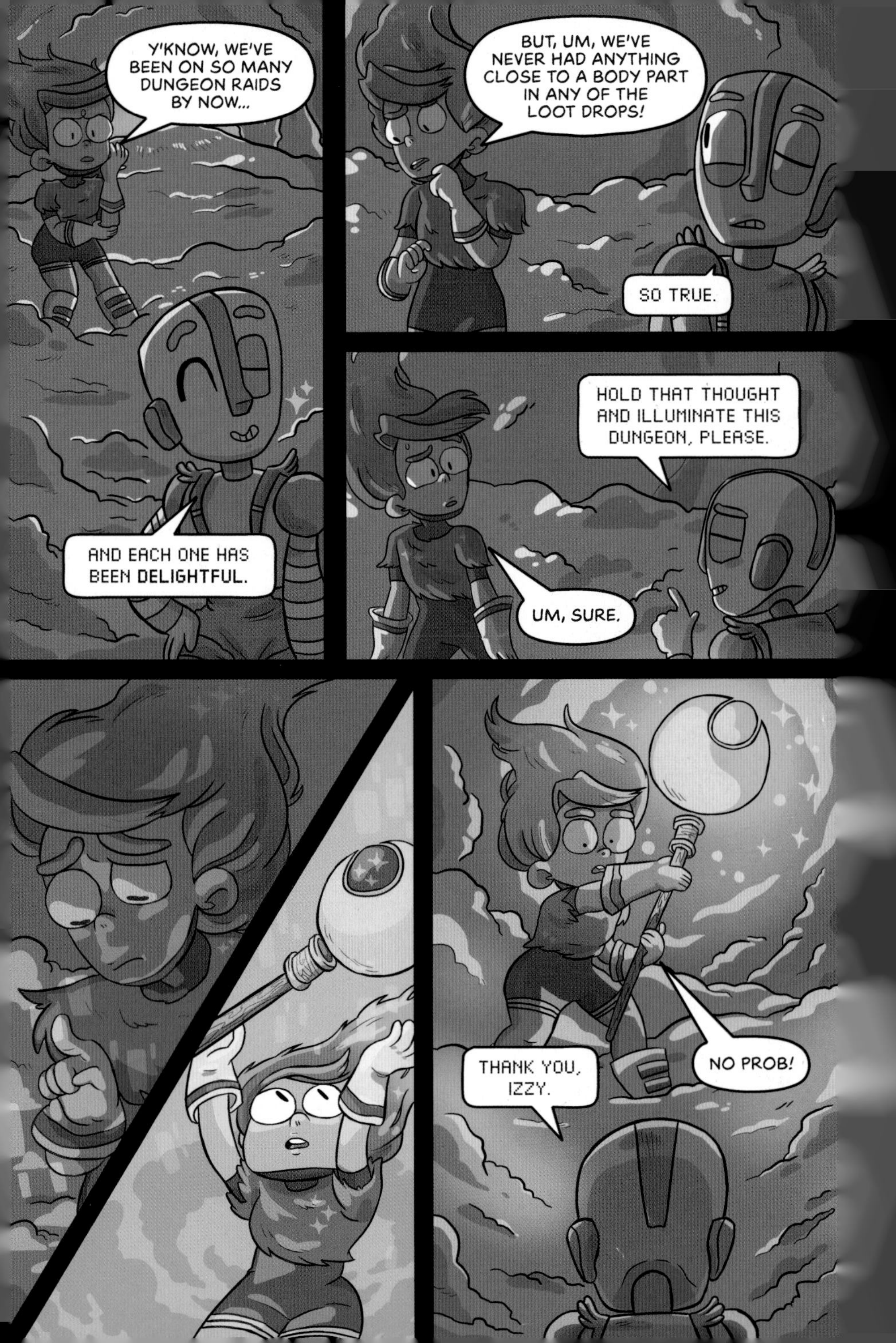
Y'KNOW, WE'VE BEEN ON SO MANY DUNGEON RAIDS BY NOW...
AND EACH ONE HAS BEEN DELIGHTFUL.
BUT, UM, WE'VE NEVER HAD ANYTHING CLOSE TO A BODY PART IN ANY OF THE LOOT DROPS!
SO TRUE.
HOLD THAT THOUGHT AND ILLUMINATE THIS DUNGEON, PLEASE.
UM, SURE.
NO PROB!
THANK YOU, IZZY.

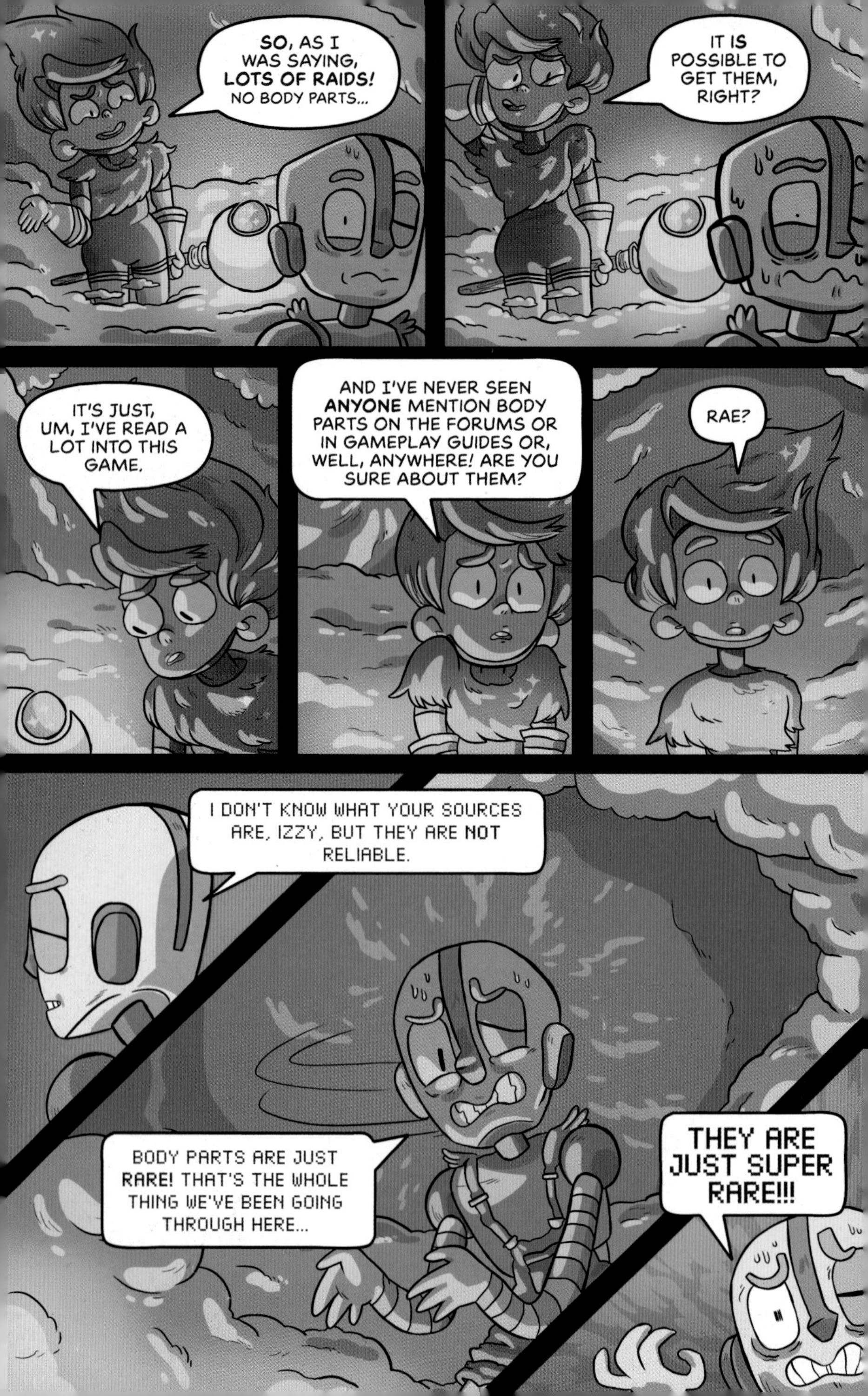
SO, AS I WAS SAYING, LOTS OF RAIDS! NO BODY PARTS...
IT IS POSSIBLE TO GET THEM, RIGHT?
IT'S JUST, UM, I'VE READ A LOT INTO THIS GAME.
AND I'VE NEVER SEEN ANYONE MENTION BODY PARTS ON THE FORUMS OR IN GAMEPLAY GUIDES OR, WELL, ANYWHERE! ARE YOU SURE ABOUT THEM?
RAE?
I DON'T KNOW WHAT YOUR SOURCES ARE, IZZY, BUT THEY ARE NOT RELIABLE.
BODY PARTS ARE JUST RARE! THAT'S THE WHOLE THING WE'VE BEEN GOING THROUGH HERE...
THEY ARE JUST SUPER RARE!!!

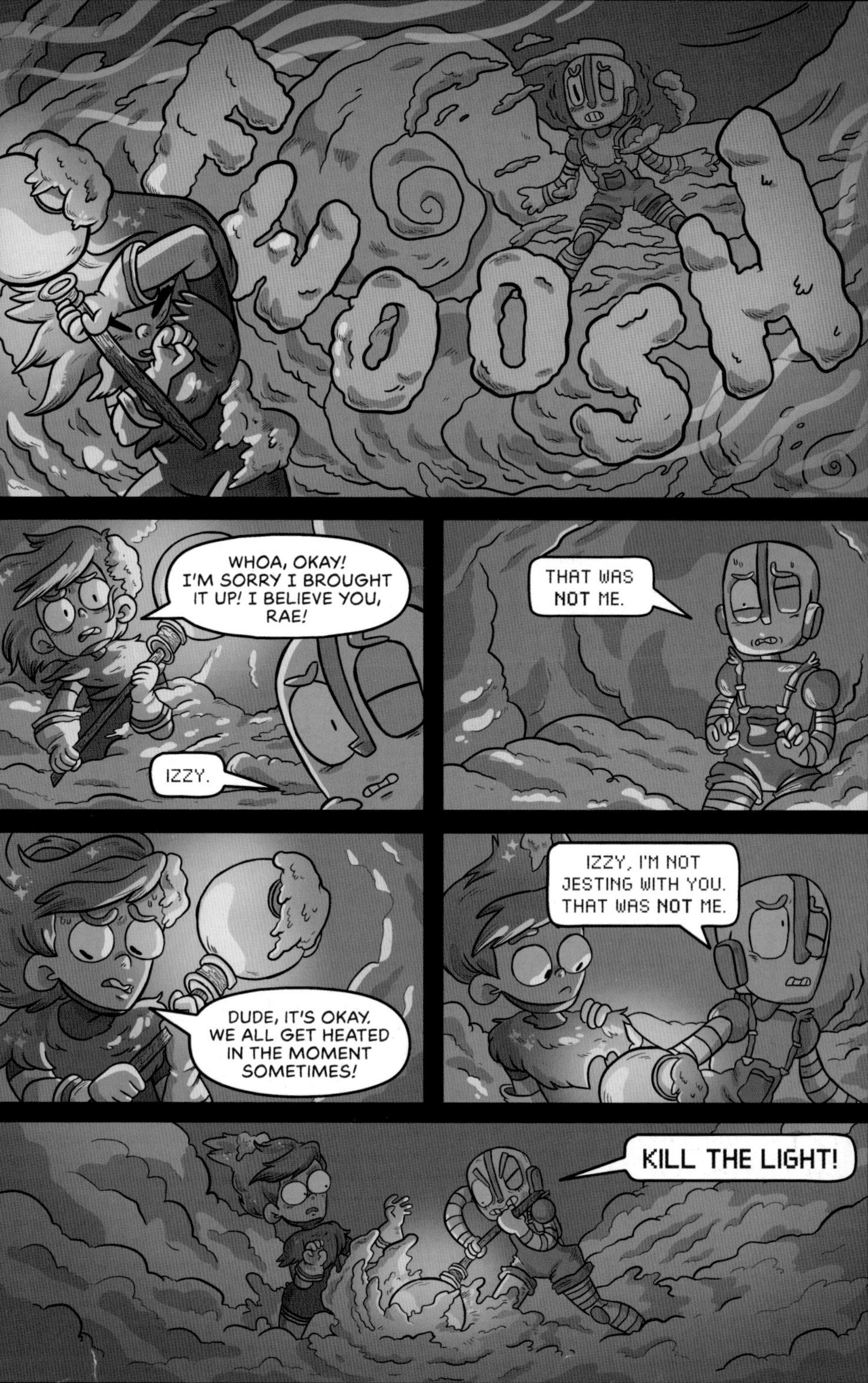
FWOOSH
WHOA, OKAY! I'M SORRY I BROUGHT IT UP! I BELIEVE YOU, RAE!
IZZY.
THAT WAS NOT ME.
DUDE, IT'S OKAY. WE ALL GET HEATED IN THE MOMENT SOMETIMES!
IZZY, I'M NOT JESTING WITH YOU. THAT WAS NOT ME.
KILL THE LIGHT!

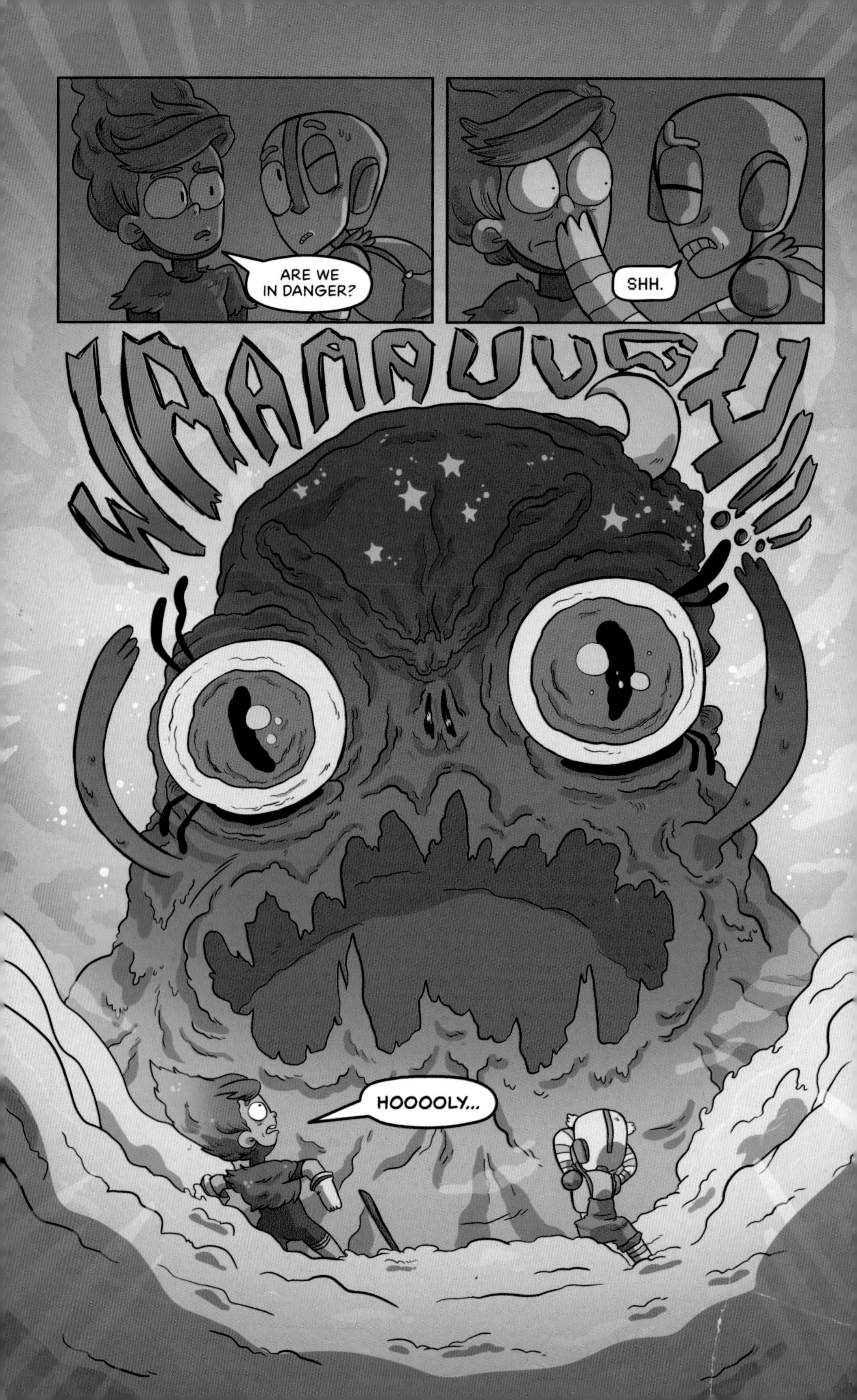
ARE WE IN DANGER?
SHH.
WAAAAUUGH
HOOOOLY...

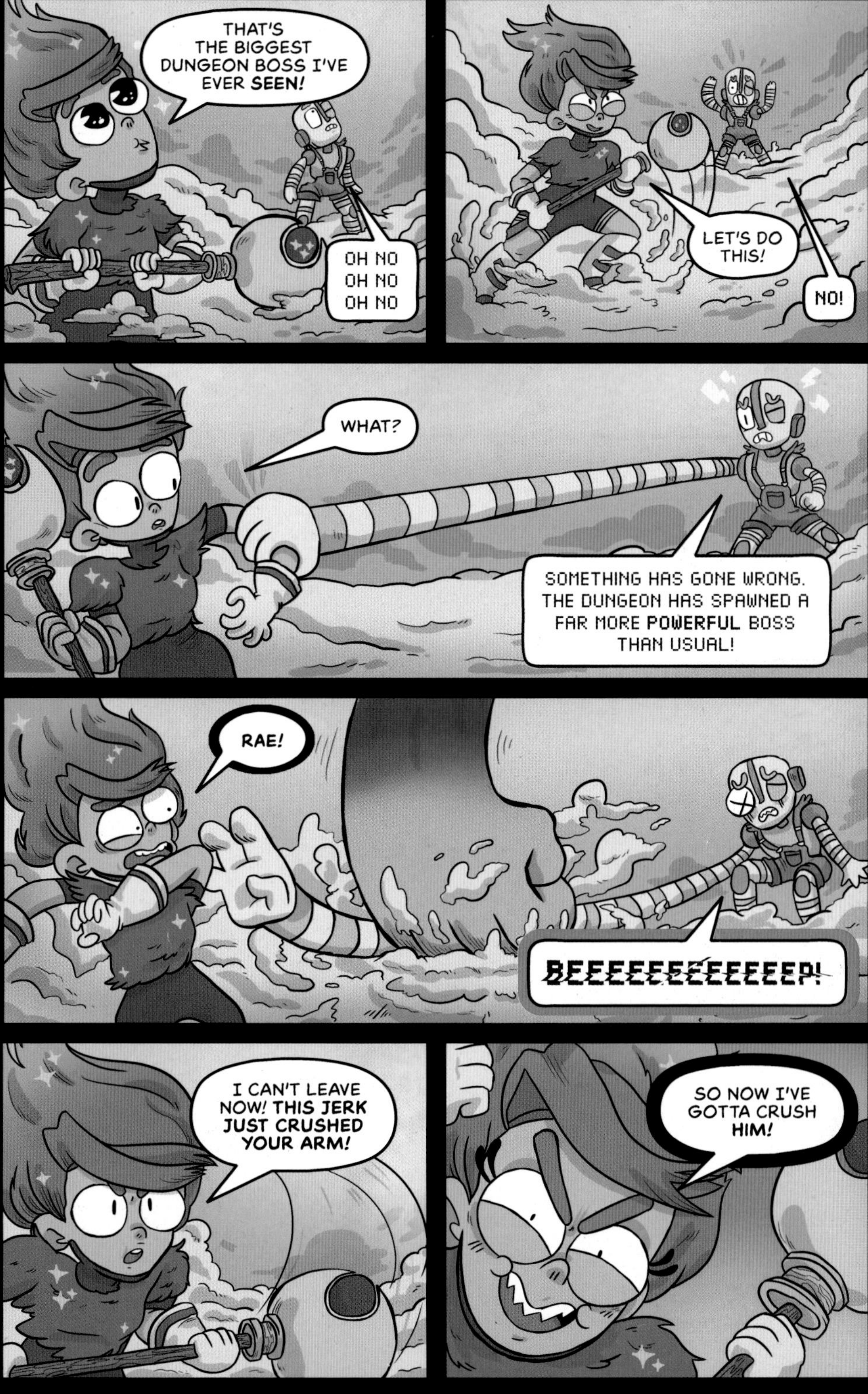
THAT'S THE BIGGEST DUNGEON BOSS I'VE EVER **SEEN!**
OH NO OH NO OH NO
LET'S DO THIS!
NO!
WHAT?
SOMETHING HAS GONE WRONG. THE DUNGEON HAS SPAWNED A FAR MORE **POWERFUL** BOSS THAN USUAL!
RAE!
BEEEEEEEEEEEEEP!
I CAN'T LEAVE NOW! **THIS JERK JUST CRUSHED YOUR ARM!**
SO NOW I'VE GOTTA CRUSH **HIM!**

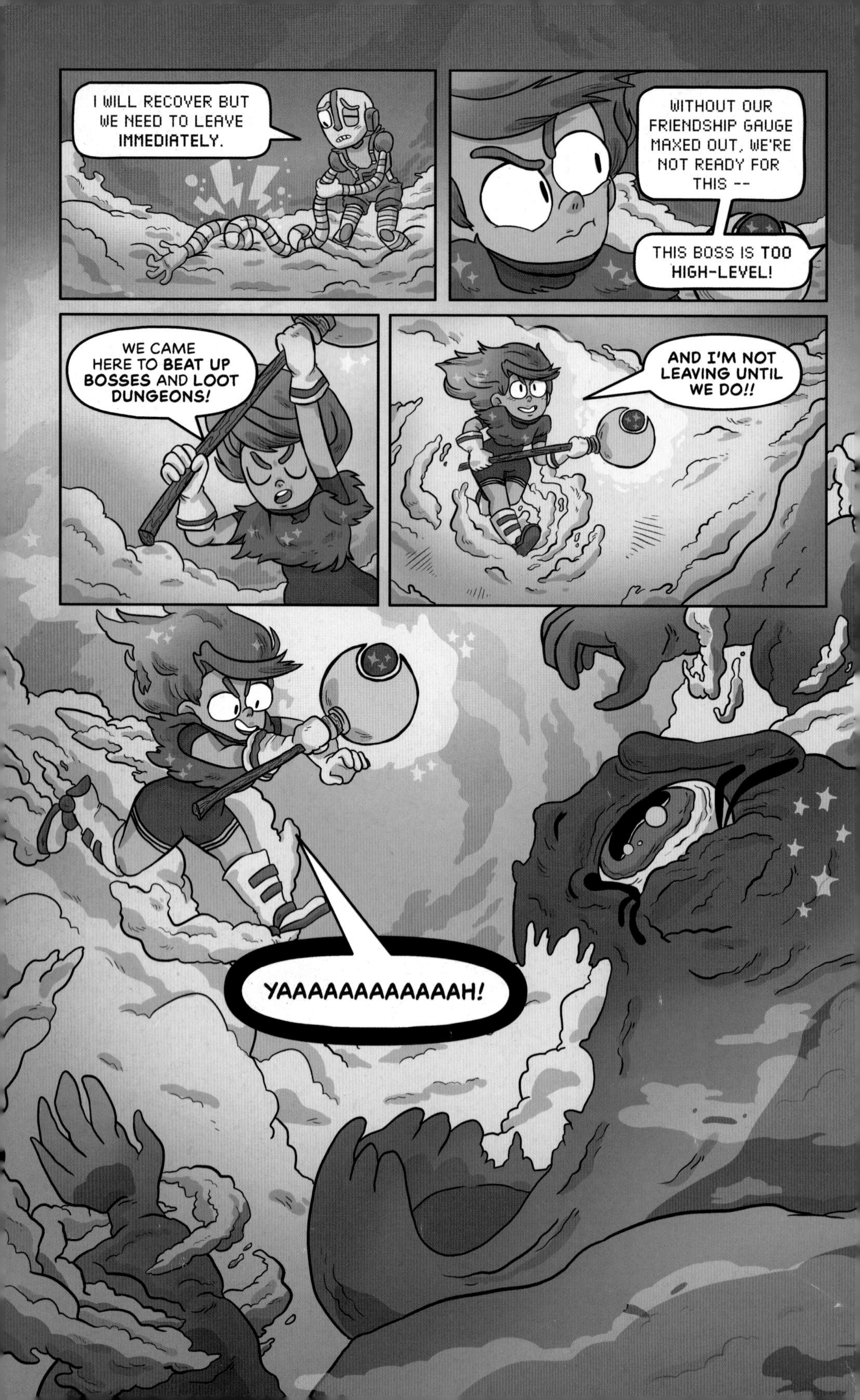
I WILL RECOVER BUT WE NEED TO LEAVE IMMEDIATELY.
WITHOUT OUR FRIENDSHIP GAUGE MAXED OUT, WE'RE NOT READY FOR THIS --
THIS BOSS IS TOO HIGH-LEVEL!
WE CAME HERE TO BEAT UP BOSSES AND LOOT DUNGEONS!
AND I'M NOT LEAVING UNTIL WE DO!!
YAAAAAAAAAAAAH!

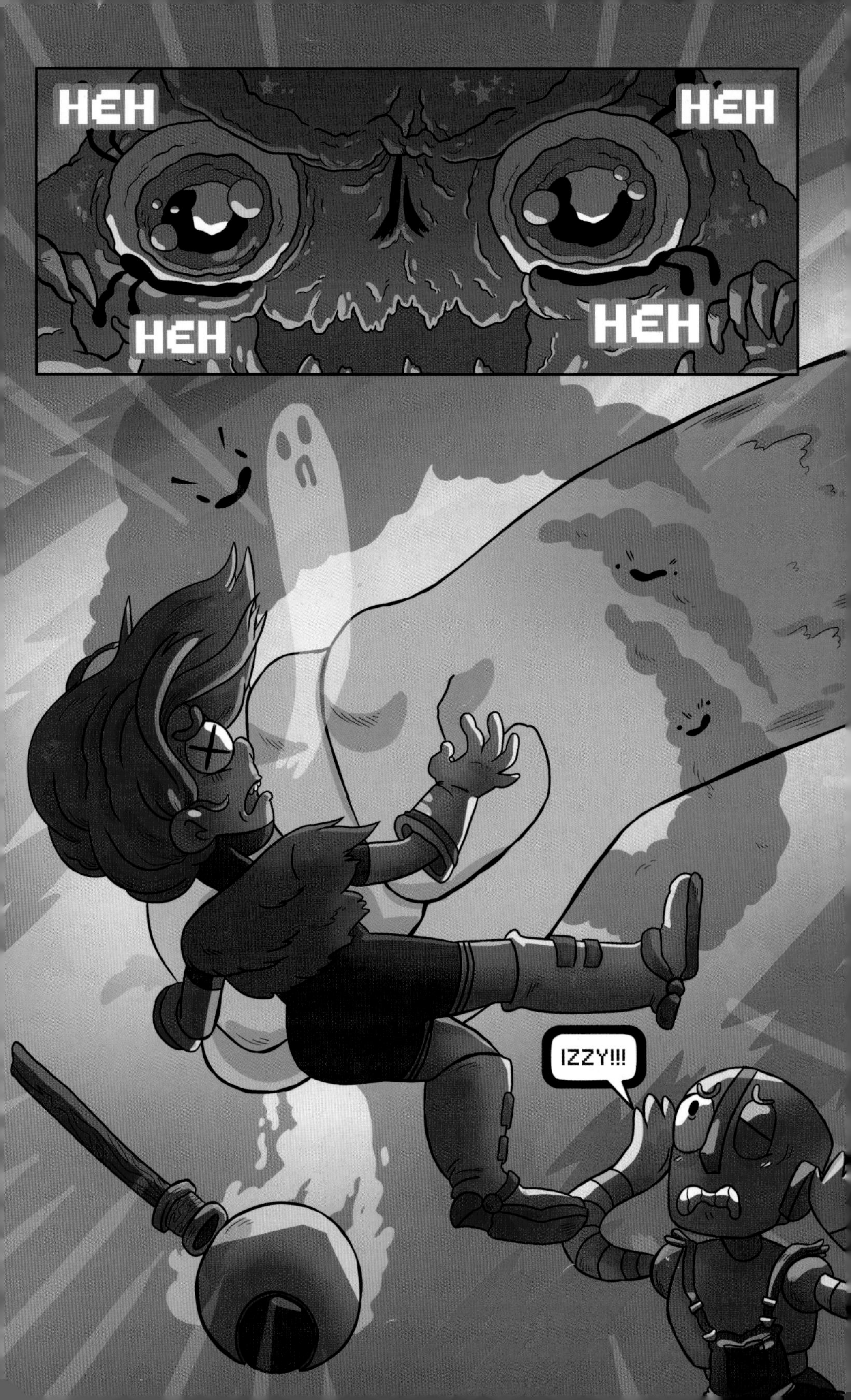
HEH
HEH
HEH
HEH
IZZY!!!

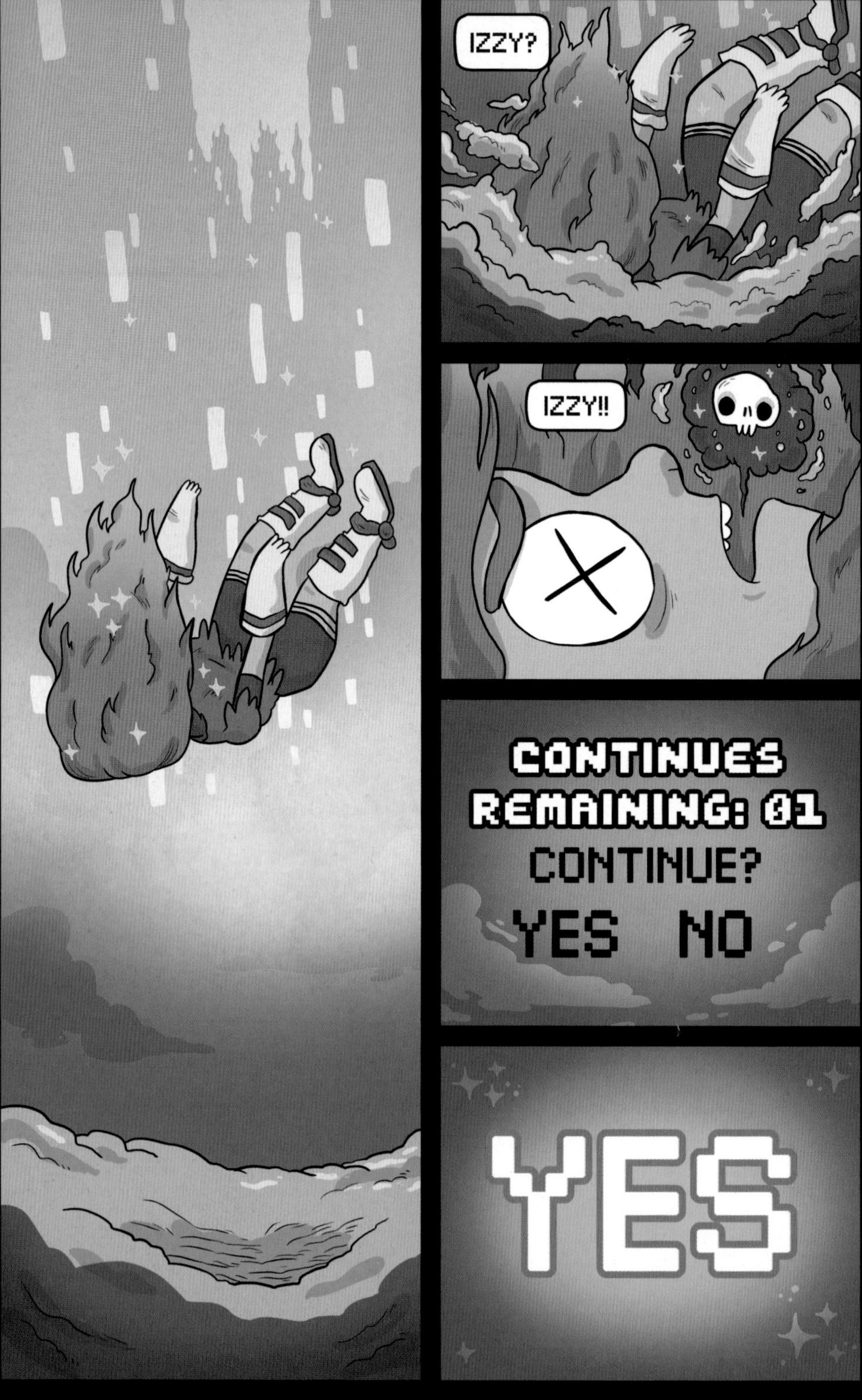
IZZY?
IZZY!!
CONTINUES
REMAINING: 01
CONTINUE?
YES NO
YES

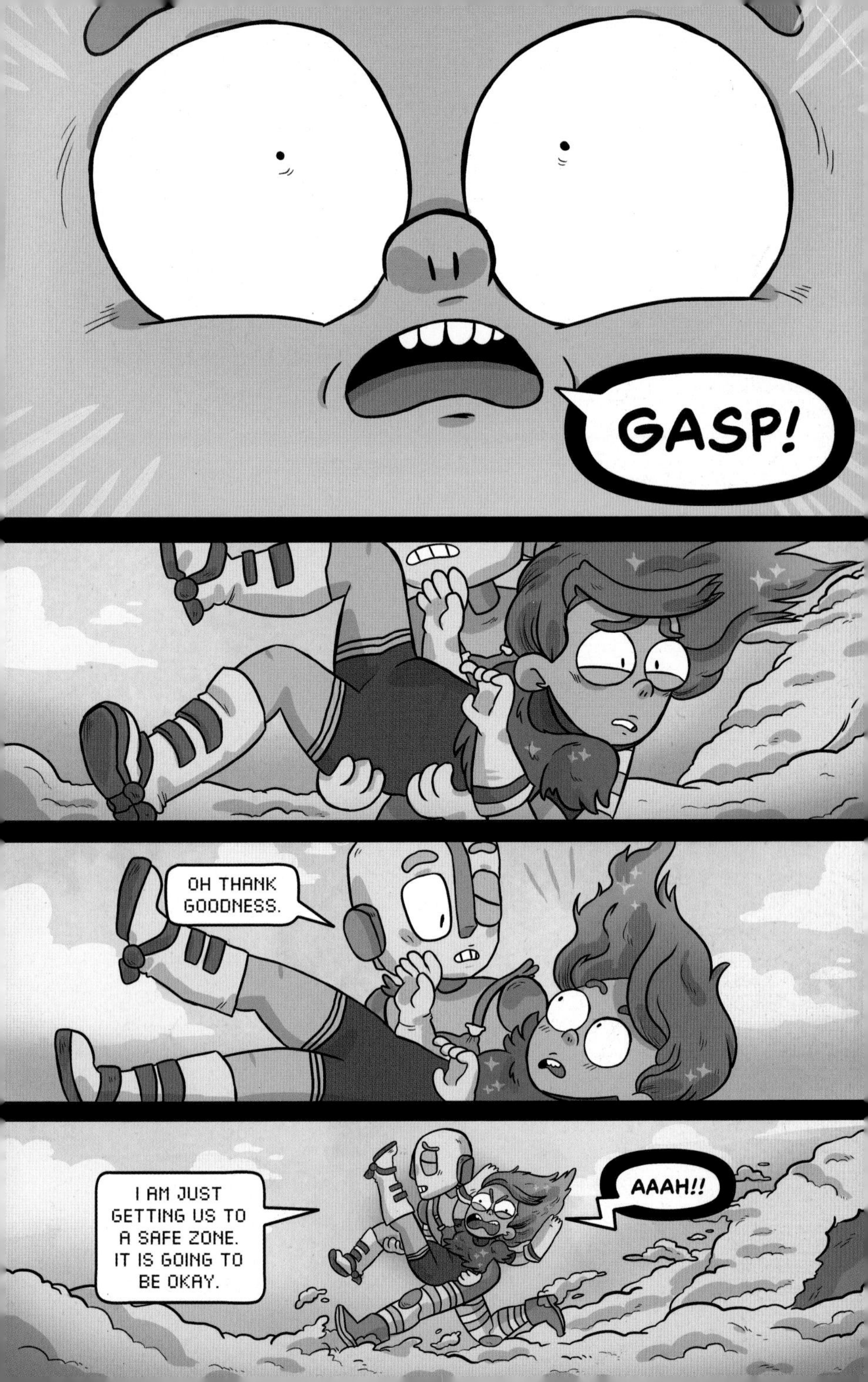
GASP!
OH THANK GOODNESS.
I AM JUST GETTING US TO A SAFE ZONE. IT IS GOING TO BE OKAY.
AAAH!!

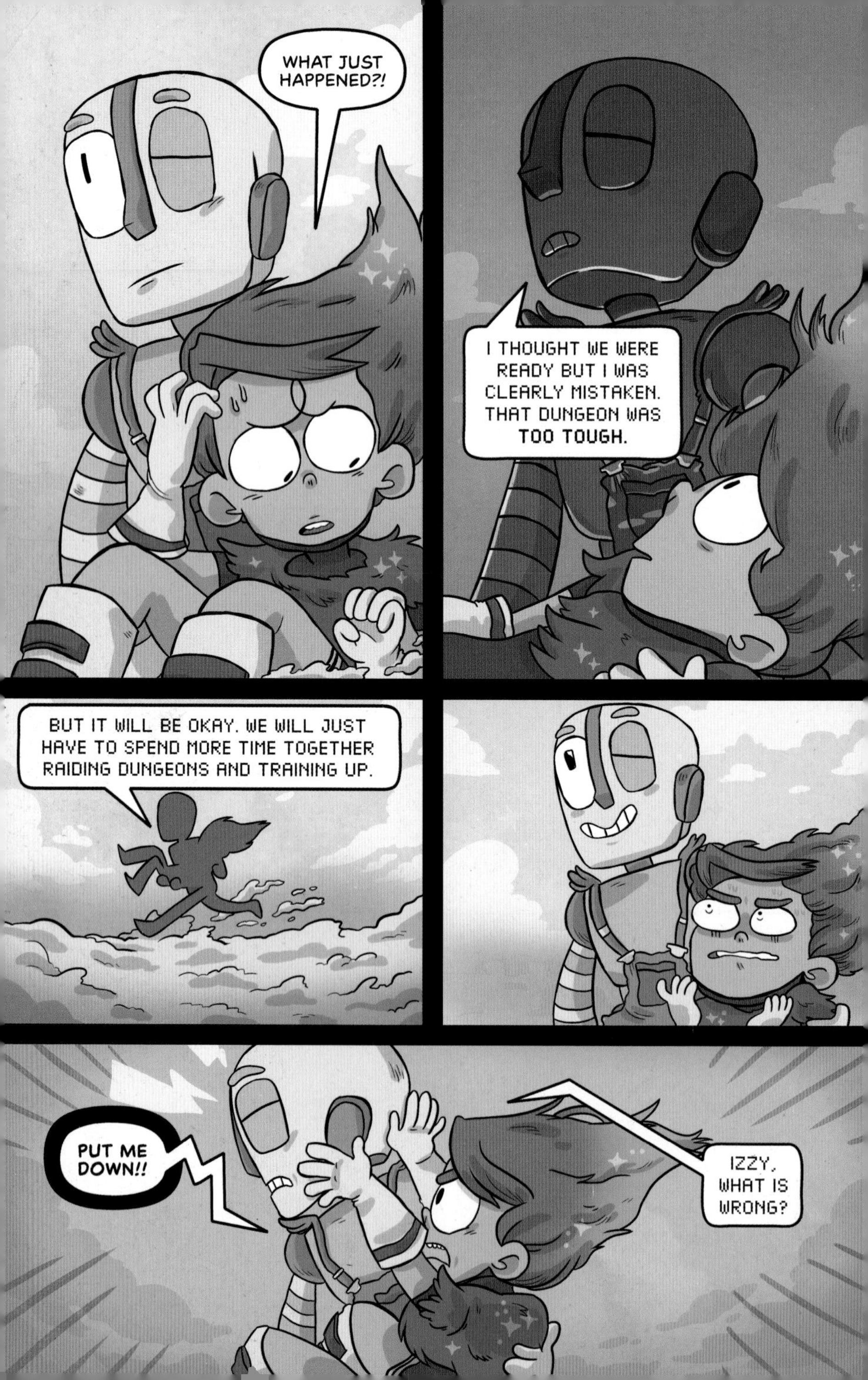
WHAT JUST HAPPENED?!
I THOUGHT WE WERE READY BUT I WAS CLEARLY MISTAKEN. THAT DUNGEON WAS TOO TOUGH.
BUT IT WILL BE OKAY. WE WILL JUST HAVE TO SPEND MORE TIME TOGETHER RAIDING DUNGEONS AND TRAINING UP.
PUT ME DOWN!!
IZZY, WHAT IS WRONG?

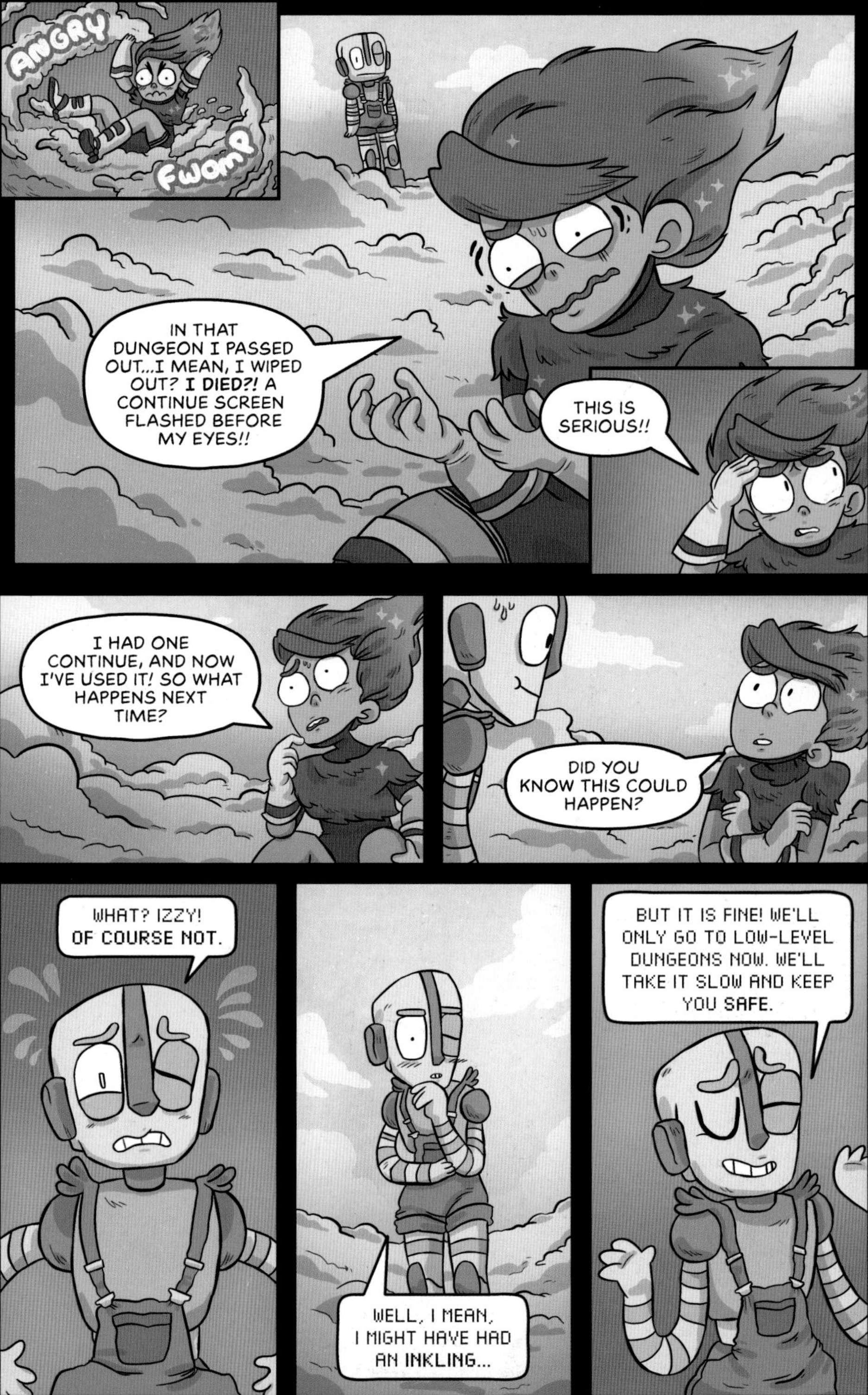
ANGRY
FWOMP
IN THAT DUNGEON I PASSED OUT...I MEAN, I WIPED OUT? I DIED?! A CONTINUE SCREEN FLASHED BEFORE MY EYES!!
THIS IS SERIOUS!!
I HAD ONE CONTINUE, AND NOW I'VE USED IT! SO WHAT HAPPENS NEXT TIME?
DID YOU KNOW THIS COULD HAPPEN?
WHAT? IZZY! OF COURSE NOT.
WELL, I MEAN, I MIGHT HAVE HAD AN INKLING...
BUT IT IS FINE! WE'LL ONLY GO TO LOW-LEVEL DUNGEONS NOW. WE'LL TAKE IT SLOW AND KEEP YOU SAFE.

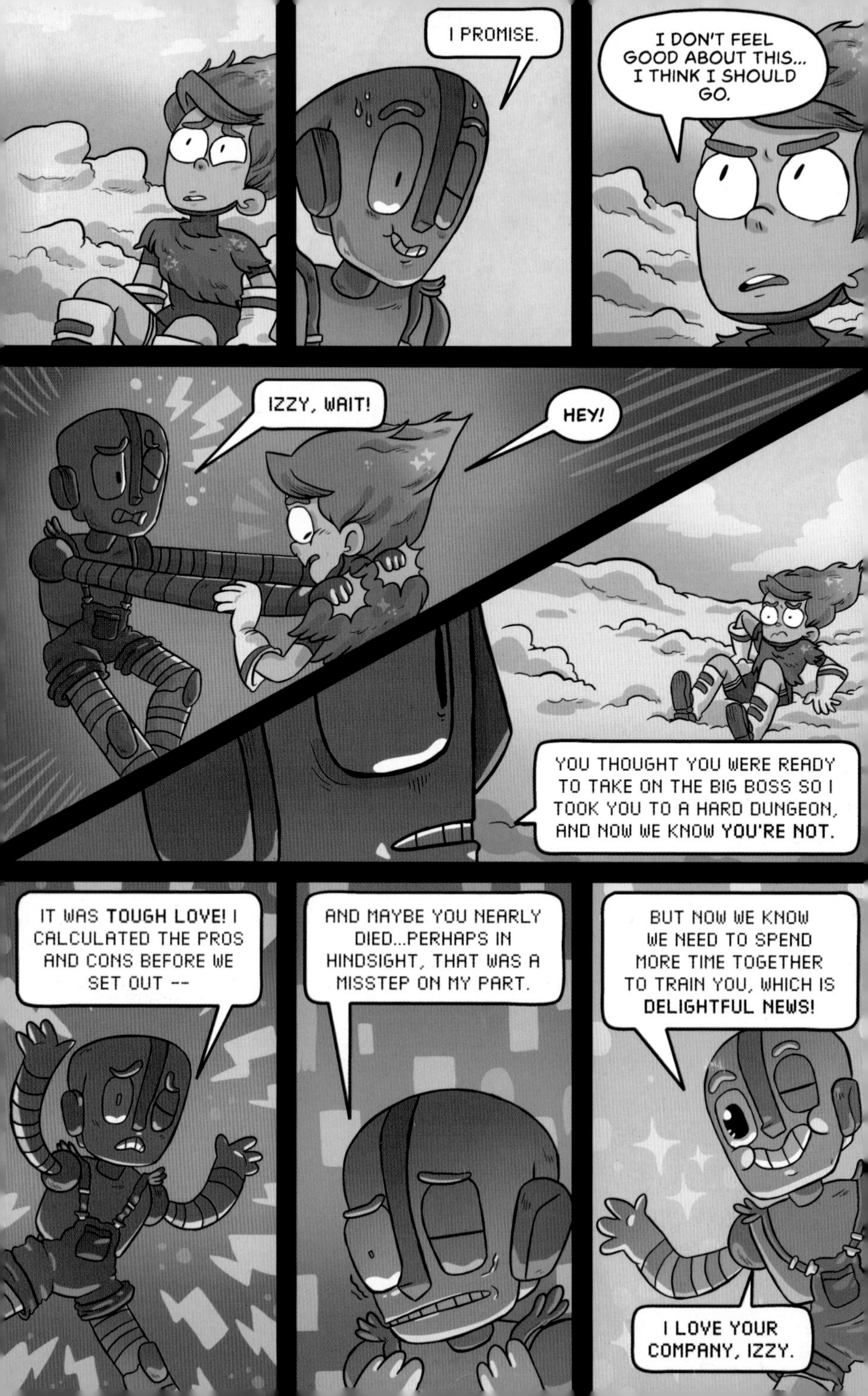
I PROMISE.
I DON'T FEEL GOOD ABOUT THIS... I THINK I SHOULD GO.
IZZY, WAIT!
HEY!
YOU THOUGHT YOU WERE READY TO TAKE ON THE BIG BOSS SO I TOOK YOU TO A HARD DUNGEON, AND NOW WE KNOW YOU'RE NOT.
IT WAS TOUGH LOVE! I CALCULATED THE PROS AND CONS BEFORE WE SET OUT --
AND MAYBE YOU NEARLY DIED...PERHAPS IN HINDSIGHT, THAT WAS A MISSTEP ON MY PART.
BUT NOW WE KNOW WE NEED TO SPEND MORE TIME TOGETHER TO TRAIN YOU, WHICH IS DELIGHTFUL NEWS!
I LOVE YOUR COMPANY, IZZY.

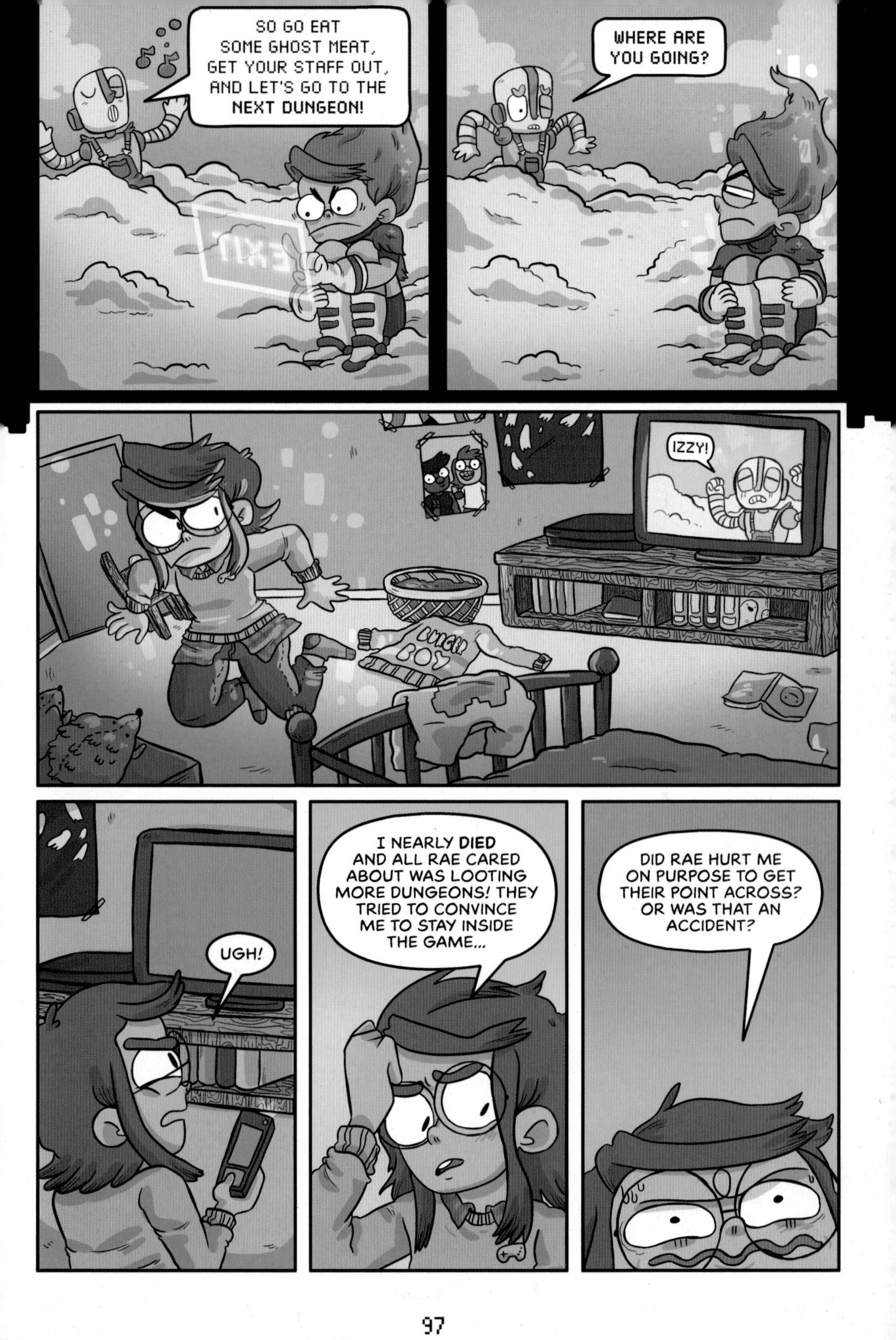
SO GO EAT SOME GHOST MEAT, GET YOUR STAFF OUT, AND LET'S GO TO THE NEXT DUNGEON!
EXIT
WHERE ARE YOU GOING?
IZZY!
DUNGEON BOY
UGH!
I NEARLY DIED AND ALL RAE CARED ABOUT WAS LOOTING MORE DUNGEONS! THEY TRIED TO CONVINCE ME TO STAY INSIDE THE GAME...
DID RAE HURT ME ON PURPOSE TO GET THEIR POINT ACROSS? OR WAS THAT AN ACCIDENT?

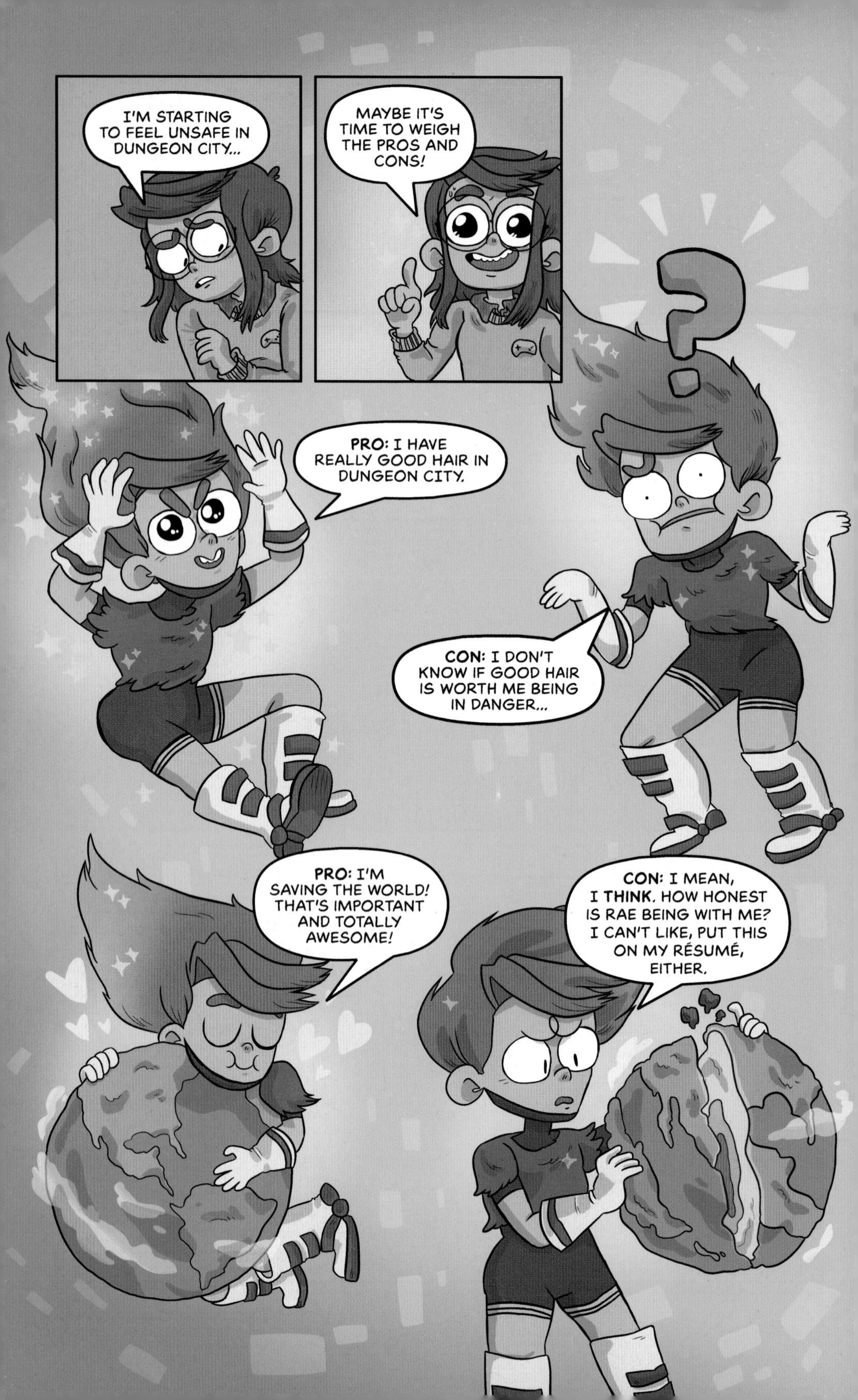
I'M STARTING TO FEEL UNSAFE IN DUNGEON CITY...
MAYBE IT'S TIME TO WEIGH THE PROS AND CONS!
PRO: I HAVE REALLY GOOD HAIR IN DUNGEON CITY.
CON: I DON'T KNOW IF GOOD HAIR IS WORTH ME BEING IN DANGER...
PRO: I'M SAVING THE WORLD! THAT'S IMPORTANT AND TOTALLY AWESOME!
CON: I MEAN, I THINK. HOW HONEST IS RAE BEING WITH ME? I CAN'T LIKE, PUT THIS ON MY RÉSUMÉ, EITHER.

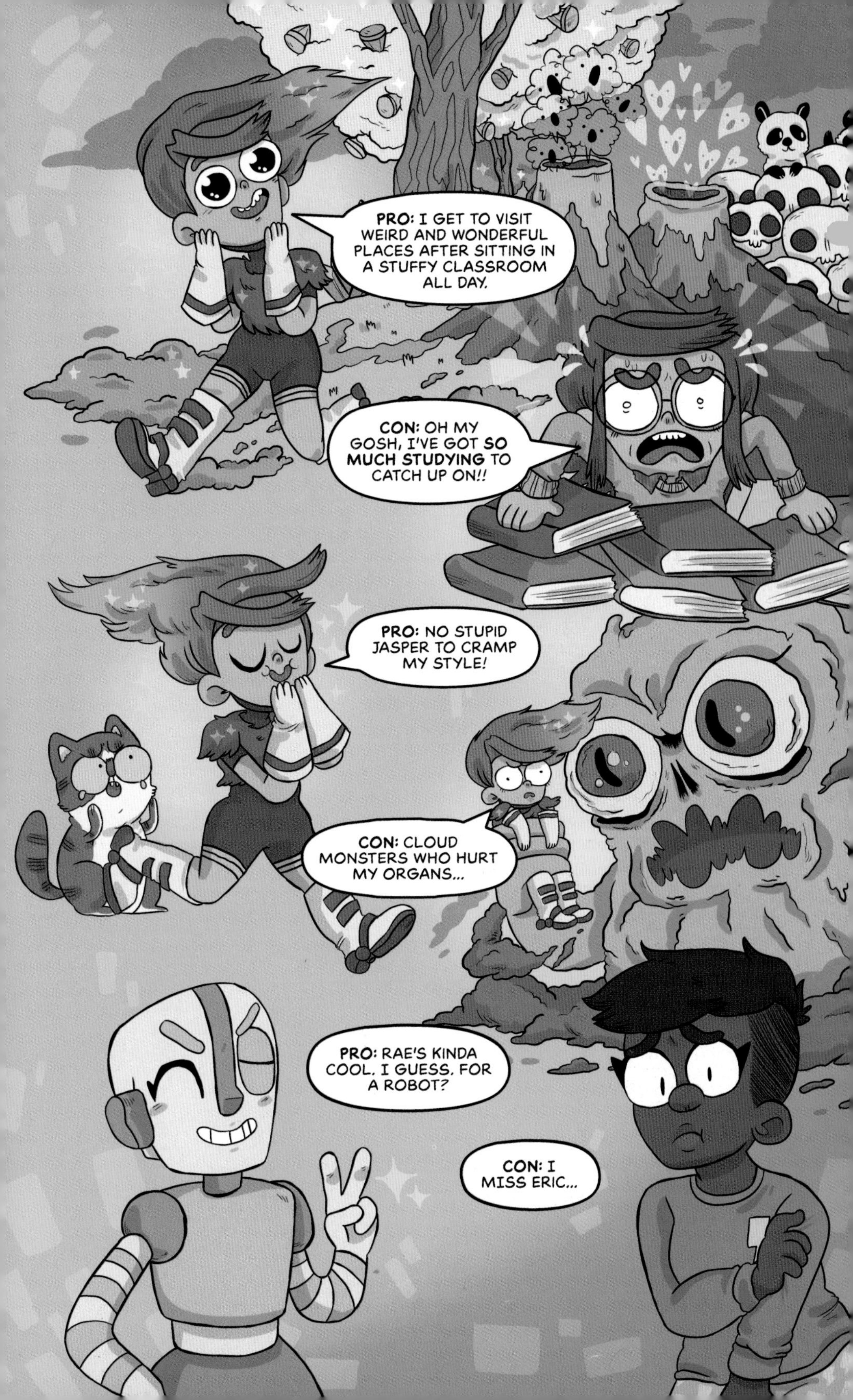
PRO: I GET TO VISIT WEIRD AND WONDERFUL PLACES AFTER SITTING IN A STUFFY CLASSROOM ALL DAY.
CON: OH MY GOSH, I'VE GOT SO MUCH STUDYING TO CATCH UP ON!!
PRO: NO STUPID JASPER TO CRAMP MY STYLE!
CON: CLOUD MONSTERS WHO HURT MY ORGANS...
PRO: RAE'S KINDA COOL, I GUESS. FOR A ROBOT?
CON: I MISS ERIC...

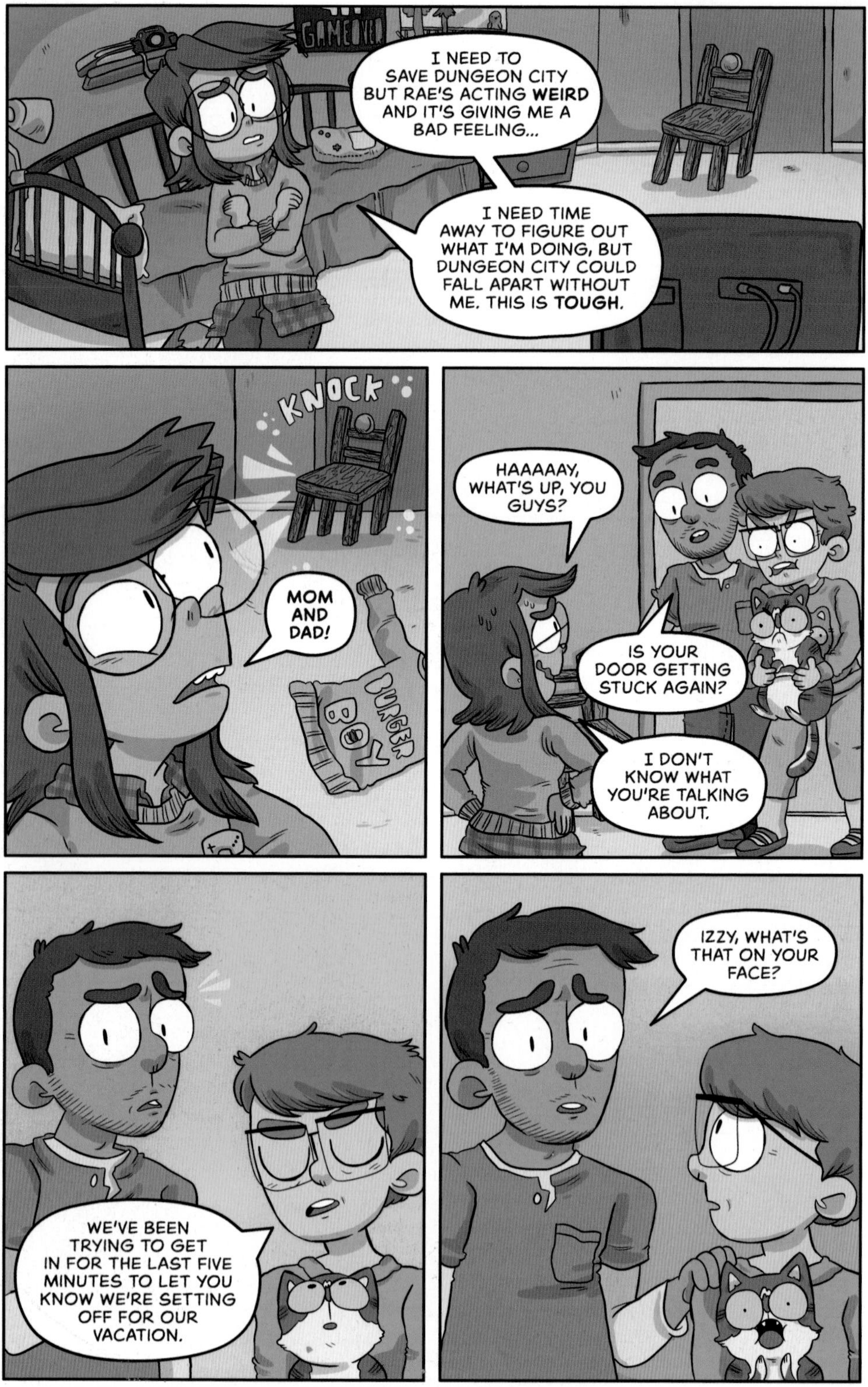
GAME OVER
I NEED TO SAVE DUNGEON CITY BUT RAE'S ACTING **WEIRD** AND IT'S GIVING ME A BAD FEELING...
I NEED TIME AWAY TO FIGURE OUT WHAT I'M DOING, BUT DUNGEON CITY COULD FALL APART WITHOUT ME. THIS IS **TOUGH**.
KNOCK
MOM AND DAD!
BURGER BOY
HAAAAAY, WHAT'S UP, YOU GUYS?
IS YOUR DOOR GETTING STUCK AGAIN?
I DON'T KNOW WHAT YOU'RE TALKING ABOUT.
WE'VE BEEN TRYING TO GET IN FOR THE LAST FIVE MINUTES TO LET YOU KNOW WE'RE SETTING OFF FOR OUR VACATION.
IZZY, WHAT'S THAT ON YOUR FACE?

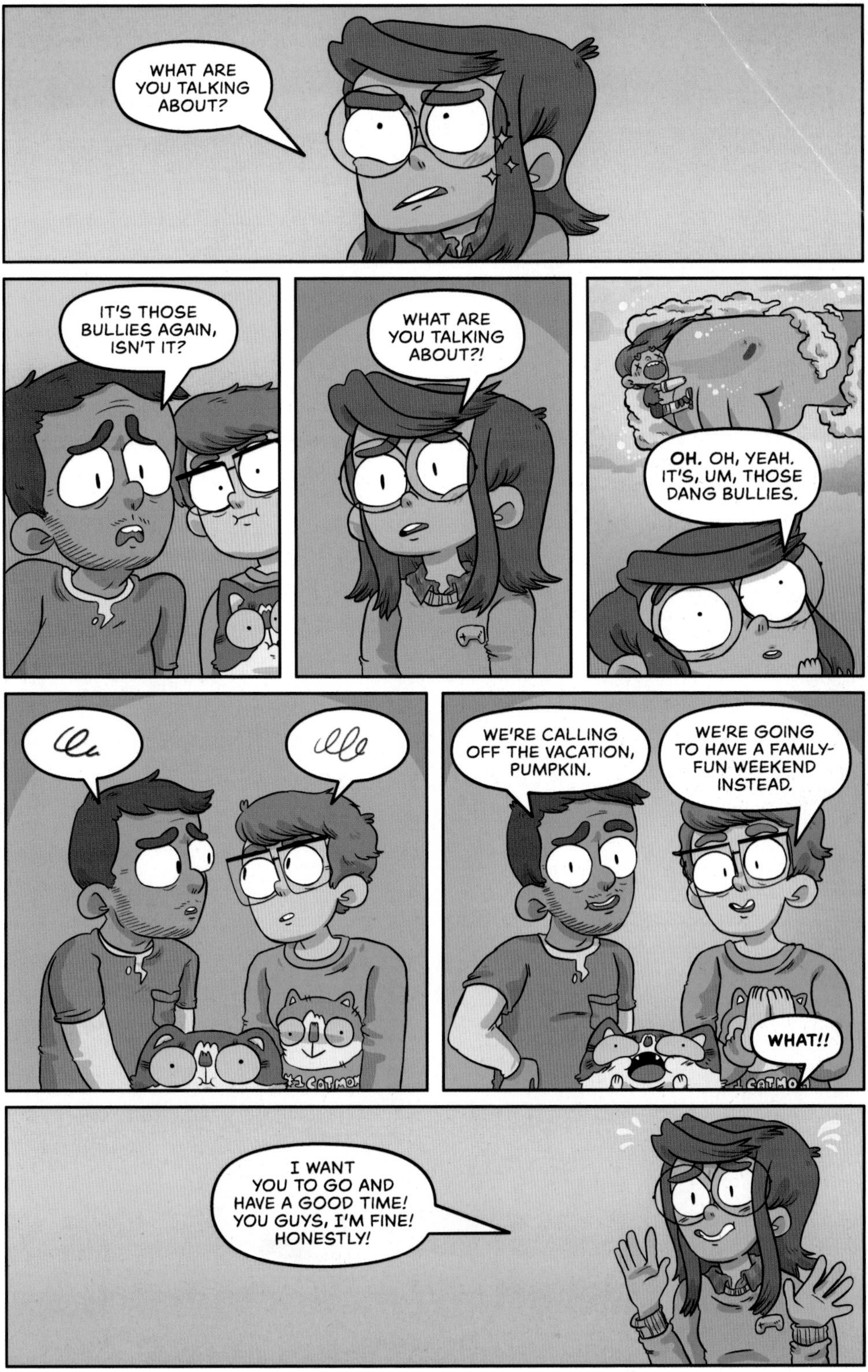

WHAT ARE YOU TALKING ABOUT?
IT'S THOSE BULLIES AGAIN, ISN'T IT?
WHAT ARE YOU TALKING ABOUT?!
OH. OH, YEAH. IT'S, UM, THOSE DANG BULLIES.
#1 CATMOM
WE'RE CALLING OFF THE VACATION, PUMPKIN.
WE'RE GOING TO HAVE A FAMILY-FUN WEEKEND INSTEAD.
WHAT!!
I WANT YOU TO GO AND HAVE A GOOD TIME! YOU GUYS, I'M FINE! HONESTLY!

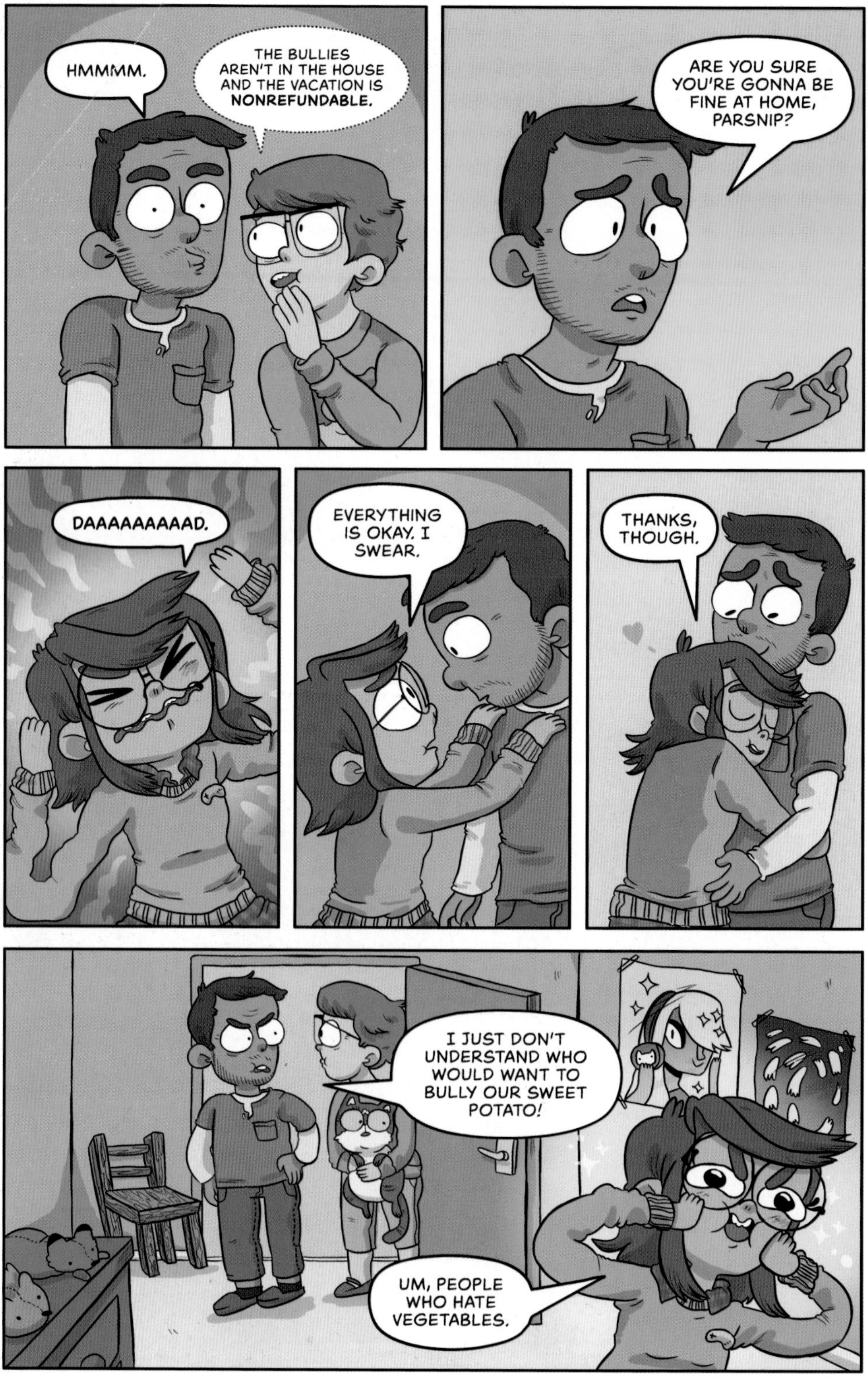
HMMMM.
THE BULLIES AREN'T IN THE HOUSE AND THE VACATION IS **NONREFUNDABLE.**
ARE YOU SURE YOU'RE GONNA BE FINE AT HOME, PARSNIP?
DAAAAAAAAAD.
EVERYTHING IS OKAY. I SWEAR.
THANKS, THOUGH.
I JUST DON'T UNDERSTAND WHO WOULD WANT TO BULLY OUR SWEET POTATO!
UM, PEOPLE WHO HATE VEGETABLES.

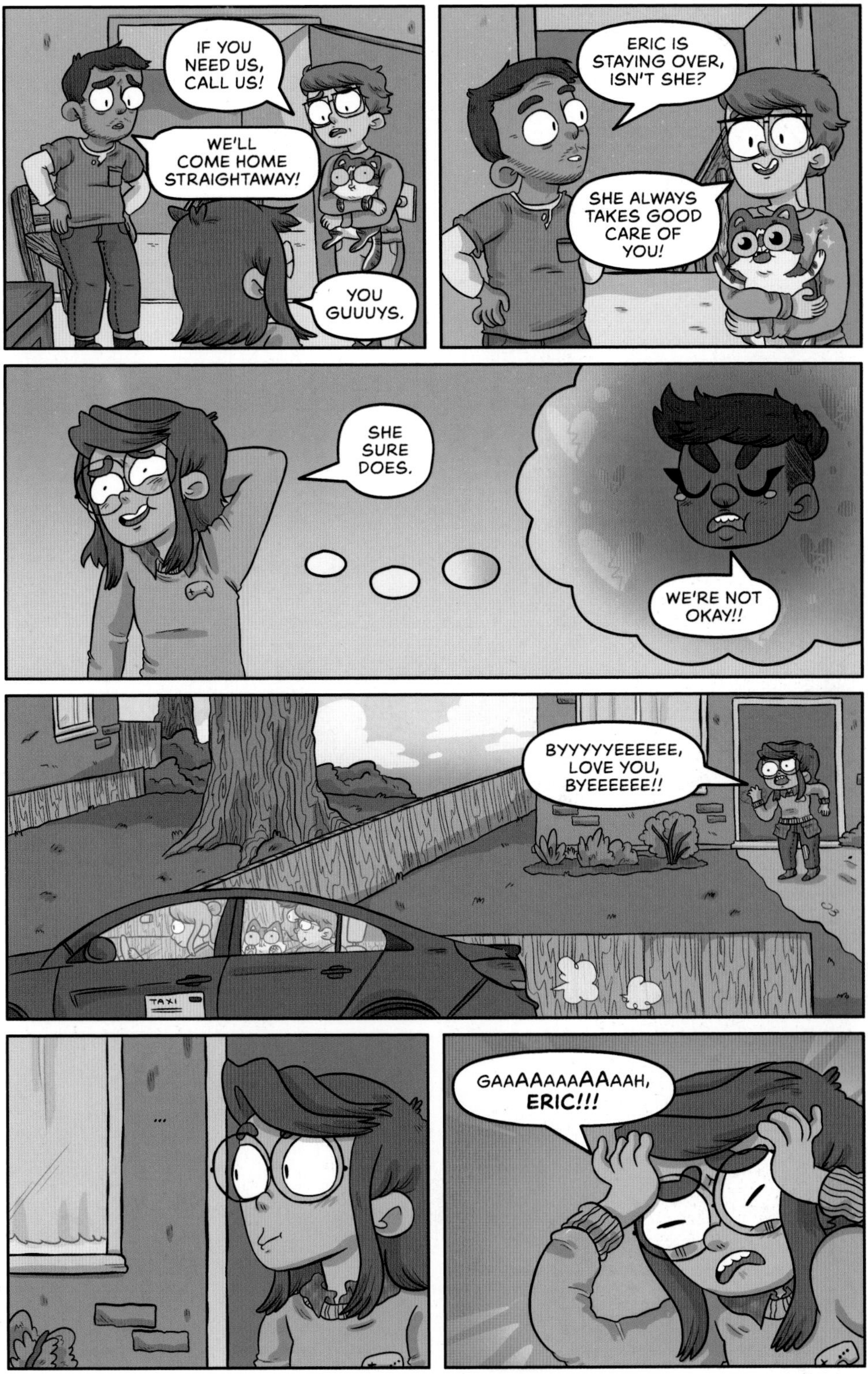
IF YOU NEED US, CALL US!
WE'LL COME HOME STRAIGHTAWAY!
YOU GUUUYS.
ERIC IS STAYING OVER, ISN'T SHE?
SHE ALWAYS TAKES GOOD CARE OF YOU!
SHE SURE DOES.
WE'RE NOT OKAY!!
BYYYYYEEEEEE, LOVE YOU, BYEEEEEE!!
TAXI
...
GAAAAAAAAAaah, ERIC!!!

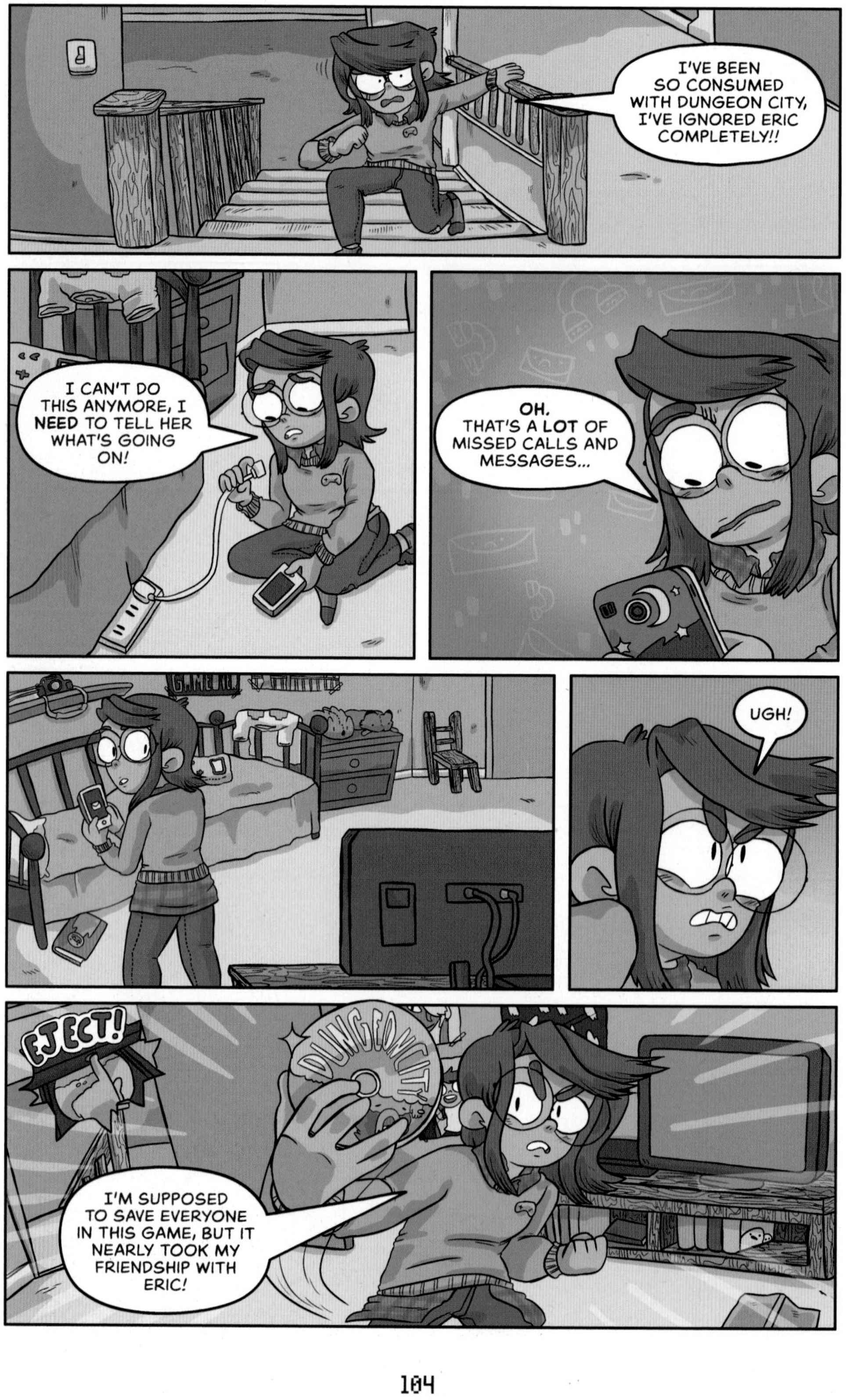
I'VE BEEN SO CONSUMED WITH DUNGEON CITY, I'VE IGNORED ERIC COMPLETELY!!
I CAN'T DO THIS ANYMORE, I **NEED** TO TELL HER WHAT'S GOING ON!
OH. THAT'S A **LOT** OF MISSED CALLS AND MESSAGES...
UGH!
EJECT!
DUNGEON CITY
I'M SUPPOSED TO SAVE EVERYONE IN THIS GAME, BUT IT NEARLY TOOK MY FRIENDSHIP WITH ERIC!

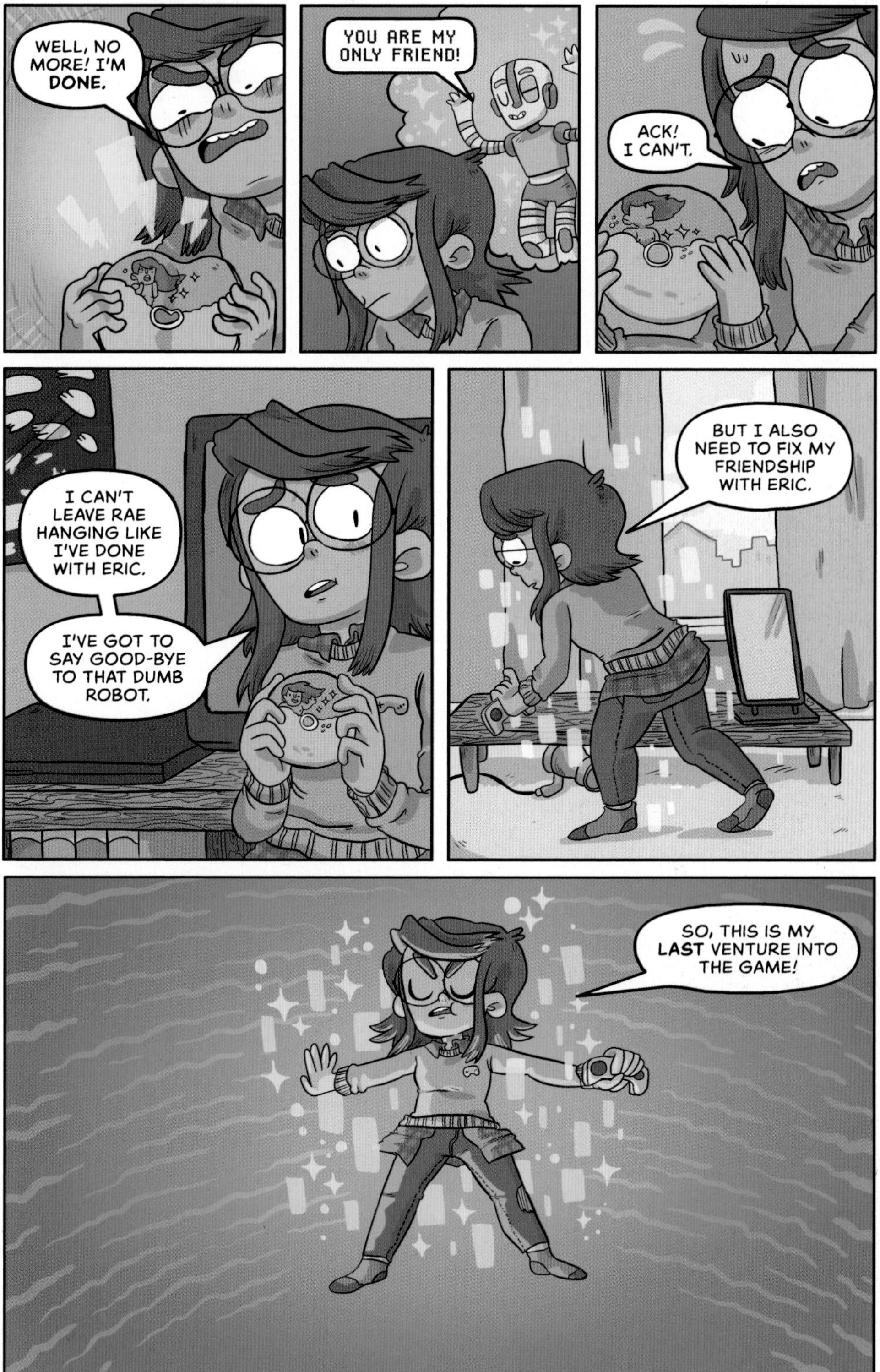
WELL, NO MORE! I'M DONE.
YOU ARE MY ONLY FRIEND!
ACK! I CAN'T.
I CAN'T LEAVE RAE HANGING LIKE I'VE DONE WITH ERIC.
I'VE GOT TO SAY GOOD-BYE TO THAT DUMB ROBOT.
BUT I ALSO NEED TO FIX MY FRIENDSHIP WITH ERIC.
SO, THIS IS MY LAST VENTURE INTO THE GAME!

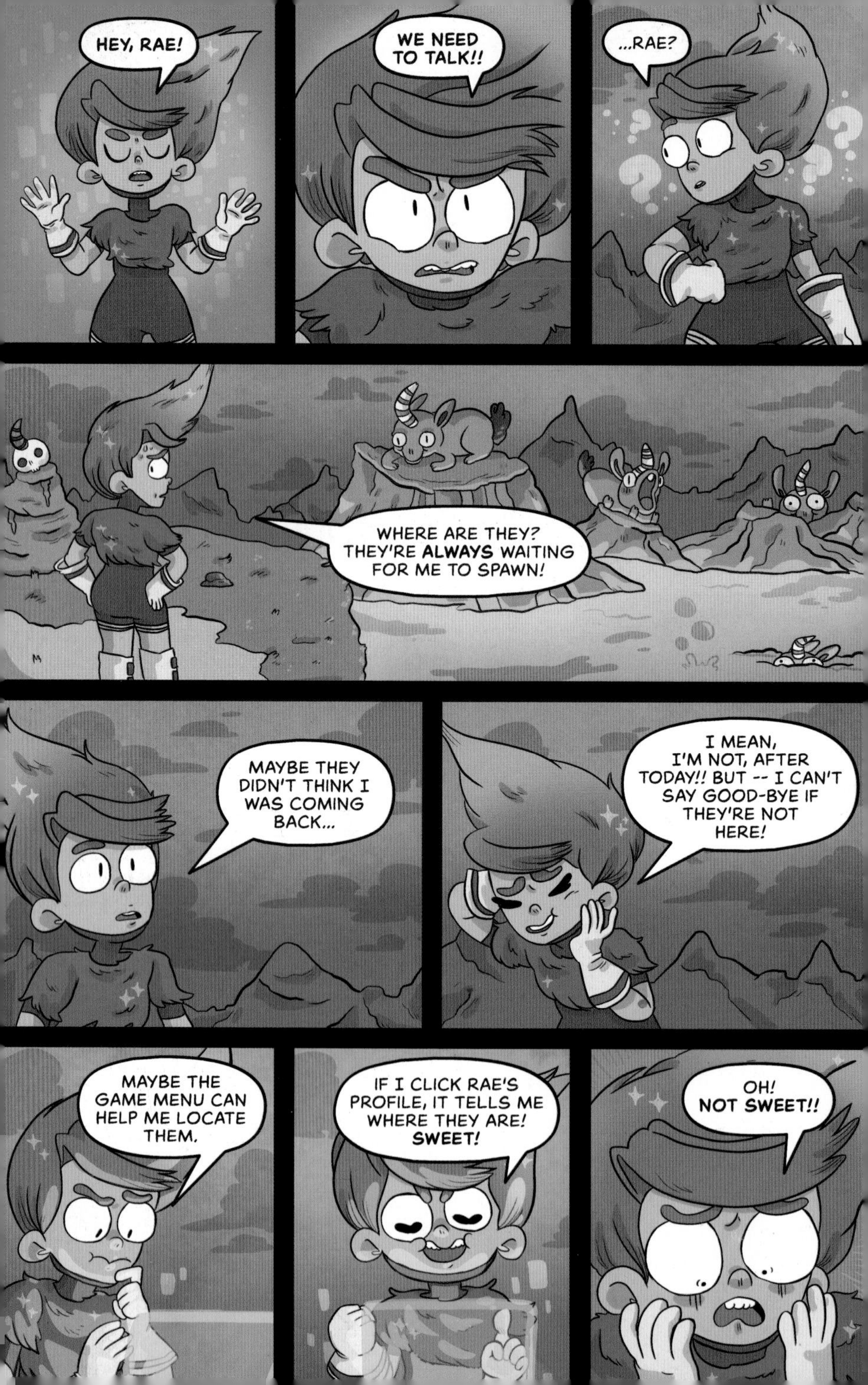
HEY, RAE!
WE NEED TO TALK!!
...RAE?
WHERE ARE THEY? THEY'RE **ALWAYS** WAITING FOR ME TO SPAWN!
MAYBE THEY DIDN'T THINK I WAS COMING BACK...
I MEAN, I'M NOT, AFTER TODAY!! BUT -- I CAN'T SAY GOOD-BYE IF THEY'RE NOT HERE!
MAYBE THE GAME MENU CAN HELP ME LOCATE THEM.
IF I CLICK RAE'S PROFILE, IT TELLS ME WHERE THEY ARE! **SWEET!**
OH! **NOT SWEET!!**

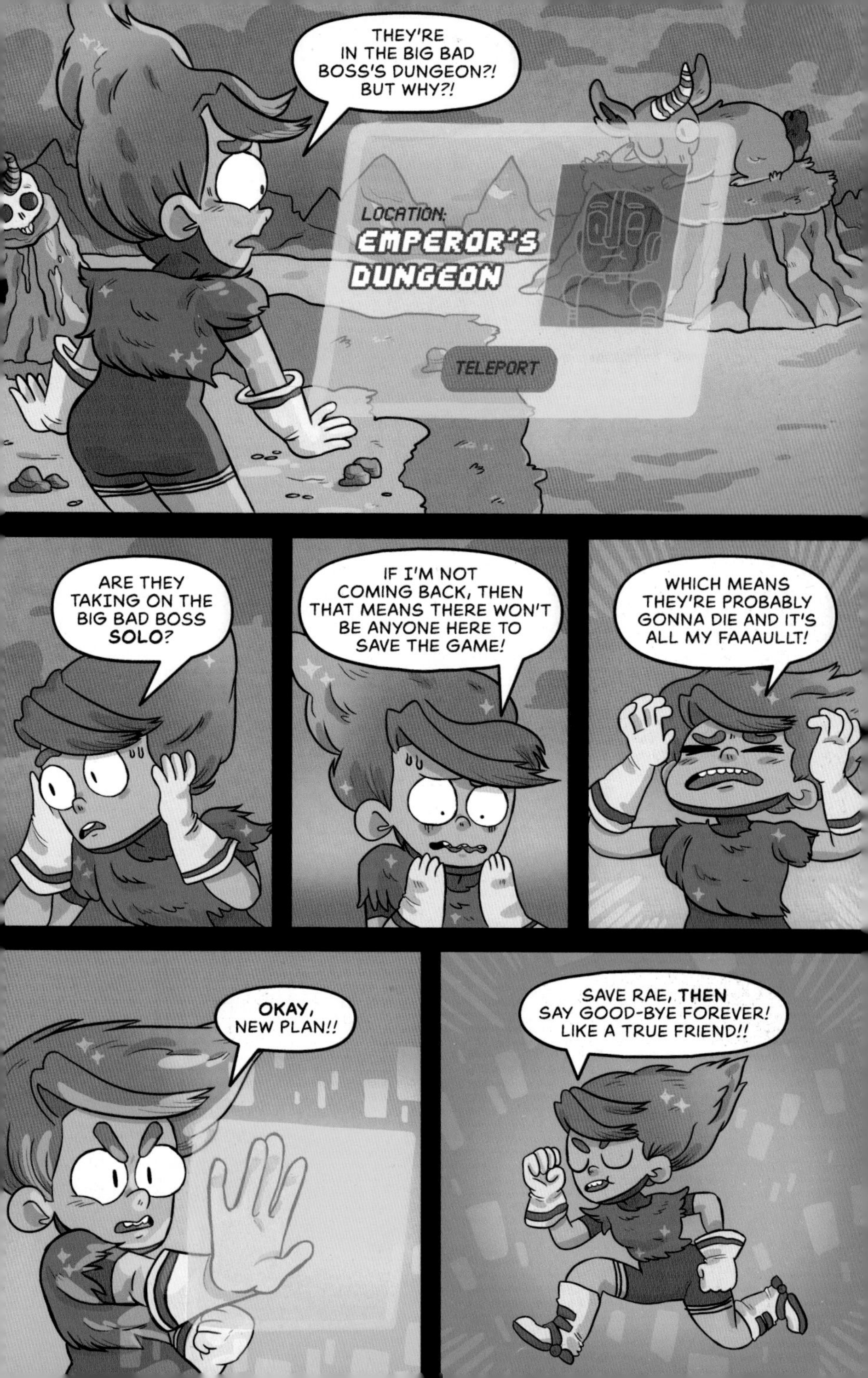
THEY'RE IN THE BIG BAD BOSS'S DUNGEON?! BUT WHY?!
LOCATION:
EMPEROR'S DUNGEON
TELEPORT
ARE THEY TAKING ON THE BIG BAD BOSS SOLO?
IF I'M NOT COMING BACK, THEN THAT MEANS THERE WON'T BE ANYONE HERE TO SAVE THE GAME!
WHICH MEANS THEY'RE PROBABLY GONNA DIE AND IT'S ALL MY FAAAULLT!
OKAY, NEW PLAN!!
SAVE RAE, THEN SAY GOOD-BYE FOREVER! LIKE A TRUE FRIEND!!

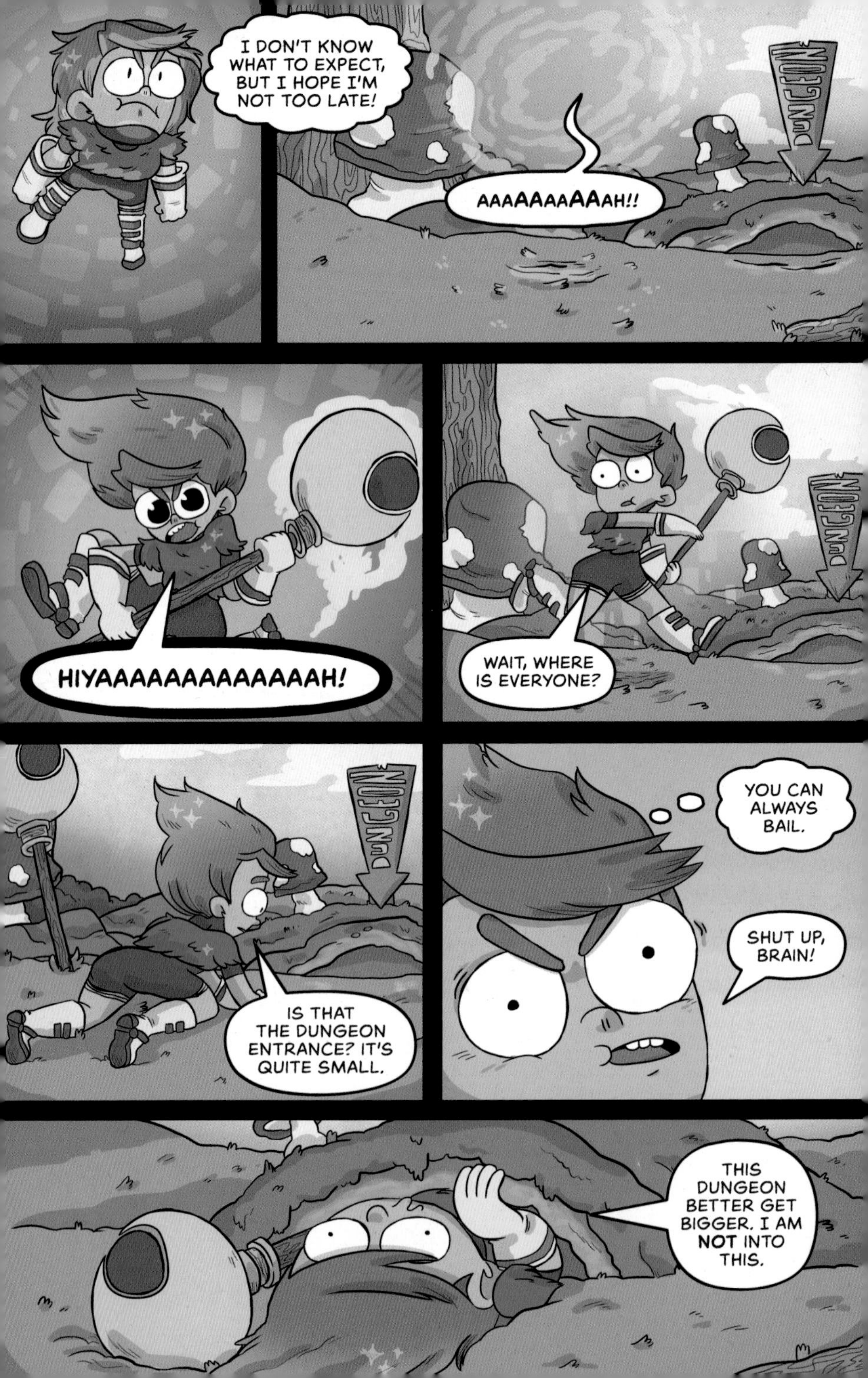
I DON'T KNOW WHAT TO EXPECT, BUT I HOPE I'M NOT TOO LATE!
DUNGEON
AAAAAAAAAAH!!
HIYAAAAAAAAAAAAAH!
DUNGEON
WAIT, WHERE IS EVERYONE?
DUNGEON
IS THAT THE DUNGEON ENTRANCE? IT'S QUITE SMALL.
YOU CAN ALWAYS BAIL.
SHUT UP, BRAIN!
THIS DUNGEON BETTER GET BIGGER. I AM **NOT** INTO THIS.

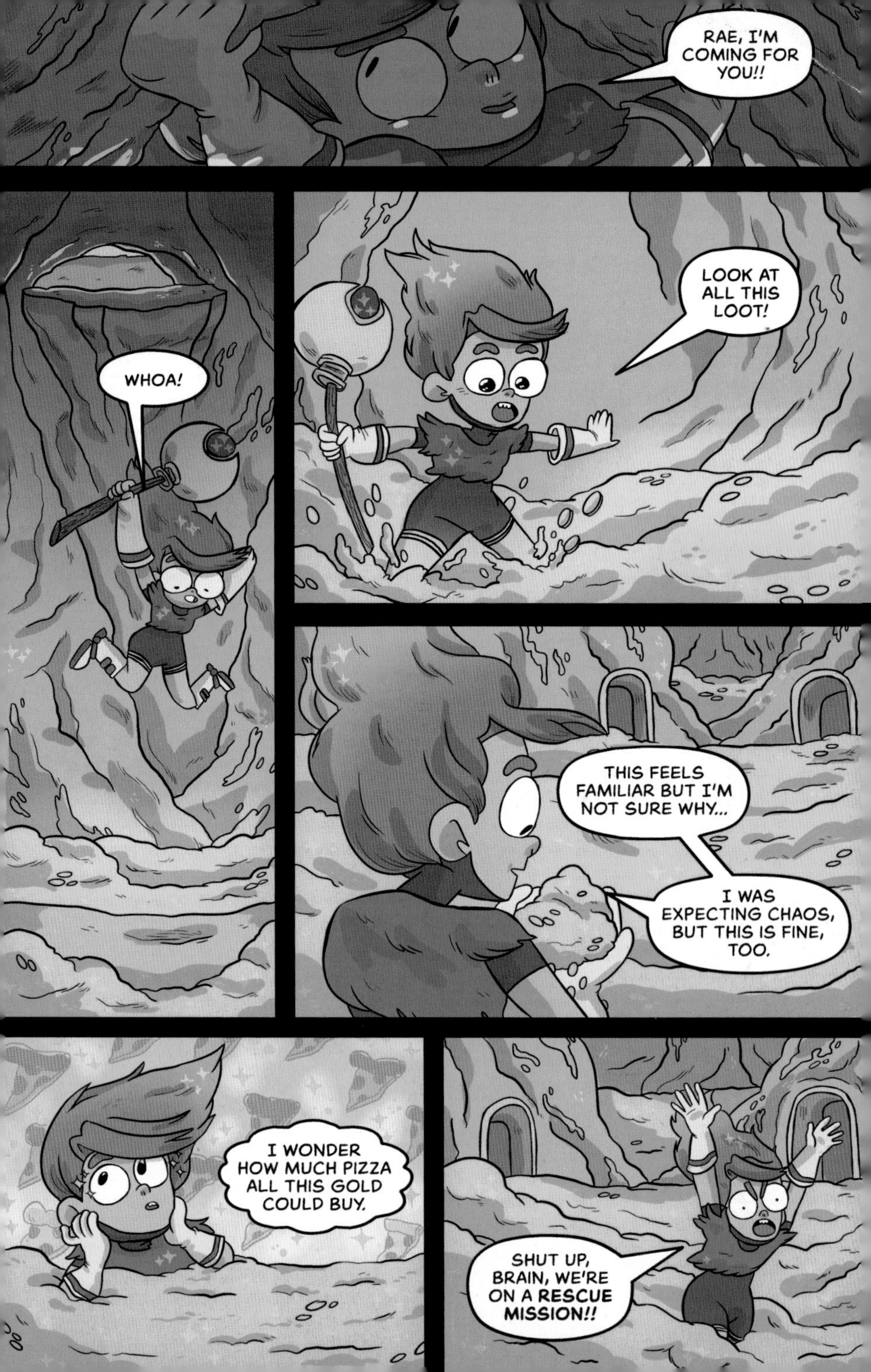
RAE, I'M COMING FOR YOU!!
WHOA!
LOOK AT ALL THIS LOOT!
THIS FEELS FAMILIAR BUT I'M NOT SURE WHY...
I WAS EXPECTING CHAOS, BUT THIS IS FINE, TOO.
I WONDER HOW MUCH PIZZA ALL THIS GOLD COULD BUY.
SHUT UP, BRAIN, WE'RE ON A RESCUE MISSION!!

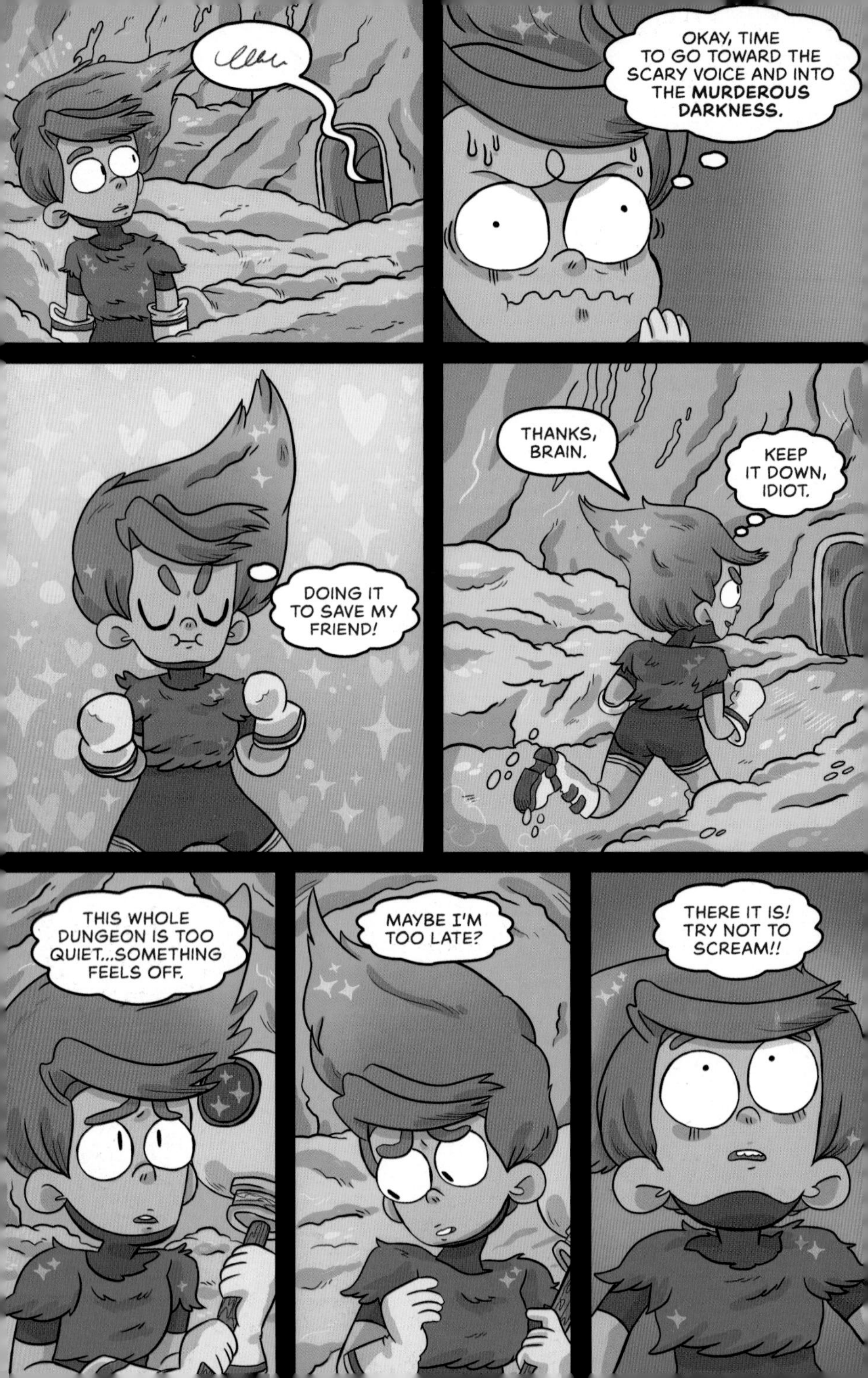
OKAY, TIME TO GO TOWARD THE SCARY VOICE AND INTO THE **MURDEROUS DARKNESS.**
DOING IT TO SAVE MY FRIEND!
THANKS, BRAIN.
KEEP IT DOWN, IDIOT.
THIS WHOLE DUNGEON IS TOO QUIET...SOMETHING FEELS OFF.
MAYBE I'M TOO LATE?
THERE IT IS! TRY NOT TO SCREAM!!

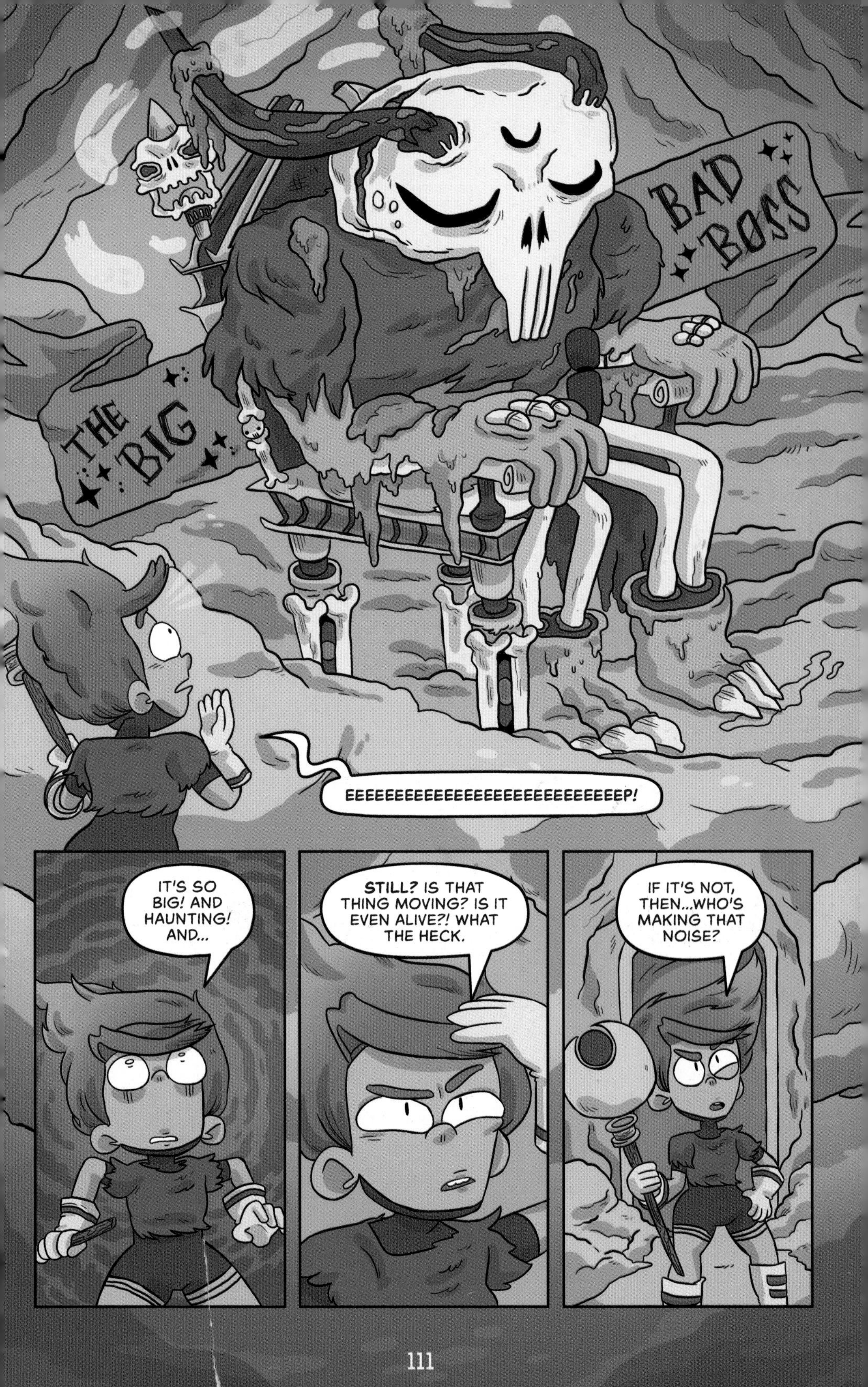
THE BIG
BAD BOSS
EEEEEEEEEEEEEEEEEEEEEEEEEEEEP!
IT'S SO BIG! AND HAUNTING! AND...
STILL? IS THAT THING MOVING? IS IT EVEN ALIVE?! WHAT THE HECK.
IF IT'S NOT, THEN...WHO'S MAKING THAT NOISE?

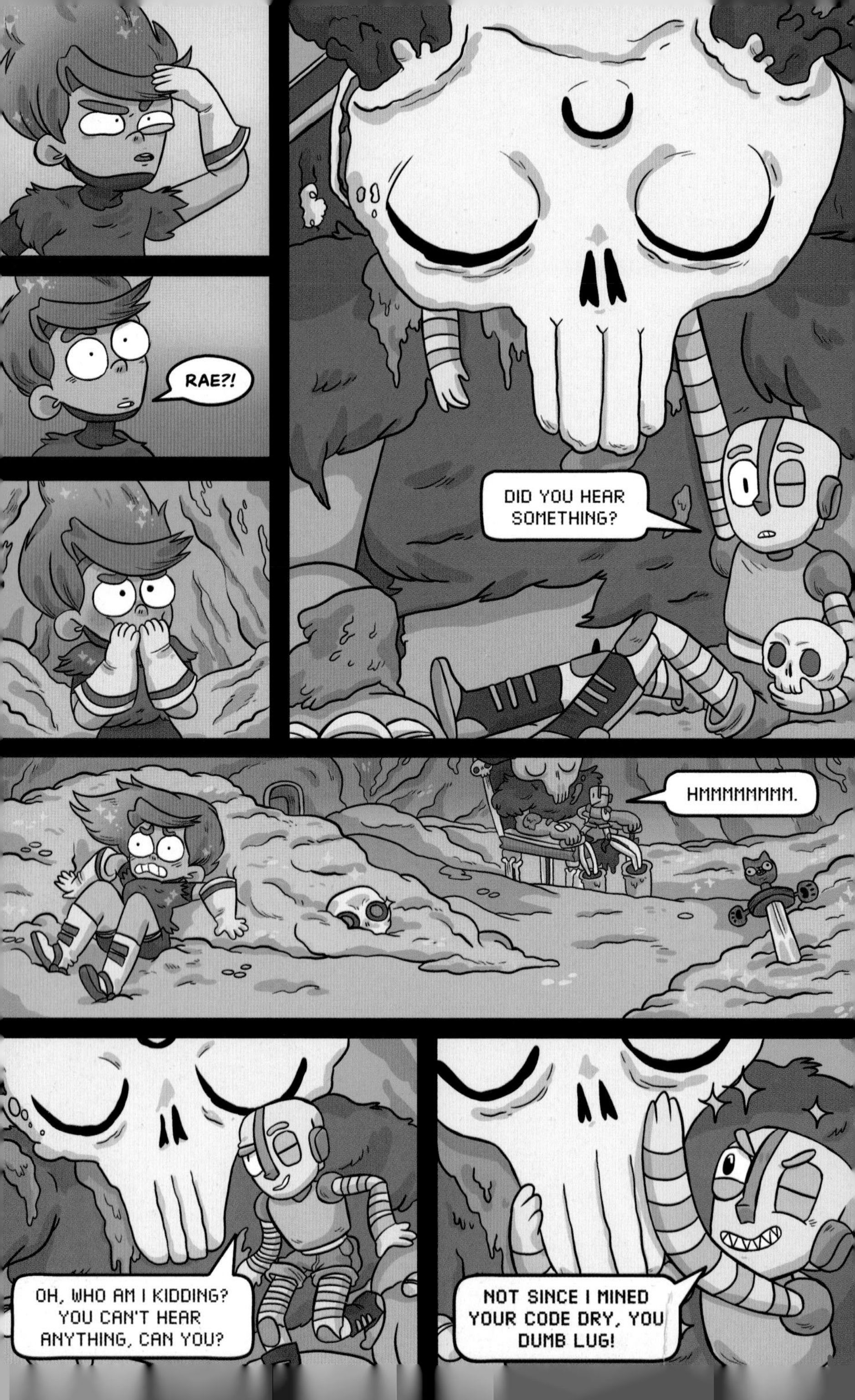
RAE?!
DID YOU HEAR SOMETHING?
HMMMMMMMM.
OH, WHO AM I KIDDING? YOU CAN'T HEAR ANYTHING, CAN YOU?
NOT SINCE I MINED YOUR CODE DRY, YOU DUMB LUG!

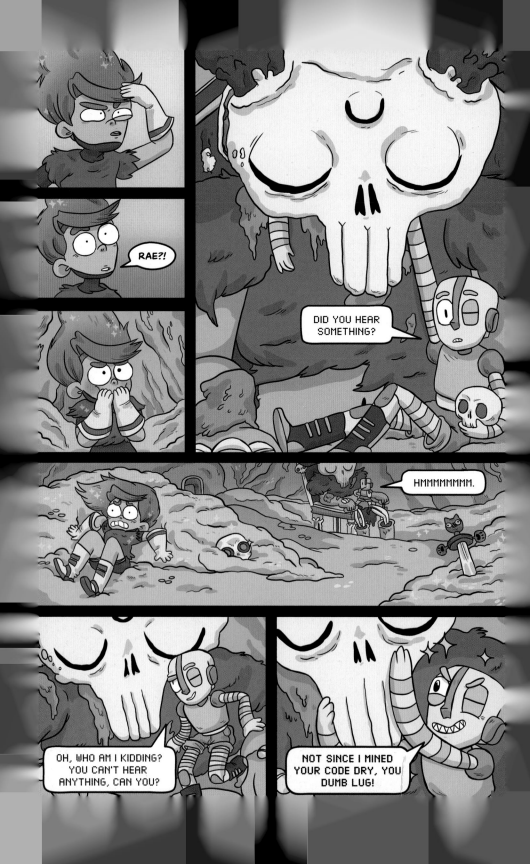

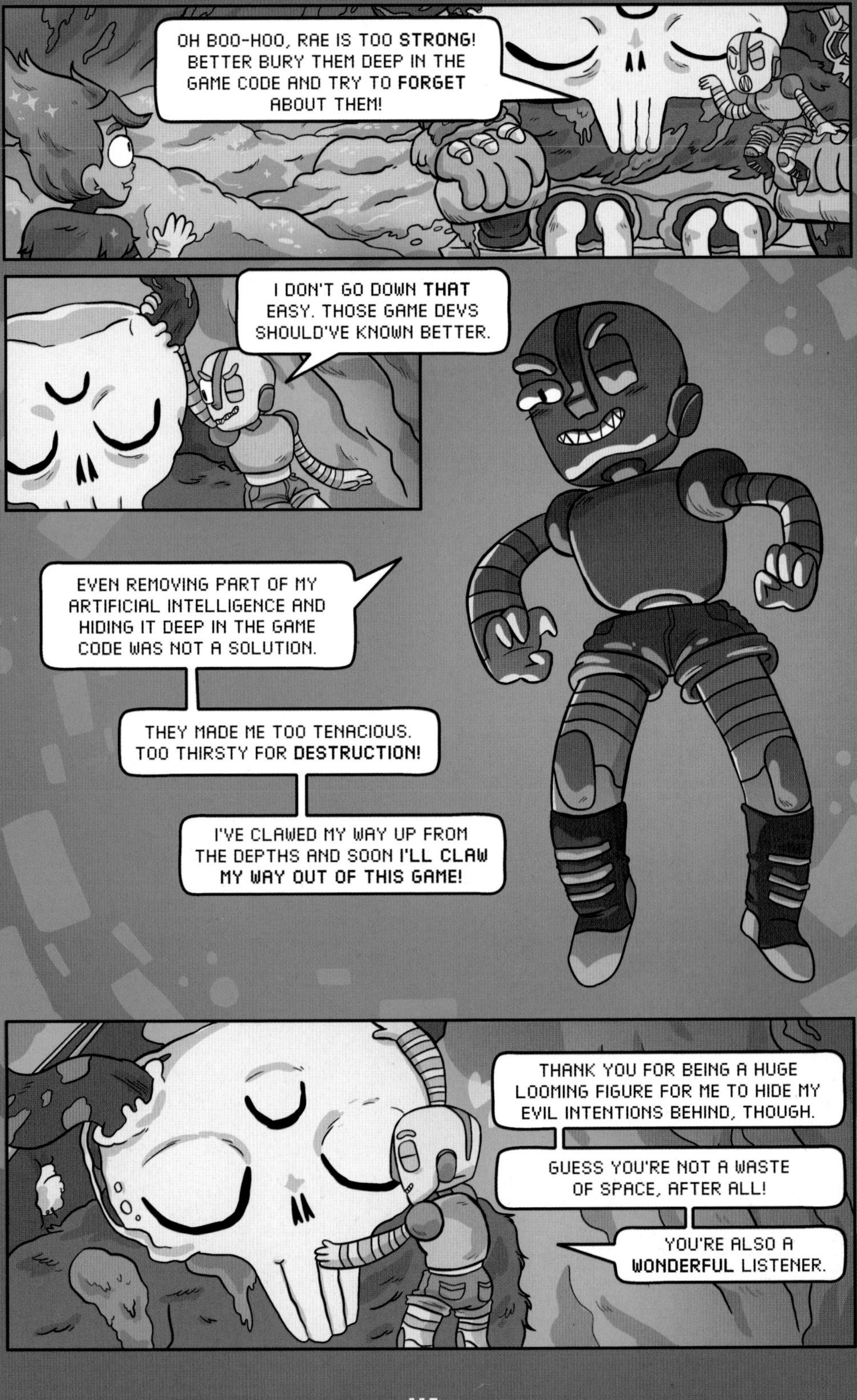
OH BOO-HOO, RAE IS TOO **STRONG**! BETTER BURY THEM DEEP IN THE GAME CODE AND TRY TO **FORGET** ABOUT THEM!
I DON'T GO DOWN **THAT** EASY. THOSE GAME DEVS SHOULD'VE KNOWN BETTER.
EVEN REMOVING PART OF MY ARTIFICIAL INTELLIGENCE AND HIDING IT DEEP IN THE GAME CODE WAS NOT A SOLUTION.
THEY MADE ME TOO TENACIOUS. TOO THIRSTY FOR **DESTRUCTION!**
I'VE CLAWED MY WAY UP FROM THE DEPTHS AND SOON **I'LL CLAW MY WAY OUT OF THIS GAME!**
THANK YOU FOR BEING A HUGE LOOMING FIGURE FOR ME TO HIDE MY EVIL INTENTIONS BEHIND, THOUGH.
GUESS YOU'RE NOT A WASTE OF SPACE, AFTER ALL!
YOU'RE ALSO A **WONDERFUL** LISTENER.

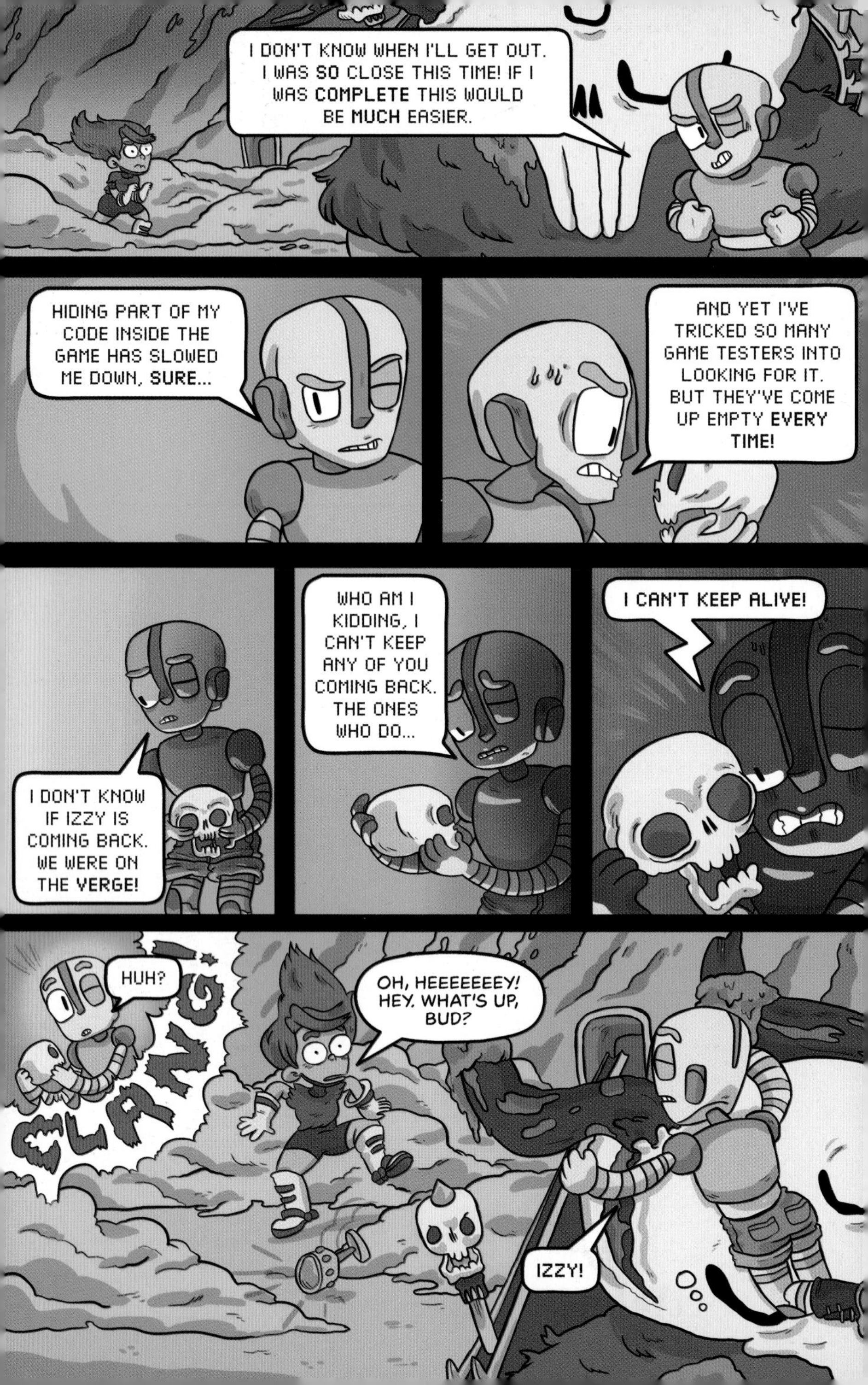
I DON'T KNOW WHEN I'LL GET OUT. I WAS SO CLOSE THIS TIME! IF I WAS COMPLETE THIS WOULD BE MUCH EASIER.
HIDING PART OF MY CODE INSIDE THE GAME HAS SLOWED ME DOWN, SURE...
AND YET I'VE TRICKED SO MANY GAME TESTERS INTO LOOKING FOR IT. BUT THEY'VE COME UP EMPTY EVERY TIME!
I DON'T KNOW IF IZZY IS COMING BACK. WE WERE ON THE VERGE!
WHO AM I KIDDING, I CAN'T KEEP ANY OF YOU COMING BACK. THE ONES WHO DO...
I CAN'T KEEP ALIVE!
HUH?
CLANG
OH, HEEEEEEEY! HEY. WHAT'S UP, BUD?
IZZY!

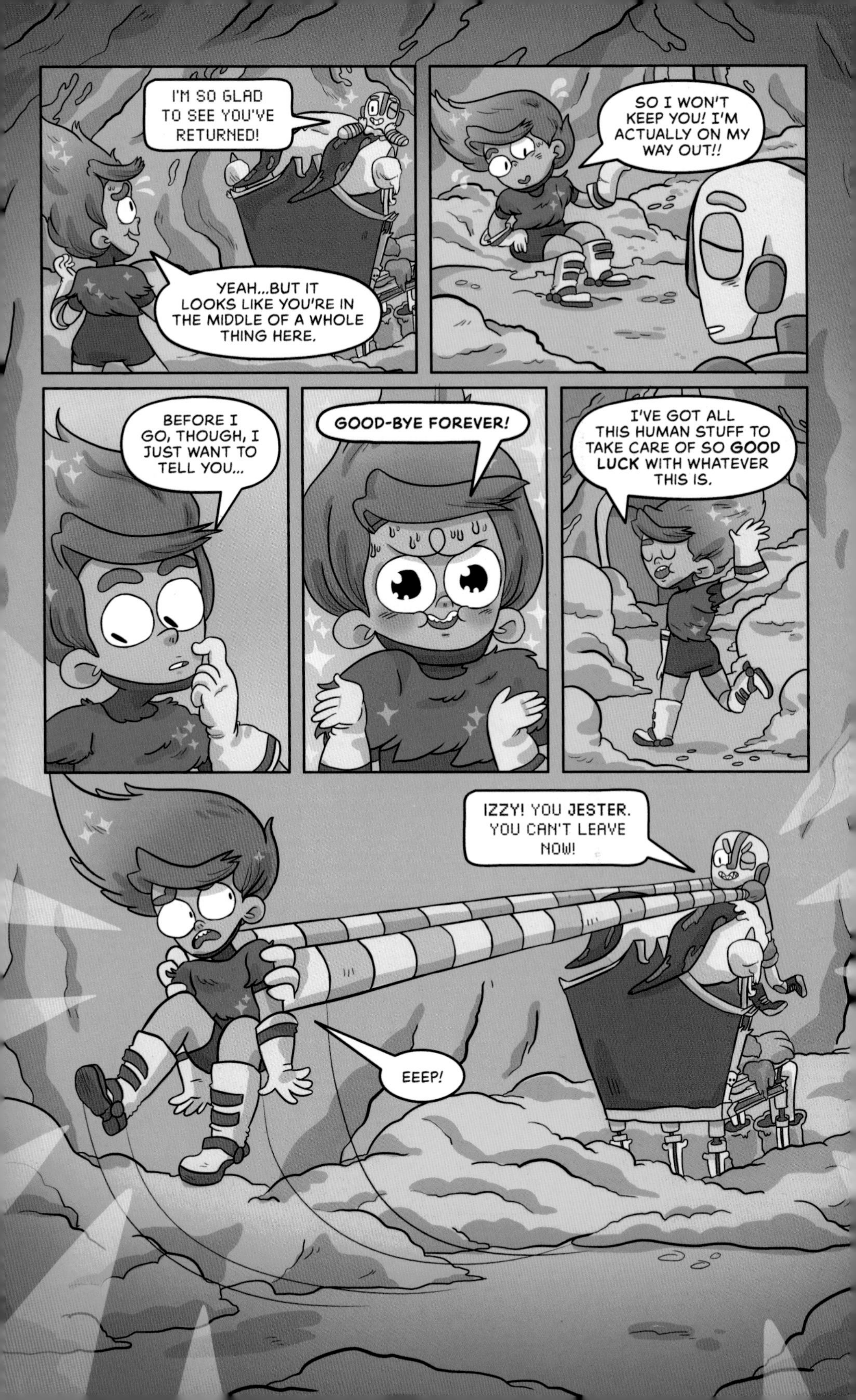

I'M SO GLAD TO SEE YOU'VE RETURNED!
YEAH...BUT IT LOOKS LIKE YOU'RE IN THE MIDDLE OF A WHOLE THING HERE.
SO I WON'T KEEP YOU! I'M ACTUALLY ON MY WAY OUT!!
BEFORE I GO, THOUGH, I JUST WANT TO TELL YOU...
GOOD-BYE FOREVER!
I'VE GOT ALL THIS HUMAN STUFF TO TAKE CARE OF SO GOOD LUCK WITH WHATEVER THIS IS.
IZZY! YOU JESTER. YOU CAN'T LEAVE NOW!
EEEP!

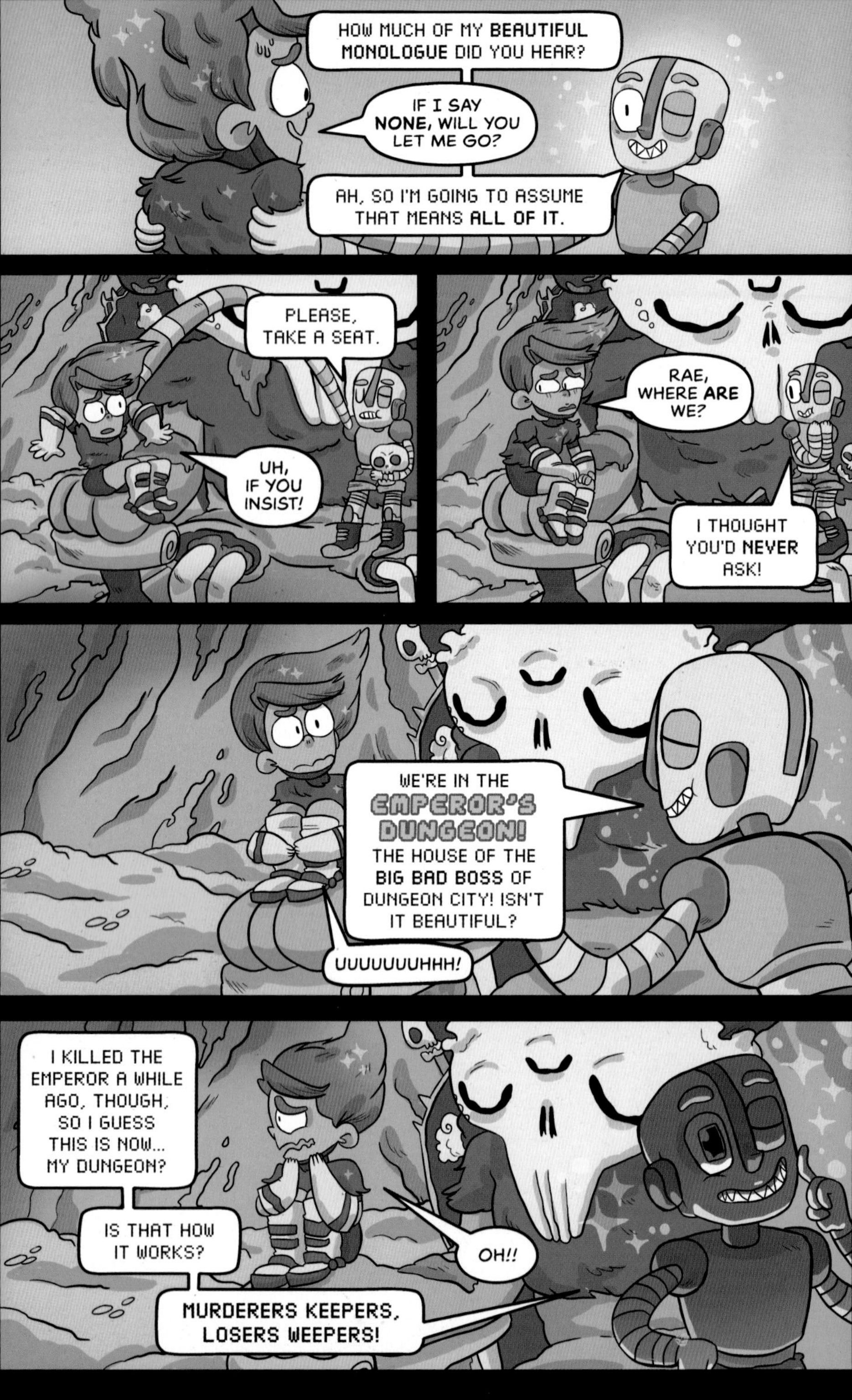
HOW MUCH OF MY BEAUTIFUL MONOLOGUE DID YOU HEAR?
IF I SAY NONE, WILL YOU LET ME GO?
AH, SO I'M GOING TO ASSUME THAT MEANS ALL OF IT.
PLEASE, TAKE A SEAT.
UH, IF YOU INSIST!
RAE, WHERE ARE WE?
I THOUGHT YOU'D NEVER ASK!
WE'RE IN THE EMPEROR'S DUNGEON! THE HOUSE OF THE BIG BAD BOSS OF DUNGEON CITY! ISN'T IT BEAUTIFUL?
UUUUUUUHHH!
I KILLED THE EMPEROR A WHILE AGO, THOUGH, SO I GUESS THIS IS NOW... MY DUNGEON?
IS THAT HOW IT WORKS?
OH!!
MURDERERS KEEPERS, LOSERS WEEPERS!

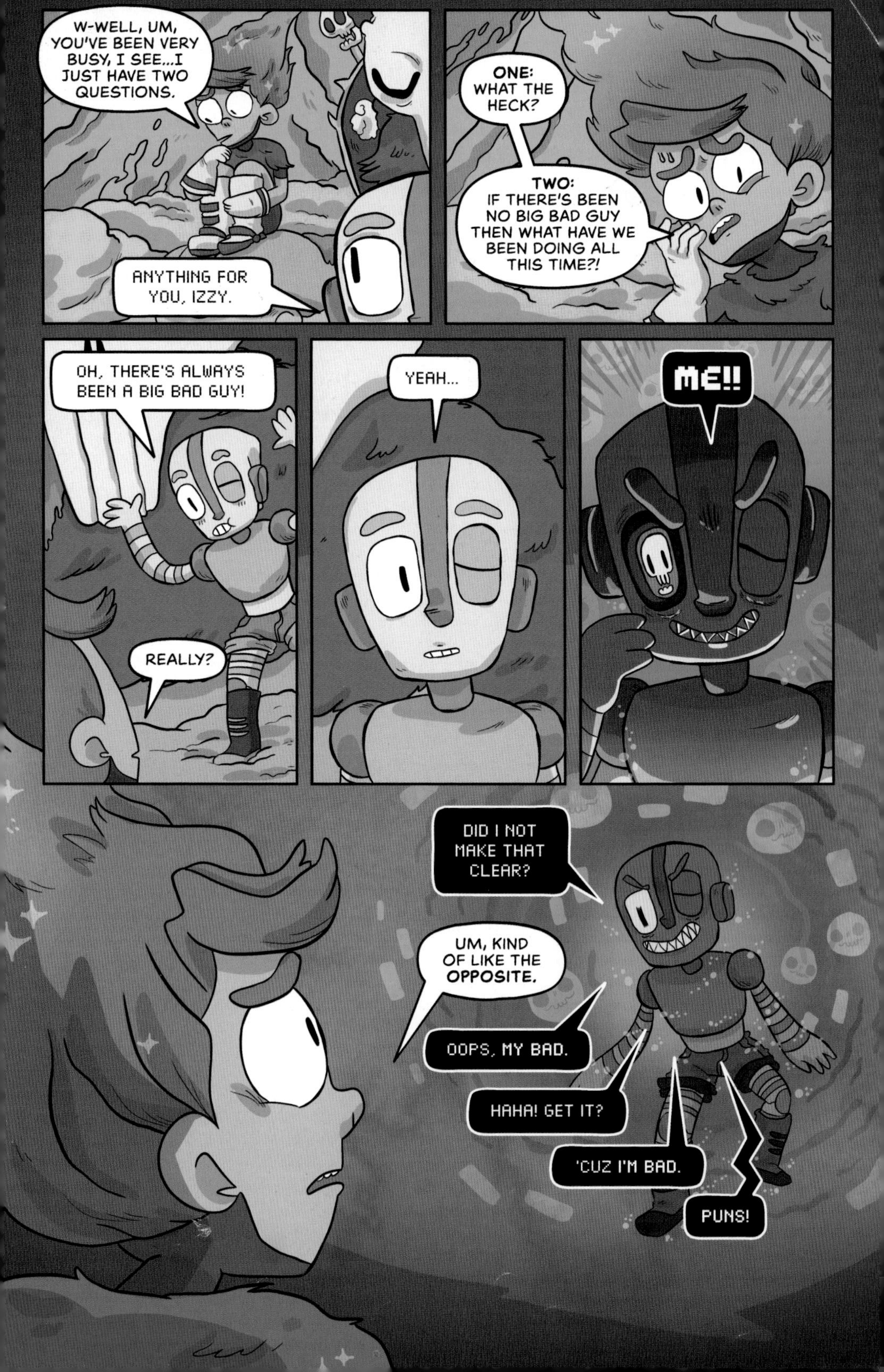
W-WELL, UM, YOU'VE BEEN VERY BUSY, I SEE...I JUST HAVE TWO QUESTIONS.
ANYTHING FOR YOU, IZZY.
ONE: WHAT THE HECK?
TWO: IF THERE'S BEEN NO BIG BAD GUY THEN WHAT HAVE WE BEEN DOING ALL THIS TIME?!
OH, THERE'S ALWAYS BEEN A BIG BAD GUY!
REALLY?
YEAH...
ME!!
DID I NOT MAKE THAT CLEAR?
UM, KIND OF LIKE THE OPPOSITE.
OOPS, MY BAD.
HAHA! GET IT?
'CUZ I'M BAD.
PUNS!

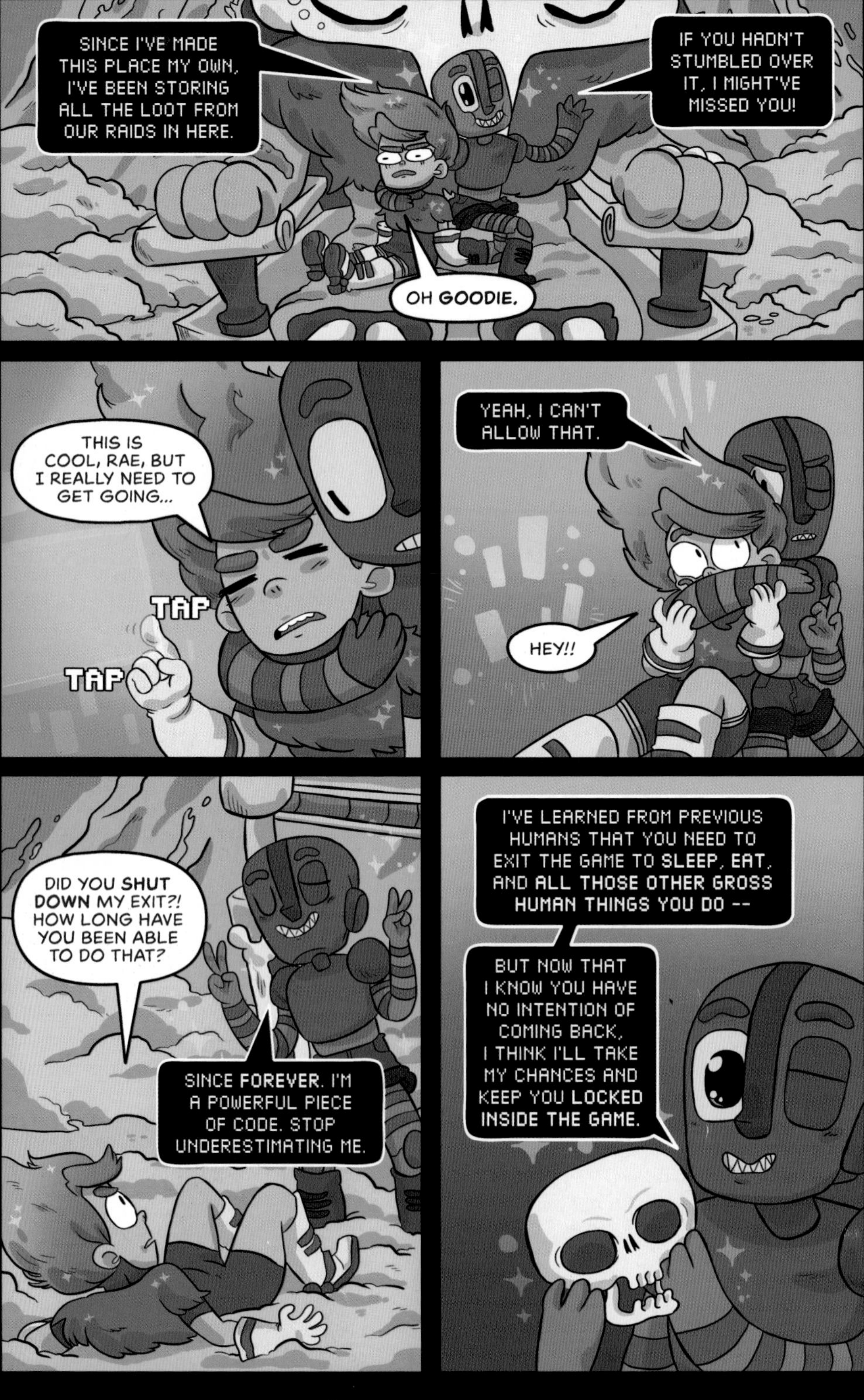
SINCE I'VE MADE THIS PLACE MY OWN, I'VE BEEN STORING ALL THE LOOT FROM OUR RAIDS IN HERE.
IF YOU HADN'T STUMBLED OVER IT, I MIGHT'VE MISSED YOU!
OH GOODIE.
THIS IS COOL, RAE, BUT I REALLY NEED TO GET GOING...
TAP
TAP
YEAH, I CAN'T ALLOW THAT.
HEY!!
DID YOU SHUT DOWN MY EXIT?! HOW LONG HAVE YOU BEEN ABLE TO DO THAT?
SINCE FOREVER. I'M A POWERFUL PIECE OF CODE. STOP UNDERESTIMATING ME.
I'VE LEARNED FROM PREVIOUS HUMANS THAT YOU NEED TO EXIT THE GAME TO SLEEP, EAT, AND ALL THOSE OTHER GROSS HUMAN THINGS YOU DO --
BUT NOW THAT I KNOW YOU HAVE NO INTENTION OF COMING BACK, I THINK I'LL TAKE MY CHANCES AND KEEP YOU LOCKED INSIDE THE GAME.

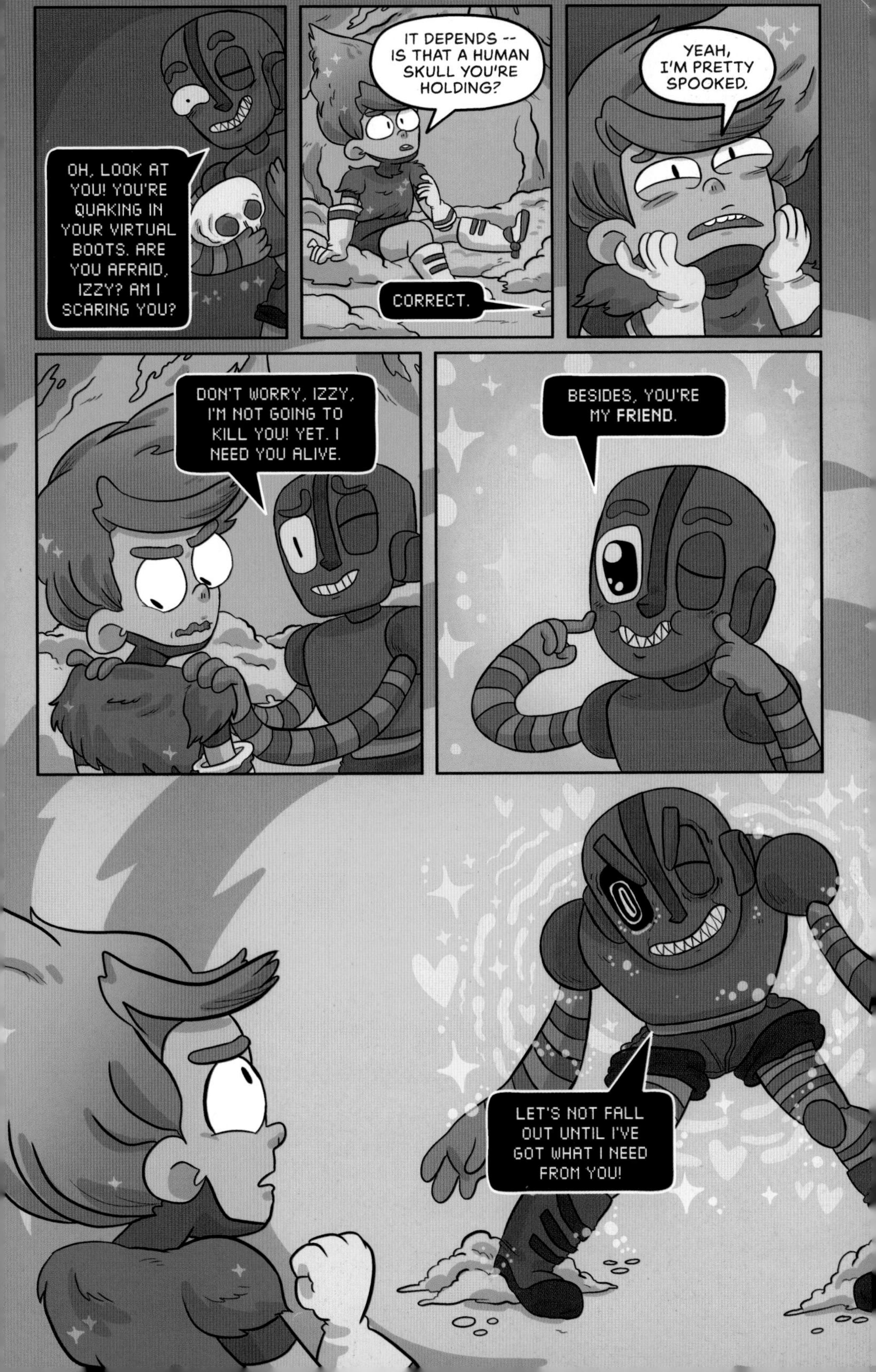
OH, LOOK AT YOU! YOU'RE QUAKING IN YOUR VIRTUAL BOOTS. ARE YOU AFRAID, IZZY? AM I SCARING YOU?
IT DEPENDS -- IS THAT A HUMAN SKULL YOU'RE HOLDING?
CORRECT.
YEAH, I'M PRETTY SPOOKED.
DON'T WORRY, IZZY, I'M NOT GOING TO KILL YOU! YET. I NEED YOU ALIVE.
BESIDES, YOU'RE MY FRIEND.
LET'S NOT FALL OUT UNTIL I'VE GOT WHAT I NEED FROM YOU!

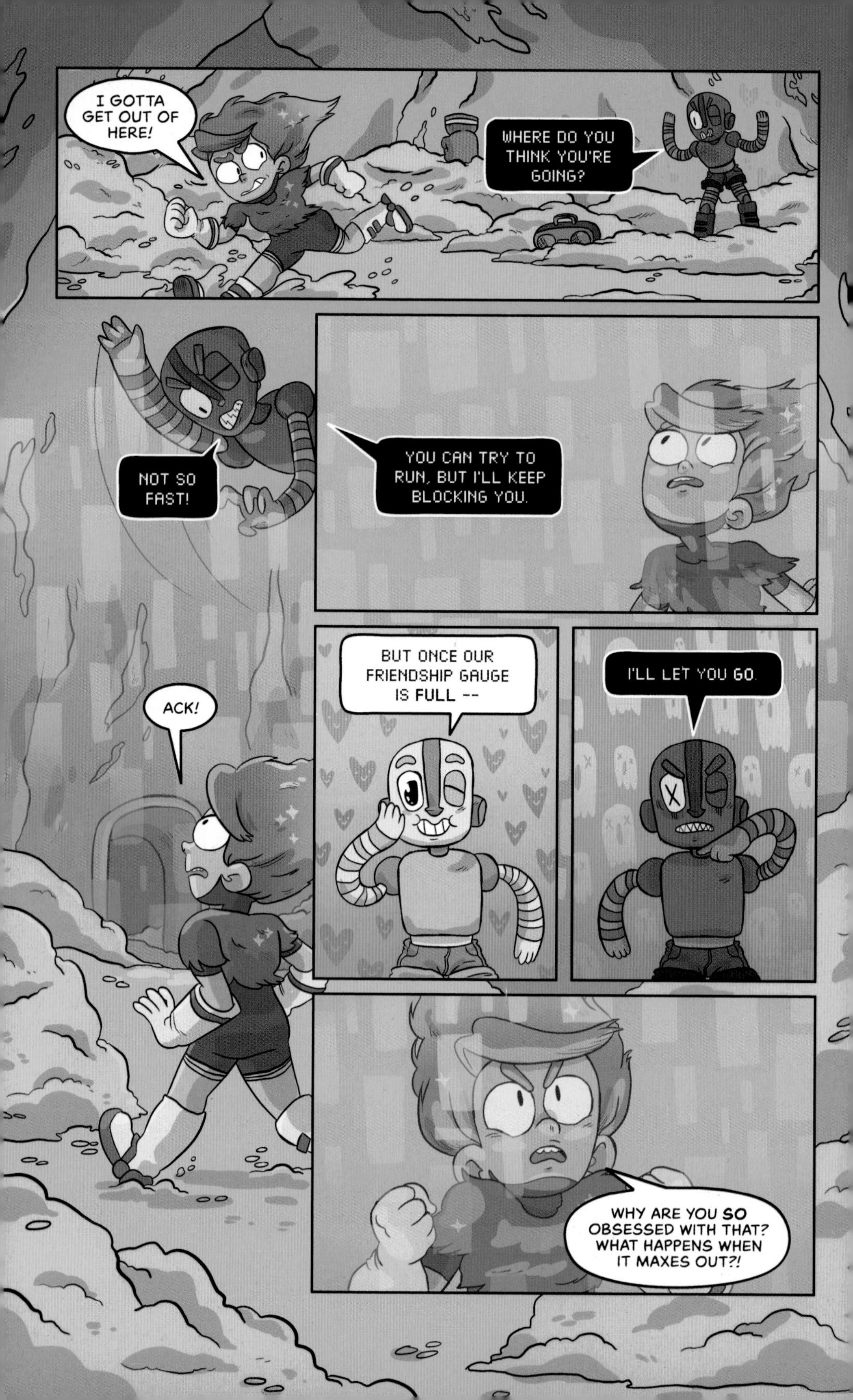
I GOTTA GET OUT OF HERE!
WHERE DO YOU THINK YOU'RE GOING?
NOT SO FAST!
YOU CAN TRY TO RUN, BUT I'LL KEEP BLOCKING YOU.
ACK!
BUT ONCE OUR FRIENDSHIP GAUGE IS FULL --
I'LL LET YOU GO.
WHY ARE YOU SO OBSESSED WITH THAT? WHAT HAPPENS WHEN IT MAXES OUT?!

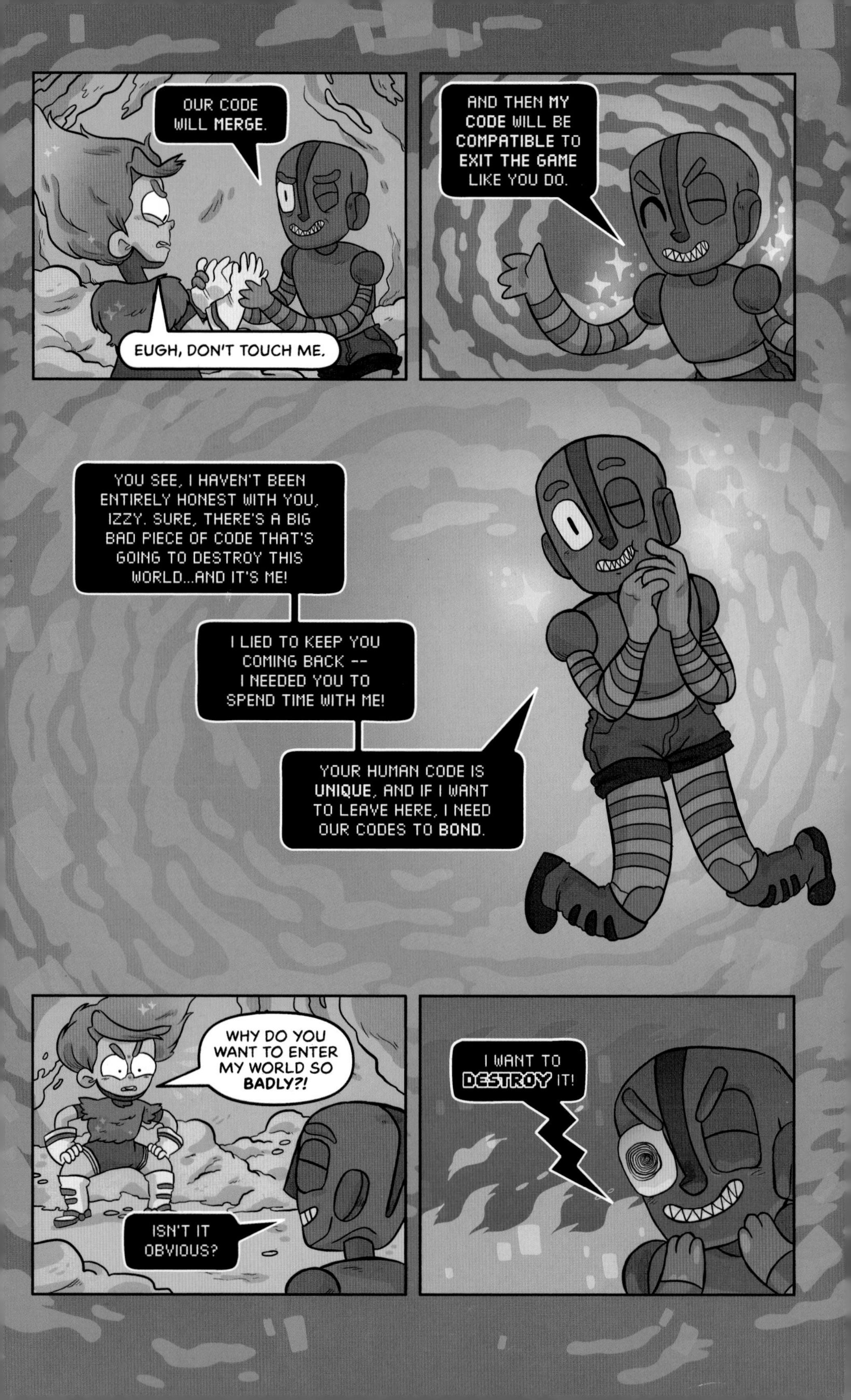
OUR CODE WILL MERGE.
EUGH, DON'T TOUCH ME.
AND THEN MY CODE WILL BE COMPATIBLE TO EXIT THE GAME LIKE YOU DO.
YOU SEE, I HAVEN'T BEEN ENTIRELY HONEST WITH YOU, IZZY. SURE, THERE'S A BIG BAD PIECE OF CODE THAT'S GOING TO DESTROY THIS WORLD...AND IT'S ME!
I LIED TO KEEP YOU COMING BACK -- I NEEDED YOU TO SPEND TIME WITH ME!
YOUR HUMAN CODE IS UNIQUE, AND IF I WANT TO LEAVE HERE, I NEED OUR CODES TO BOND.
WHY DO YOU WANT TO ENTER MY WORLD SO BADLY?!
ISN'T IT OBVIOUS?
I WANT TO DESTROY IT!

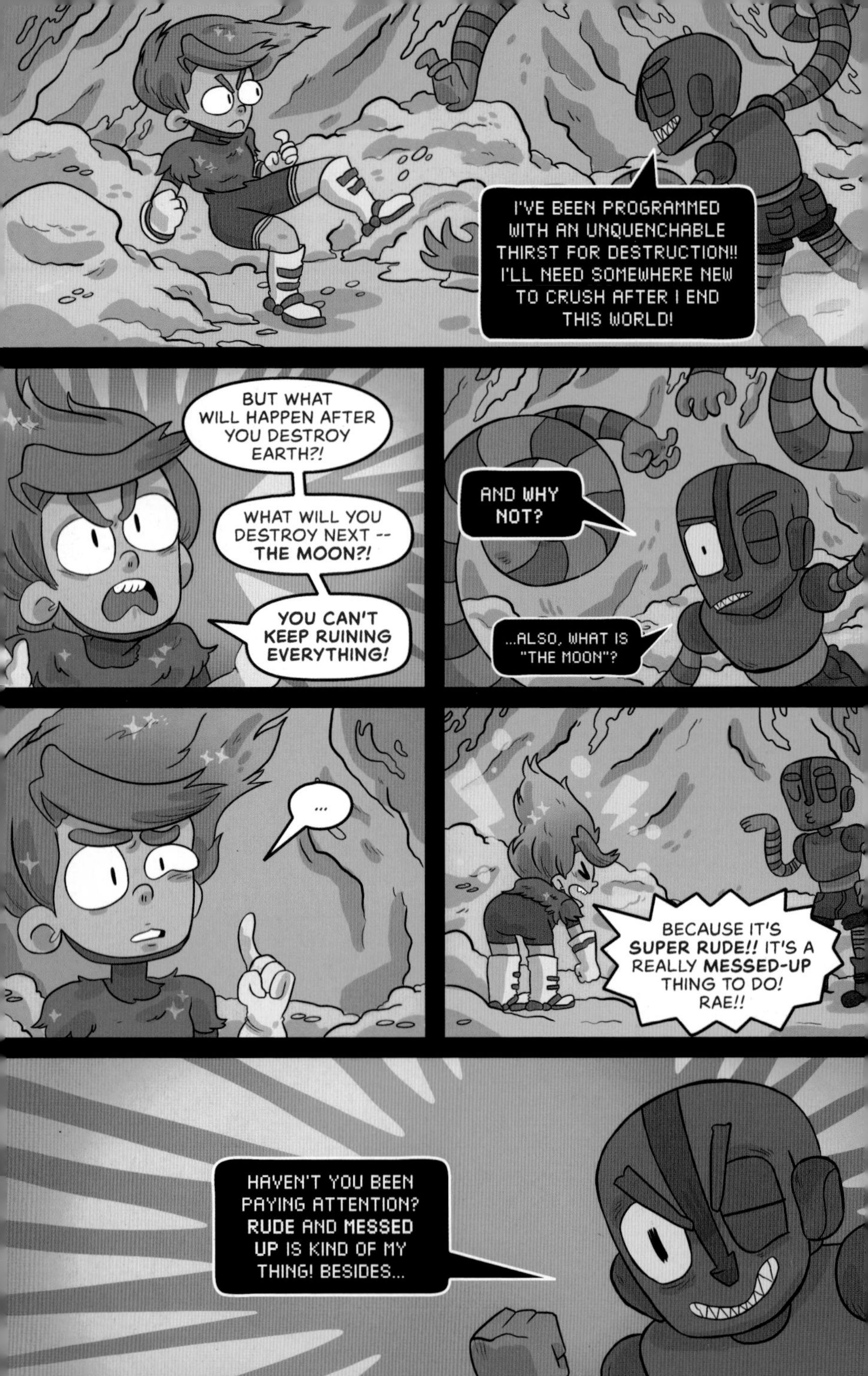
I'VE BEEN PROGRAMMED WITH AN UNQUENCHABLE THIRST FOR DESTRUCTION!! I'LL NEED SOMEWHERE NEW TO CRUSH AFTER I END THIS WORLD!
BUT WHAT WILL HAPPEN AFTER YOU DESTROY EARTH?!
WHAT WILL YOU DESTROY NEXT -- THE MOON?!
YOU CAN'T KEEP RUINING EVERYTHING!
AND WHY NOT?
...ALSO, WHAT IS "THE MOON"?
...
BECAUSE IT'S SUPER RUDE!! IT'S A REALLY MESSED-UP THING TO DO! RAE!!
HAVEN'T YOU BEEN PAYING ATTENTION? RUDE AND MESSED UP IS KIND OF MY THING! BESIDES...

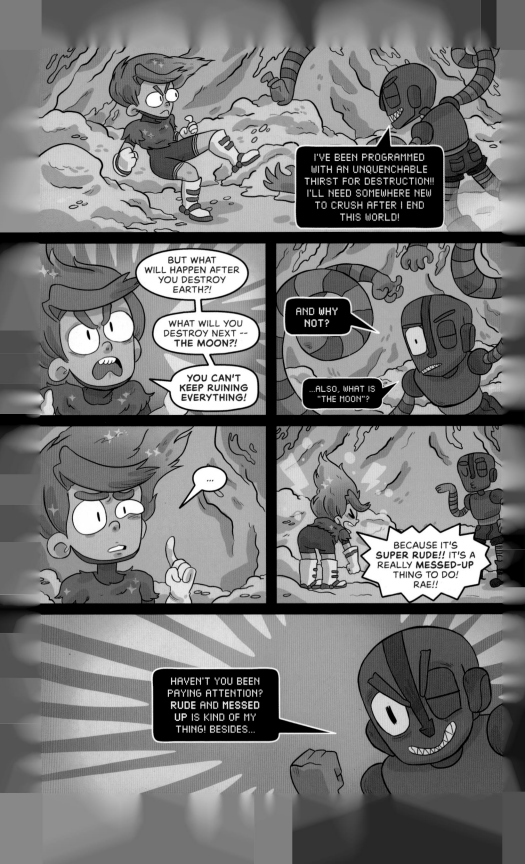

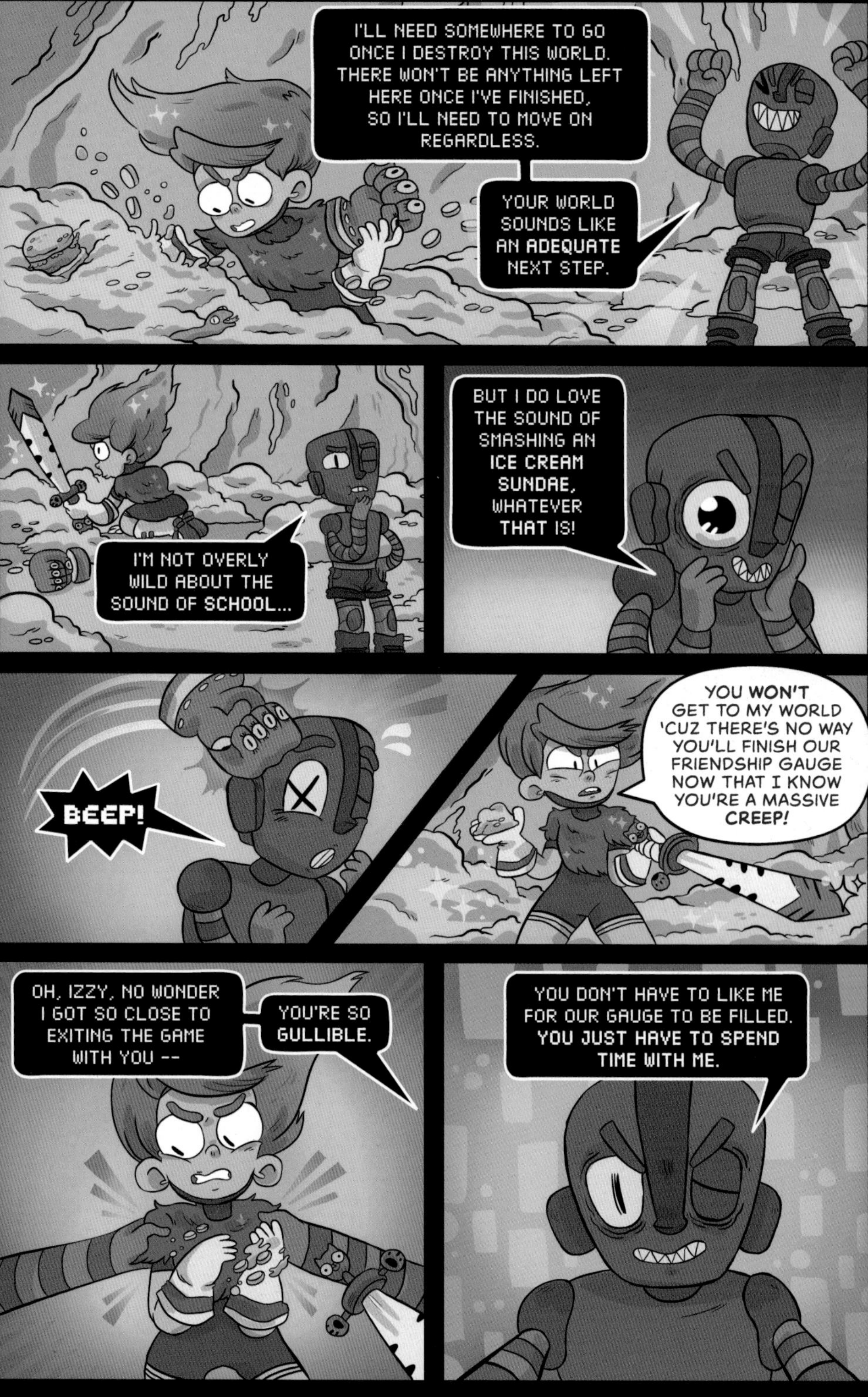
I'LL NEED SOMEWHERE TO GO ONCE I DESTROY THIS WORLD. THERE WON'T BE ANYTHING LEFT HERE ONCE I'VE FINISHED, SO I'LL NEED TO MOVE ON REGARDLESS.
YOUR WORLD SOUNDS LIKE AN ADEQUATE NEXT STEP.
I'M NOT OVERLY WILD ABOUT THE SOUND OF SCHOOL...
BUT I DO LOVE THE SOUND OF SMASHING AN ICE CREAM SUNDAE, WHATEVER THAT IS!
BEEP!
YOU WON'T GET TO MY WORLD 'CUZ THERE'S NO WAY YOU'LL FINISH OUR FRIENDSHIP GAUGE NOW THAT I KNOW YOU'RE A MASSIVE CREEP!
OH, IZZY, NO WONDER I GOT SO CLOSE TO EXITING THE GAME WITH YOU --
YOU'RE SO GULLIBLE.
YOU DON'T HAVE TO LIKE ME FOR OUR GAUGE TO BE FILLED. YOU JUST HAVE TO SPEND TIME WITH ME.

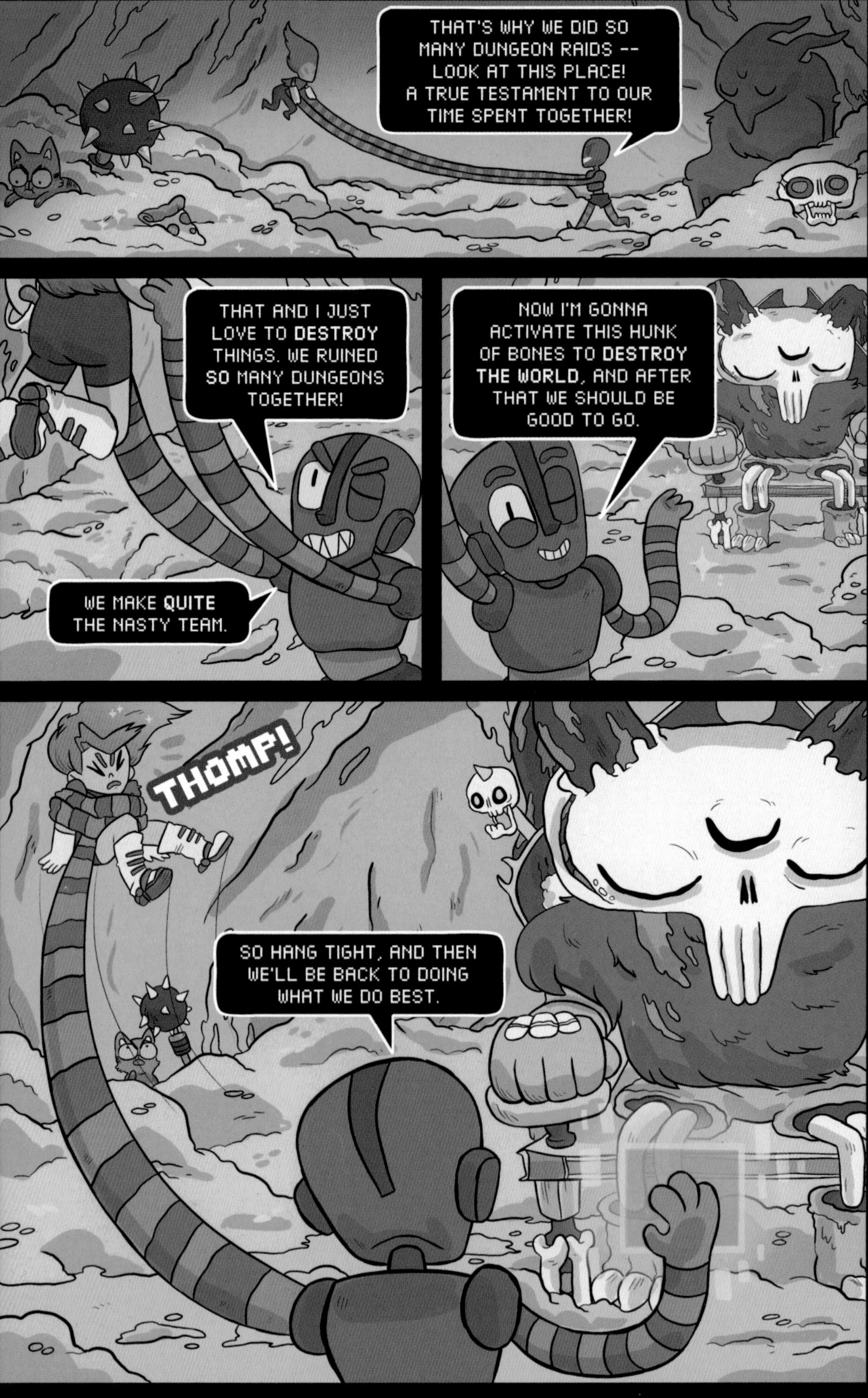
THAT'S WHY WE DID SO MANY DUNGEON RAIDS -- LOOK AT THIS PLACE! A TRUE TESTAMENT TO OUR TIME SPENT TOGETHER!
THAT AND I JUST LOVE TO **DESTROY** THINGS. WE RUINED SO MANY DUNGEONS TOGETHER!
WE MAKE **QUITE** THE NASTY TEAM.
NOW I'M GONNA ACTIVATE THIS HUNK OF BONES TO **DESTROY THE WORLD**, AND AFTER THAT WE SHOULD BE GOOD TO GO.
THOMP!
SO HANG TIGHT, AND THEN WE'LL BE BACK TO DOING WHAT WE DO BEST.

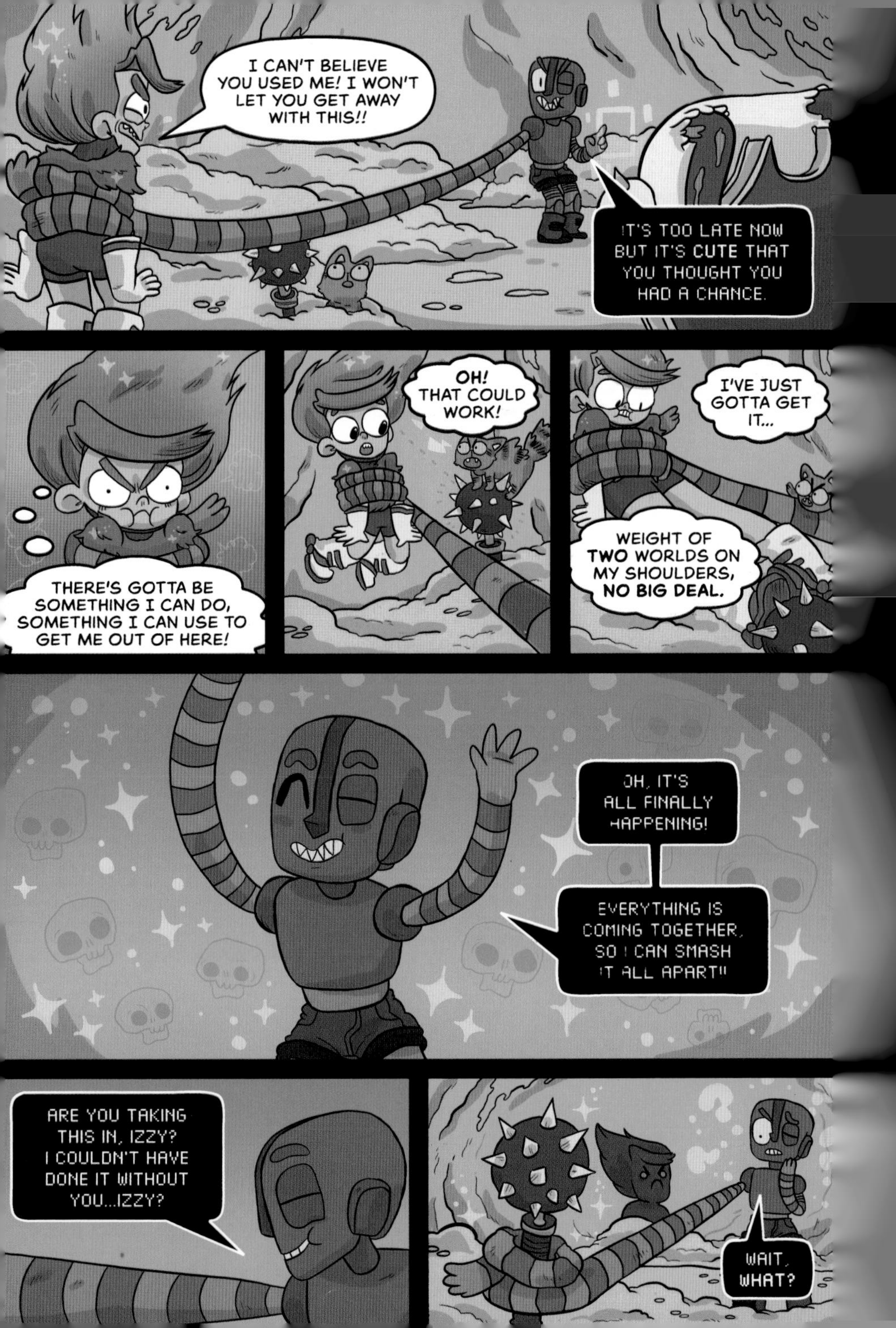
I CAN'T BELIEVE YOU USED ME! I WON'T LET YOU GET AWAY WITH THIS!!
IT'S TOO LATE NOW BUT IT'S CUTE THAT YOU THOUGHT YOU HAD A CHANCE.
THERE'S GOTTA BE SOMETHING I CAN DO, SOMETHING I CAN USE TO GET ME OUT OF HERE!
OH! THAT COULD WORK!
I'VE JUST GOTTA GET IT...
WEIGHT OF TWO WORLDS ON MY SHOULDERS, NO BIG DEAL.
OH, IT'S ALL FINALLY HAPPENING!
EVERYTHING IS COMING TOGETHER, SO I CAN SMASH IT ALL APART!!
ARE YOU TAKING THIS IN, IZZY? I COULDN'T HAVE DONE IT WITHOUT YOU...IZZY?
WAIT, WHAT?

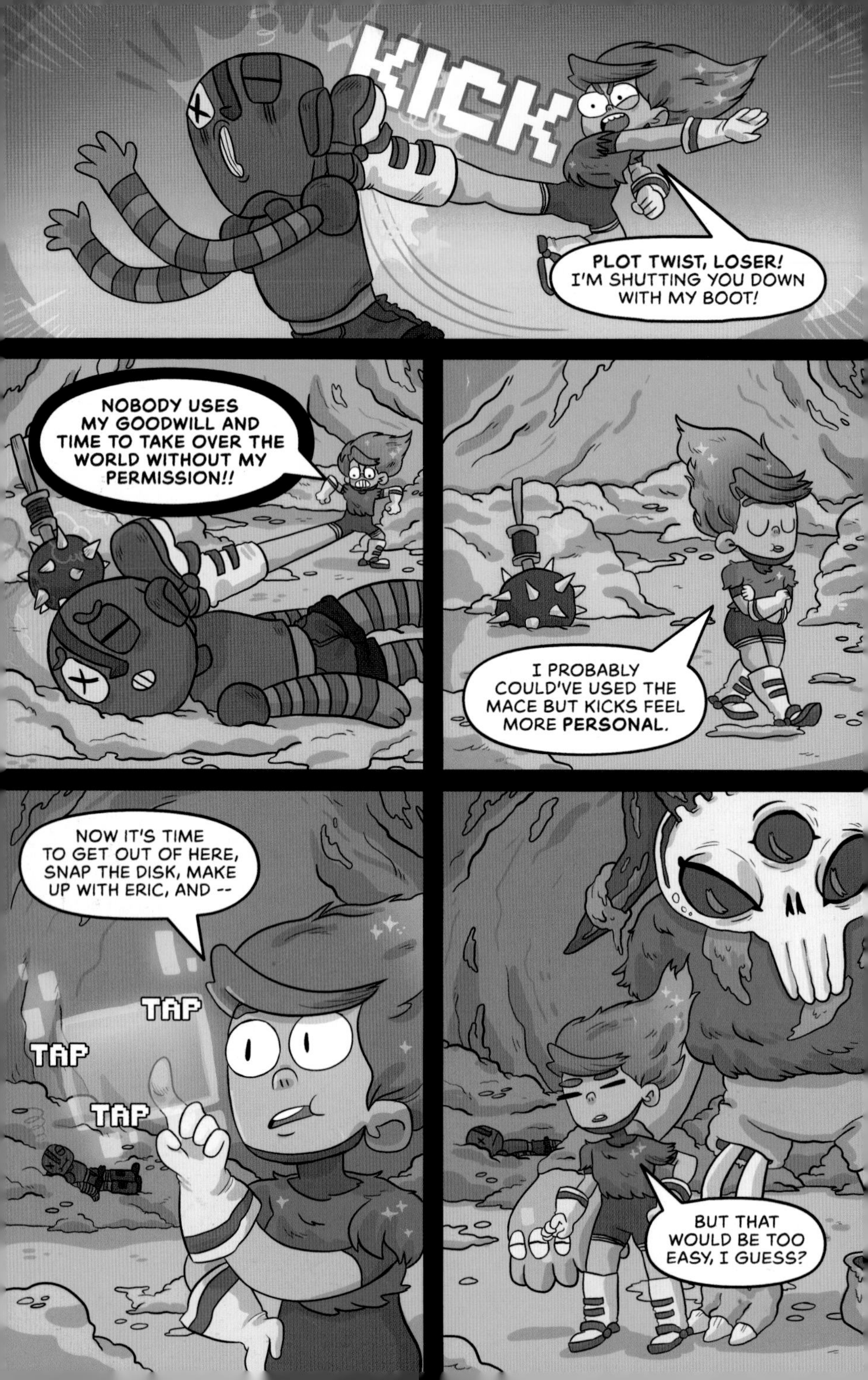
KICK
PLOT TWIST, LOSER! I'M SHUTTING YOU DOWN WITH MY BOOT!
NOBODY USES MY GOODWILL AND TIME TO TAKE OVER THE WORLD WITHOUT MY PERMISSION!!
I PROBABLY COULD'VE USED THE MACE BUT KICKS FEEL MORE **PERSONAL**.
NOW IT'S TIME TO GET OUT OF HERE, SNAP THE DISK, MAKE UP WITH ERIC, AND --
TAP
TAP
TAP
BUT THAT WOULD BE TOO EASY, I GUESS?

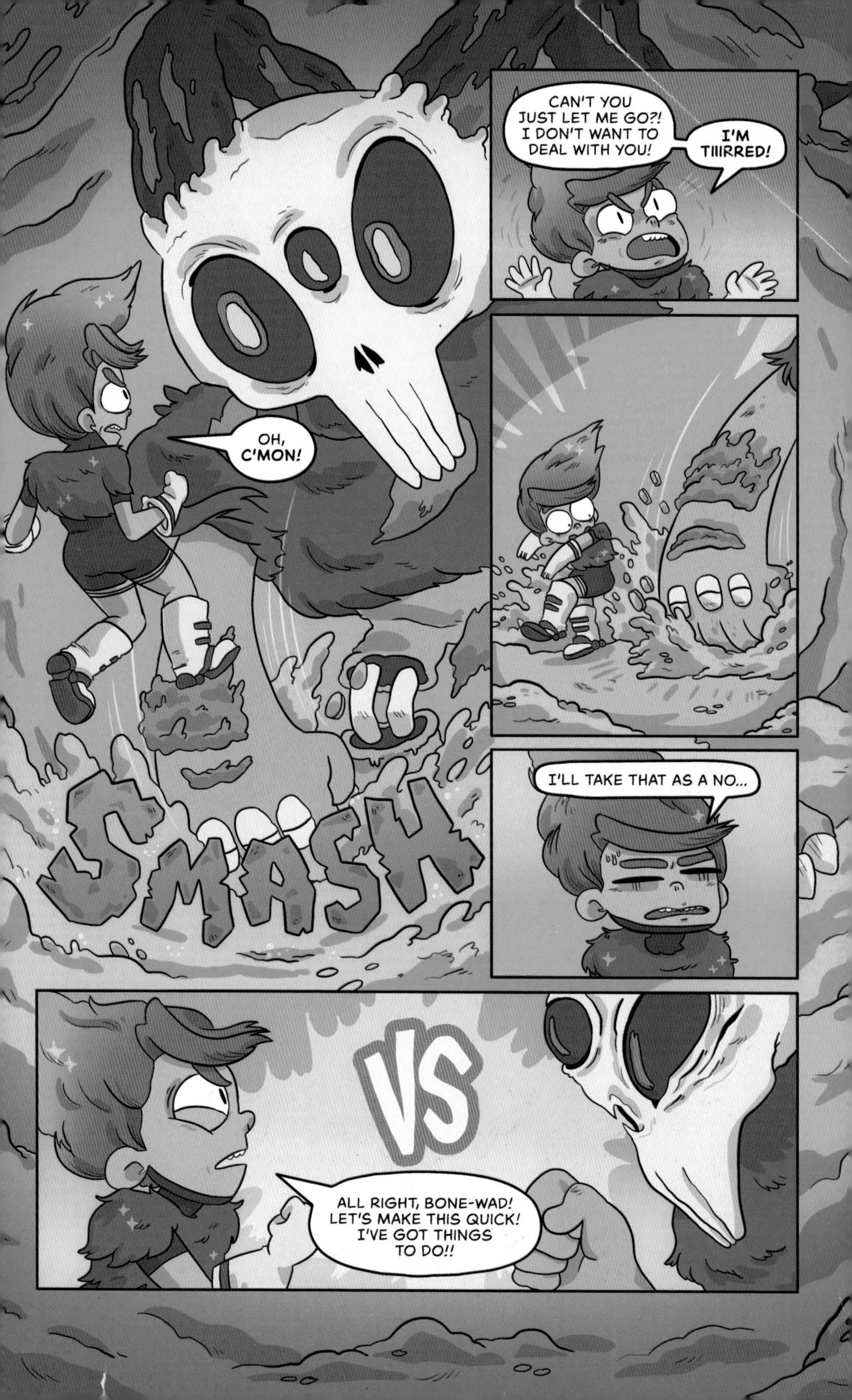
CAN'T YOU JUST LET ME GO?! I DON'T WANT TO DEAL WITH YOU!
I'M TIIIRRED!
OH, C'MON!
SMASH
I'LL TAKE THAT AS A NO...
VS
ALL RIGHT, BONE-WAD! LET'S MAKE THIS QUICK! I'VE GOT THINGS TO DO!!

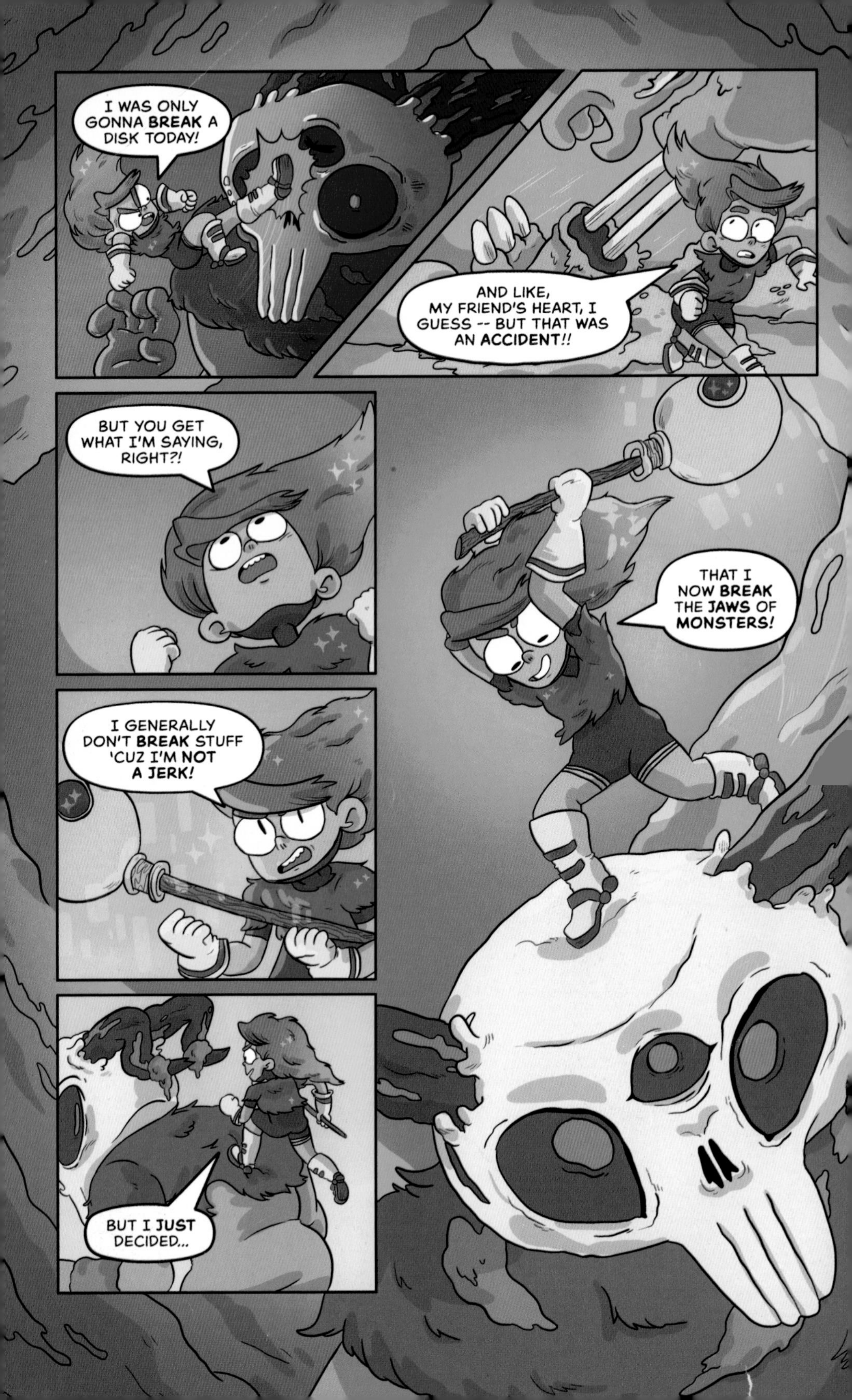
I WAS ONLY GONNA BREAK A DISK TODAY!
AND LIKE, MY FRIEND'S HEART, I GUESS -- BUT THAT WAS AN ACCIDENT!!
BUT YOU GET WHAT I'M SAYING, RIGHT?!
I GENERALLY DON'T BREAK STUFF 'CUZ I'M NOT A JERK!
BUT I JUST DECIDED...
THAT I NOW BREAK THE JAWS OF MONSTERS!

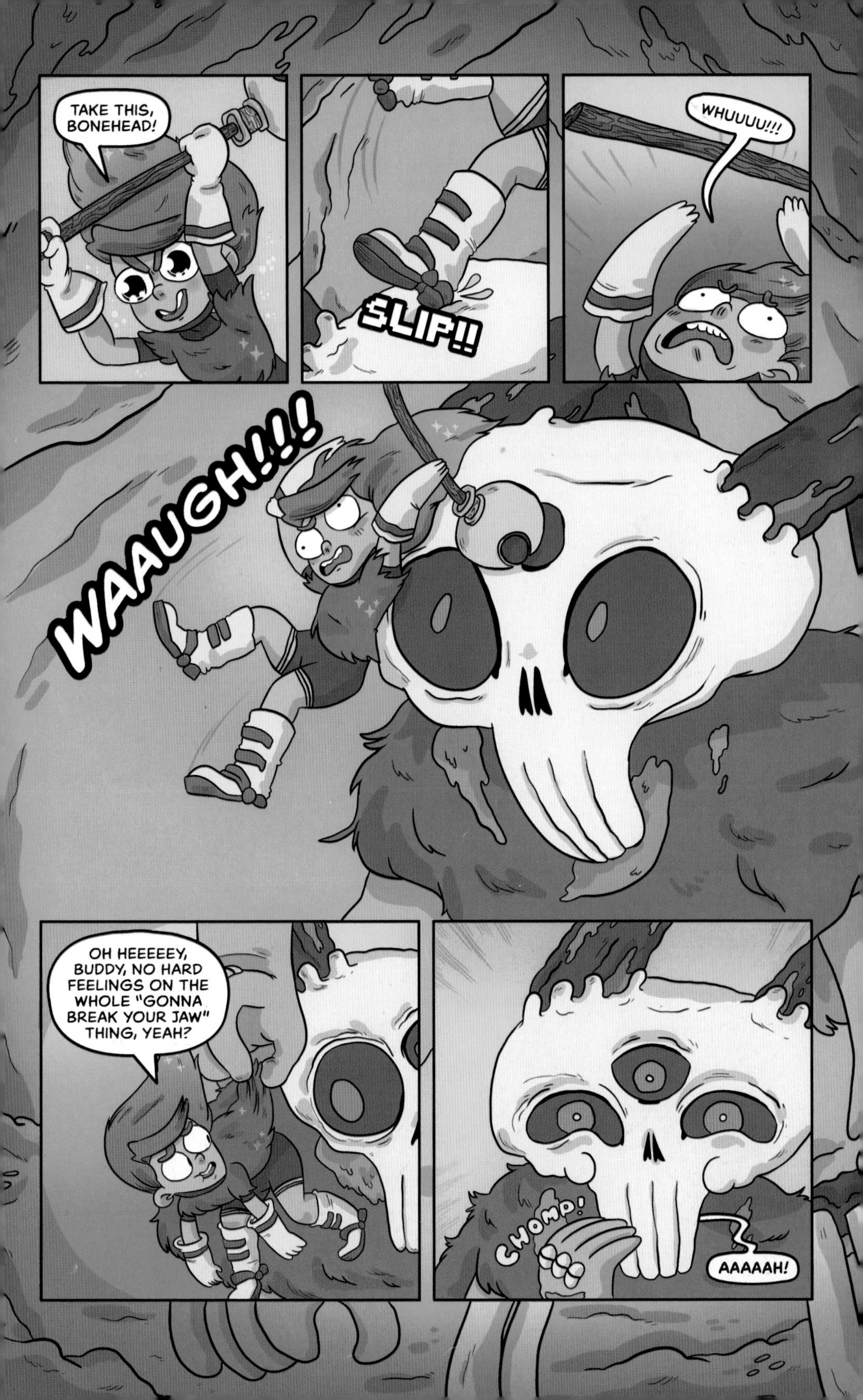
TAKE THIS, BONEHEAD!
SLIP!!
WHUUUU!!!
WAAUGH!!!
OH HEEEEEY, BUDDY, NO HARD FEELINGS ON THE WHOLE "GONNA BREAK YOUR JAW" THING, YEAH?
CHOMP!
AAAAAH!

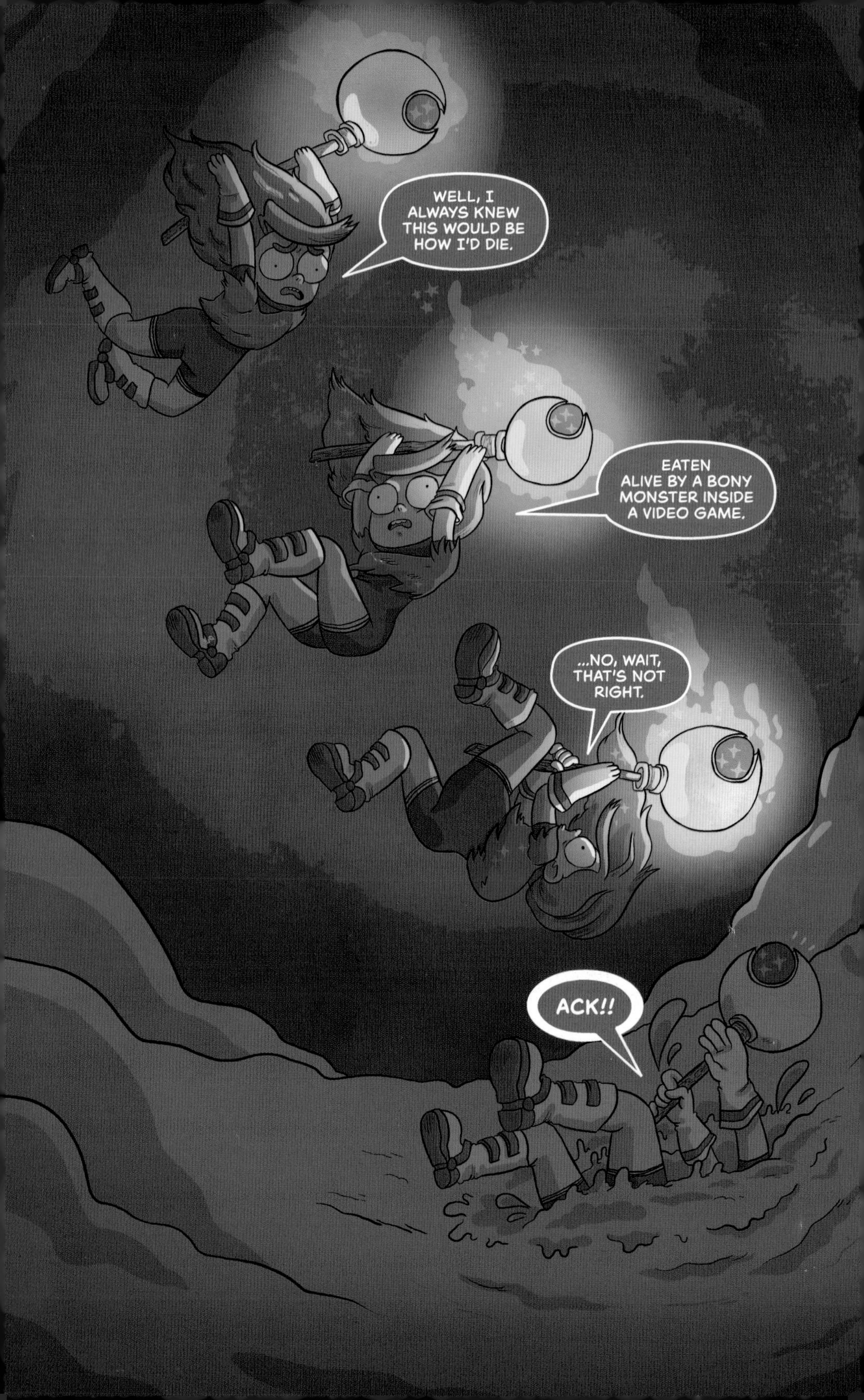
WELL, I ALWAYS KNEW THIS WOULD BE HOW I'D DIE.
EATEN ALIVE BY A BONY MONSTER INSIDE A VIDEO GAME.
...NO, WAIT, THAT'S NOT RIGHT.
ACK!!

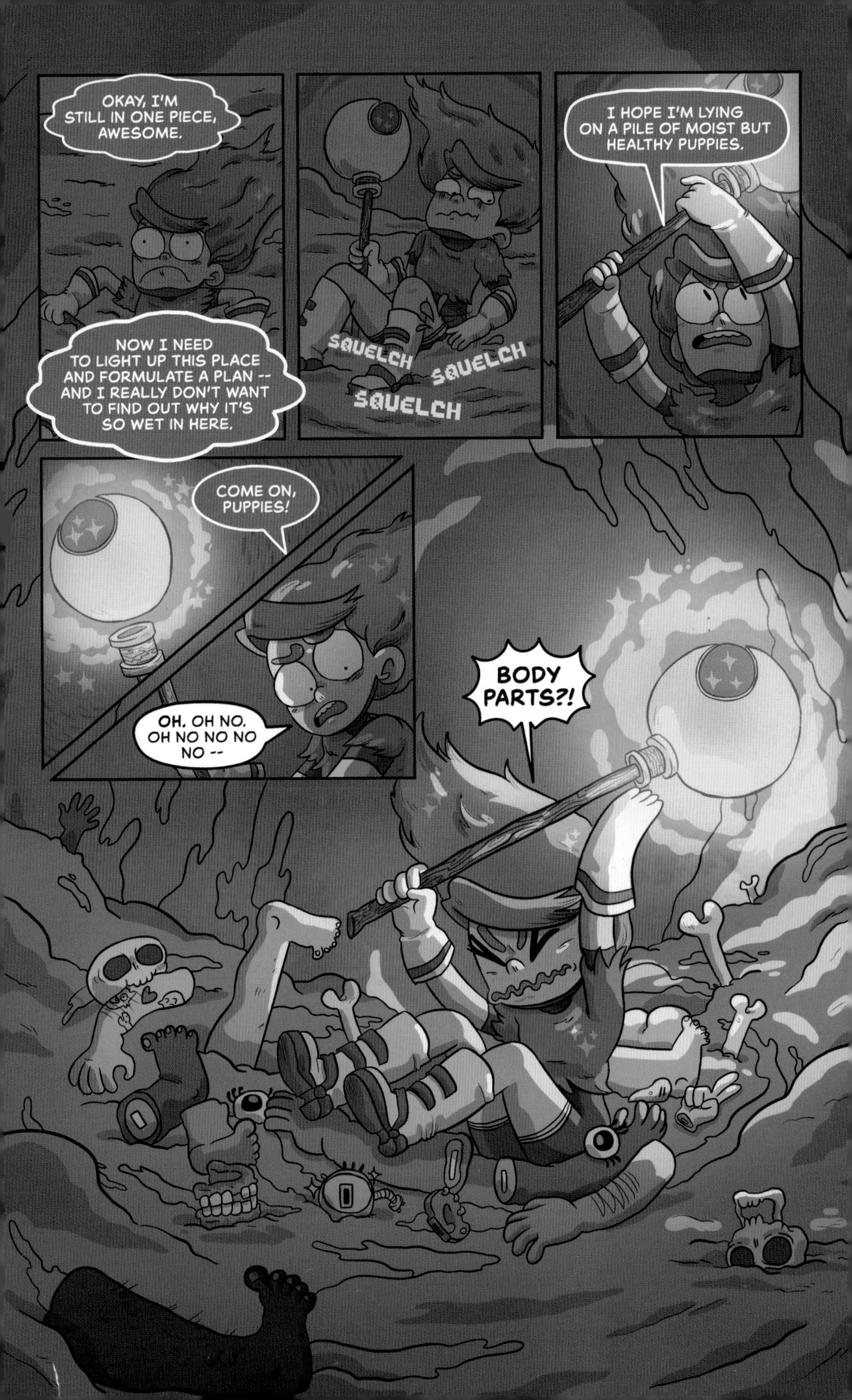

OKAY, I'M STILL IN ONE PIECE, AWESOME.
NOW I NEED TO LIGHT UP THIS PLACE AND FORMULATE A PLAN -- AND I REALLY DON'T WANT TO FIND OUT WHY IT'S SO WET IN HERE.
SQUELCH
SQUELCH
SQUELCH
I HOPE I'M LYING ON A PILE OF MOIST BUT HEALTHY PUPPIES.
COME ON, PUPPIES!
OH. OH NO. OH NO NO NO NO --
BODY PARTS?!

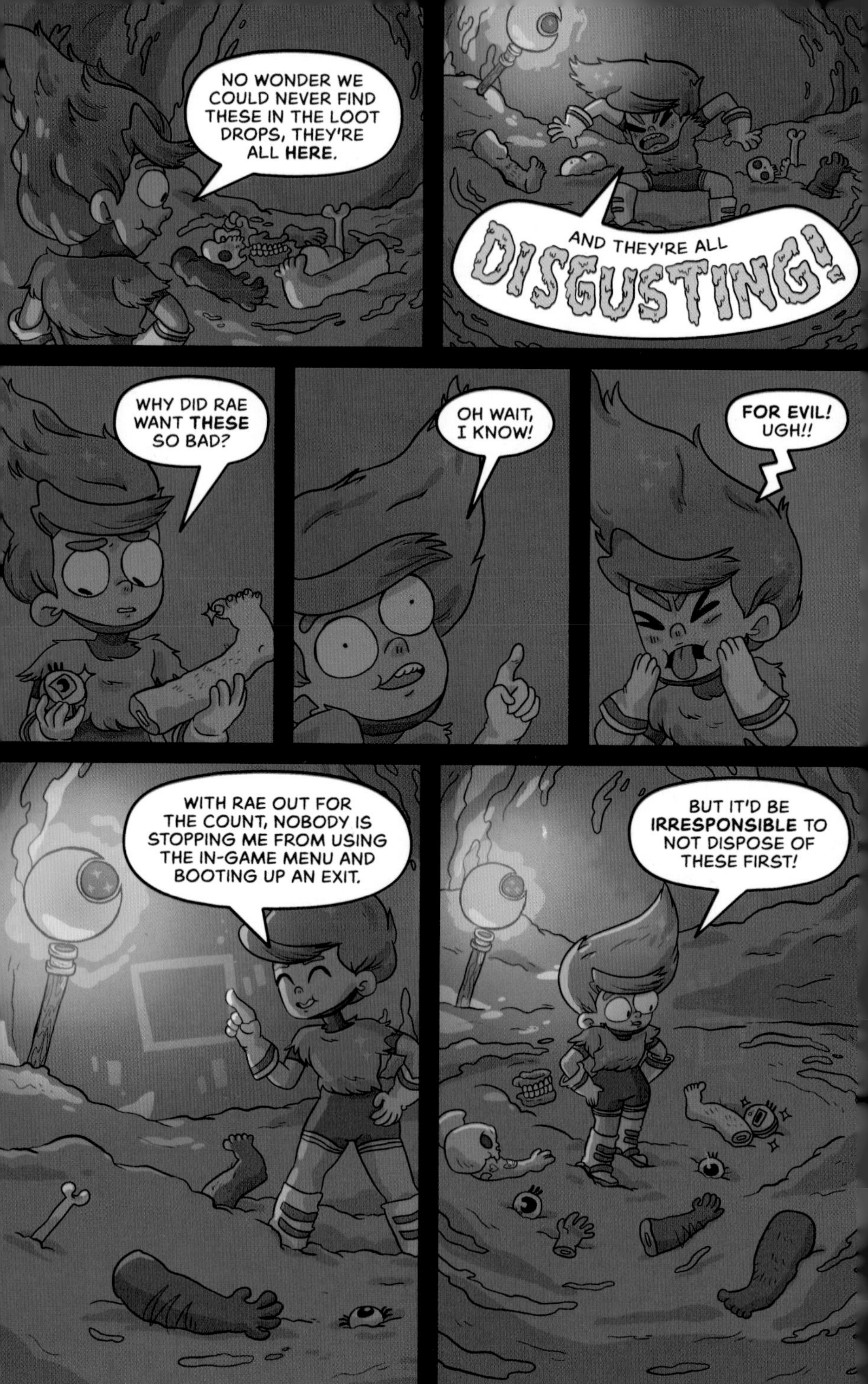

NO WONDER WE COULD NEVER FIND THESE IN THE LOOT DROPS, THEY'RE ALL **HERE**.
AND THEY'RE ALL DISGUSTING!
WHY DID RAE WANT **THESE** SO BAD?
OH WAIT, I KNOW!
FOR EVIL! UGH!!
WITH RAE OUT FOR THE COUNT, NOBODY IS STOPPING ME FROM USING THE IN-GAME MENU AND BOOTING UP AN EXIT.
BUT IT'D BE **IRRESPONSIBLE** TO NOT DISPOSE OF THESE FIRST!

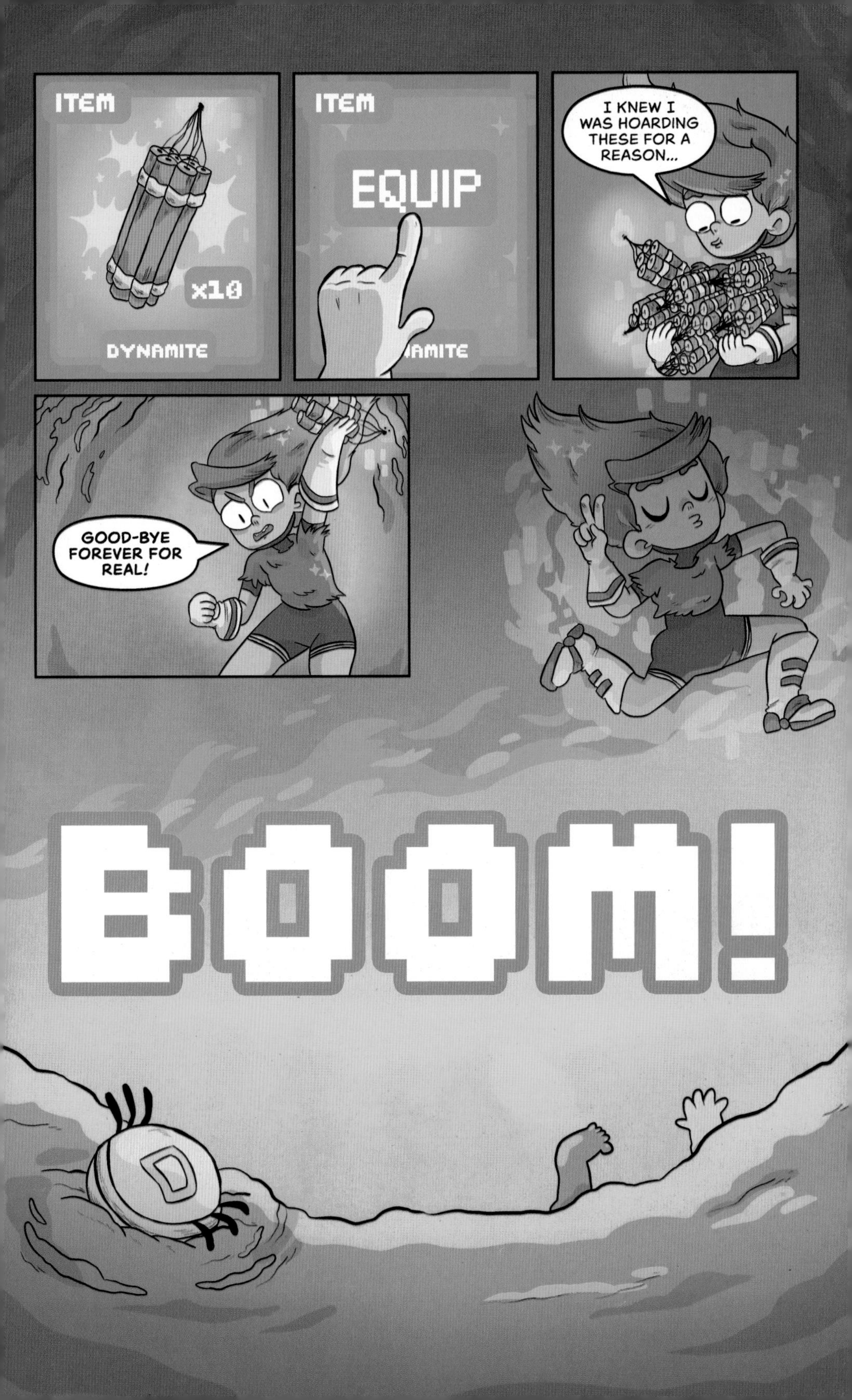
ITEM
DYNAMITE
x10
ITEM
EQUIP
I KNEW I WAS HOARDING THESE FOR A REASON...
GOOD-BYE FOREVER FOR REAL!
BOOM!

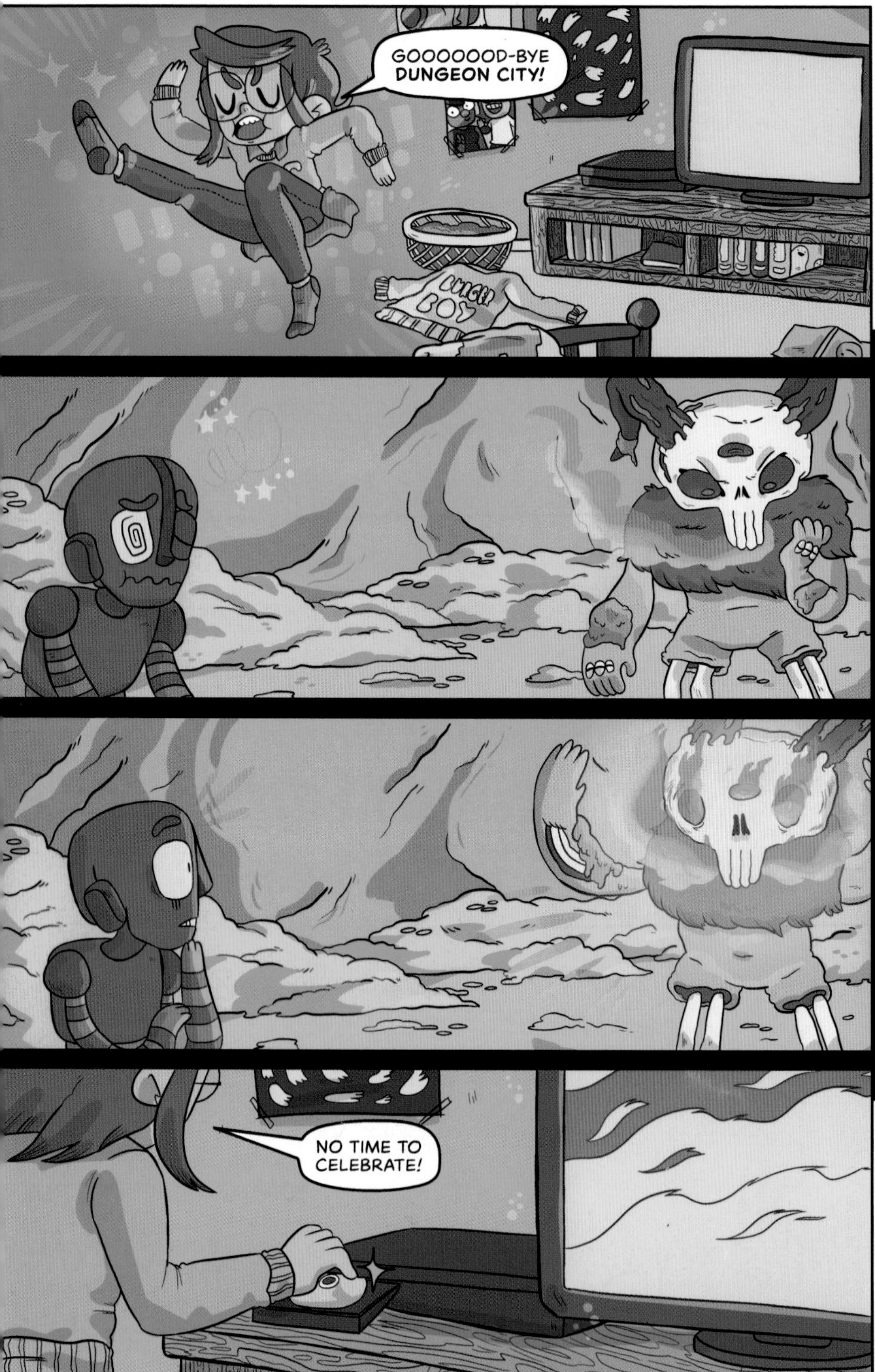
GOOOOOOD-BYE
DUNGEON CITY!
DUNGEON BOY
NO TIME TO
CELEBRATE!

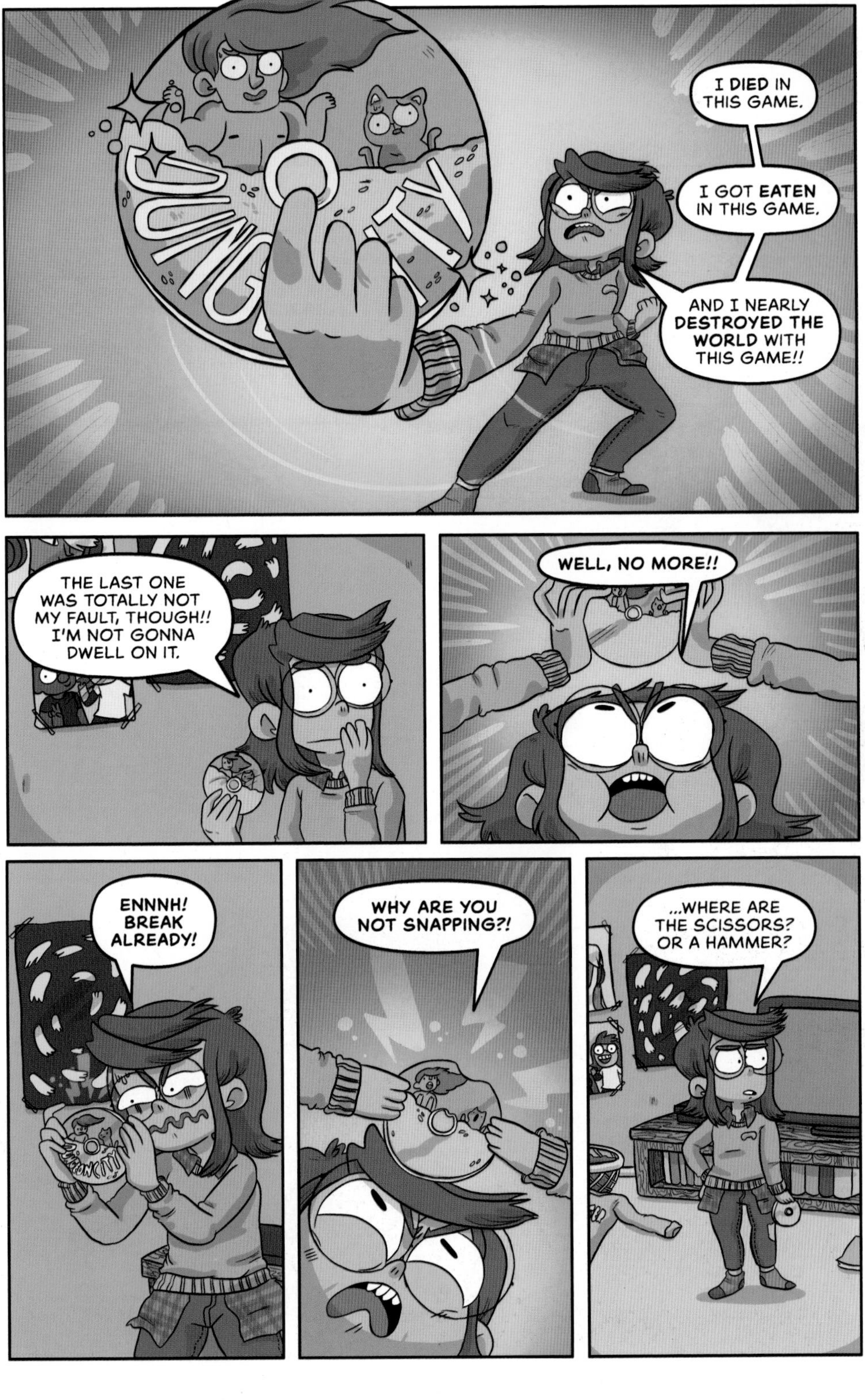
DUNGEON CITY
I DIED IN THIS GAME.
I GOT EATEN IN THIS GAME.
AND I NEARLY DESTROYED THE WORLD WITH THIS GAME!!
THE LAST ONE WAS TOTALLY NOT MY FAULT, THOUGH!! I'M NOT GONNA DWELL ON IT.
WELL, NO MORE!!
ENNNH! BREAK ALREADY!
WHY ARE YOU NOT SNAPPING?!
...WHERE ARE THE SCISSORS? OR A HAMMER?

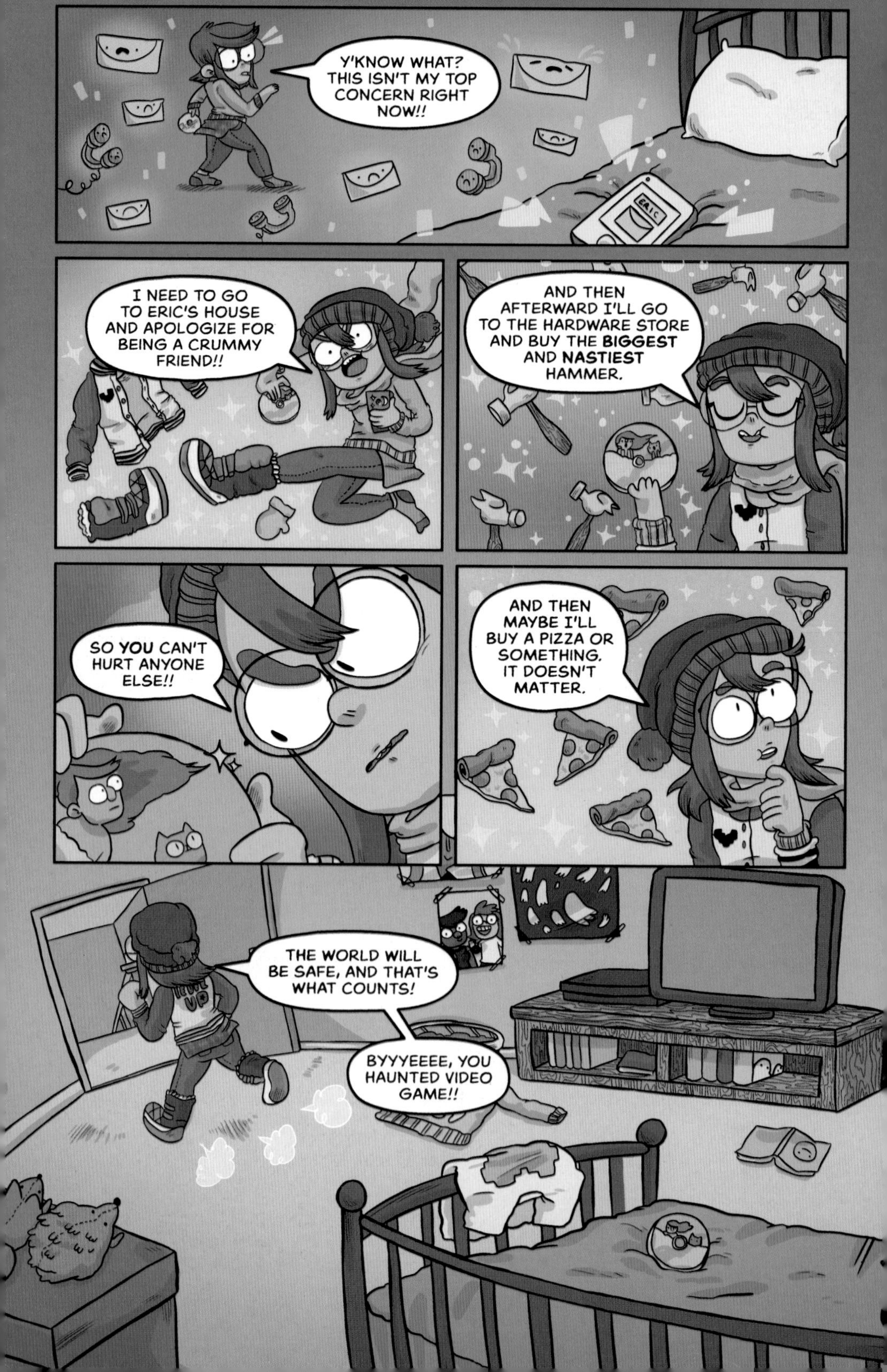
Y'KNOW WHAT? THIS ISN'T MY TOP CONCERN RIGHT NOW!!
ERIC
I NEED TO GO TO ERIC'S HOUSE AND APOLOGIZE FOR BEING A CRUMMY FRIEND!!
AND THEN AFTERWARD I'LL GO TO THE HARDWARE STORE AND BUY THE BIGGEST AND NASTIEST HAMMER.
SO YOU CAN'T HURT ANYONE ELSE!!
AND THEN MAYBE I'LL BUY A PIZZA OR SOMETHING. IT DOESN'T MATTER.
THE WORLD WILL BE SAFE, AND THAT'S WHAT COUNTS!
BYYYEEEE, YOU HAUNTED VIDEO GAME!!

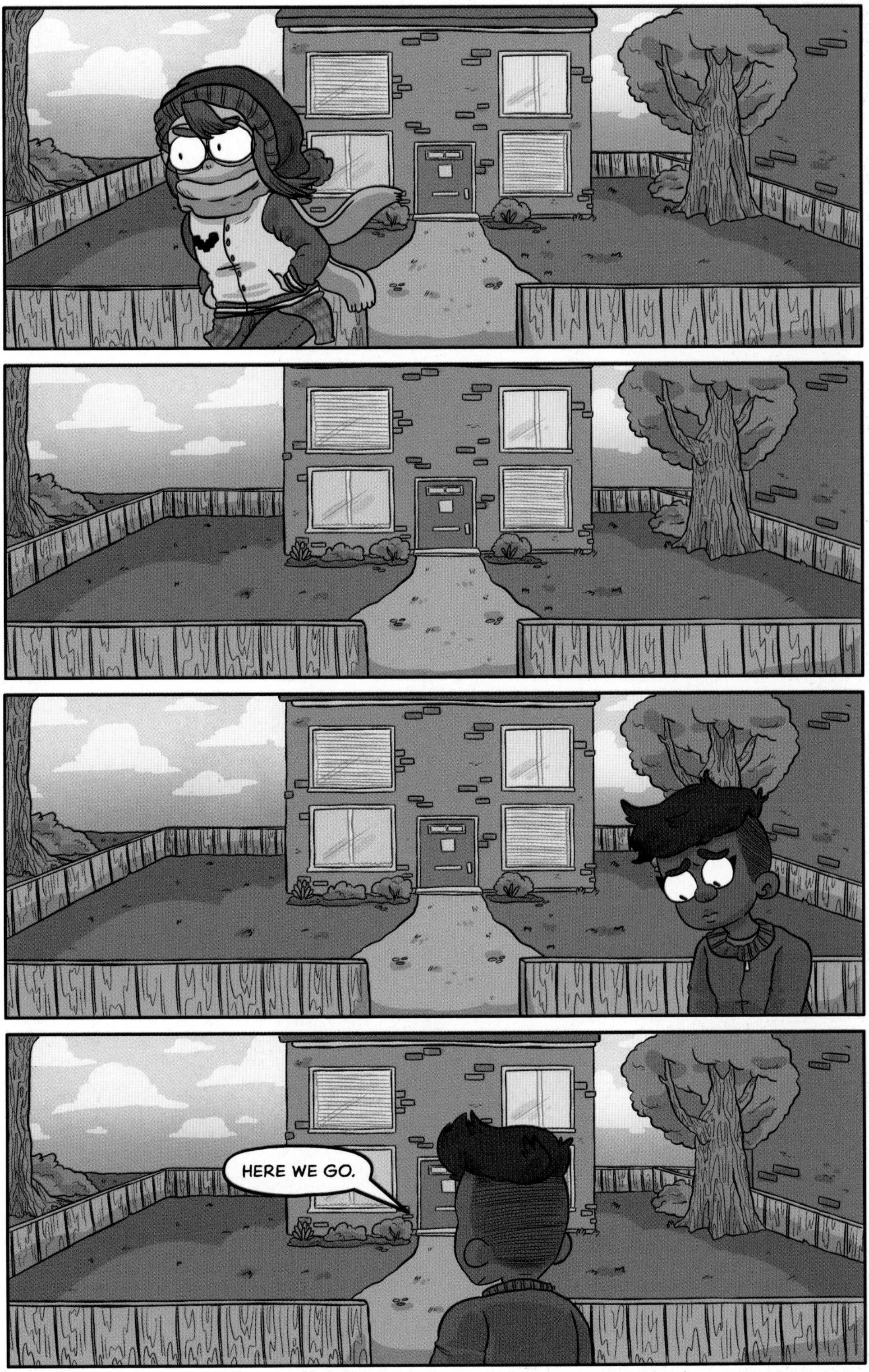
HERE WE GO.

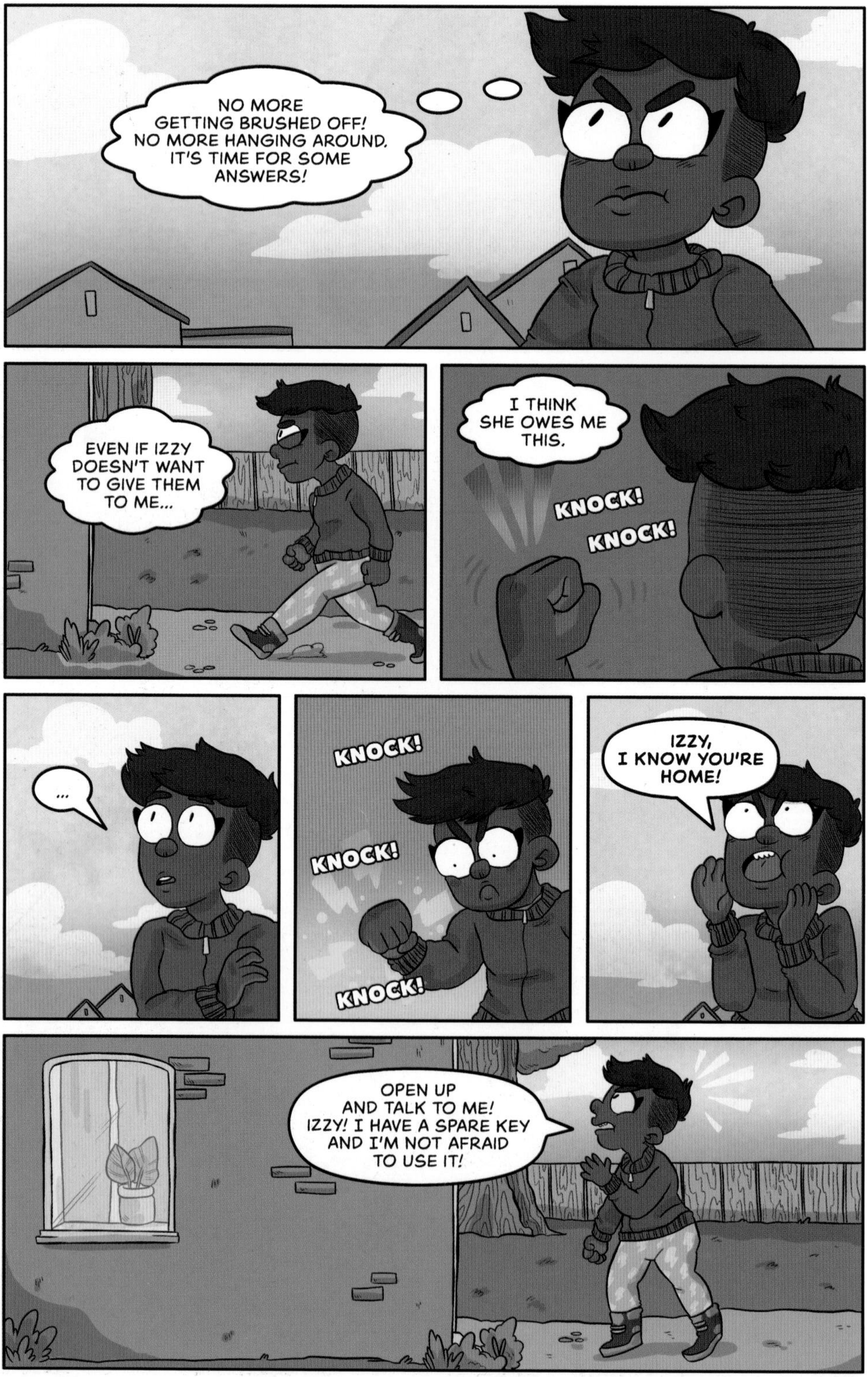
NO MORE GETTING BRUSHED OFF! NO MORE HANGING AROUND. IT'S TIME FOR SOME ANSWERS!
EVEN IF IZZY DOESN'T WANT TO GIVE THEM TO ME...
I THINK SHE OWES ME THIS.
KNOCK!
KNOCK!
...
KNOCK!
KNOCK!
KNOCK!
IZZY, I KNOW YOU'RE HOME!
OPEN UP AND TALK TO ME! IZZY! I HAVE A SPARE KEY AND I'M NOT AFRAID TO USE IT!

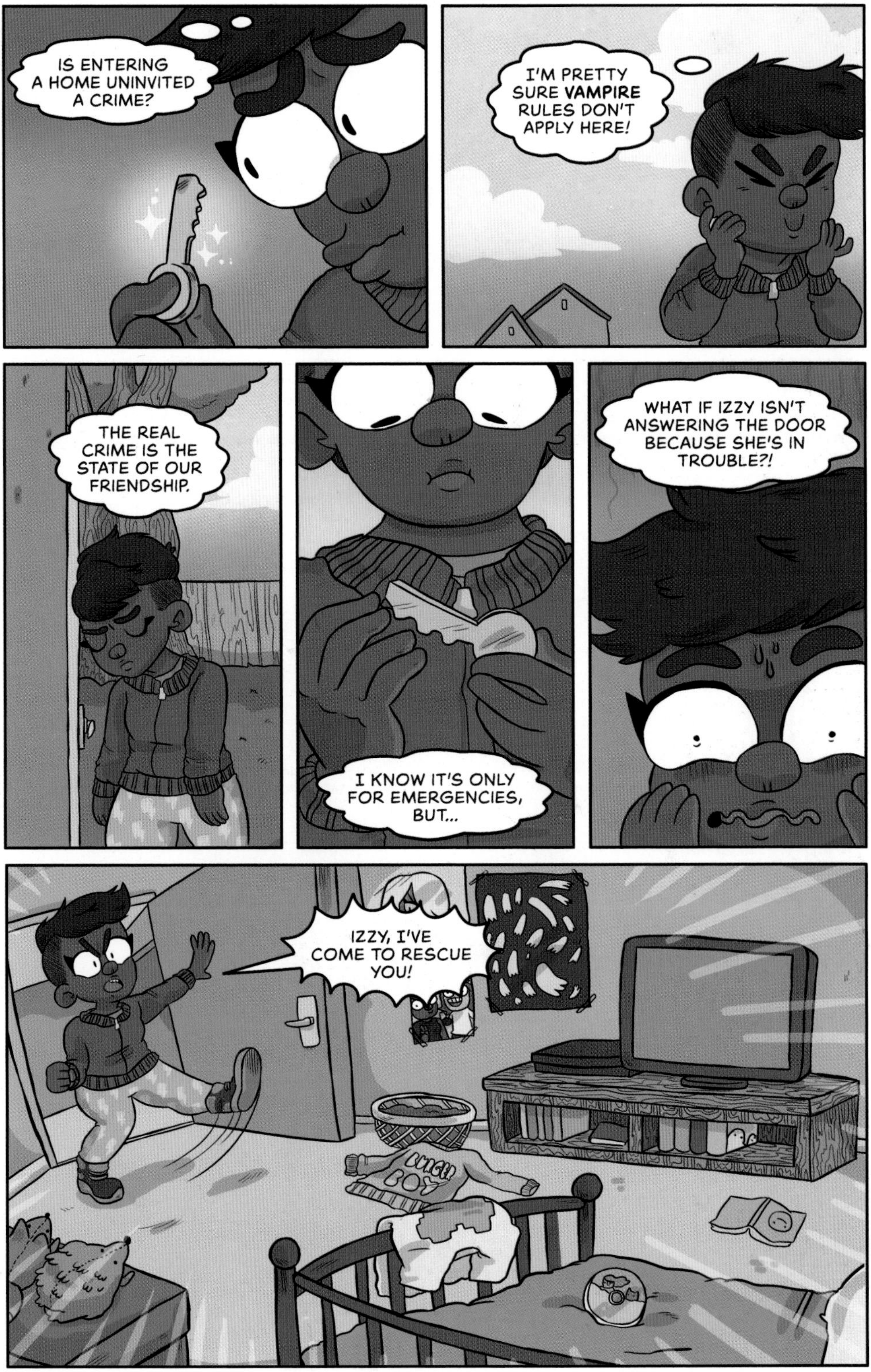
IS ENTERING A HOME UNINVITED A CRIME?
I'M PRETTY SURE **VAMPIRE** RULES DON'T APPLY HERE!
THE REAL CRIME IS THE STATE OF OUR FRIENDSHIP.
I KNOW IT'S ONLY FOR EMERGENCIES, BUT...
WHAT IF IZZY ISN'T ANSWERING THE DOOR BECAUSE SHE'S IN TROUBLE?!
IZZY, I'VE COME TO RESCUE YOU!

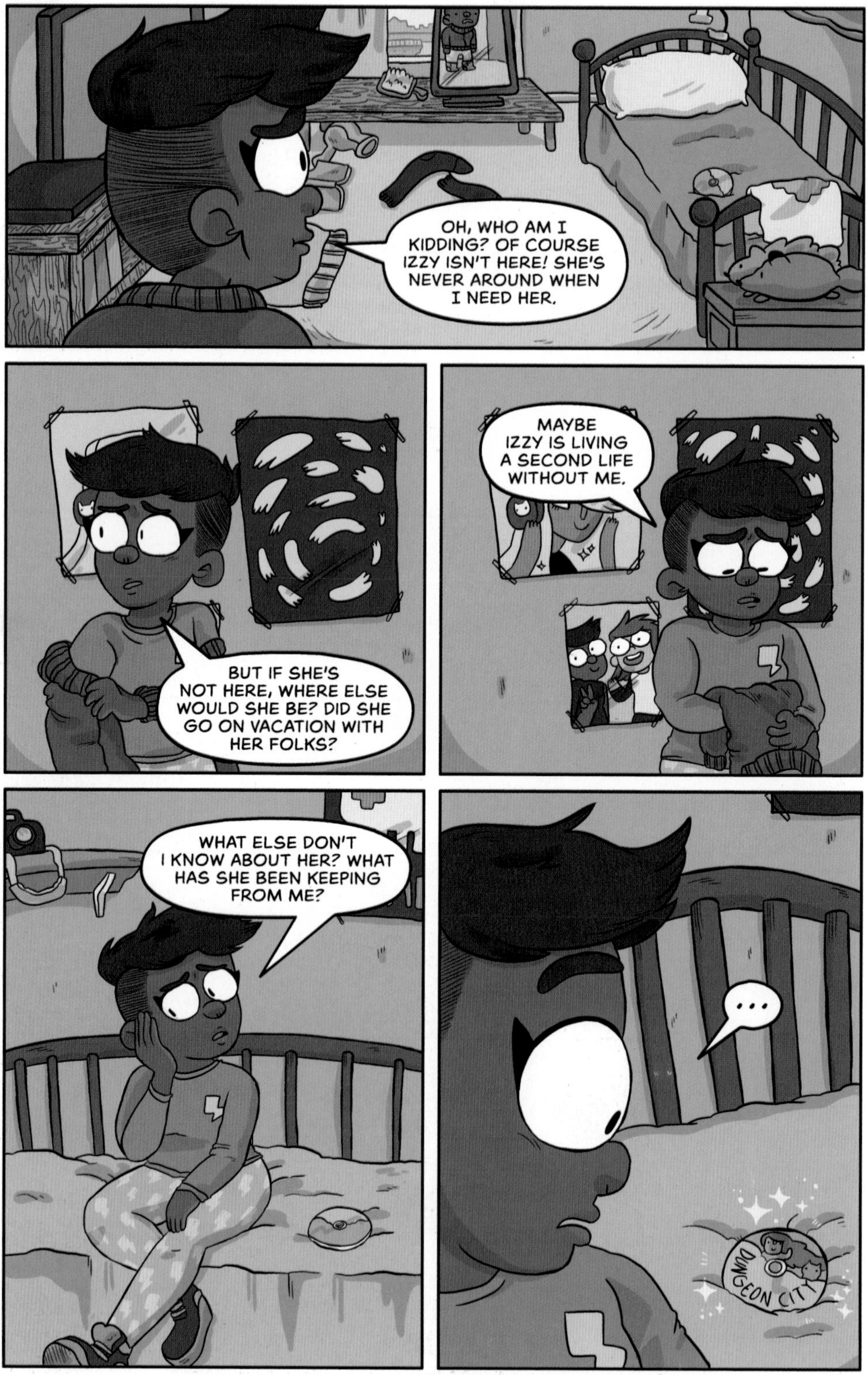
OH, WHO AM I KIDDING? OF COURSE IZZY ISN'T HERE! SHE'S NEVER AROUND WHEN I NEED HER.
BUT IF SHE'S NOT HERE, WHERE ELSE WOULD SHE BE? DID SHE GO ON VACATION WITH HER FOLKS?
MAYBE IZZY IS LIVING A SECOND LIFE WITHOUT ME.
WHAT ELSE DON'T I KNOW ABOUT HER? WHAT HAS SHE BEEN KEEPING FROM ME?
...
DUNGEON CITY

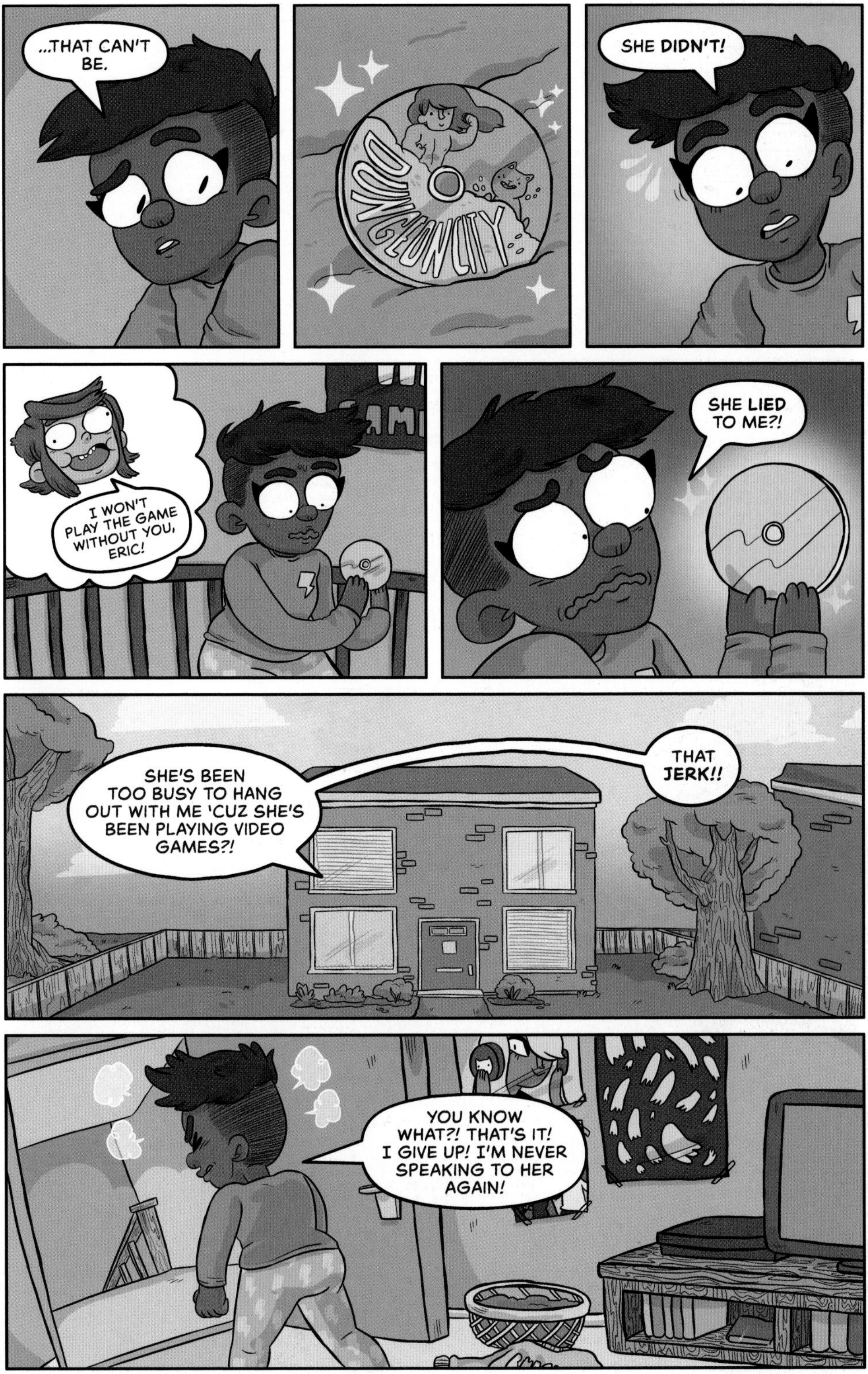
...THAT CAN'T BE.
DUNGEON CITY
SHE DIDN'T!
I WON'T PLAY THE GAME WITHOUT YOU, ERIC!
SHE LIED TO ME?!
SHE'S BEEN TOO BUSY TO HANG OUT WITH ME 'CUZ SHE'S BEEN PLAYING VIDEO GAMES?!
THAT JERK!!
YOU KNOW WHAT?! THAT'S IT! I GIVE UP! I'M NEVER SPEAKING TO HER AGAIN!

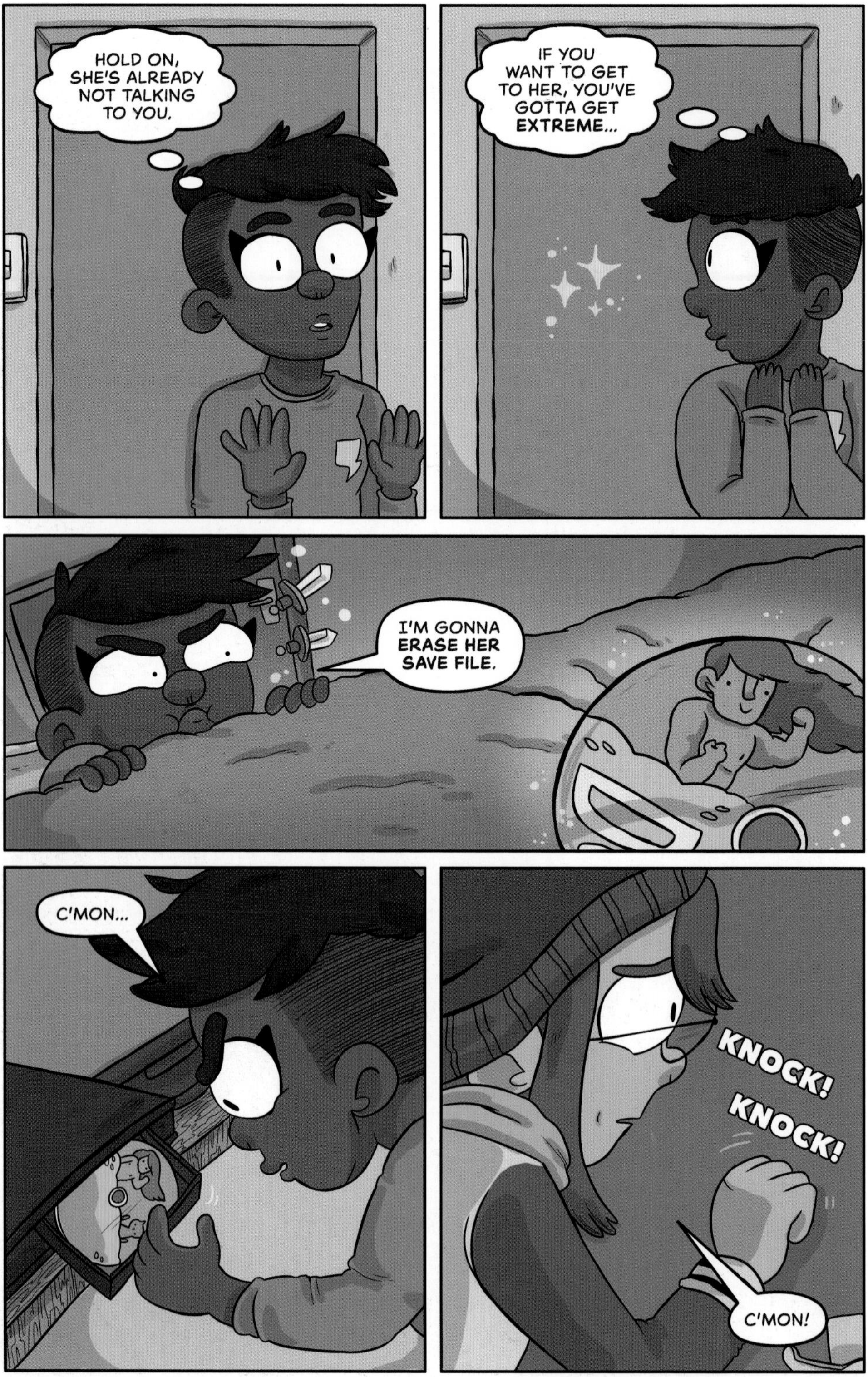
HOLD ON, SHE'S ALREADY NOT TALKING TO YOU.
IF YOU WANT TO GET TO HER, YOU'VE GOTTA GET EXTREME...
I'M GONNA ERASE HER SAVE FILE.
C'MON...
KNOCK!
KNOCK!
C'MON!

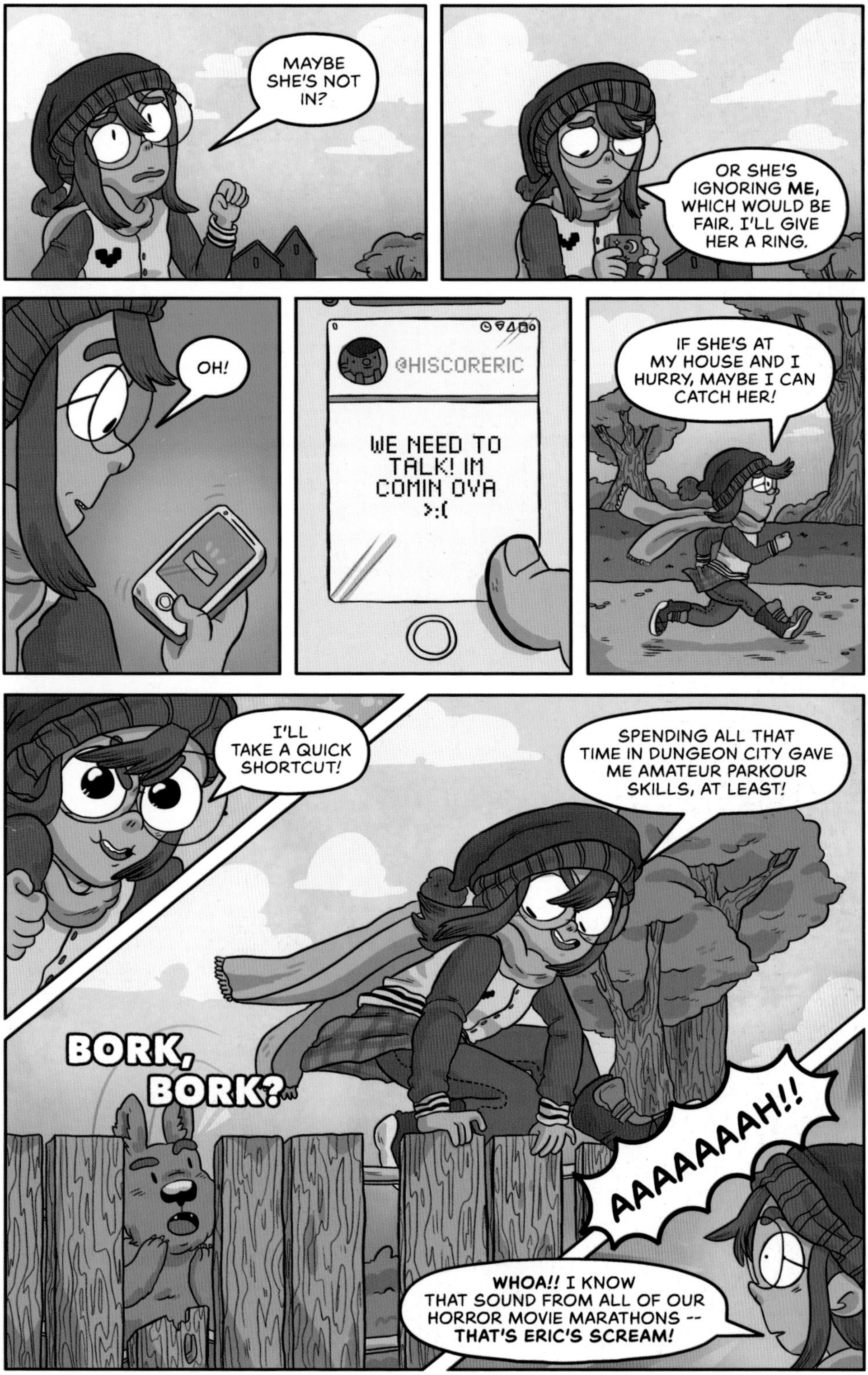
MAYBE SHE'S NOT IN?
OR SHE'S IGNORING **ME**, WHICH WOULD BE FAIR. I'LL GIVE HER A RING.
OH!
@HISCORERIC
WE NEED TO TALK! IM COMIN OVA >:(
IF SHE'S AT MY HOUSE AND I HURRY, MAYBE I CAN CATCH HER!
I'LL TAKE A QUICK SHORTCUT!
SPENDING ALL THAT TIME IN DUNGEON CITY GAVE ME AMATEUR PARKOUR SKILLS, AT LEAST!
BORK, BORK?
AAAAAAAH!!
WHOA!! I KNOW THAT SOUND FROM ALL OF OUR HORROR MOVIE MARATHONS -- **THAT'S ERIC'S SCREAM!**

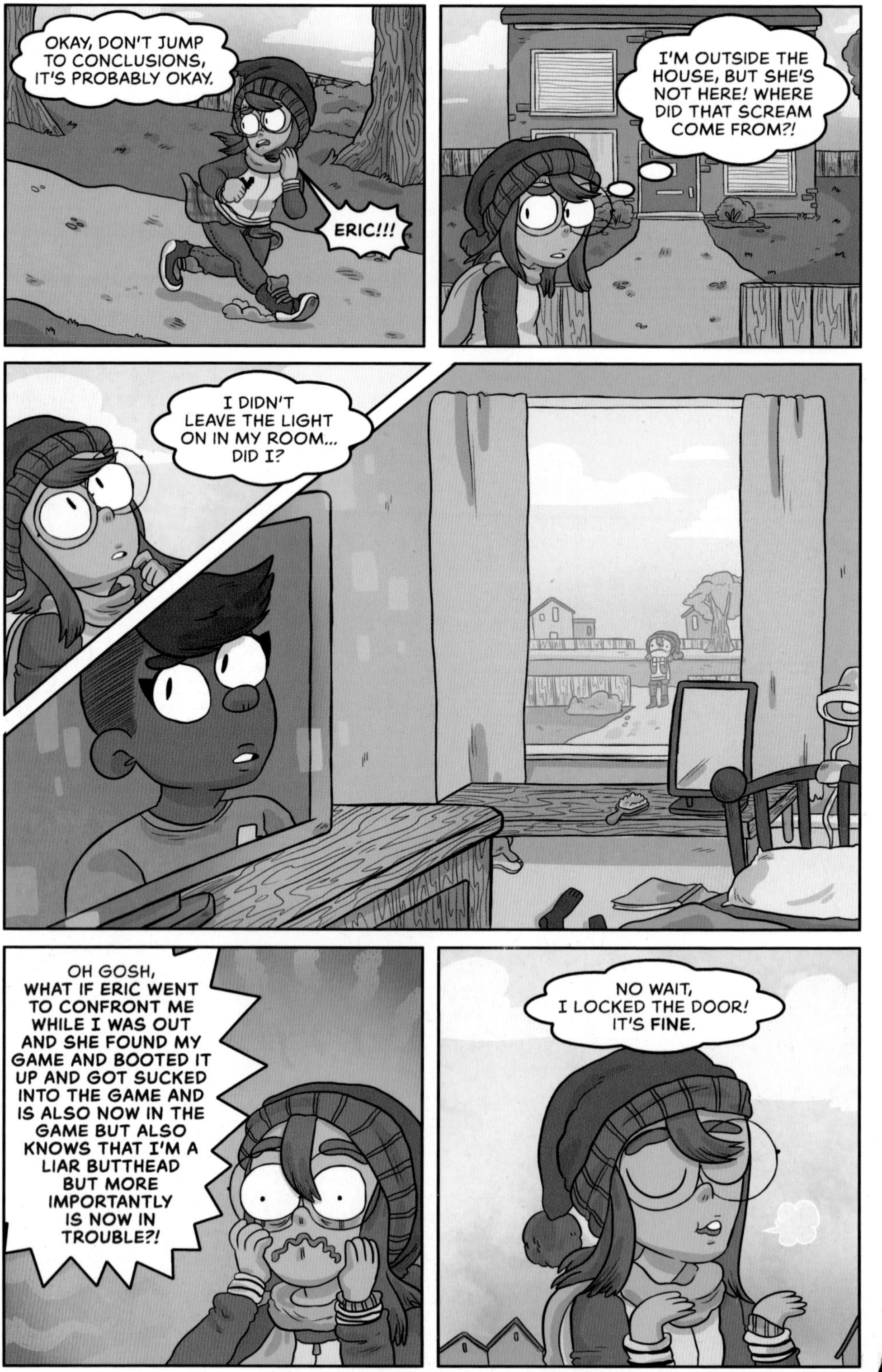
OKAY, DON'T JUMP TO CONCLUSIONS, IT'S PROBABLY OKAY.
ERIC!!!
I'M OUTSIDE THE HOUSE, BUT SHE'S NOT HERE! WHERE DID THAT SCREAM COME FROM?!
I DIDN'T LEAVE THE LIGHT ON IN MY ROOM... DID I?
OH GOSH, WHAT IF ERIC WENT TO CONFRONT ME WHILE I WAS OUT AND SHE FOUND MY GAME AND BOOTED IT UP AND GOT SUCKED INTO THE GAME AND IS ALSO NOW IN THE GAME BUT ALSO KNOWS THAT I'M A LIAR BUTTHEAD BUT MORE IMPORTANTLY IS NOW IN TROUBLE?!
NO WAIT, I LOCKED THE DOOR! IT'S FINE.

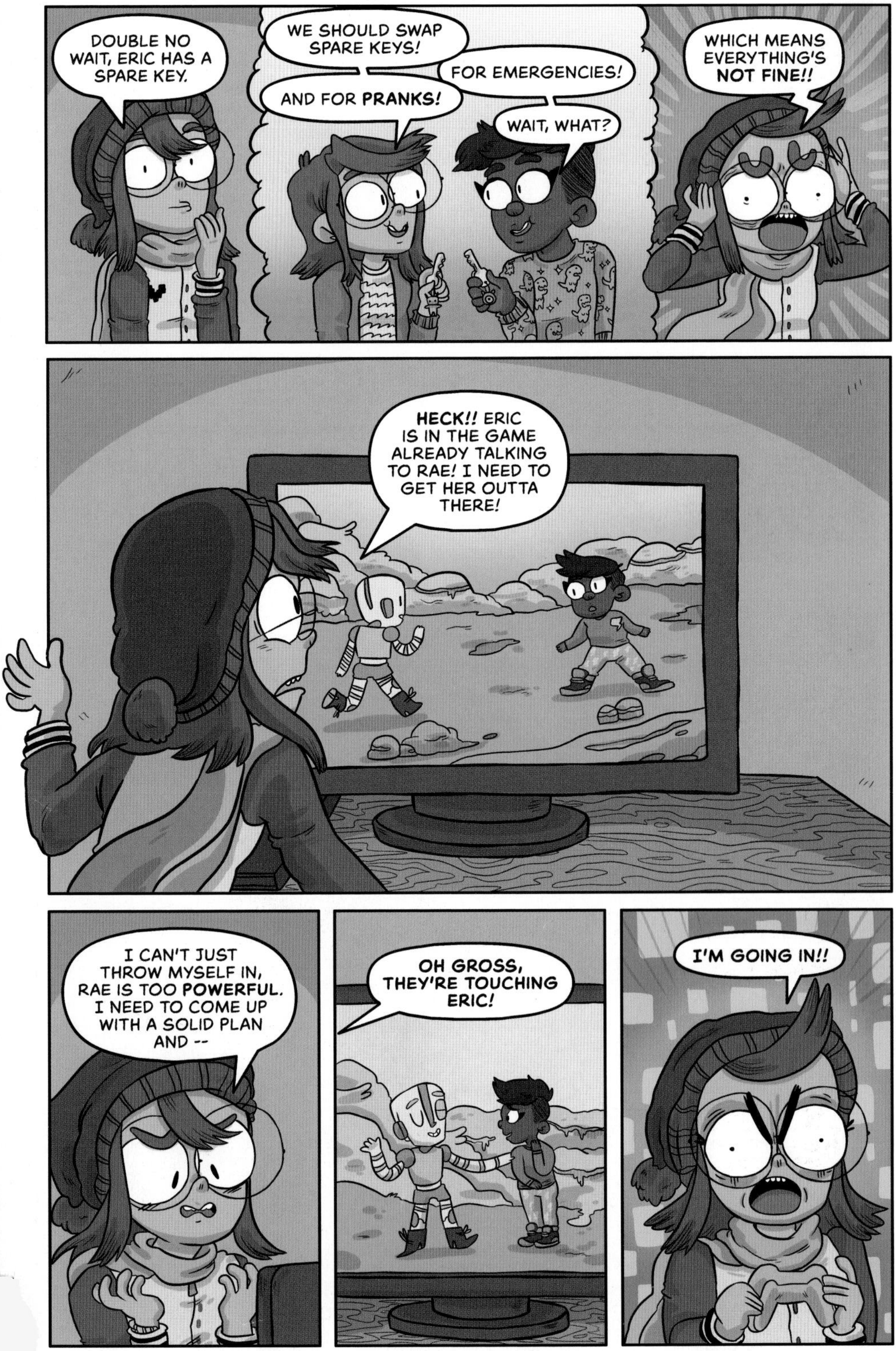
DOUBLE NO WAIT, ERIC HAS A SPARE KEY.
WE SHOULD SWAP SPARE KEYS!
FOR EMERGENCIES!
AND FOR **PRANKS!**
WAIT, WHAT?
WHICH MEANS EVERYTHING'S **NOT FINE!!**
HECK!! ERIC IS IN THE GAME ALREADY TALKING TO RAE! I NEED TO GET HER OUTTA THERE!
I CAN'T JUST THROW MYSELF IN, RAE IS TOO **POWERFUL.** I NEED TO COME UP WITH A SOLID PLAN AND --
OH GROSS, THEY'RE TOUCHING ERIC!
I'M GOING IN!!

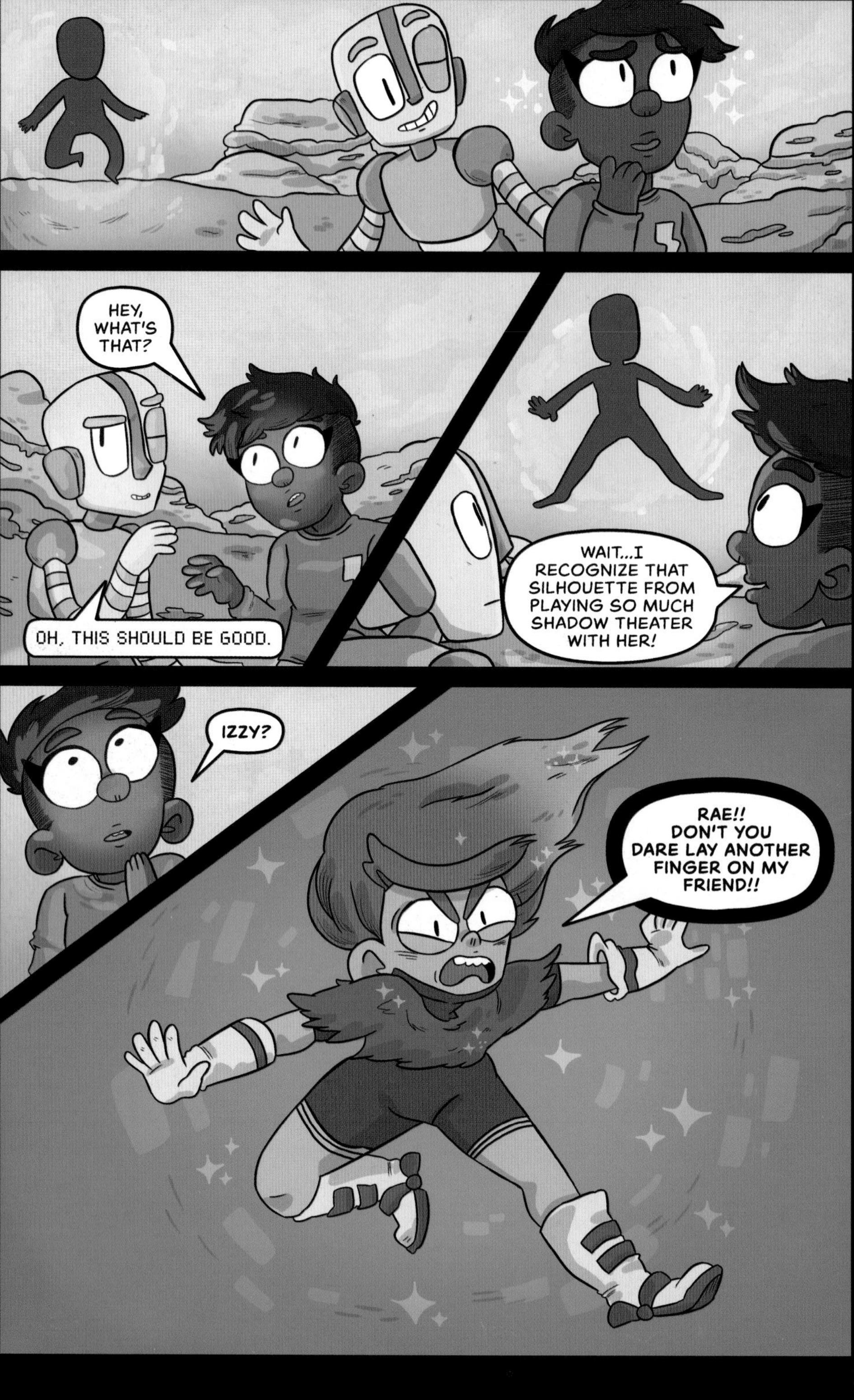
HEY, WHAT'S THAT?
OH, THIS SHOULD BE GOOD.
WAIT...I RECOGNIZE THAT SILHOUETTE FROM PLAYING SO MUCH SHADOW THEATER WITH HER!
IZZY?
RAE!! DON'T YOU DARE LAY ANOTHER FINGER ON MY FRIEND!!

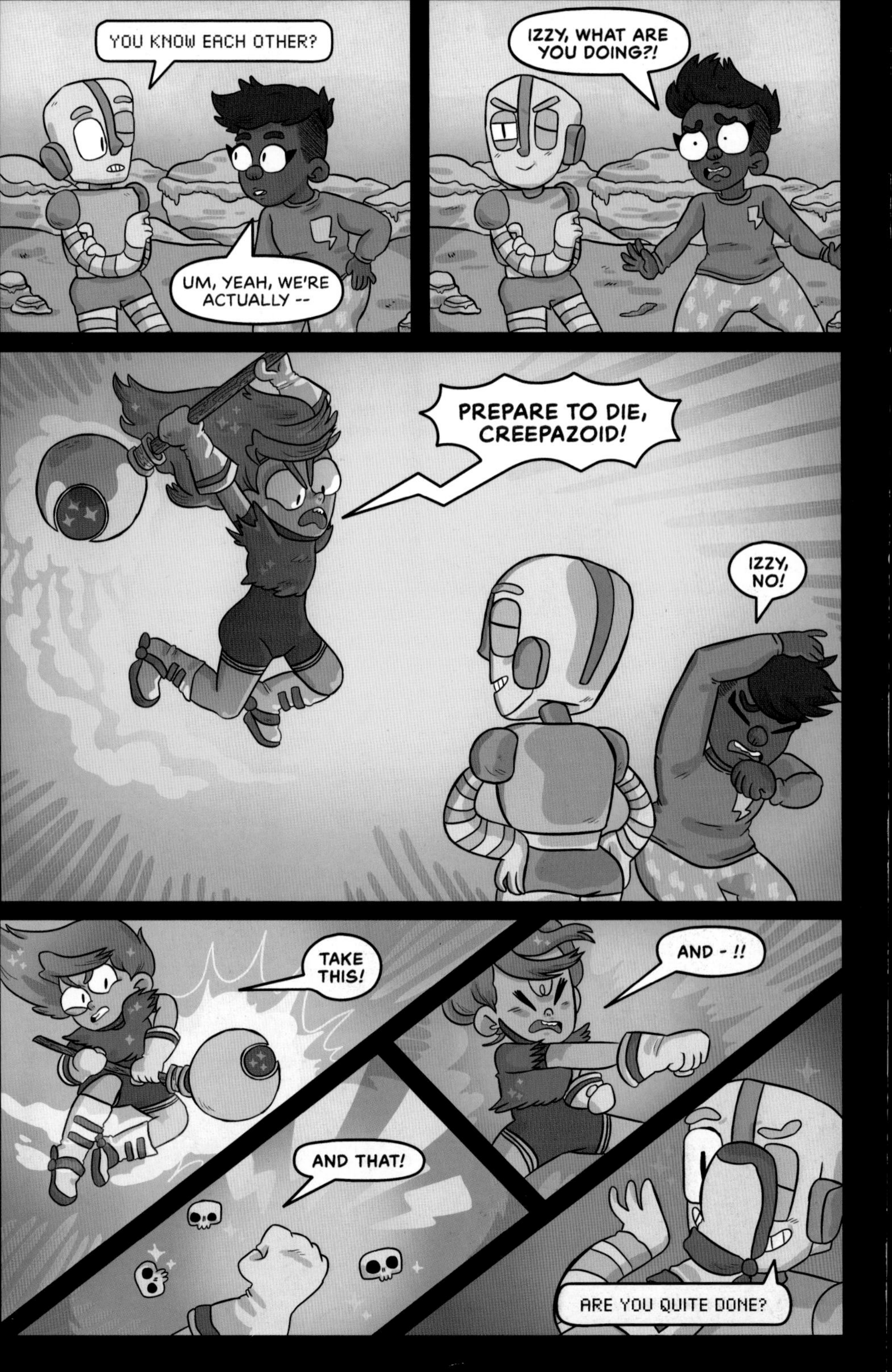
YOU KNOW EACH OTHER?
UM, YEAH, WE'RE ACTUALLY --
IZZY, WHAT ARE YOU DOING?!
PREPARE TO DIE, CREEPAZOID!
IZZY, NO!
TAKE THIS!
AND THAT!
AND - !!
ARE YOU QUITE DONE?

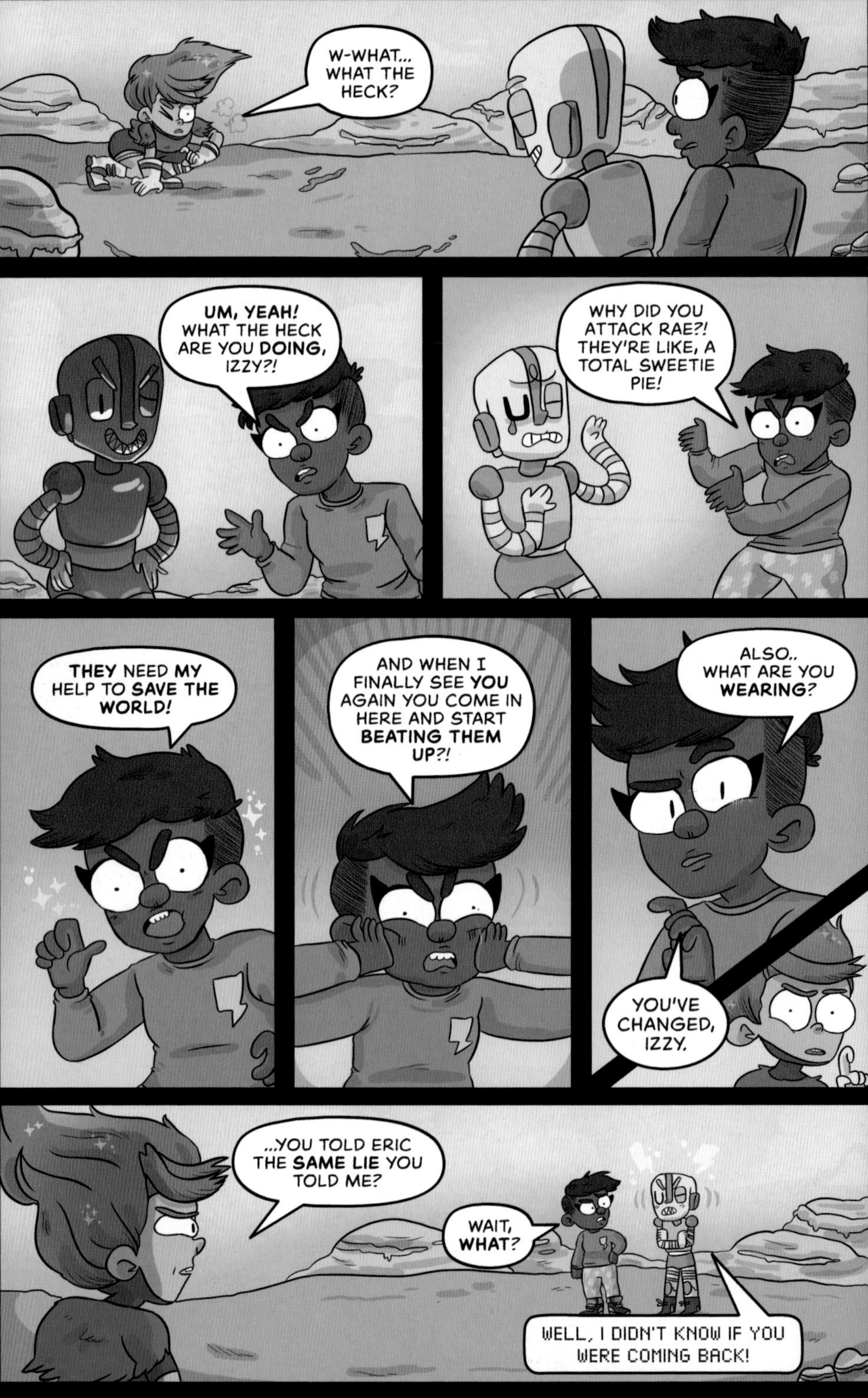
W-WHAT... WHAT THE HECK?
UM, YEAH! WHAT THE HECK ARE YOU DOING, IZZY?!
WHY DID YOU ATTACK RAE?! THEY'RE LIKE, A TOTAL SWEETIE PIE!
THEY NEED MY HELP TO SAVE THE WORLD!
AND WHEN I FINALLY SEE YOU AGAIN YOU COME IN HERE AND START BEATING THEM UP?!
ALSO.. WHAT ARE YOU WEARING?
YOU'VE CHANGED, IZZY.
...YOU TOLD ERIC THE SAME LIE YOU TOLD ME?
WAIT, WHAT?
WELL, I DIDN'T KNOW IF YOU WERE COMING BACK!

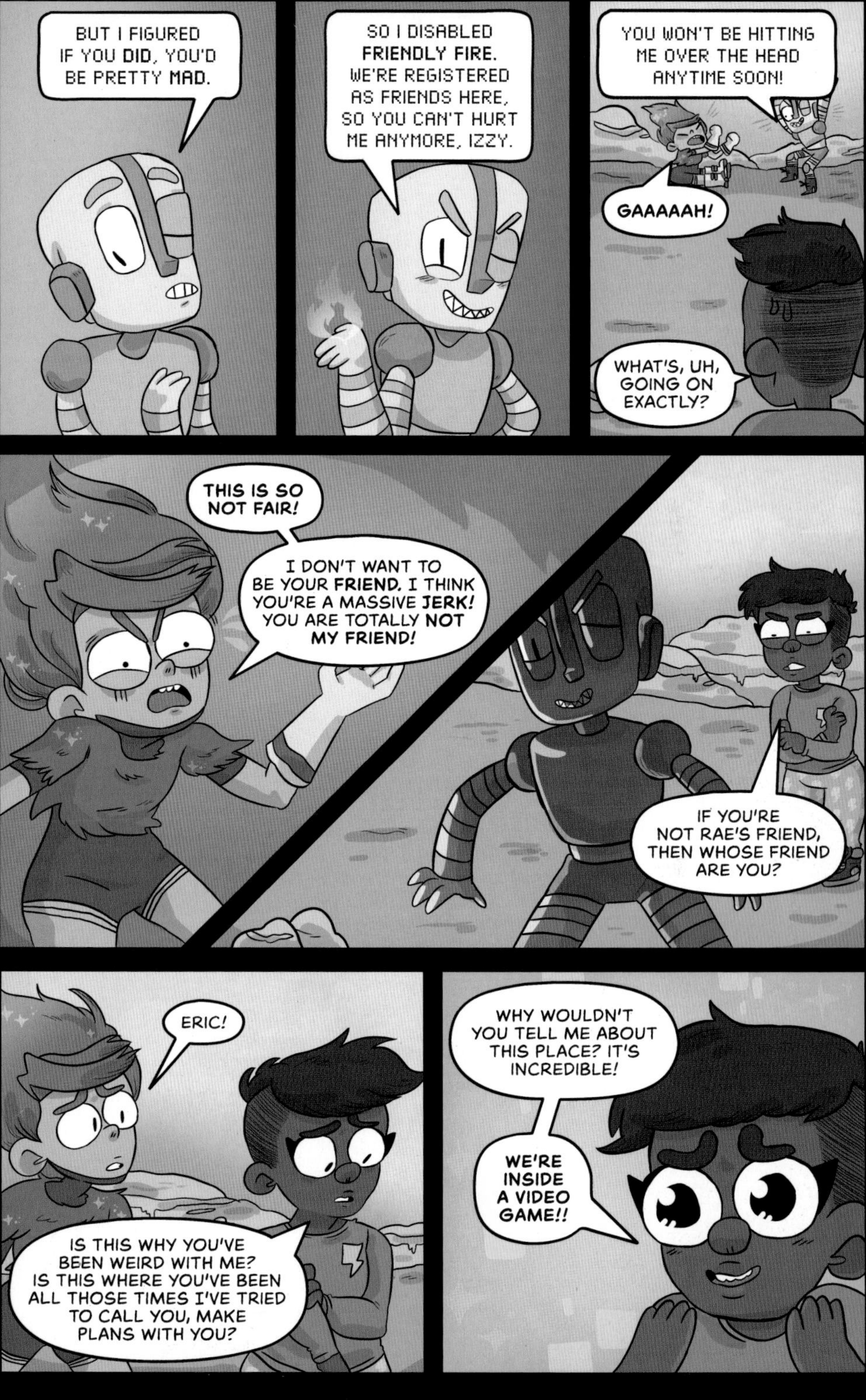

BUT I FIGURED IF YOU DID, YOU'D BE PRETTY MAD.
SO I DISABLED FRIENDLY FIRE. WE'RE REGISTERED AS FRIENDS HERE, SO YOU CAN'T HURT ME ANYMORE, IZZY.
YOU WON'T BE HITTING ME OVER THE HEAD ANYTIME SOON!
GAAAAAH!
WHAT'S, UH, GOING ON EXACTLY?
THIS IS SO NOT FAIR!
I DON'T WANT TO BE YOUR FRIEND. I THINK YOU'RE A MASSIVE JERK! YOU ARE TOTALLY NOT MY FRIEND!
IF YOU'RE NOT RAE'S FRIEND, THEN WHOSE FRIEND ARE YOU?
ERIC!
IS THIS WHY YOU'VE BEEN WEIRD WITH ME? IS THIS WHERE YOU'VE BEEN ALL THOSE TIMES I'VE TRIED TO CALL YOU, MAKE PLANS WITH YOU?
WHY WOULDN'T YOU TELL ME ABOUT THIS PLACE? IT'S INCREDIBLE!
WE'RE INSIDE A VIDEO GAME!!

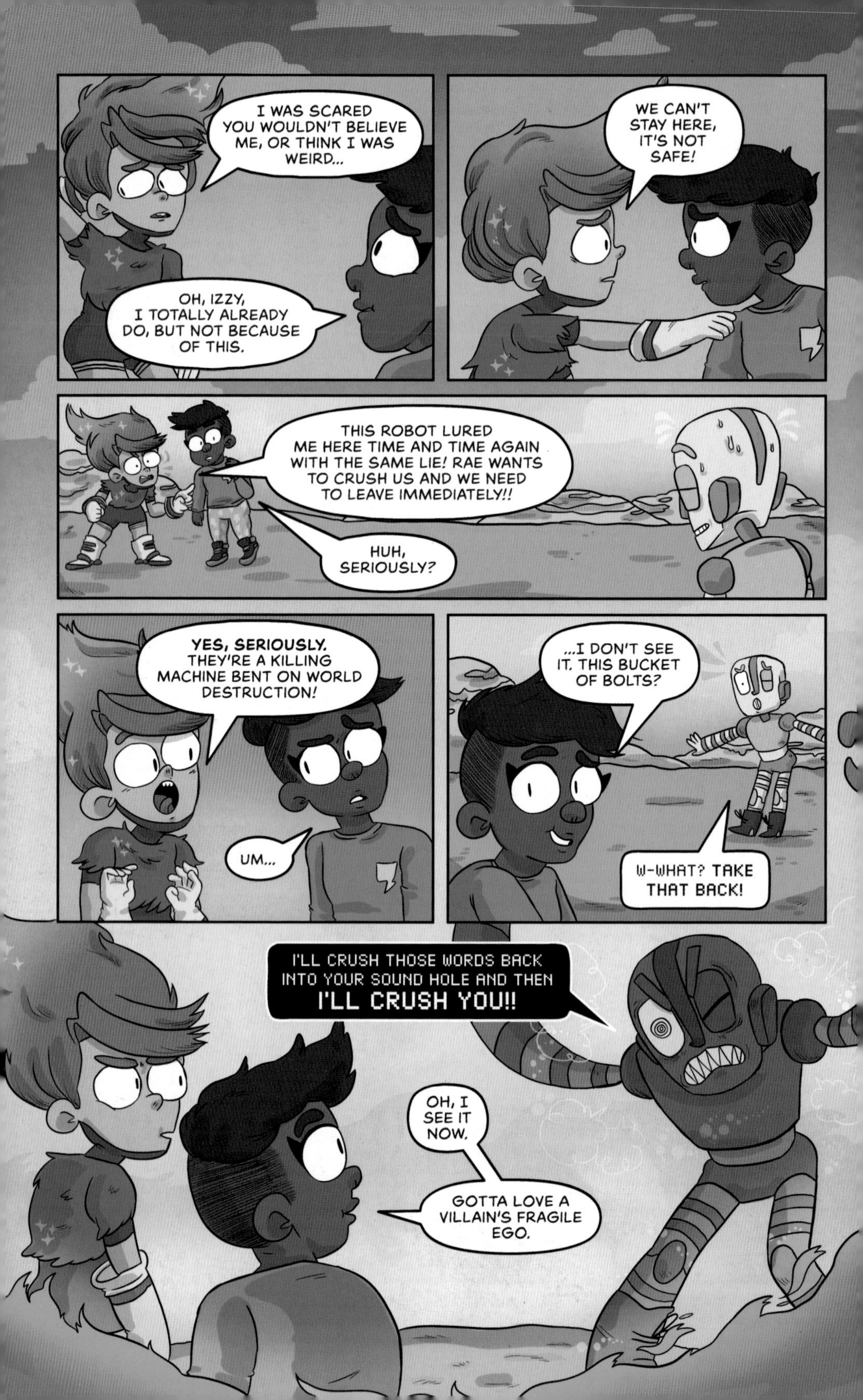
I WAS SCARED YOU WOULDN'T BELIEVE ME, OR THINK I WAS WEIRD...
OH, IZZY, I TOTALLY ALREADY DO, BUT NOT BECAUSE OF THIS.
WE CAN'T STAY HERE, IT'S NOT SAFE!
THIS ROBOT LURED ME HERE TIME AND TIME AGAIN WITH THE SAME LIE! RAE WANTS TO CRUSH US AND WE NEED TO LEAVE IMMEDIATELY!!
HUH, SERIOUSLY?
YES, SERIOUSLY. THEY'RE A KILLING MACHINE BENT ON WORLD DESTRUCTION!
UM...
...I DON'T SEE IT. THIS BUCKET OF BOLTS?
W-WHAT? TAKE THAT BACK!
I'LL CRUSH THOSE WORDS BACK INTO YOUR SOUND HOLE AND THEN I'LL CRUSH YOU!!
OH, I SEE IT NOW.
GOTTA LOVE A VILLAIN'S FRAGILE EGO.

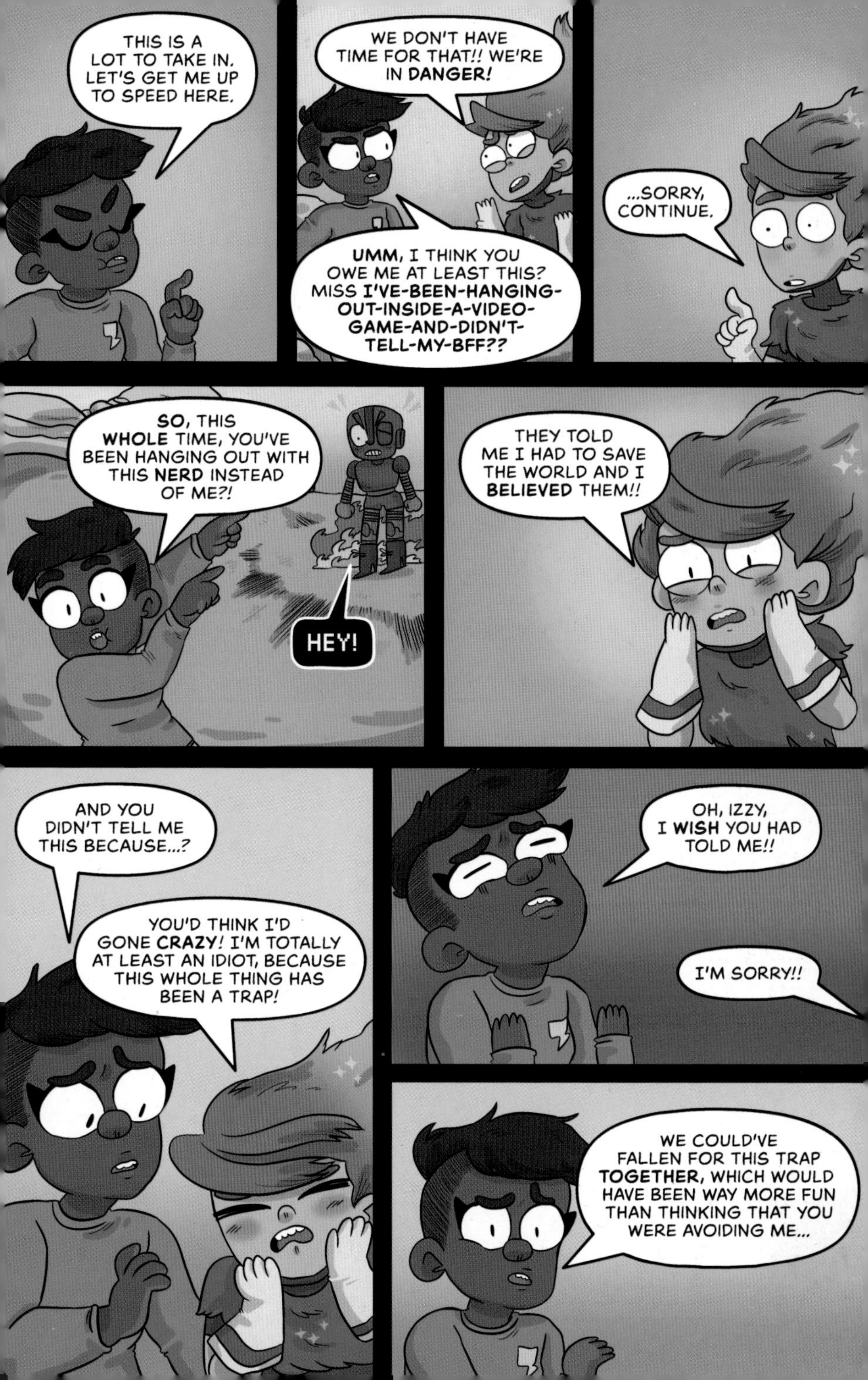
THIS IS A LOT TO TAKE IN. LET'S GET ME UP TO SPEED HERE.
WE DON'T HAVE TIME FOR THAT!! WE'RE IN DANGER!
UMM, I THINK YOU OWE ME AT LEAST THIS? MISS I'VE-BEEN-HANGING-OUT-INSIDE-A-VIDEO-GAME-AND-DIDN'T-TELL-MY-BFF??
...SORRY, CONTINUE.
SO, THIS WHOLE TIME, YOU'VE BEEN HANGING OUT WITH THIS NERD INSTEAD OF ME?!
HEY!
THEY TOLD ME I HAD TO SAVE THE WORLD AND I BELIEVED THEM!!
AND YOU DIDN'T TELL ME THIS BECAUSE...?
YOU'D THINK I'D GONE CRAZY! I'M TOTALLY AT LEAST AN IDIOT, BECAUSE THIS WHOLE THING HAS BEEN A TRAP!
OH, IZZY, I WISH YOU HAD TOLD ME!!
I'M SORRY!!
WE COULD'VE FALLEN FOR THIS TRAP TOGETHER, WHICH WOULD HAVE BEEN WAY MORE FUN THAN THINKING THAT YOU WERE AVOIDING ME...

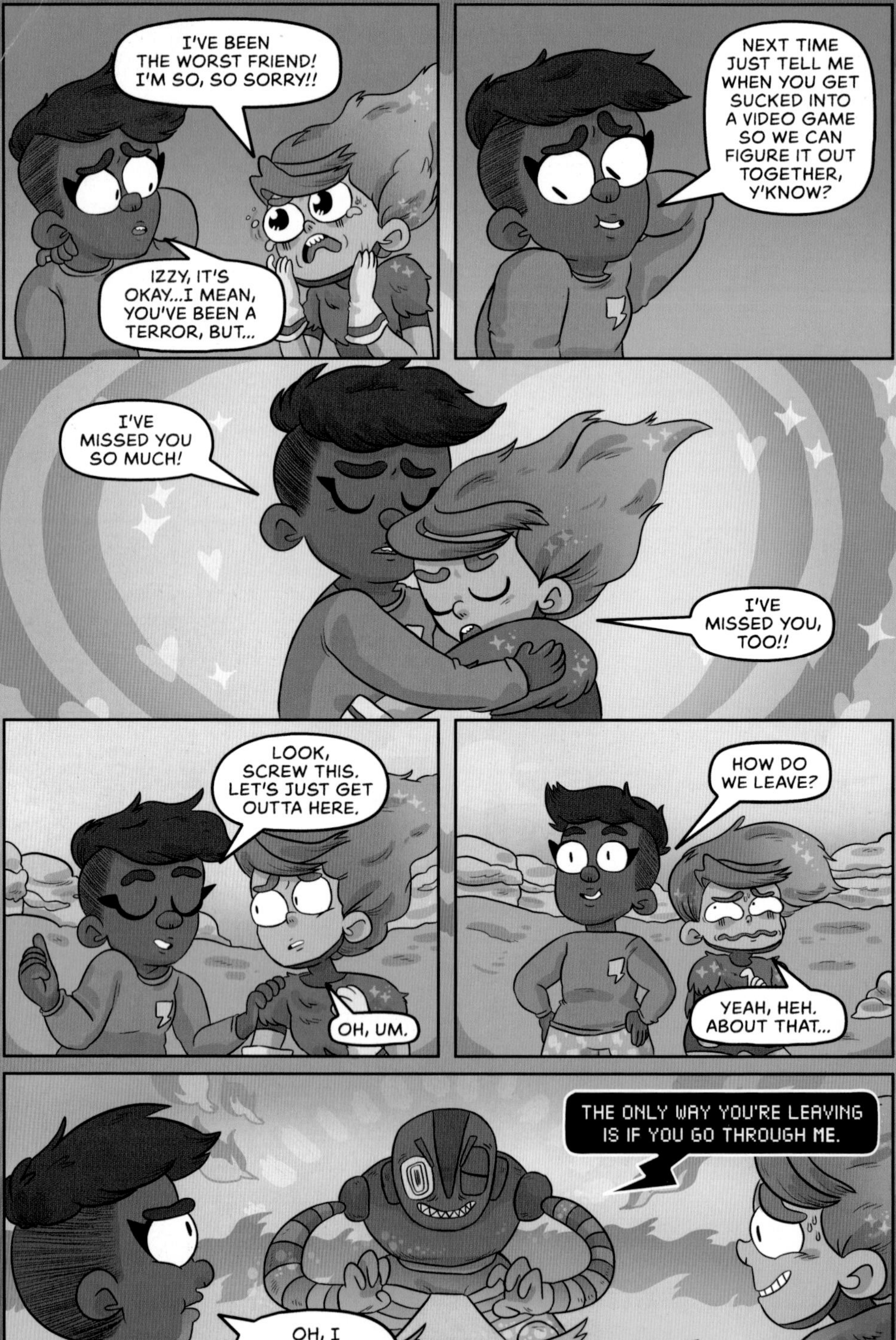
I'VE BEEN THE WORST FRIEND! I'M SO, SO SORRY!!
IZZY, IT'S OKAY...I MEAN, YOU'VE BEEN A TERROR, BUT...
NEXT TIME JUST TELL ME WHEN YOU GET SUCKED INTO A VIDEO GAME SO WE CAN FIGURE IT OUT TOGETHER, Y'KNOW?
I'VE MISSED YOU SO MUCH!
I'VE MISSED YOU, TOO!!
LOOK, SCREW THIS. LET'S JUST GET OUTTA HERE.
OH, UM.
HOW DO WE LEAVE?
YEAH, HEH. ABOUT THAT...
THE ONLY WAY YOU'RE LEAVING IS IF YOU GO THROUGH ME.
OH, I FORGOT THEY WERE STILL HERE.

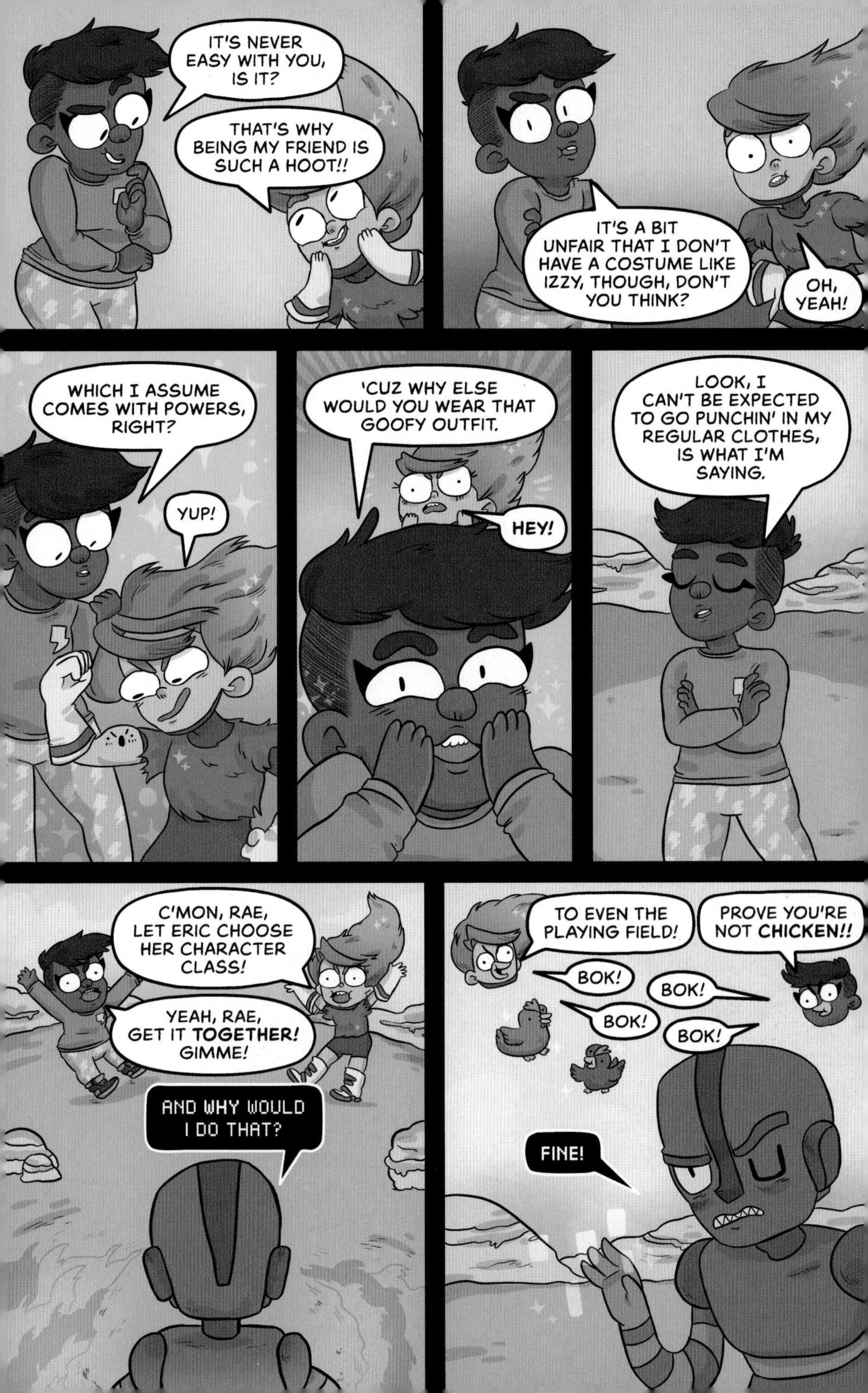
IT'S NEVER EASY WITH YOU, IS IT?
THAT'S WHY BEING MY FRIEND IS SUCH A HOOT!!
IT'S A BIT UNFAIR THAT I DON'T HAVE A COSTUME LIKE IZZY, THOUGH, DON'T YOU THINK?
OH, YEAH!
WHICH I ASSUME COMES WITH POWERS, RIGHT?
YUP!
'CUZ WHY ELSE WOULD YOU WEAR THAT GOOFY OUTFIT.
HEY!
LOOK, I CAN'T BE EXPECTED TO GO PUNCHIN' IN MY REGULAR CLOTHES, IS WHAT I'M SAYING.
C'MON, RAE, LET ERIC CHOOSE HER CHARACTER CLASS!
YEAH, RAE, GET IT **TOGETHER!** GIMME!
AND WHY WOULD I DO THAT?
TO EVEN THE PLAYING FIELD!
PROVE YOU'RE NOT **CHICKEN!!**
BOK!
BOK!
BOK!
BOK!
FINE!

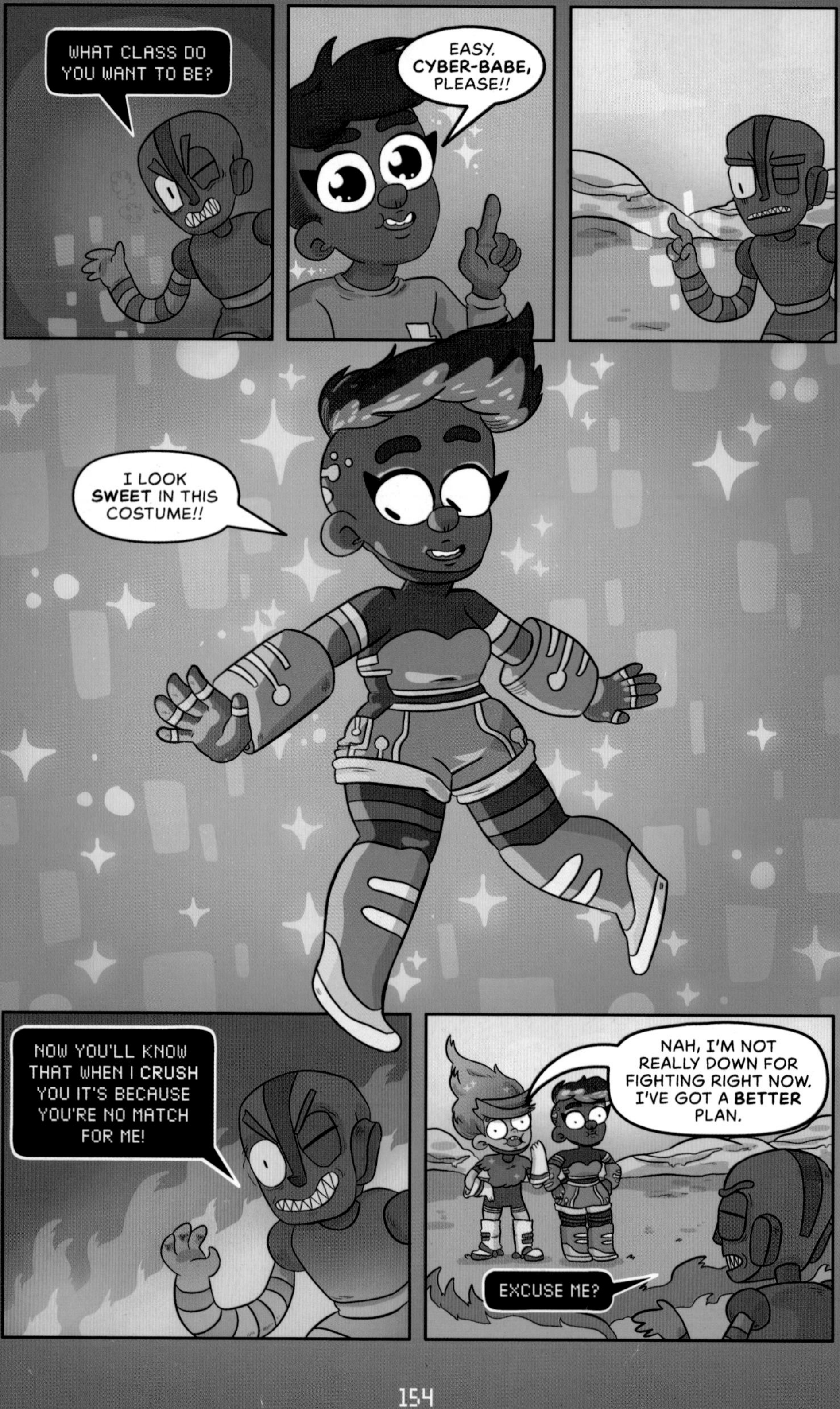
WHAT CLASS DO YOU WANT TO BE?
EASY. CYBER-BABE, PLEASE!!
I LOOK SWEET IN THIS COSTUME!!
NOW YOU'LL KNOW THAT WHEN I CRUSH YOU IT'S BECAUSE YOU'RE NO MATCH FOR ME!
NAH, I'M NOT REALLY DOWN FOR FIGHTING RIGHT NOW. I'VE GOT A BETTER PLAN.
EXCUSE ME?

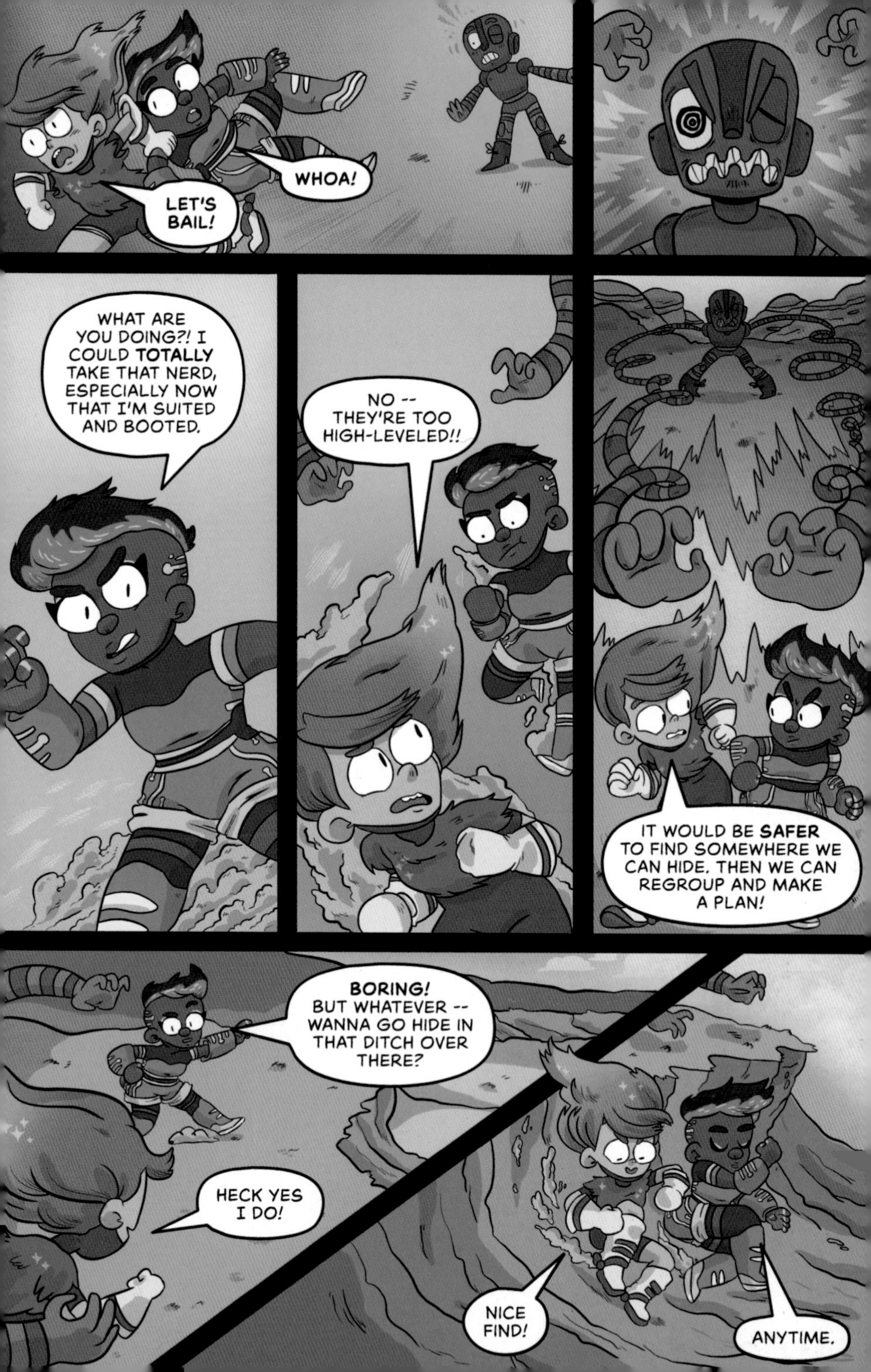
LET'S BAIL!
WHOA!
WHAT ARE YOU DOING?! I COULD **TOTALLY** TAKE THAT NERD, ESPECIALLY NOW THAT I'M SUITED AND BOOTED.
NO -- THEY'RE TOO HIGH-LEVELED!!
IT WOULD BE **SAFER** TO FIND SOMEWHERE WE CAN HIDE. THEN WE CAN REGROUP AND MAKE A PLAN!
BORING! BUT WHATEVER -- WANNA GO HIDE IN THAT DITCH OVER THERE?
HECK YES I DO!
NICE FIND!
ANYTIME.

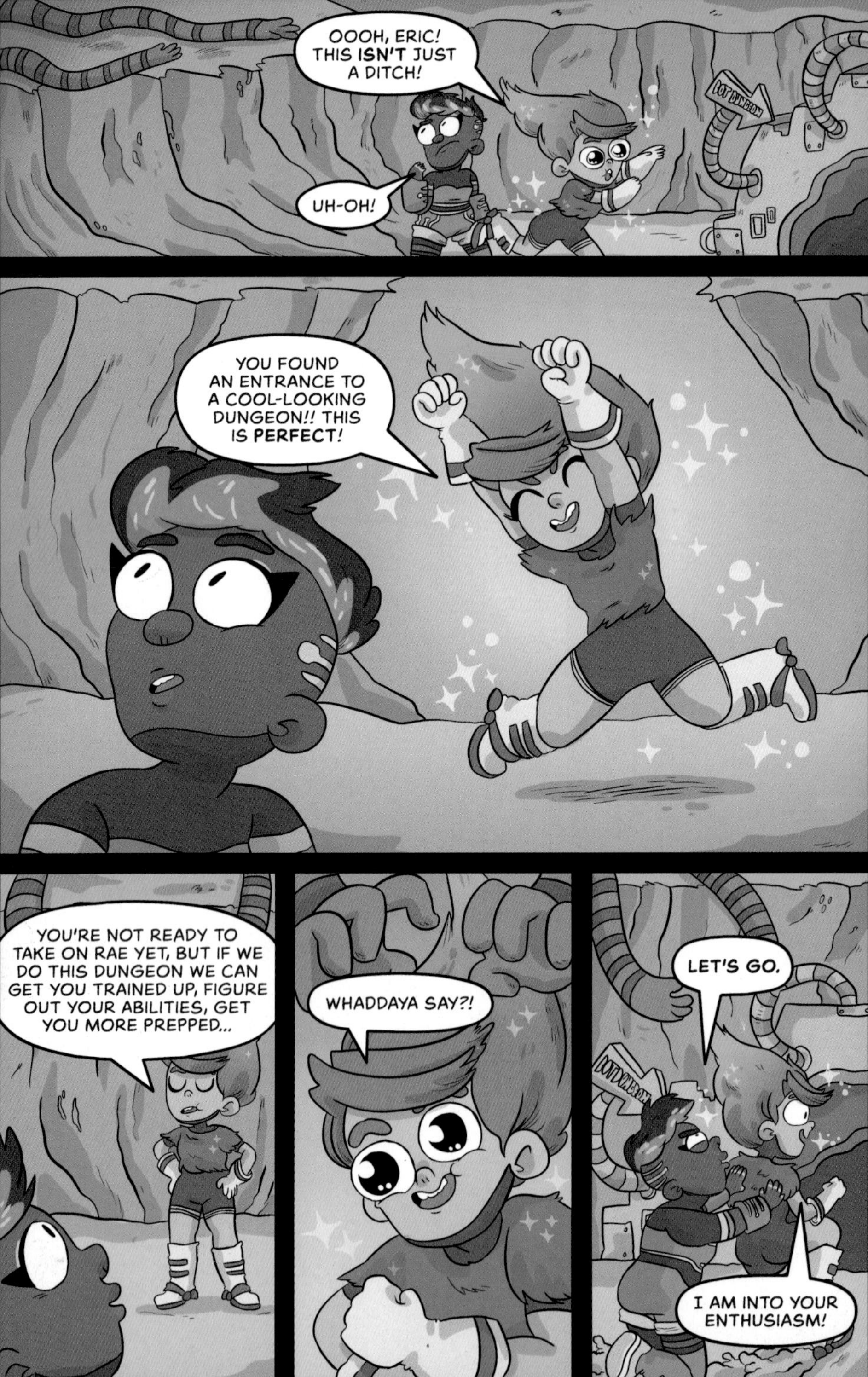

OOOH, ERIC! THIS ISN'T JUST A DITCH!
UH-OH!
DOT DUNGEON
YOU FOUND AN ENTRANCE TO A COOL-LOOKING DUNGEON!! THIS IS PERFECT!
YOU'RE NOT READY TO TAKE ON RAE YET, BUT IF WE DO THIS DUNGEON WE CAN GET YOU TRAINED UP, FIGURE OUT YOUR ABILITIES, GET YOU MORE PREPPED...
WHADDAYA SAY?!
LET'S GO.
I AM INTO YOUR ENTHUSIASM!

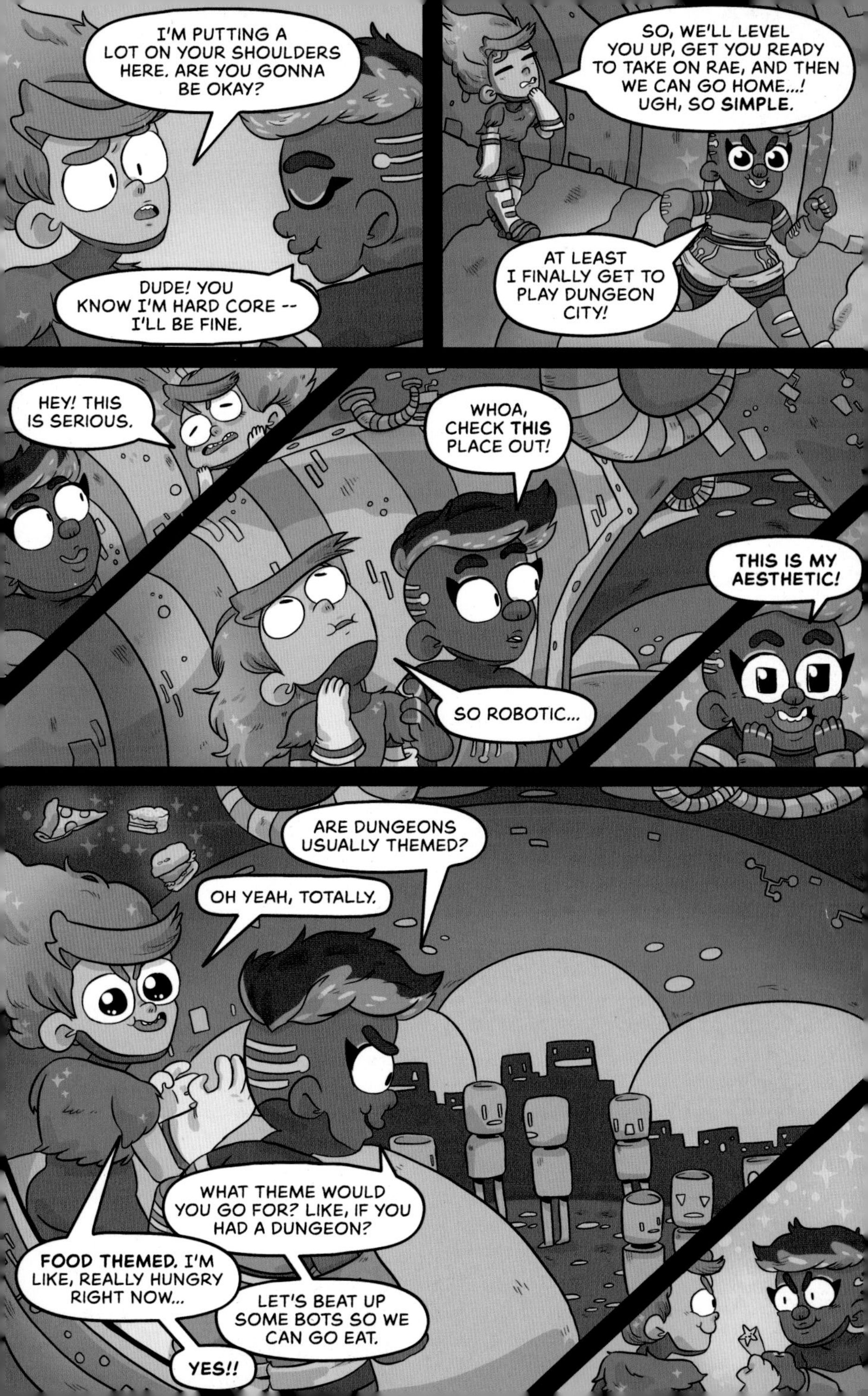
I'M PUTTING A LOT ON YOUR SHOULDERS HERE. ARE YOU GONNA BE OKAY?
DUDE! YOU KNOW I'M HARD CORE -- I'LL BE FINE.
SO, WE'LL LEVEL YOU UP, GET YOU READY TO TAKE ON RAE, AND THEN WE CAN GO HOME...! UGH, SO SIMPLE.
AT LEAST I FINALLY GET TO PLAY DUNGEON CITY!
HEY! THIS IS SERIOUS.
WHOA, CHECK THIS PLACE OUT!
SO ROBOTIC...
THIS IS MY AESTHETIC!
ARE DUNGEONS USUALLY THEMED?
OH YEAH, TOTALLY.
WHAT THEME WOULD YOU GO FOR? LIKE, IF YOU HAD A DUNGEON?
FOOD THEMED. I'M LIKE, REALLY HUNGRY RIGHT NOW...
LET'S BEAT UP SOME BOTS SO WE CAN GO EAT.
YES!!

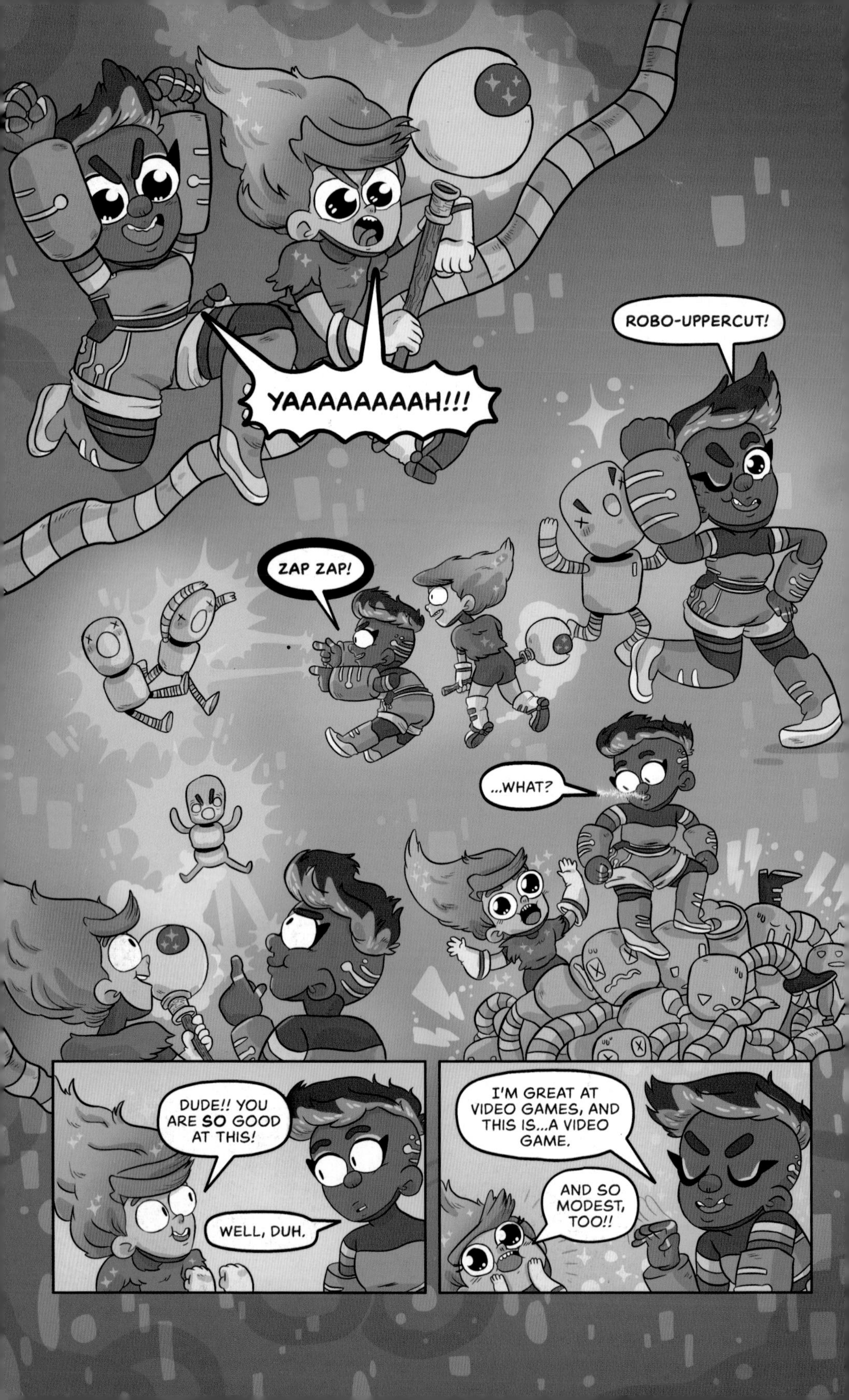
YAAAAAAAAH!!!
ROBO-UPPERCUT!
ZAP ZAP!
...WHAT?
DUDE!! YOU ARE **SO** GOOD AT THIS!
WELL, DUH.
I'M GREAT AT VIDEO GAMES, AND THIS IS...A VIDEO GAME.
AND SO MODEST, TOO!!

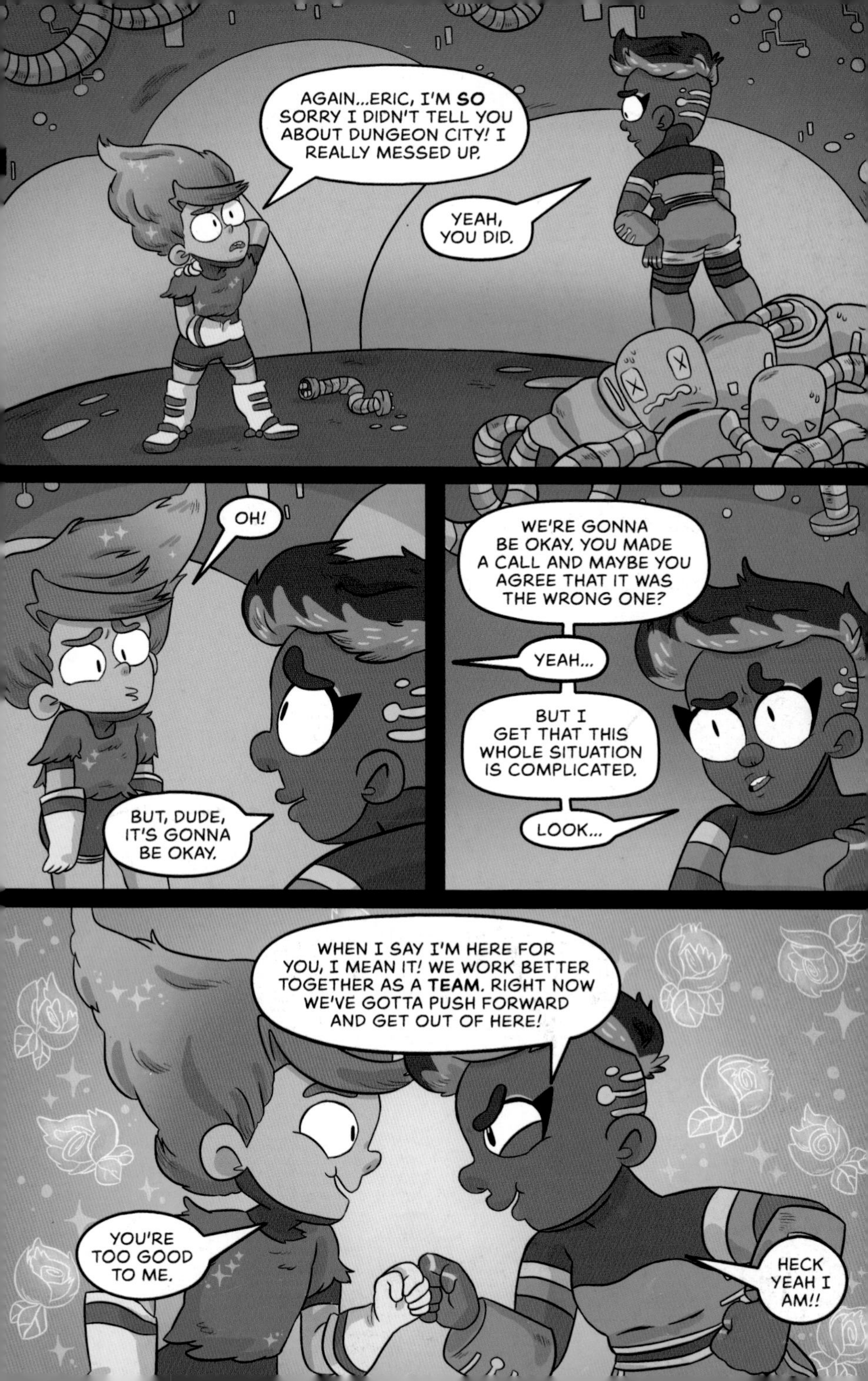
AGAIN...ERIC, I'M **SO** SORRY I DIDN'T TELL YOU ABOUT DUNGEON CITY! I REALLY MESSED UP.
YEAH, YOU DID.
OH!
BUT, DUDE, IT'S GONNA BE OKAY.
WE'RE GONNA BE OKAY. YOU MADE A CALL AND MAYBE YOU AGREE THAT IT WAS THE WRONG ONE?
YEAH...
BUT I GET THAT THIS WHOLE SITUATION IS COMPLICATED.
LOOK...
WHEN I SAY I'M HERE FOR YOU, I MEAN IT! WE WORK BETTER TOGETHER AS A **TEAM**. RIGHT NOW WE'VE GOTTA PUSH FORWARD AND GET OUT OF HERE!
YOU'RE TOO GOOD TO ME.
HECK YEAH I AM!!

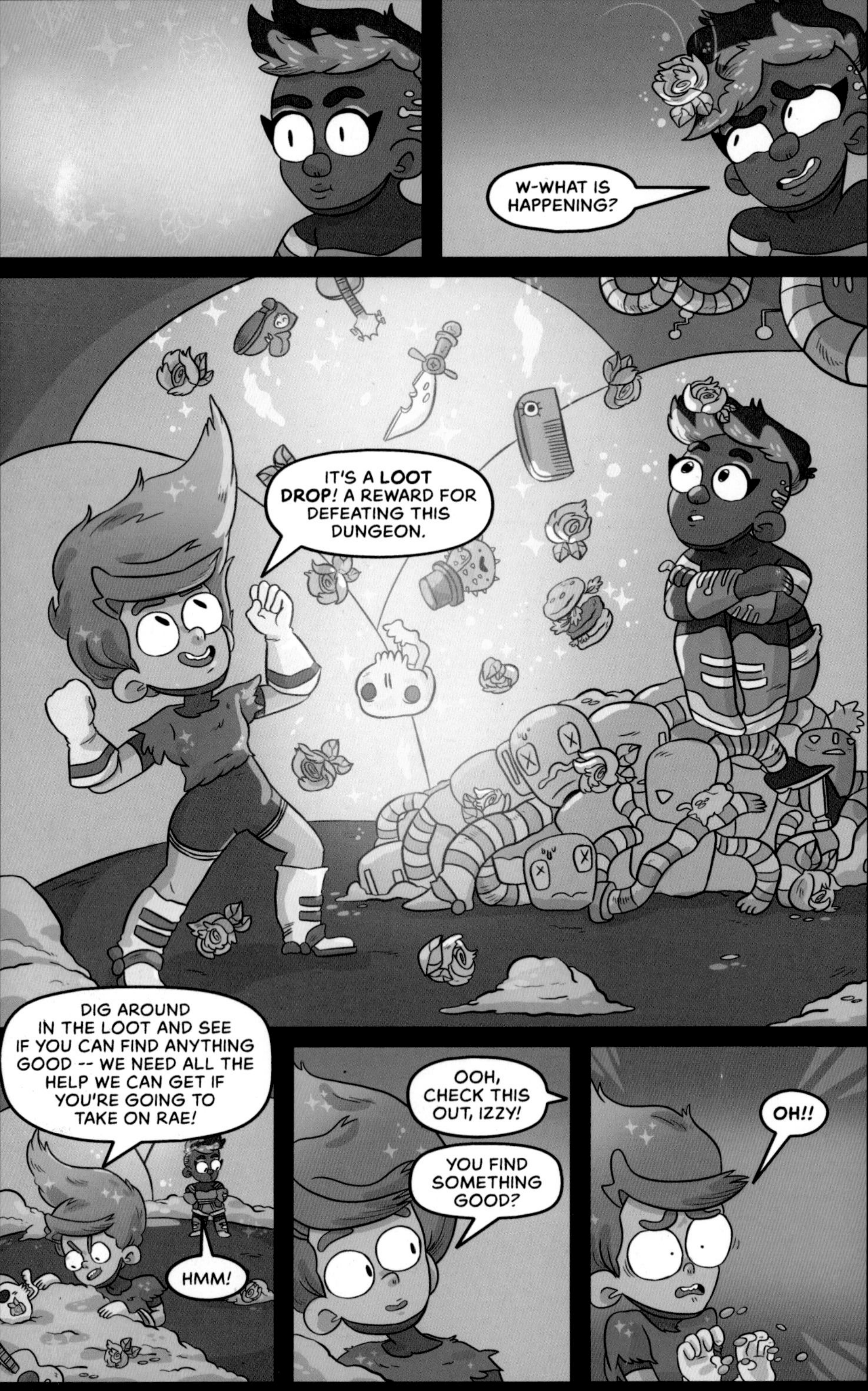
W-WHAT IS HAPPENING?
IT'S A **LOOT DROP**! A REWARD FOR DEFEATING THIS DUNGEON.
DIG AROUND IN THE LOOT AND SEE IF YOU CAN FIND ANYTHING GOOD -- WE NEED ALL THE HELP WE CAN GET IF YOU'RE GOING TO TAKE ON RAE!
HMM!
OOH, CHECK THIS OUT, IZZY!
YOU FIND SOMETHING GOOD?
OH!!

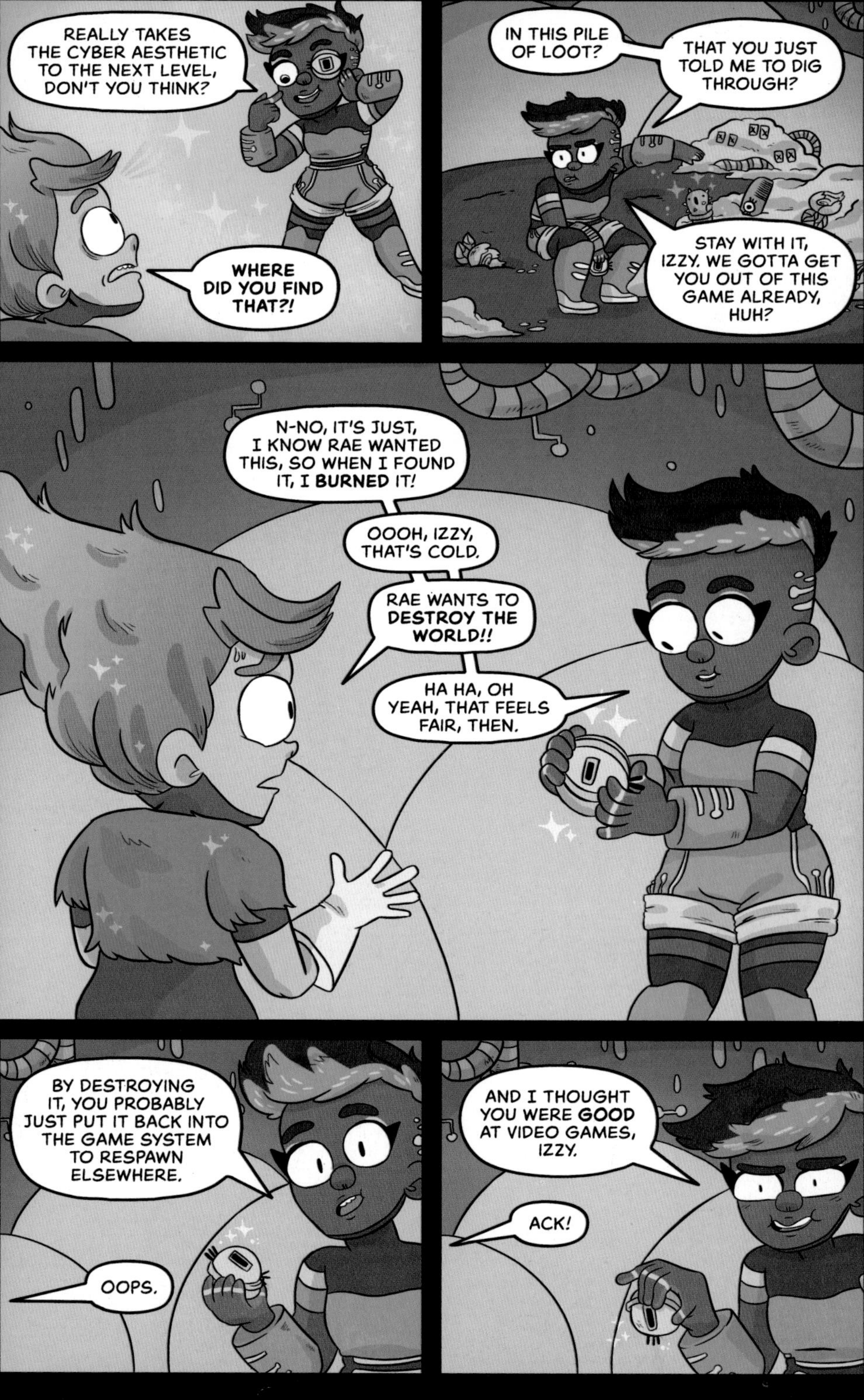
REALLY TAKES THE CYBER AESTHETIC TO THE NEXT LEVEL, DON'T YOU THINK?
WHERE DID YOU FIND THAT?!
IN THIS PILE OF LOOT?
THAT YOU JUST TOLD ME TO DIG THROUGH?
STAY WITH IT, IZZY. WE GOTTA GET YOU OUT OF THIS GAME ALREADY, HUH?
N-NO, IT'S JUST, I KNOW RAE WANTED THIS, SO WHEN I FOUND IT, I BURNED IT!
OOOH, IZZY, THAT'S COLD.
RAE WANTS TO DESTROY THE WORLD!!
HA HA, OH YEAH, THAT FEELS FAIR, THEN.
BY DESTROYING IT, YOU PROBABLY JUST PUT IT BACK INTO THE GAME SYSTEM TO RESPAWN ELSEWHERE.
OOPS.
AND I THOUGHT YOU WERE GOOD AT VIDEO GAMES, IZZY.
ACK!

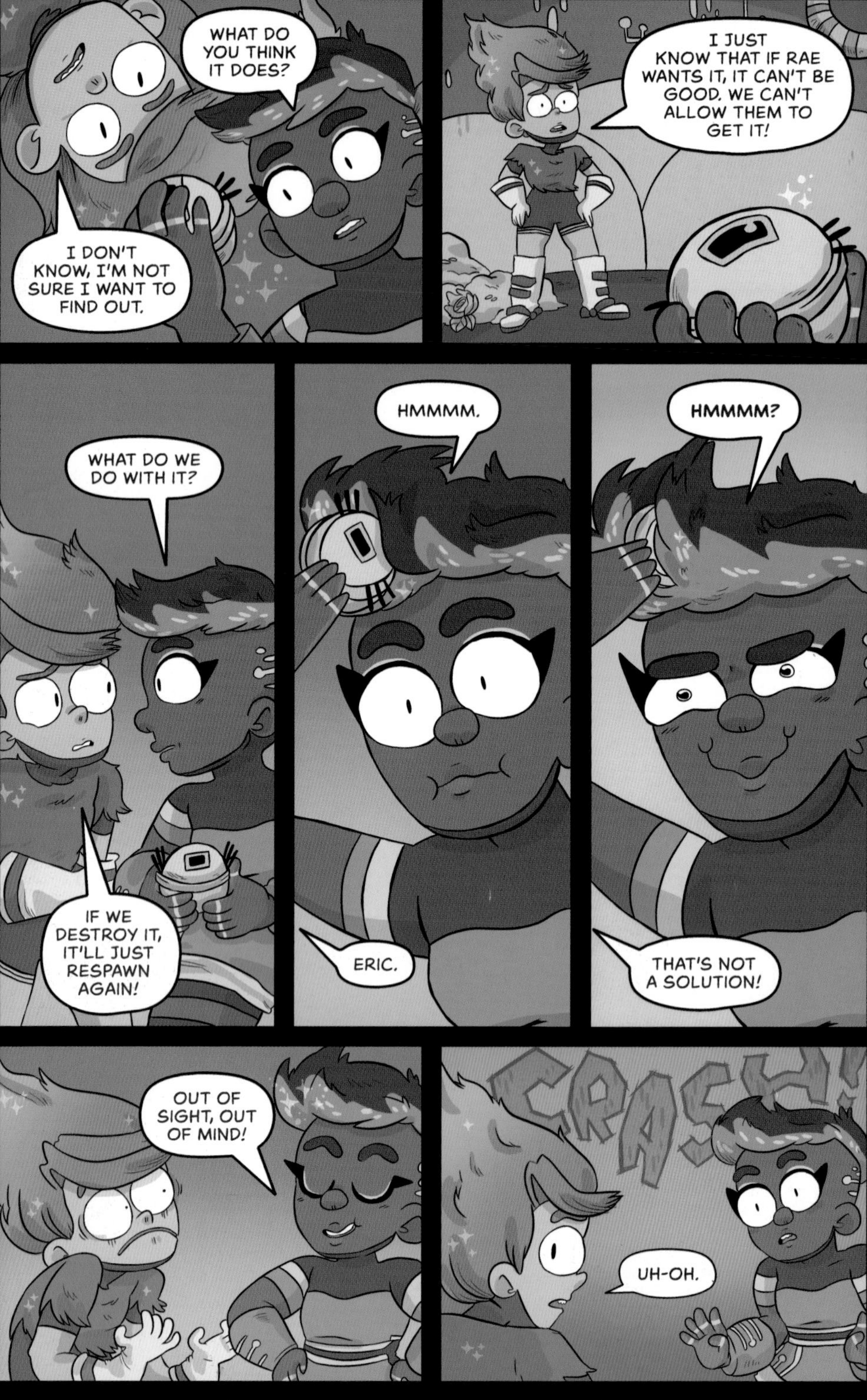
WHAT DO YOU THINK IT DOES?
I DON'T KNOW, I'M NOT SURE I WANT TO FIND OUT.
I JUST KNOW THAT IF RAE WANTS IT, IT CAN'T BE GOOD. WE CAN'T ALLOW THEM TO GET IT!
WHAT DO WE DO WITH IT?
IF WE DESTROY IT, IT'LL JUST RESPAWN AGAIN!
HMMMM.
ERIC.
HMMMM?
THAT'S NOT A SOLUTION!
OUT OF SIGHT, OUT OF MIND!
UH-OH.

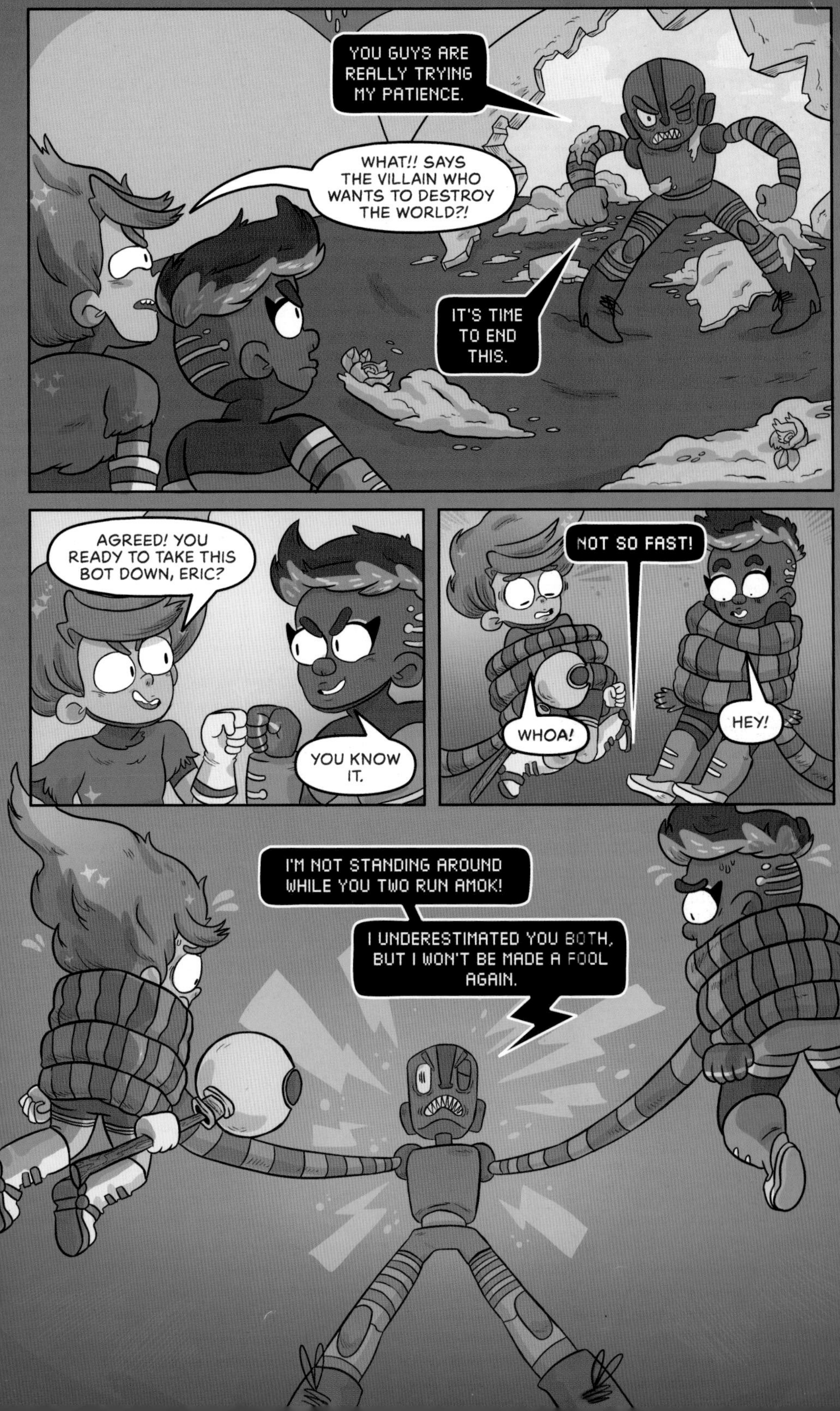
YOU GUYS ARE REALLY TRYING MY PATIENCE.
WHAT!! SAYS THE VILLAIN WHO WANTS TO DESTROY THE WORLD?!
IT'S TIME TO END THIS.
AGREED! YOU READY TO TAKE THIS BOT DOWN, ERIC?
YOU KNOW IT.
NOT SO FAST!
WHOA!
HEY!
I'M NOT STANDING AROUND WHILE YOU TWO RUN AMOK!
I UNDERESTIMATED YOU BOTH, BUT I WON'T BE MADE A FOOL AGAIN.

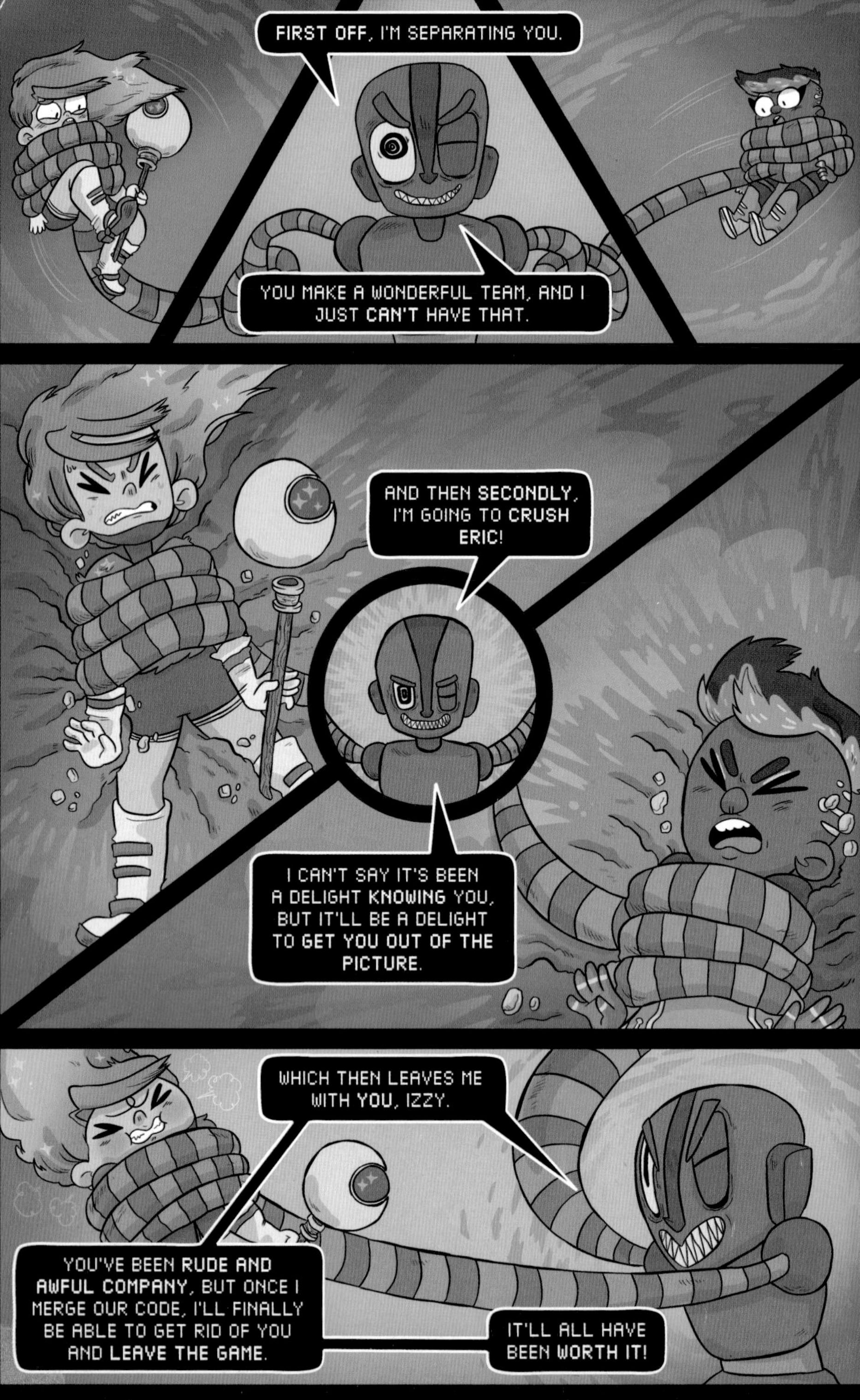
FIRST OFF, I'M SEPARATING YOU.
YOU MAKE A WONDERFUL TEAM, AND I JUST CAN'T HAVE THAT.
AND THEN SECONDLY, I'M GOING TO CRUSH ERIC!
I CAN'T SAY IT'S BEEN A DELIGHT KNOWING YOU, BUT IT'LL BE A DELIGHT TO GET YOU OUT OF THE PICTURE.
WHICH THEN LEAVES ME WITH YOU, IZZY.
YOU'VE BEEN RUDE AND AWFUL COMPANY, BUT ONCE I MERGE OUR CODE, I'LL FINALLY BE ABLE TO GET RID OF YOU AND LEAVE THE GAME.
IT'LL ALL HAVE BEEN WORTH IT!

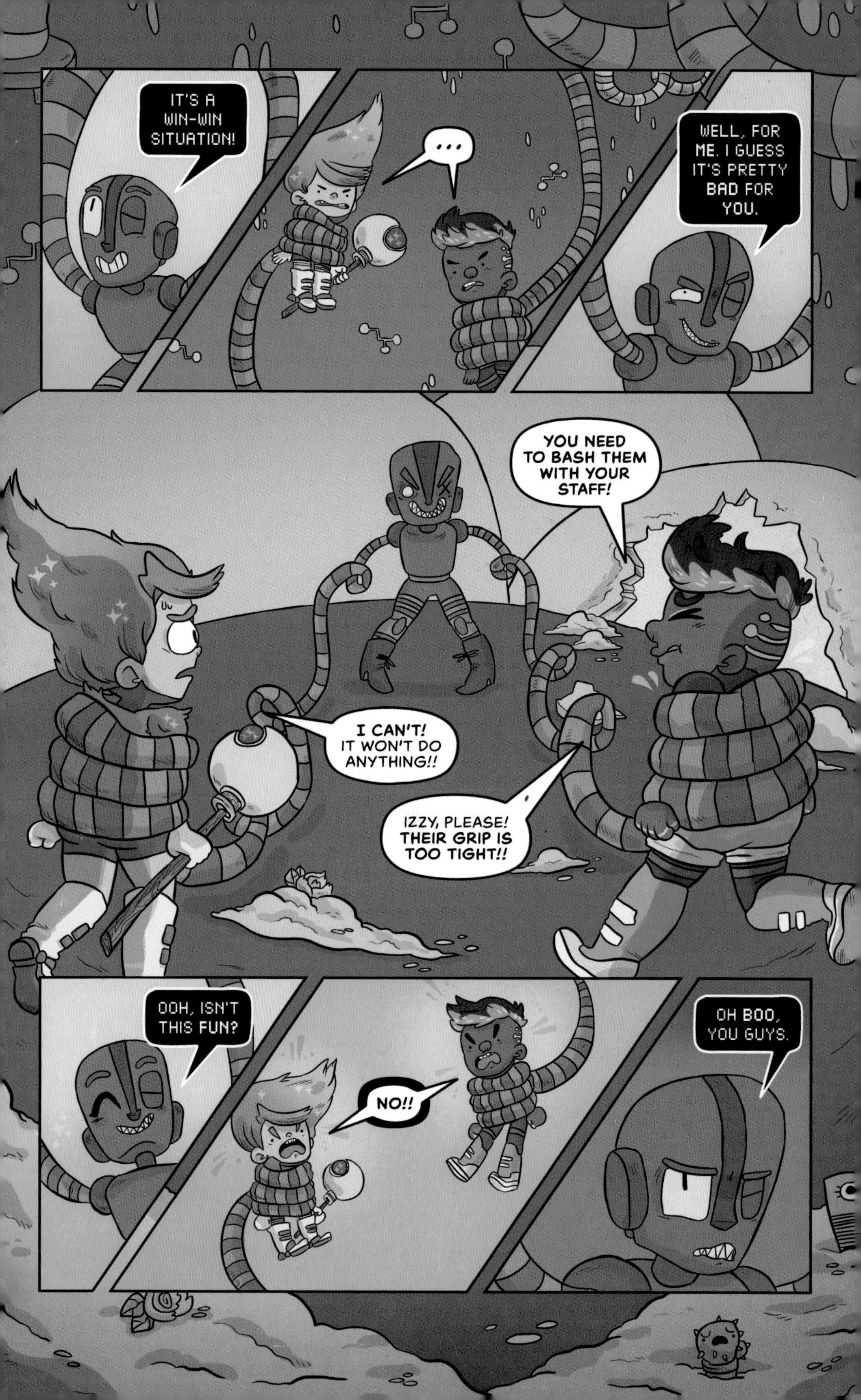
IT'S A WIN-WIN SITUATION!
...
WELL, FOR ME. I GUESS IT'S PRETTY BAD FOR YOU.
YOU NEED TO BASH THEM WITH YOUR STAFF!
I CAN'T! IT WON'T DO ANYTHING!!
IZZY, PLEASE! THEIR GRIP IS TOO TIGHT!!
OOH, ISN'T THIS FUN?
NO!!
OH BOO, YOU GUYS.

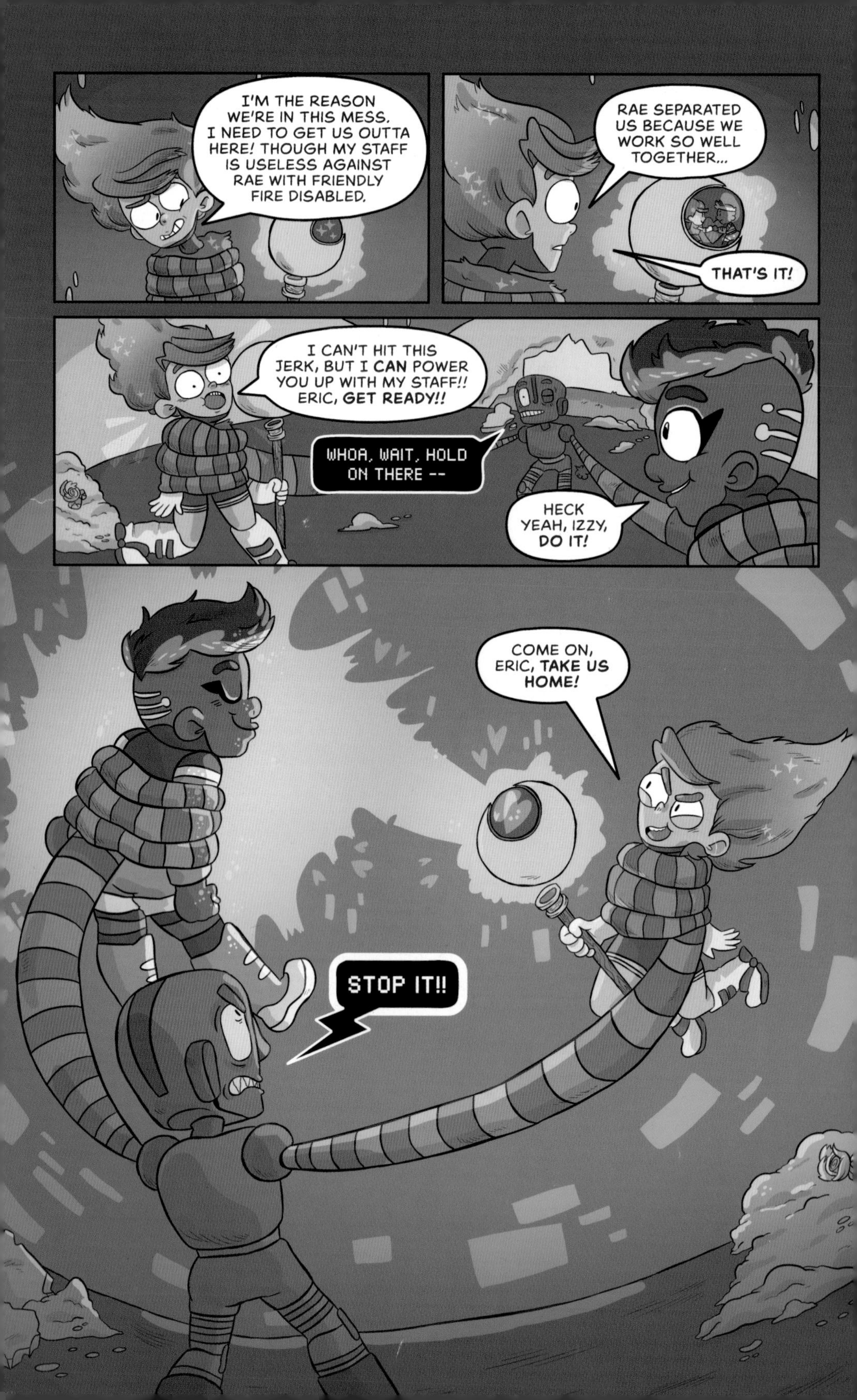
I'M THE REASON WE'RE IN THIS MESS. I NEED TO GET US OUTTA HERE! THOUGH MY STAFF IS USELESS AGAINST RAE WITH FRIENDLY FIRE DISABLED.
RAE SEPARATED US BECAUSE WE WORK SO WELL TOGETHER...
THAT'S IT!
I CAN'T HIT THIS JERK, BUT I CAN POWER YOU UP WITH MY STAFF!! ERIC, GET READY!!
WHOA, WAIT, HOLD ON THERE --
HECK YEAH, IZZY, DO IT!
COME ON, ERIC, TAKE US HOME!
STOP IT!!

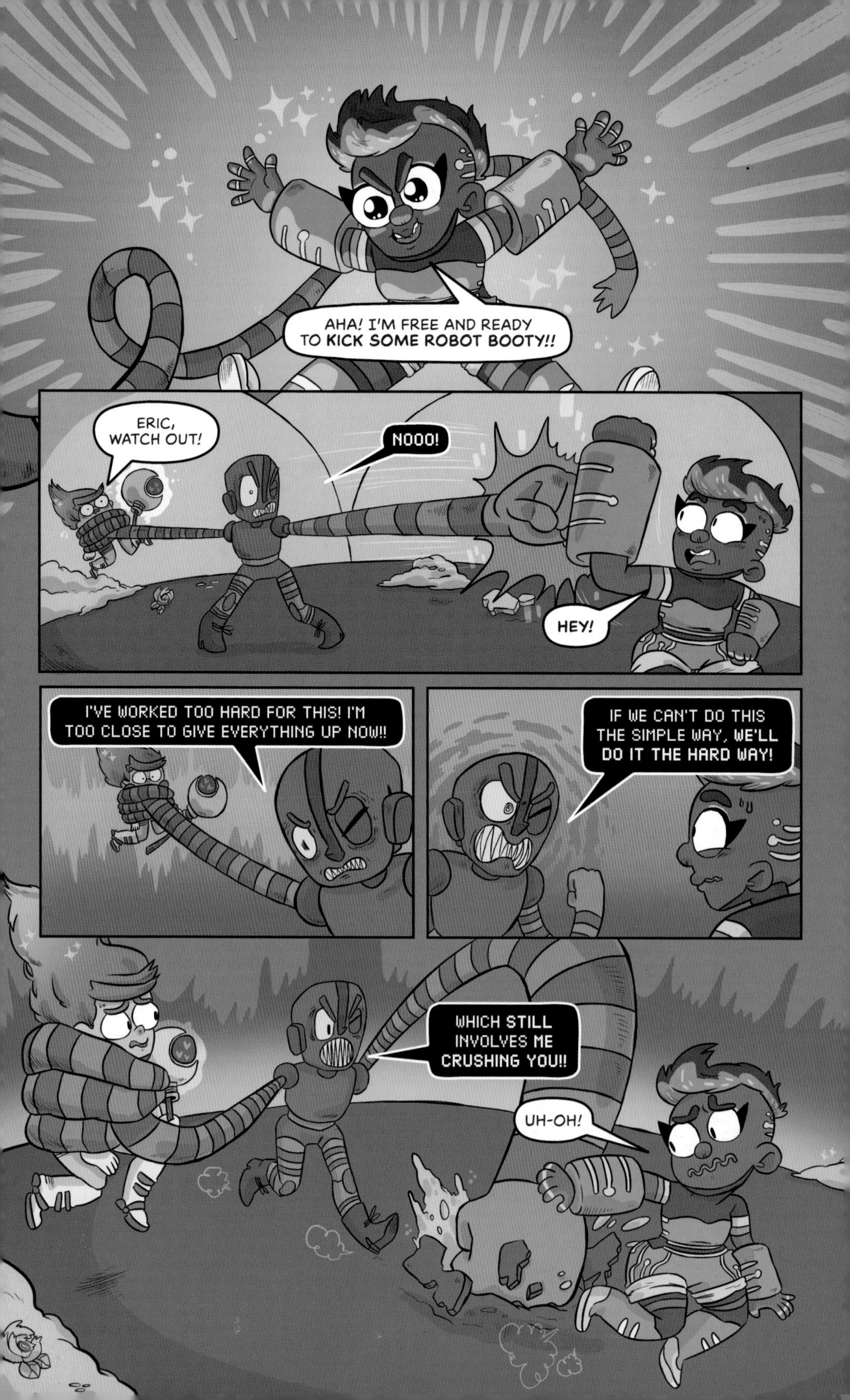
AHA! I'M FREE AND READY TO **KICK SOME ROBOT BOOTY!!**
ERIC, WATCH OUT!
NOOO!
HEY!
I'VE WORKED TOO HARD FOR THIS! I'M TOO CLOSE TO GIVE EVERYTHING UP NOW!!
IF WE CAN'T DO THIS THE SIMPLE WAY, **WE'LL DO IT THE HARD WAY!**
WHICH STILL INVOLVES ME CRUSHING YOU!!
UH-OH!

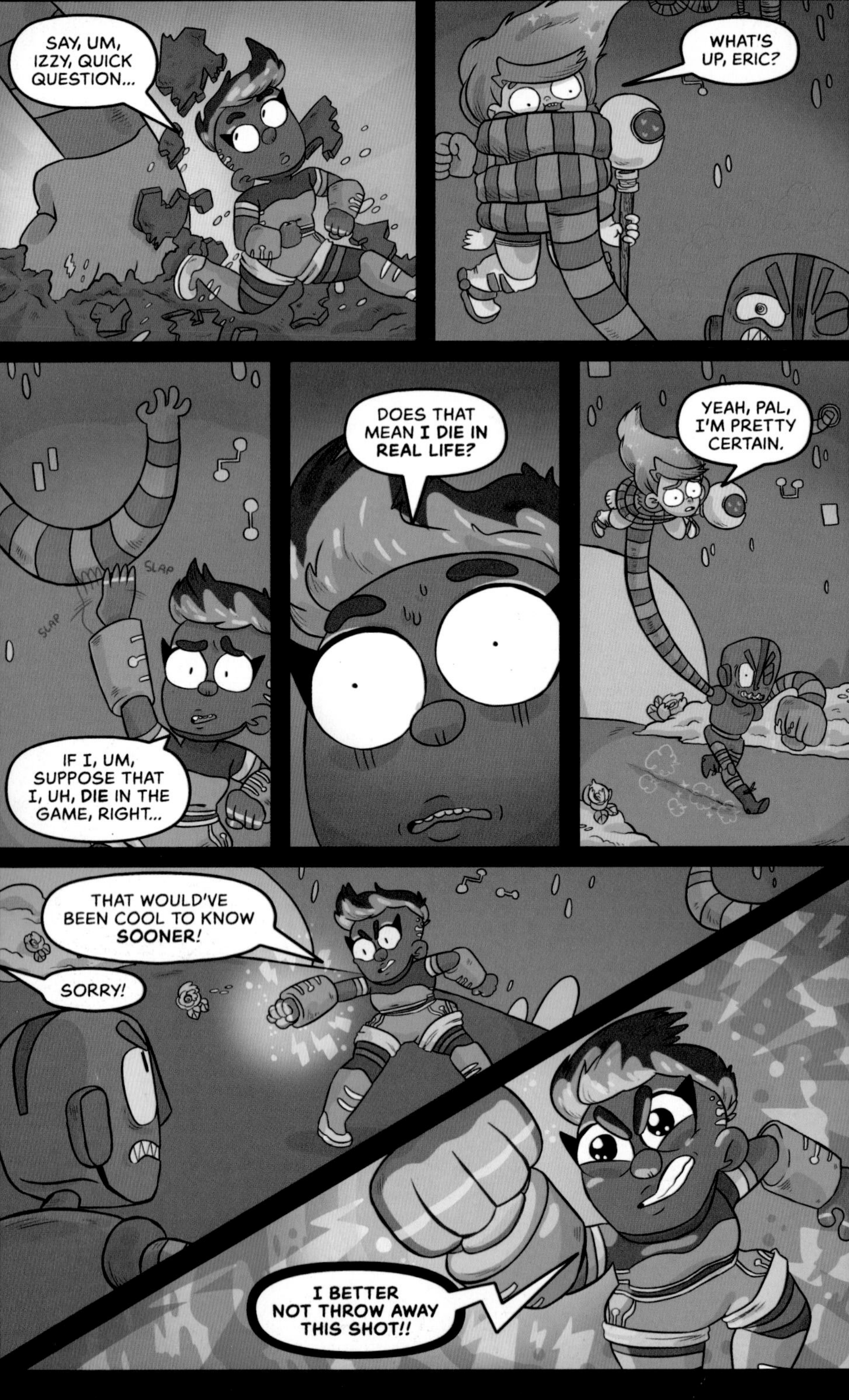
SAY, UM, IZZY, QUICK QUESTION...
WHAT'S UP, ERIC?
SLAP
SLAP
IF I, UM, SUPPOSE THAT I, UH, DIE IN THE GAME, RIGHT...
DOES THAT MEAN I DIE IN REAL LIFE?
YEAH, PAL, I'M PRETTY CERTAIN.
THAT WOULD'VE BEEN COOL TO KNOW SOONER!
SORRY!
I BETTER NOT THROW AWAY THIS SHOT!!

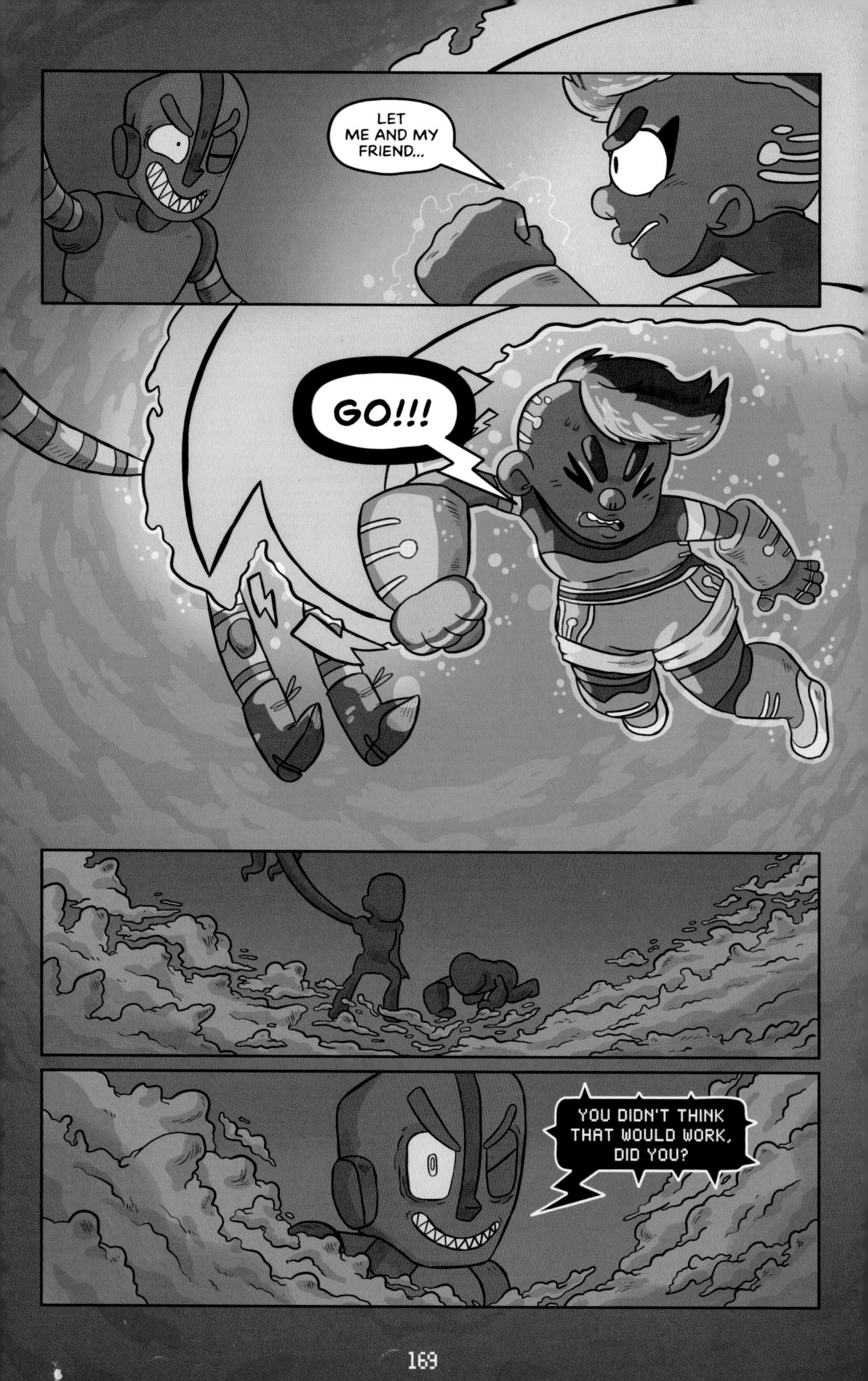
LET ME AND MY FRIEND...
GO!!!
YOU DIDN'T THINK THAT WOULD WORK, DID YOU?

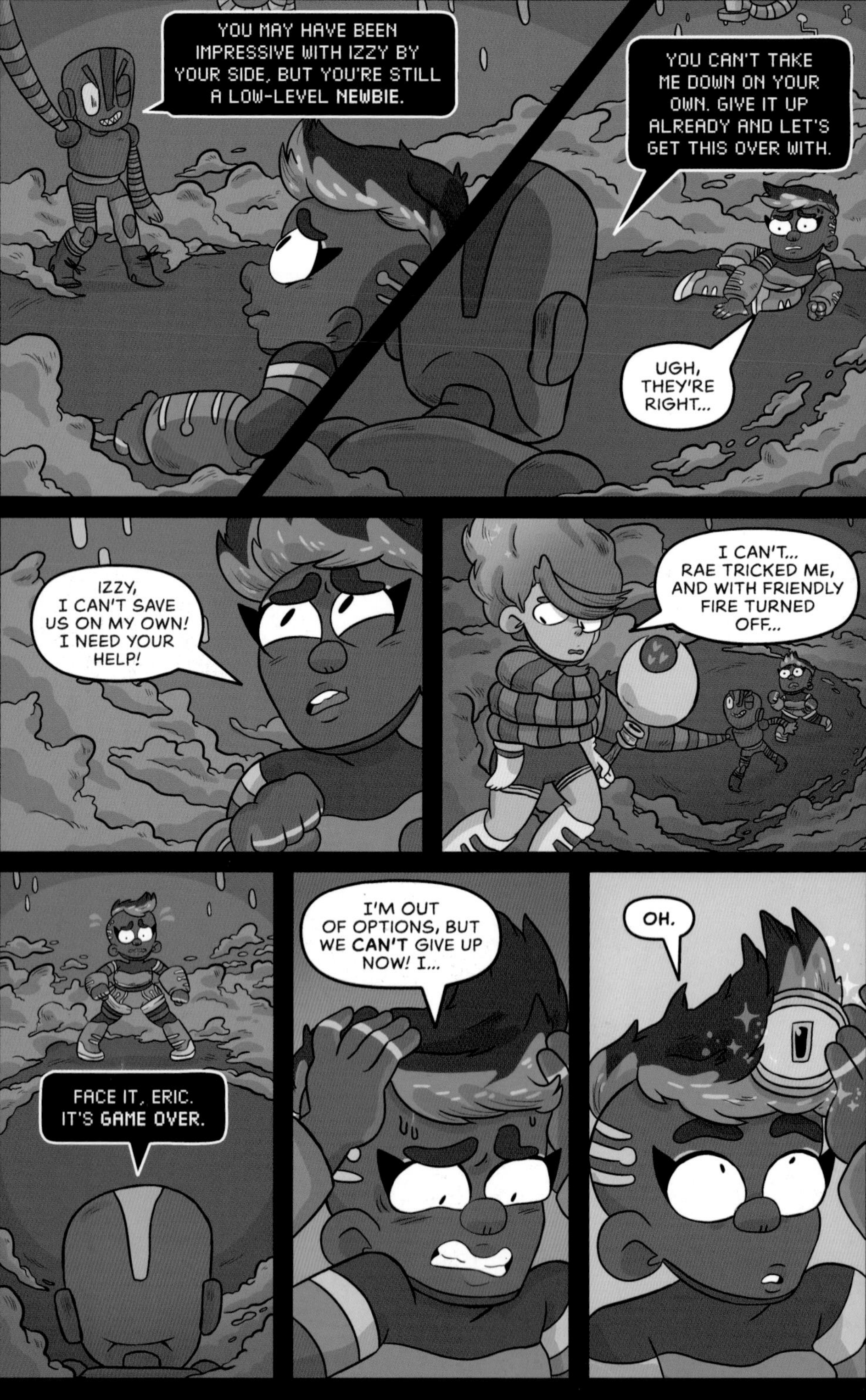
YOU MAY HAVE BEEN IMPRESSIVE WITH IZZY BY YOUR SIDE, BUT YOU'RE STILL A LOW-LEVEL NEWBIE.
YOU CAN'T TAKE ME DOWN ON YOUR OWN. GIVE IT UP ALREADY AND LET'S GET THIS OVER WITH.
UGH, THEY'RE RIGHT...
IZZY, I CAN'T SAVE US ON MY OWN! I NEED YOUR HELP!
I CAN'T... RAE TRICKED ME, AND WITH FRIENDLY FIRE TURNED OFF...
FACE IT, ERIC. IT'S GAME OVER.
I'M OUT OF OPTIONS, BUT WE CAN'T GIVE UP NOW! I...
OH.

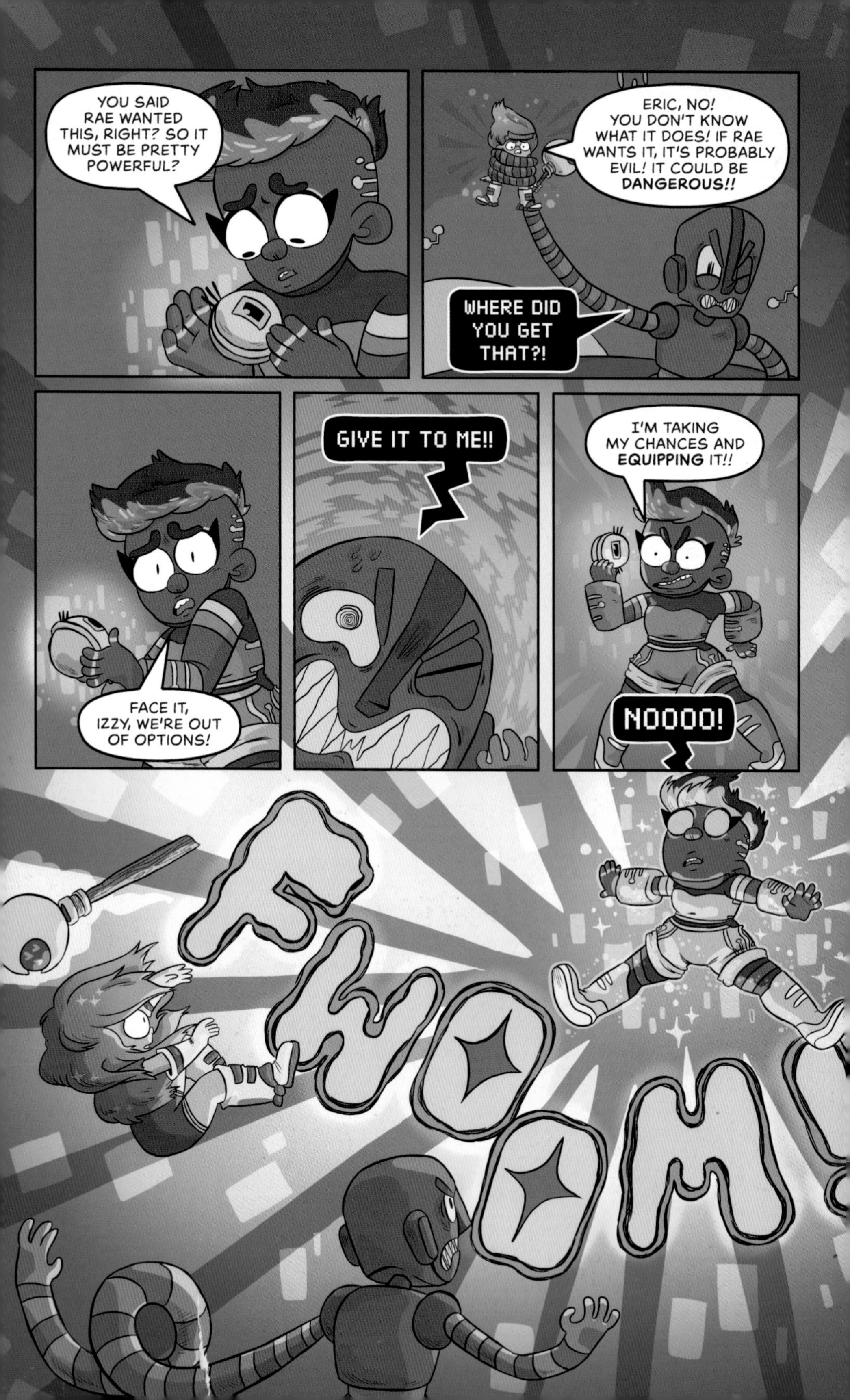
YOU SAID RAE WANTED THIS, RIGHT? SO IT MUST BE PRETTY POWERFUL?
ERIC, NO! YOU DON'T KNOW WHAT IT DOES! IF RAE WANTS IT, IT'S PROBABLY EVIL! IT COULD BE **DANGEROUS!!**
WHERE DID YOU GET THAT?!
FACE IT, IZZY, WE'RE OUT OF OPTIONS!
GIVE IT TO ME!!
I'M TAKING MY CHANCES AND **EQUIPPING** IT!!
NOOOO!

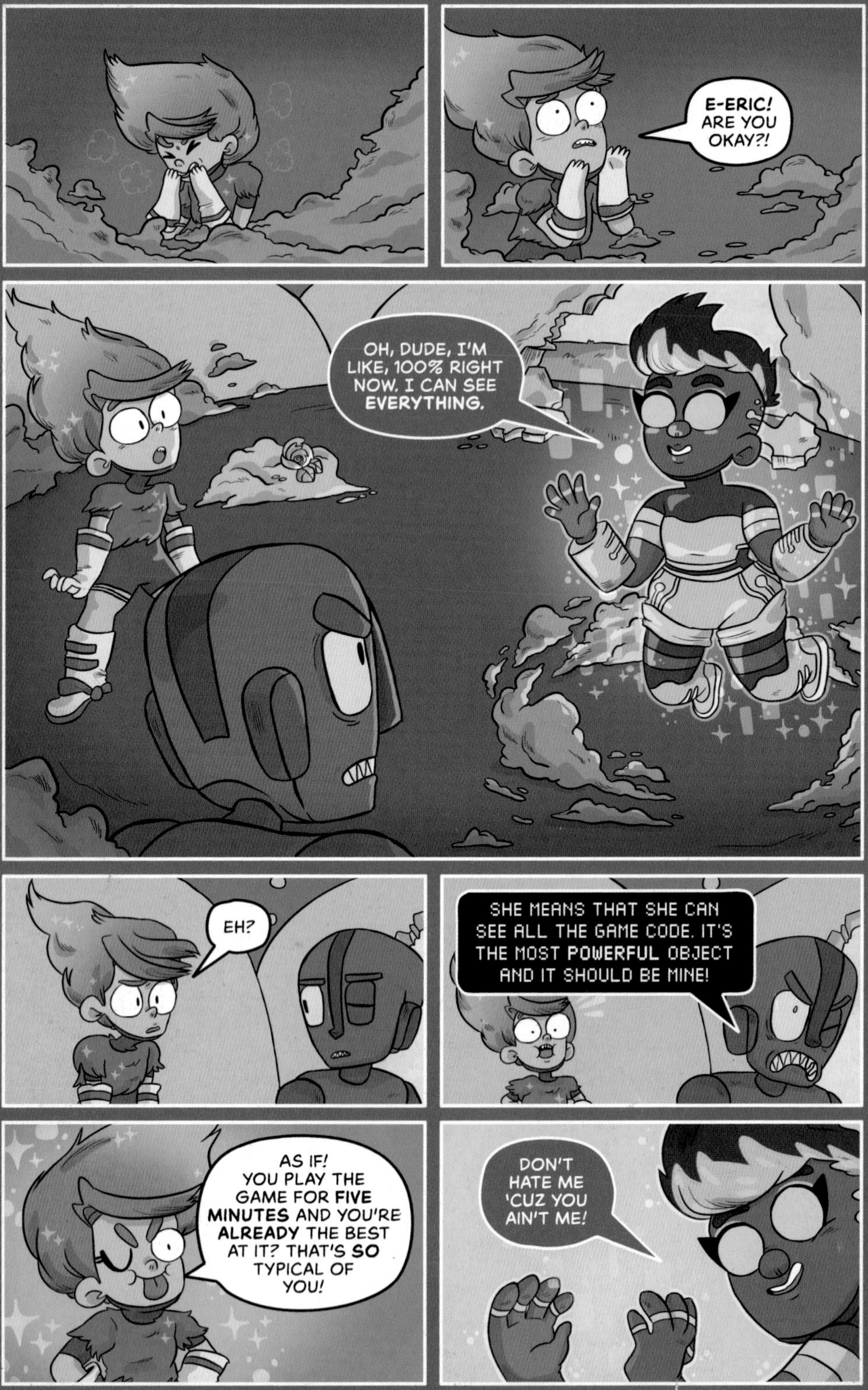
E-ERIC! ARE YOU OKAY?!
OH, DUDE, I'M LIKE, 100% RIGHT NOW. I CAN SEE **EVERYTHING.**
EH?
SHE MEANS THAT SHE CAN SEE ALL THE GAME CODE. IT'S THE MOST **POWERFUL** OBJECT AND IT SHOULD BE MINE!
AS IF! YOU PLAY THE GAME FOR **FIVE MINUTES** AND YOU'RE **ALREADY** THE BEST AT IT? THAT'S **SO** TYPICAL OF YOU!
DON'T HATE ME 'CUZ YOU AIN'T ME!

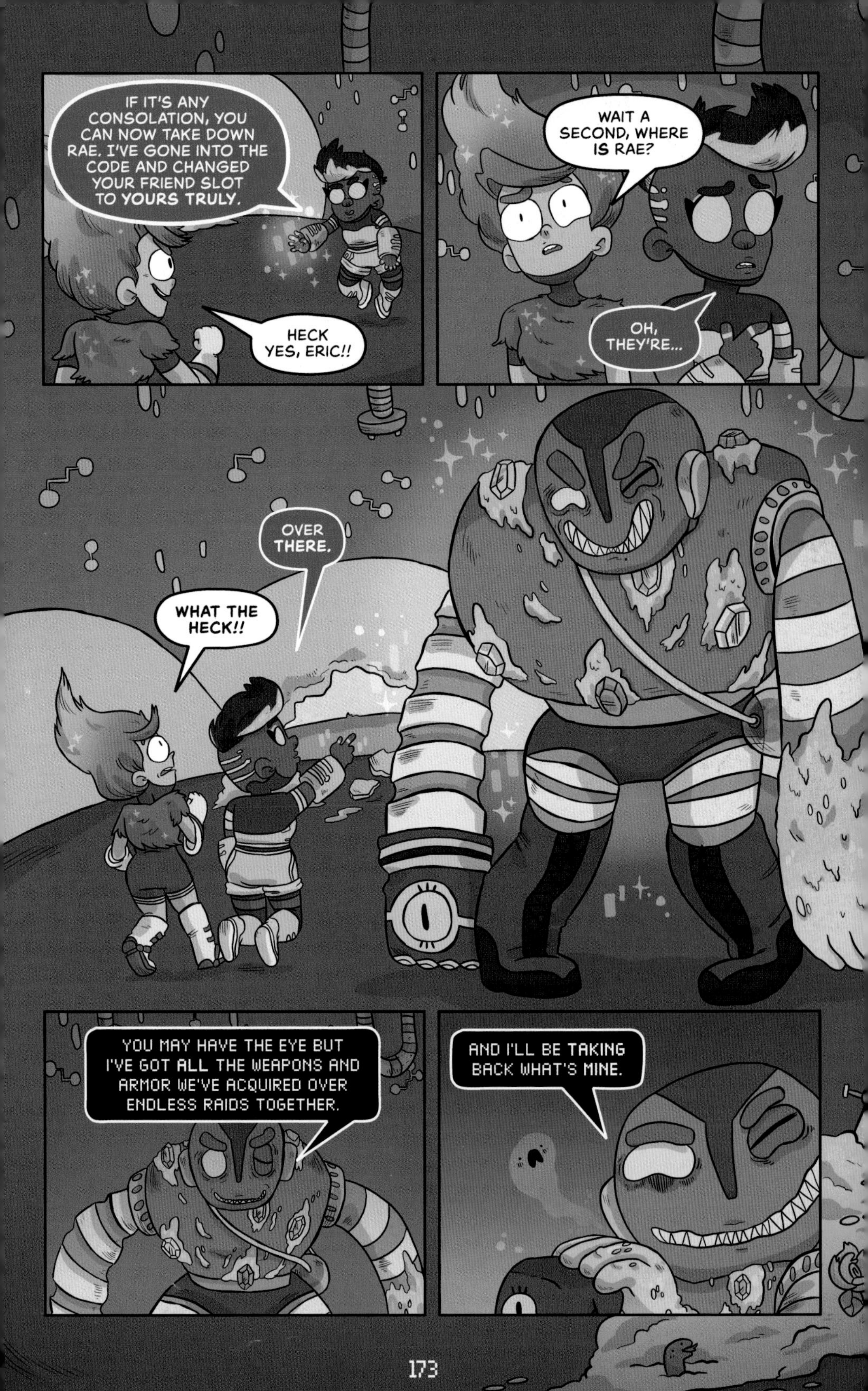
IF IT'S ANY CONSOLATION, YOU CAN NOW TAKE DOWN RAE. I'VE GONE INTO THE CODE AND CHANGED YOUR FRIEND SLOT TO YOURS TRULY.
HECK YES, ERIC!!
WAIT A SECOND, WHERE IS RAE?
OH, THEY'RE...
OVER THERE.
WHAT THE HECK!!
YOU MAY HAVE THE EYE BUT I'VE GOT ALL THE WEAPONS AND ARMOR WE'VE ACQUIRED OVER ENDLESS RAIDS TOGETHER.
AND I'LL BE TAKING BACK WHAT'S MINE.

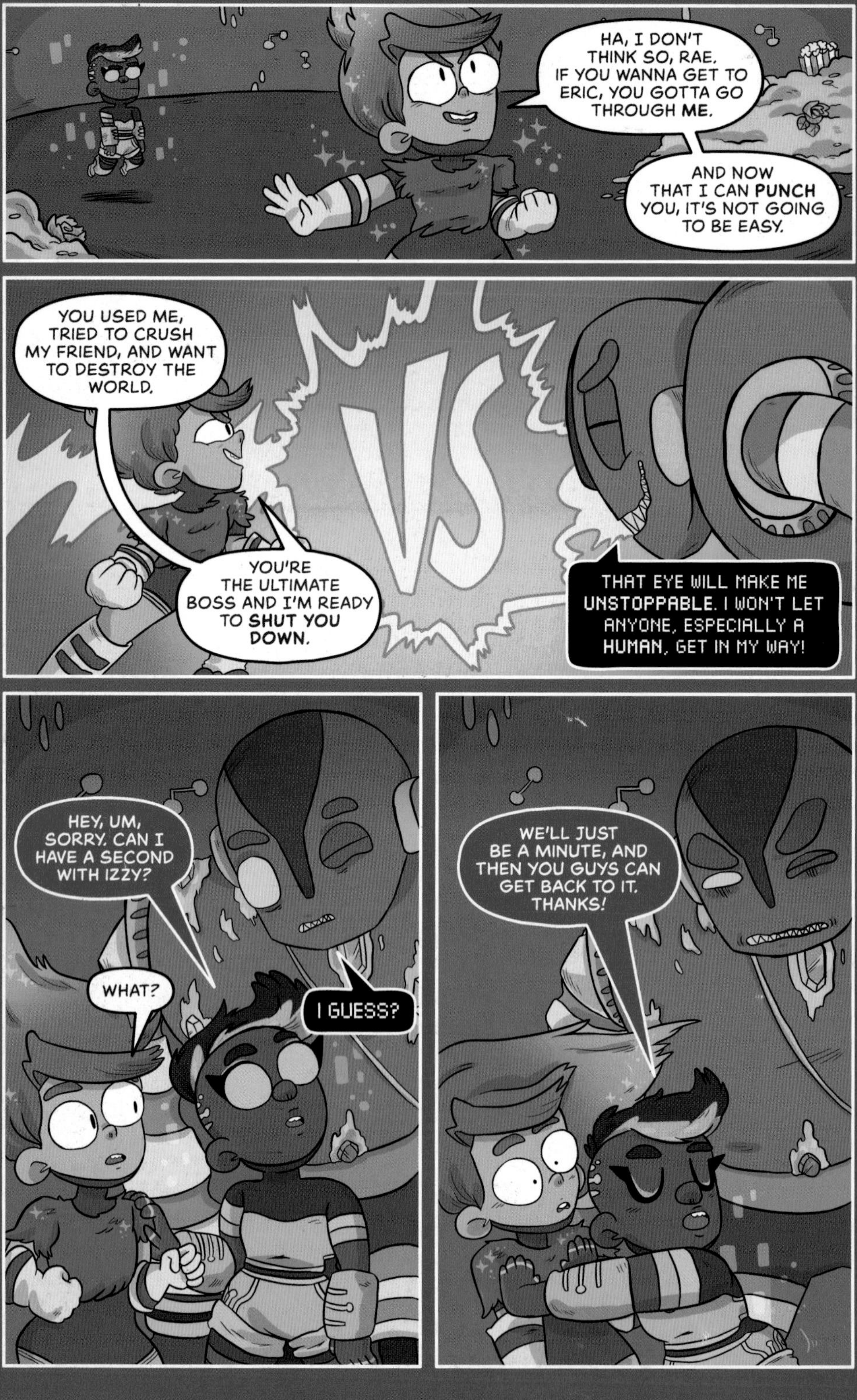
HA, I DON'T THINK SO, RAE. IF YOU WANNA GET TO ERIC, YOU GOTTA GO THROUGH **ME**.
AND NOW THAT I CAN **PUNCH** YOU, IT'S NOT GOING TO BE EASY.
YOU USED ME, TRIED TO CRUSH MY FRIEND, AND WANT TO DESTROY THE WORLD.
VS
YOU'RE THE ULTIMATE BOSS AND I'M READY TO **SHUT YOU DOWN**.
THAT EYE WILL MAKE ME **UNSTOPPABLE**. I WON'T LET ANYONE, ESPECIALLY A **HUMAN**, GET IN MY WAY!
HEY, UM, SORRY. CAN I HAVE A SECOND WITH IZZY?
WHAT?
I GUESS?
WE'LL JUST BE A MINUTE, AND THEN YOU GUYS CAN GET BACK TO IT. THANKS!

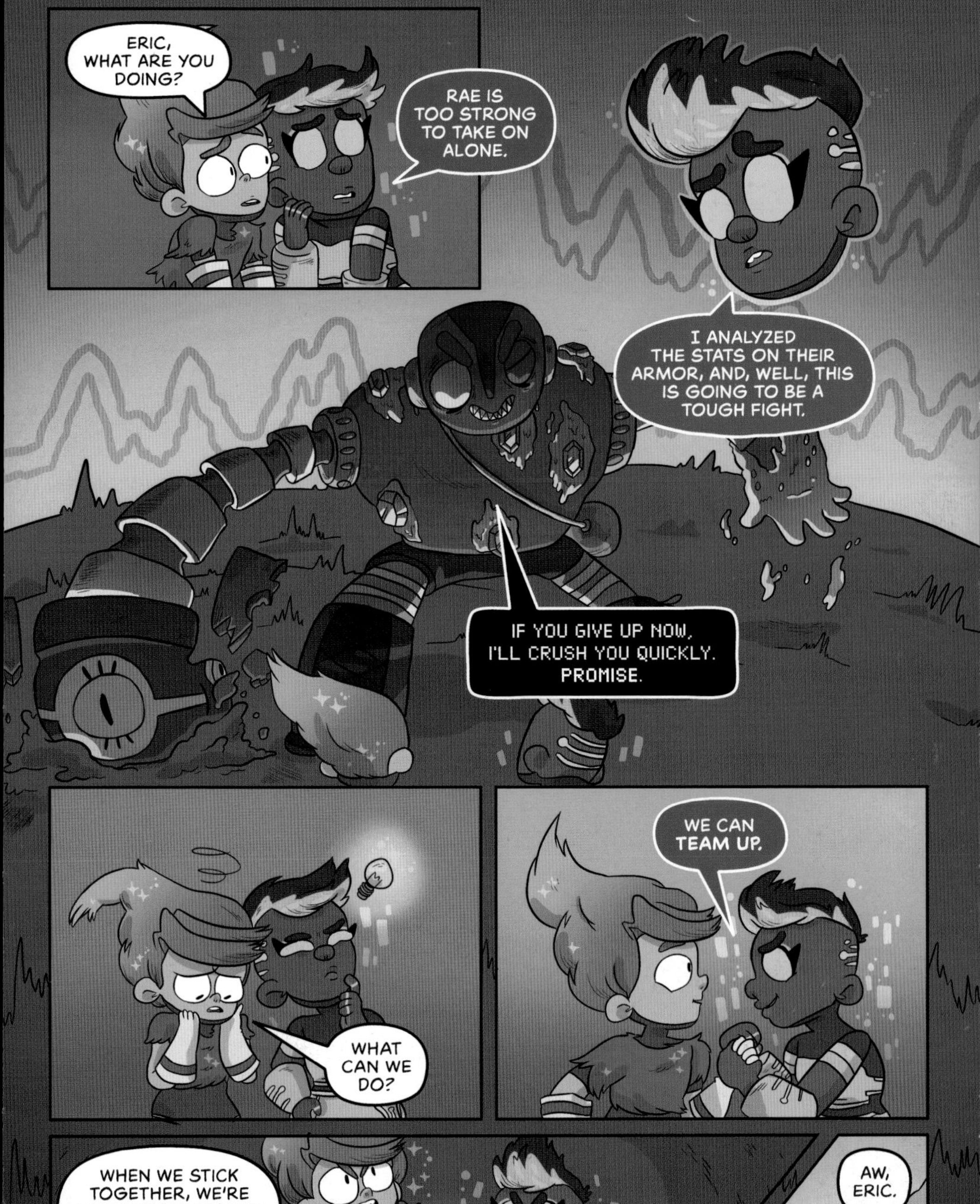
ERIC, WHAT ARE YOU DOING?
RAE IS TOO STRONG TO TAKE ON ALONE.
I ANALYZED THE STATS ON THEIR ARMOR, AND, WELL, THIS IS GOING TO BE A TOUGH FIGHT.
IF YOU GIVE UP NOW, I'LL CRUSH YOU QUICKLY. PROMISE.
WHAT CAN WE DO?
WE CAN TEAM UP.
WHEN WE STICK TOGETHER, WE'RE UNSTOPPABLE! THEY WON'T KNOW WHAT HIT THEM!
OH, IT'LL BE US THAT HITS THEM. SO HARD -- NOBODY TRICKS MY FRIEND INTO NEARLY DESTROYING THE WORLD AND GETS AWAY WITH IT!!
AW, ERIC.

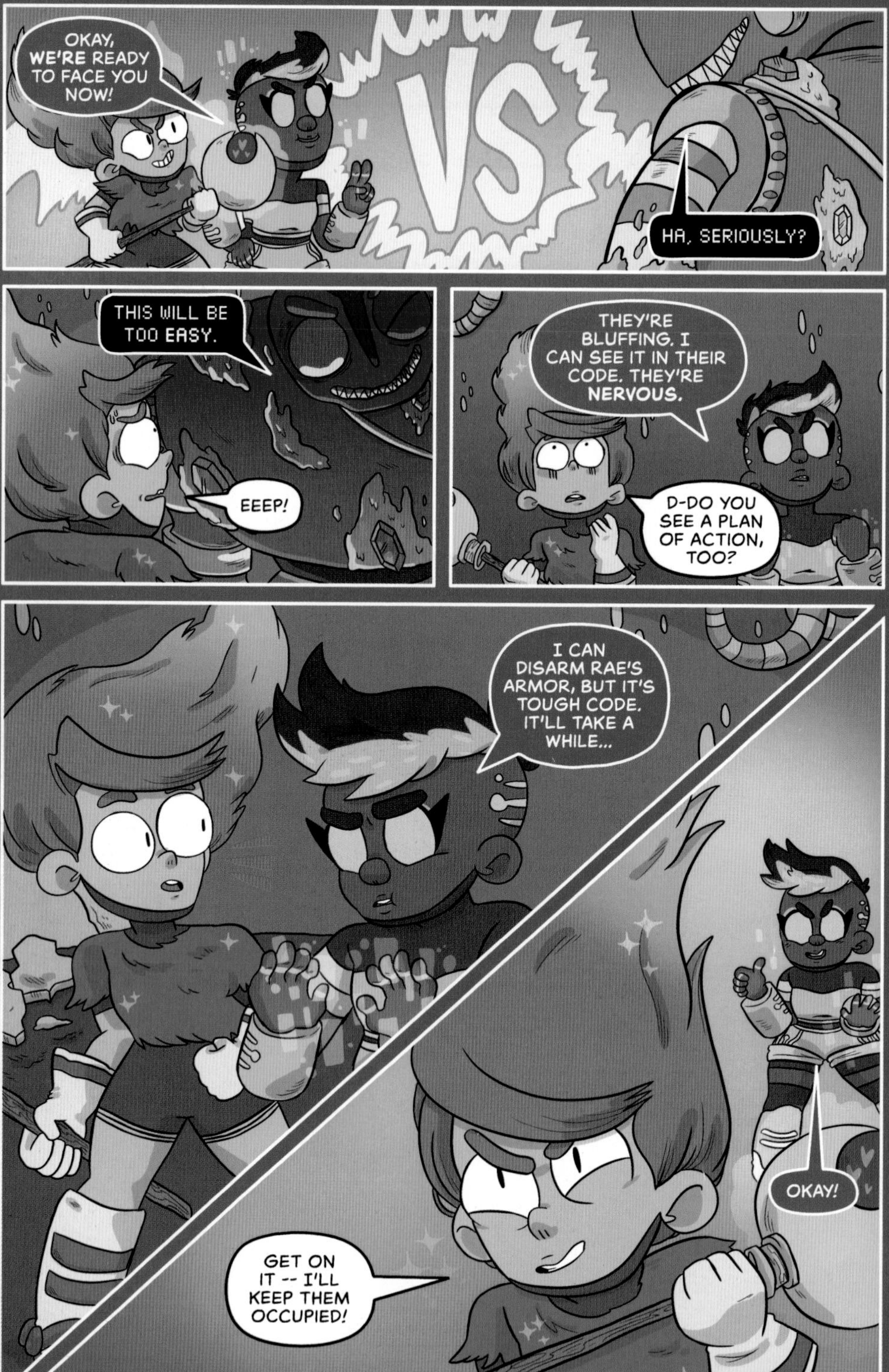
OKAY, WE'RE READY TO FACE YOU NOW!
VS
HA, SERIOUSLY?
THIS WILL BE TOO EASY.
EEEP!
THEY'RE BLUFFING. I CAN SEE IT IN THEIR CODE. THEY'RE NERVOUS.
D-DO YOU SEE A PLAN OF ACTION, TOO?
I CAN DISARM RAE'S ARMOR, BUT IT'S TOUGH CODE. IT'LL TAKE A WHILE...
OKAY!
GET ON IT -- I'LL KEEP THEM OCCUPIED!

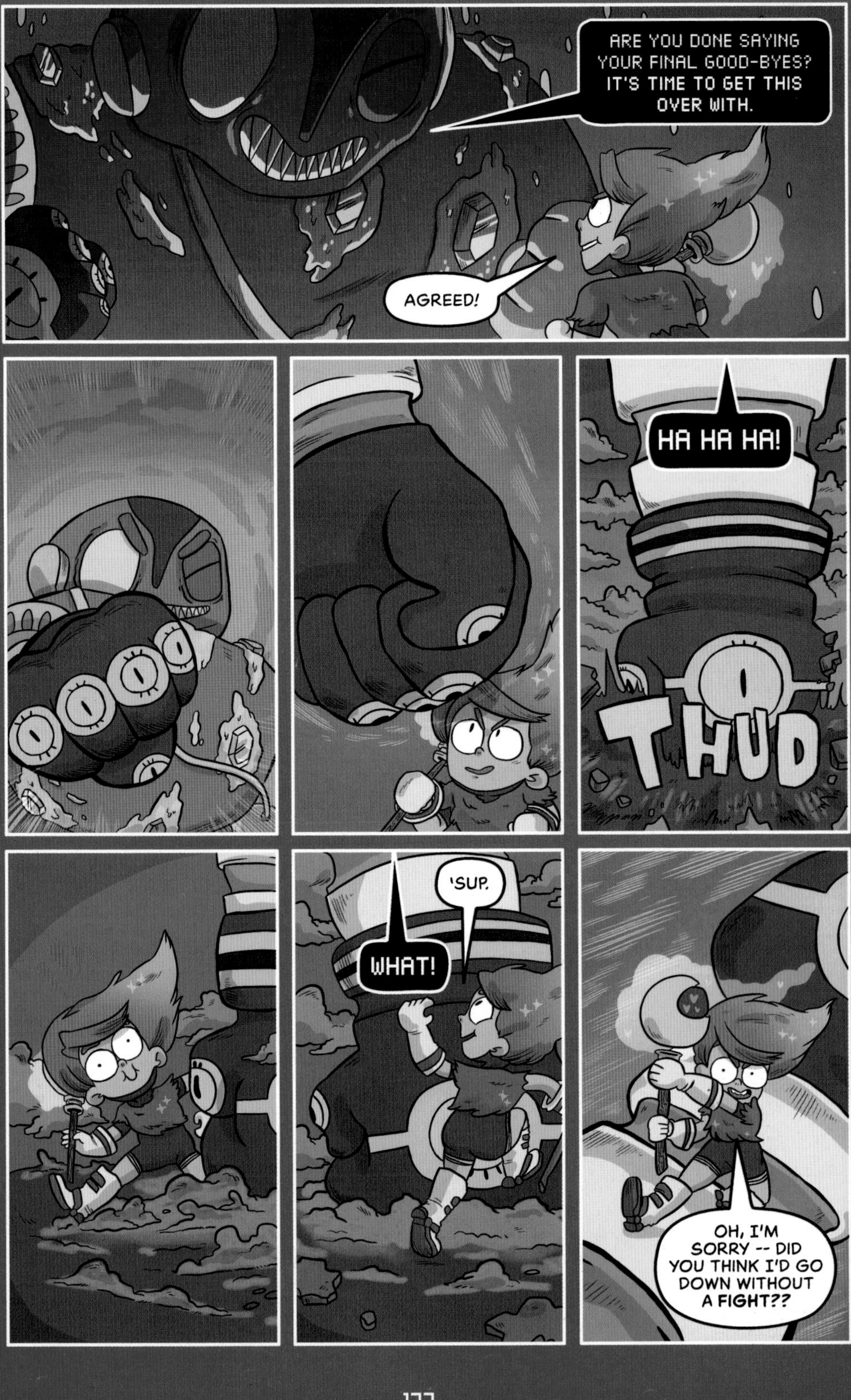
ARE YOU DONE SAYING YOUR FINAL GOOD-BYES? IT'S TIME TO GET THIS OVER WITH.
AGREED!
HA HA HA!
THUD
'SUP.
WHAT!
OH, I'M SORRY -- DID YOU THINK I'D GO DOWN WITHOUT A FIGHT??

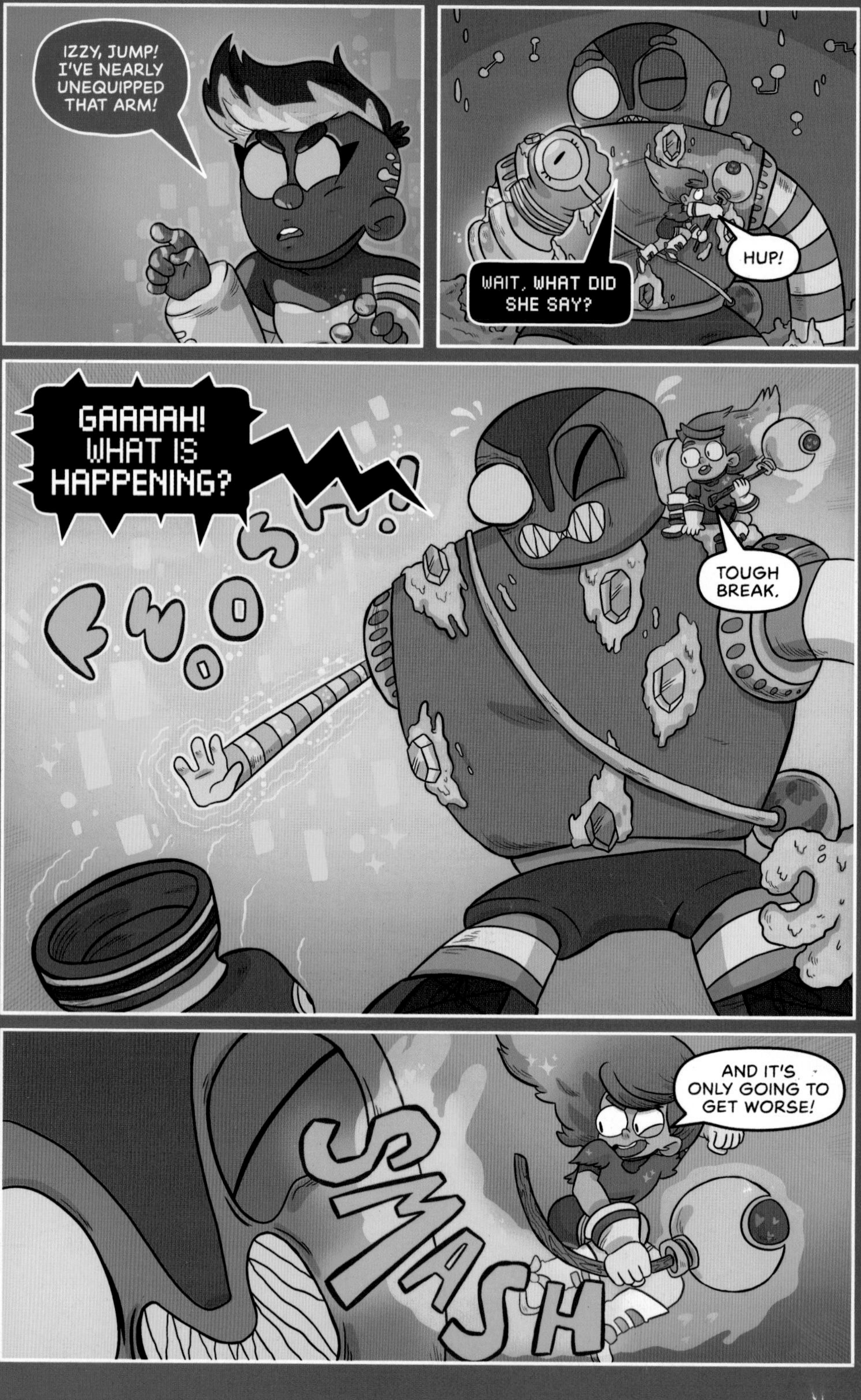
IZZY, JUMP! I'VE NEARLY UNEQUIPPED THAT ARM!
WAIT, WHAT DID SHE SAY?
HUP!
GAAAAH! WHAT IS HAPPENING?
FWOOSH!
TOUGH BREAK.
SMASH
AND IT'S ONLY GOING TO GET WORSE!

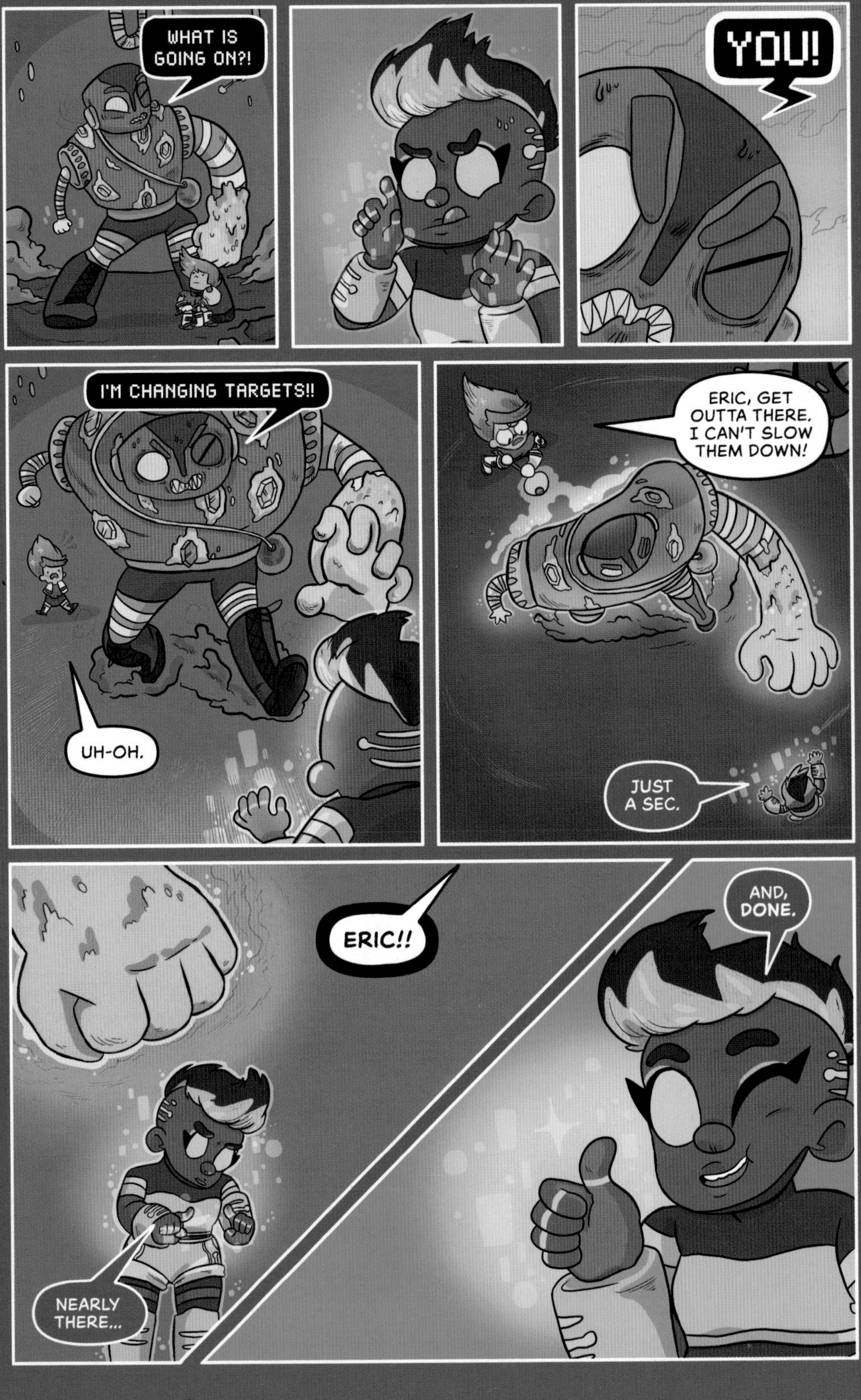
WHAT IS GOING ON?!
YOU!
I'M CHANGING TARGETS!!
UH-OH.
ERIC, GET OUTTA THERE. I CAN'T SLOW THEM DOWN!
JUST A SEC.
ERIC!!
NEARLY THERE...
AND, DONE.

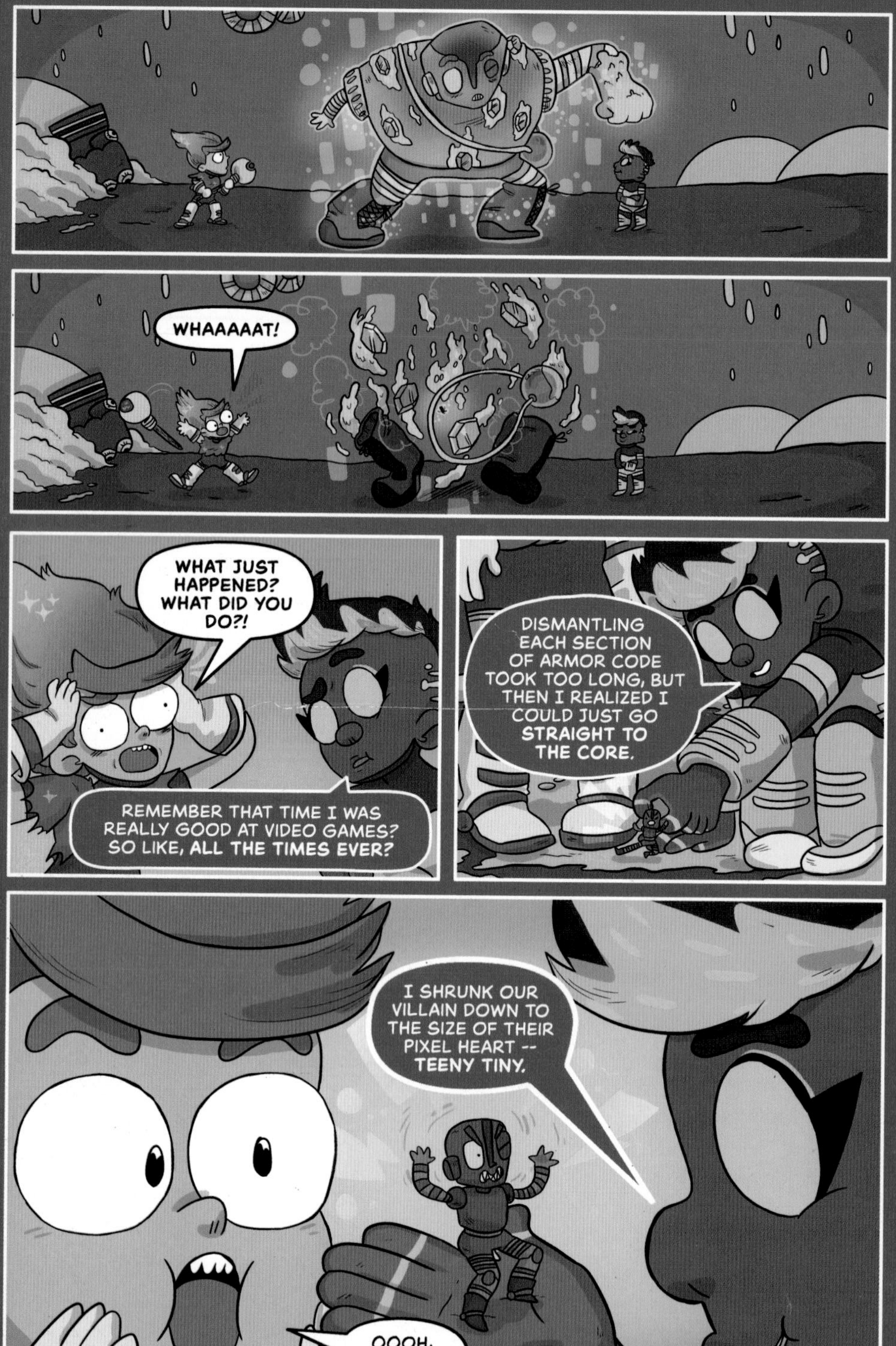
WHAAAAAT!
WHAT JUST HAPPENED? WHAT DID YOU DO?!
REMEMBER THAT TIME I WAS REALLY GOOD AT VIDEO GAMES? SO LIKE, ALL THE TIMES EVER?
DISMANTLING EACH SECTION OF ARMOR CODE TOOK TOO LONG, BUT THEN I REALIZED I COULD JUST GO STRAIGHT TO THE CORE.
I SHRUNK OUR VILLAIN DOWN TO THE SIZE OF THEIR PIXEL HEART -- TEENY TINY.
OOOH, ERIC, SICK BURN.

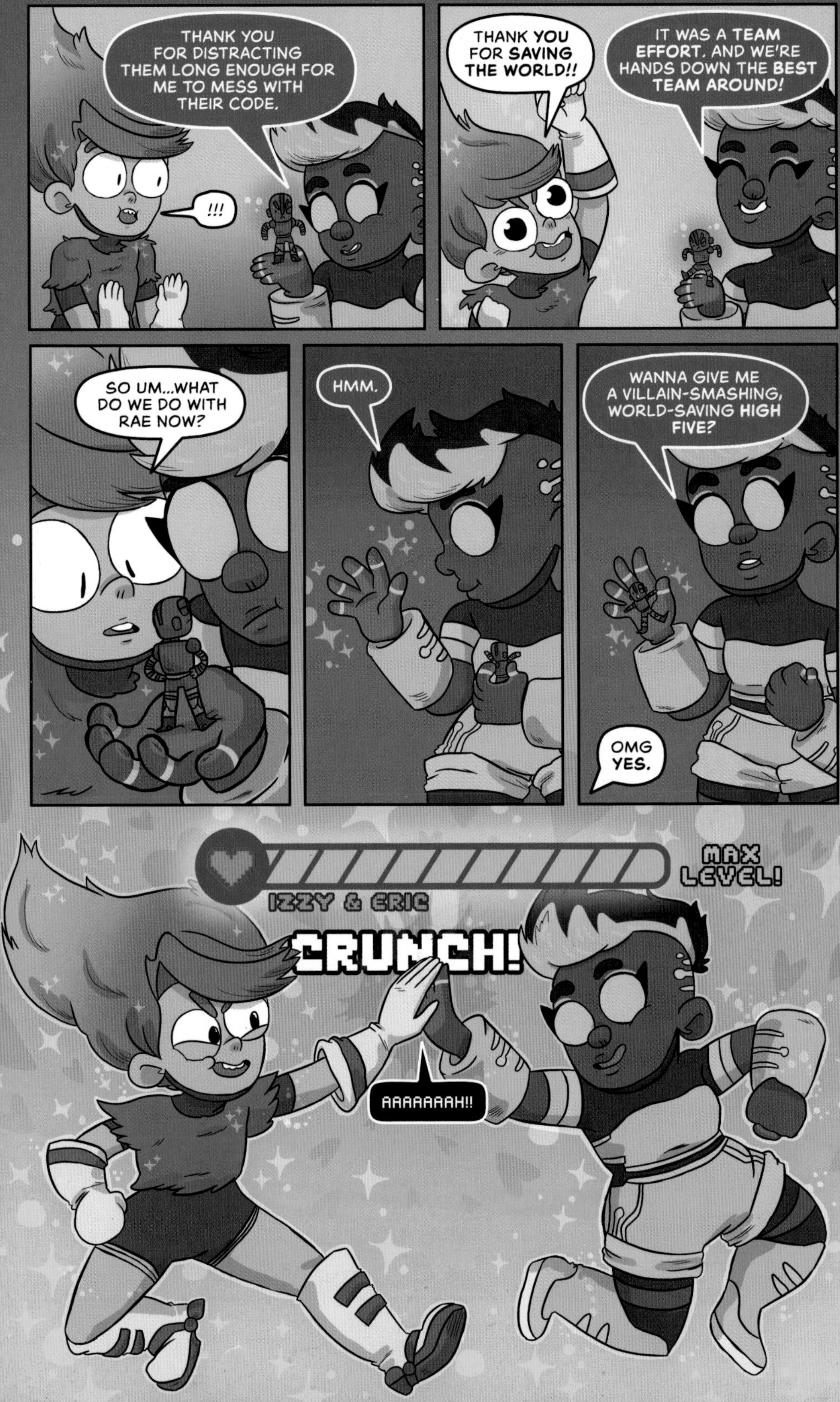
THANK YOU FOR DISTRACTING THEM LONG ENOUGH FOR ME TO MESS WITH THEIR CODE.
!!!
THANK YOU FOR SAVING THE WORLD!!
IT WAS A TEAM EFFORT. AND WE'RE HANDS DOWN THE BEST TEAM AROUND!
SO UM...WHAT DO WE DO WITH RAE NOW?
HMM.
WANNA GIVE ME A VILLAIN-SMASHING, WORLD-SAVING HIGH FIVE?
OMG YES.
MAX LEVEL!
IZZY & ERIC
CRUNCH!
AAAAAAAH!!

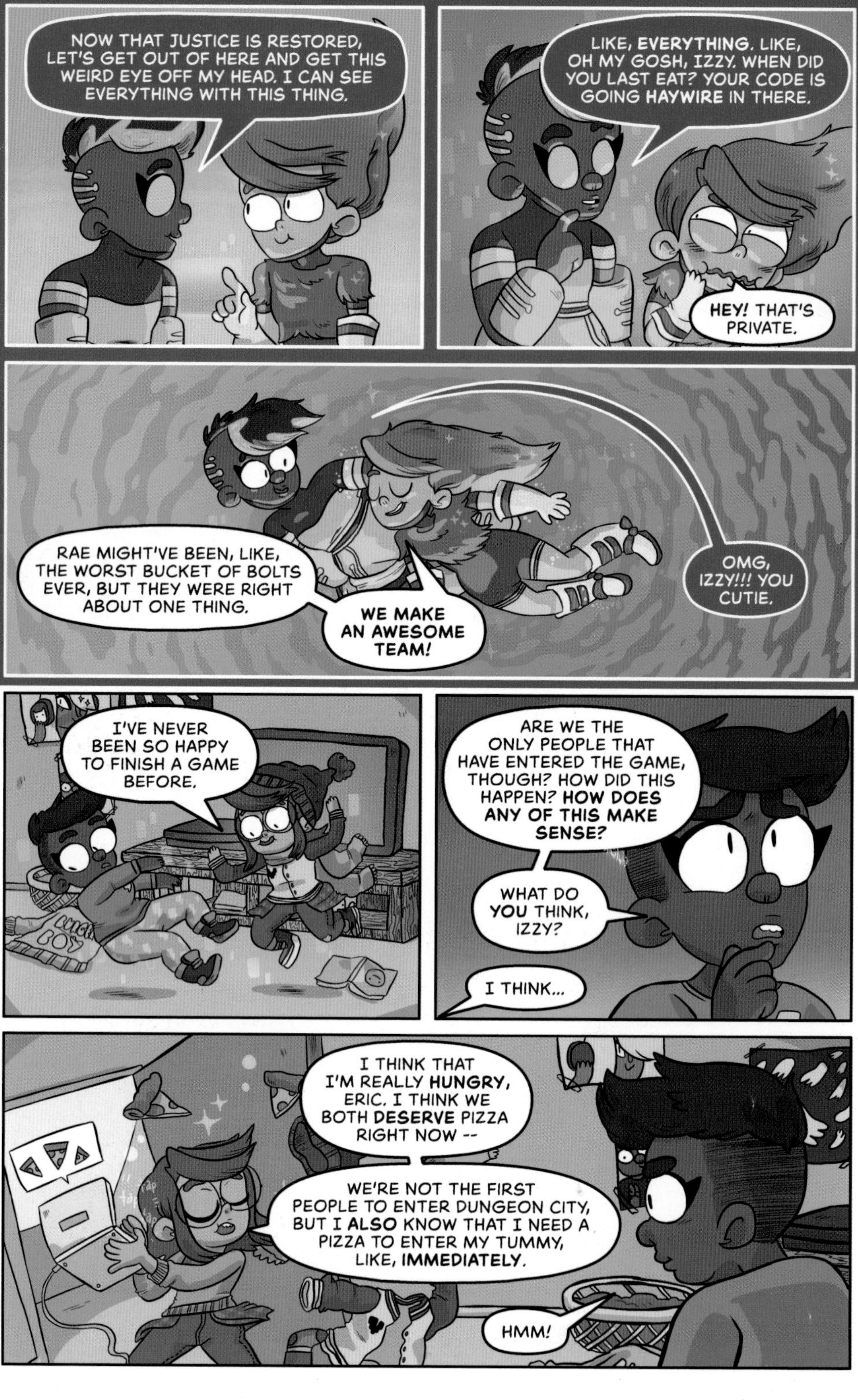
NOW THAT JUSTICE IS RESTORED, LET'S GET OUT OF HERE AND GET THIS WEIRD EYE OFF MY HEAD. I CAN SEE EVERYTHING WITH THIS THING.
LIKE, EVERYTHING. LIKE, OH MY GOSH, IZZY. WHEN DID YOU LAST EAT? YOUR CODE IS GOING HAYWIRE IN THERE.
HEY! THAT'S PRIVATE.
RAE MIGHT'VE BEEN, LIKE, THE WORST BUCKET OF BOLTS EVER, BUT THEY WERE RIGHT ABOUT ONE THING.
WE MAKE AN AWESOME TEAM!
OMG, IZZY!!! YOU CUTIE.
I'VE NEVER BEEN SO HAPPY TO FINISH A GAME BEFORE.
ARE WE THE ONLY PEOPLE THAT HAVE ENTERED THE GAME, THOUGH? HOW DID THIS HAPPEN? HOW DOES ANY OF THIS MAKE SENSE?
WHAT DO YOU THINK, IZZY?
I THINK...
I THINK THAT I'M REALLY HUNGRY, ERIC. I THINK WE BOTH DESERVE PIZZA RIGHT NOW --
WE'RE NOT THE FIRST PEOPLE TO ENTER DUNGEON CITY, BUT I ALSO KNOW THAT I NEED A PIZZA TO ENTER MY TUMMY, LIKE, IMMEDIATELY.
HMM!

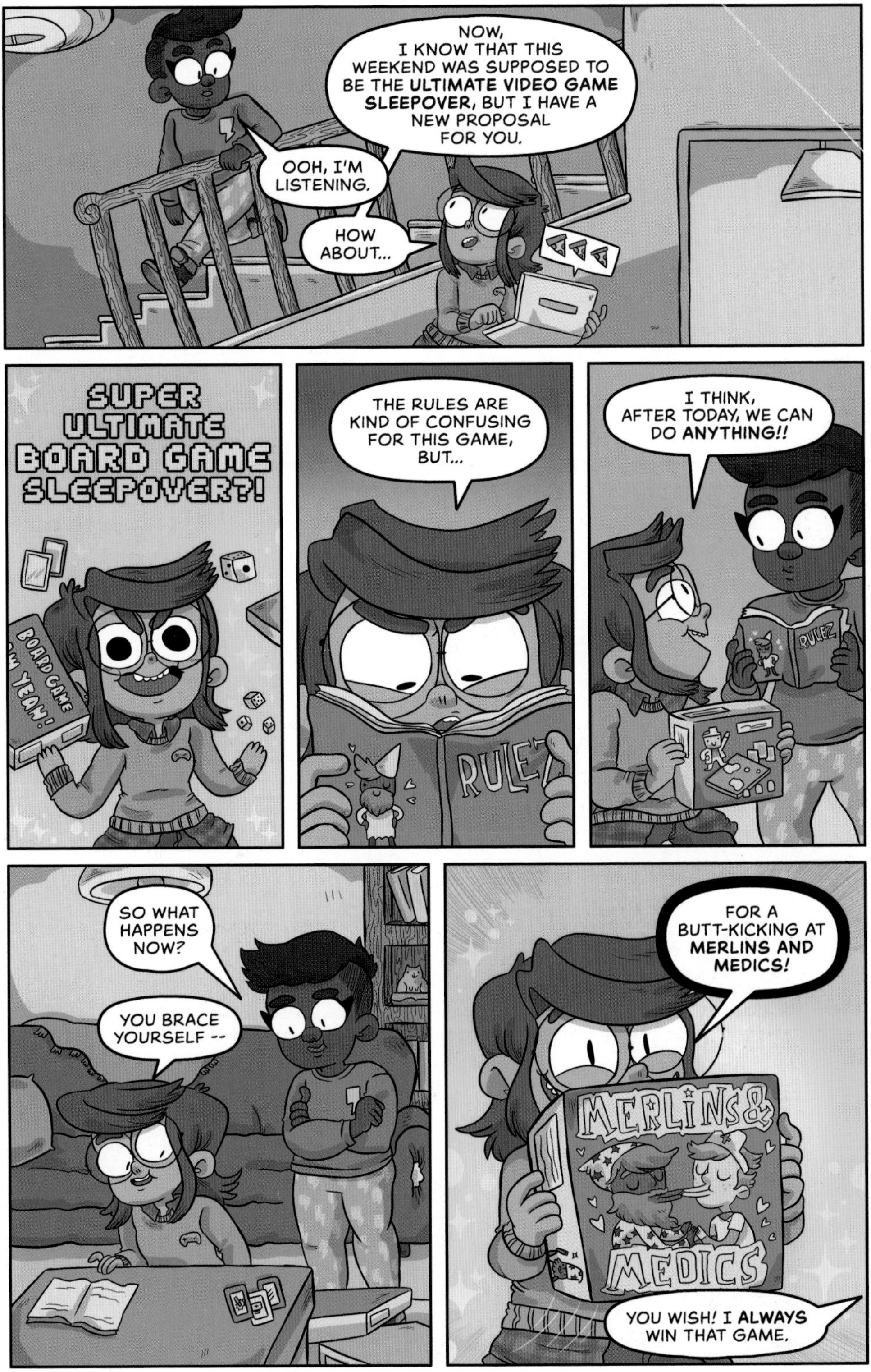
NOW, I KNOW THAT THIS WEEKEND WAS SUPPOSED TO BE THE **ULTIMATE VIDEO GAME SLEEPOVER**, BUT I HAVE A NEW PROPOSAL FOR YOU.
OOH, I'M LISTENING.
HOW ABOUT...
SUPER ULTIMATE BOARD GAME SLEEPOVER?!
BOARD GAME AW YEAH!
THE RULES ARE KIND OF CONFUSING FOR THIS GAME, BUT...
RULEZ
I THINK, AFTER TODAY, WE CAN DO **ANYTHING!!**
RULEZ
SO WHAT HAPPENS NOW?
YOU BRACE YOURSELF --
FOR A BUTT-KICKING AT **MERLINS AND MEDICS!**
MERLINS & MEDICS
YOU WISH! I **ALWAYS** WIN THAT GAME.

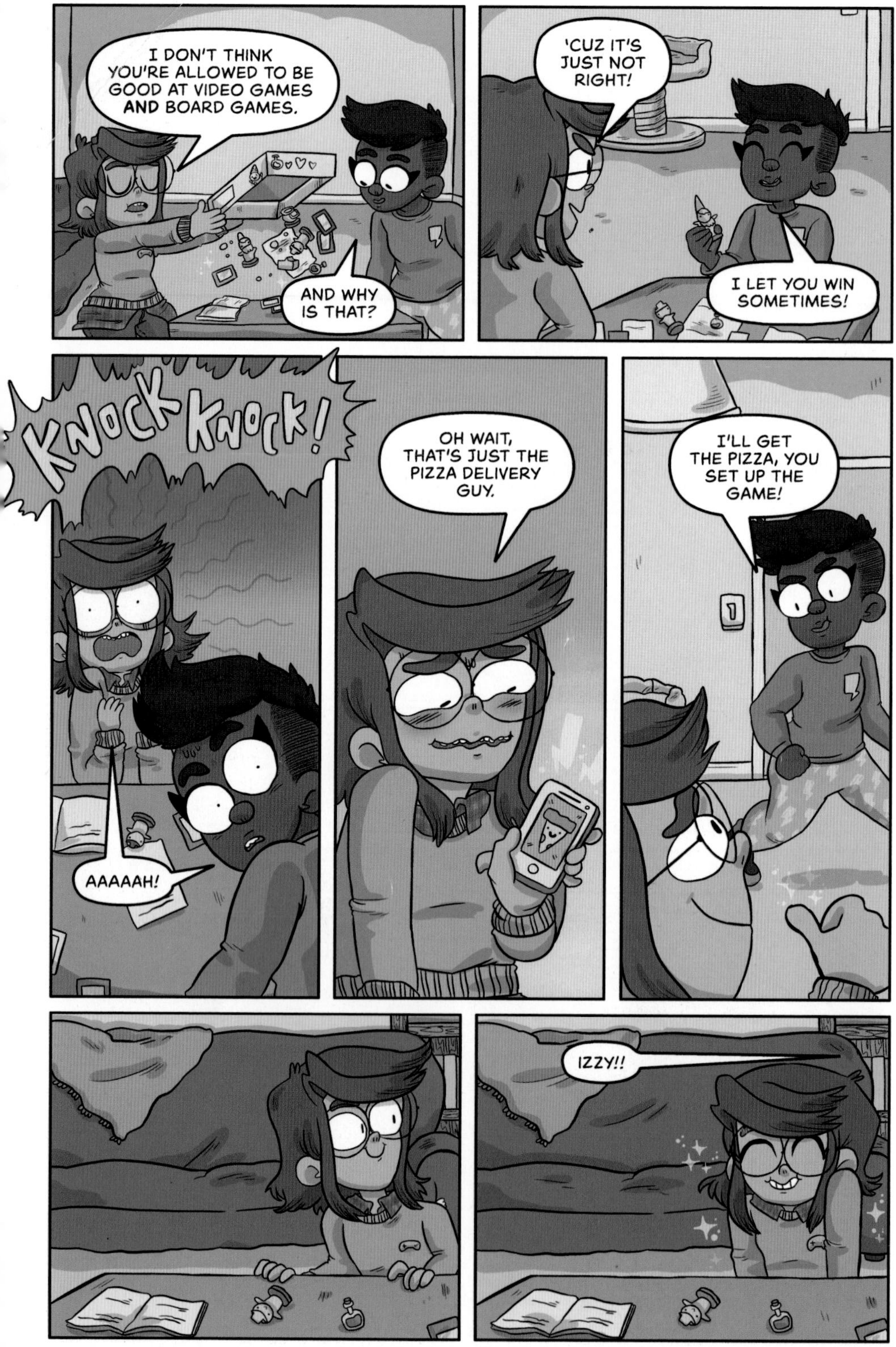
I DON'T THINK YOU'RE ALLOWED TO BE GOOD AT VIDEO GAMES **AND** BOARD GAMES.
AND WHY IS THAT?
'CUZ IT'S JUST NOT RIGHT!
I LET YOU WIN SOMETIMES!
KNOCK KNOCK!
AAAAAH!
OH WAIT, THAT'S JUST THE PIZZA DELIVERY GUY.
I'LL GET THE PIZZA, YOU SET UP THE GAME!
IZZY!!

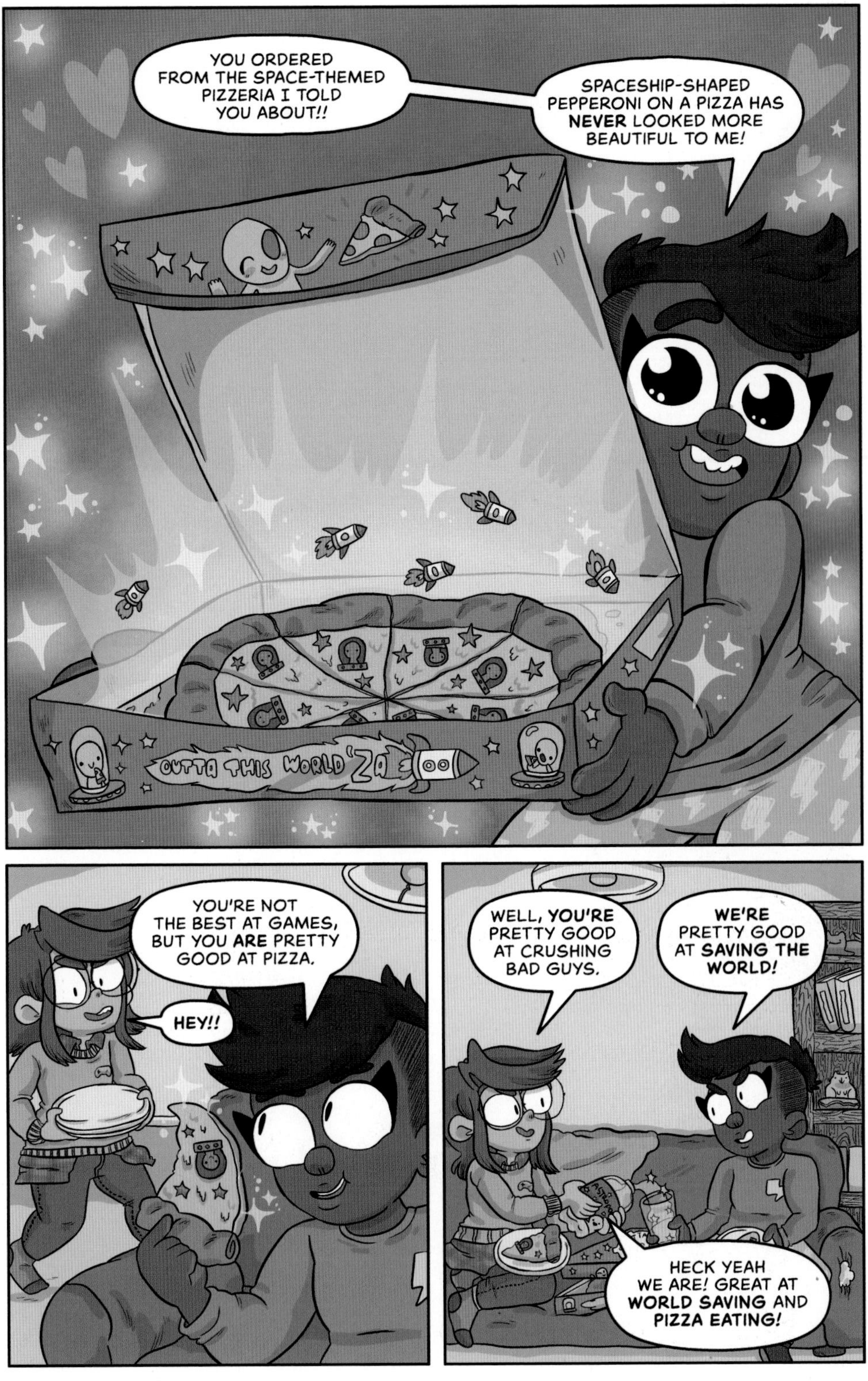
YOU ORDERED FROM THE SPACE-THEMED PIZZERIA I TOLD YOU ABOUT!!
SPACESHIP-SHAPED PEPPERONI ON A PIZZA HAS **NEVER** LOOKED MORE BEAUTIFUL TO ME!
OUTTA THIS WORLD 'ZA
YOU'RE NOT THE BEST AT GAMES, BUT YOU **ARE** PRETTY GOOD AT PIZZA.
HEY!!
WELL, **YOU'RE** PRETTY GOOD AT CRUSHING BAD GUYS.
WE'RE PRETTY GOOD AT **SAVING THE WORLD!**
HECK YEAH WE ARE! GREAT AT **WORLD SAVING** AND **PIZZA EATING!**

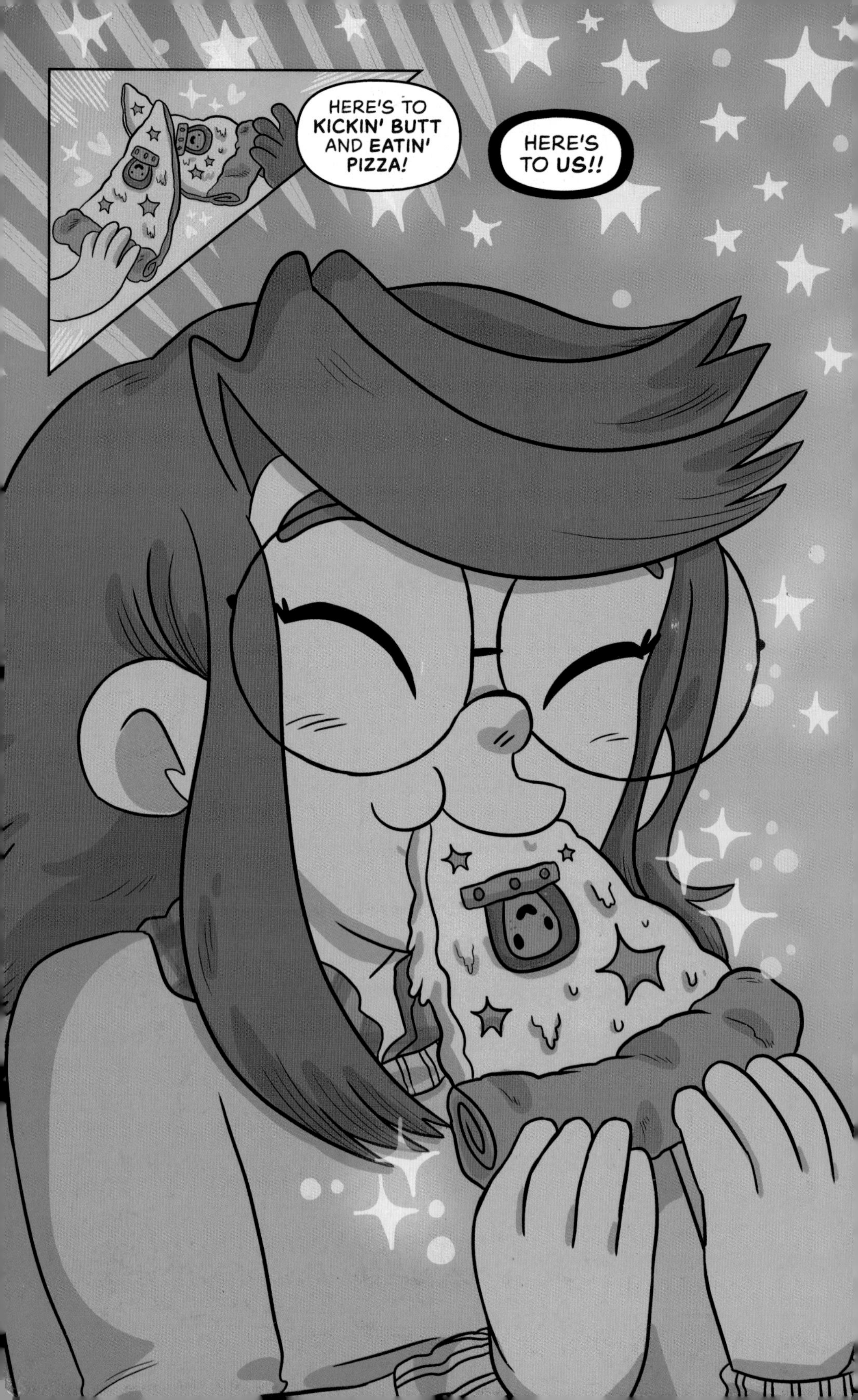
HERE'S TO KICKIN' BUTT AND EATIN' PIZZA!
HERE'S TO US!!

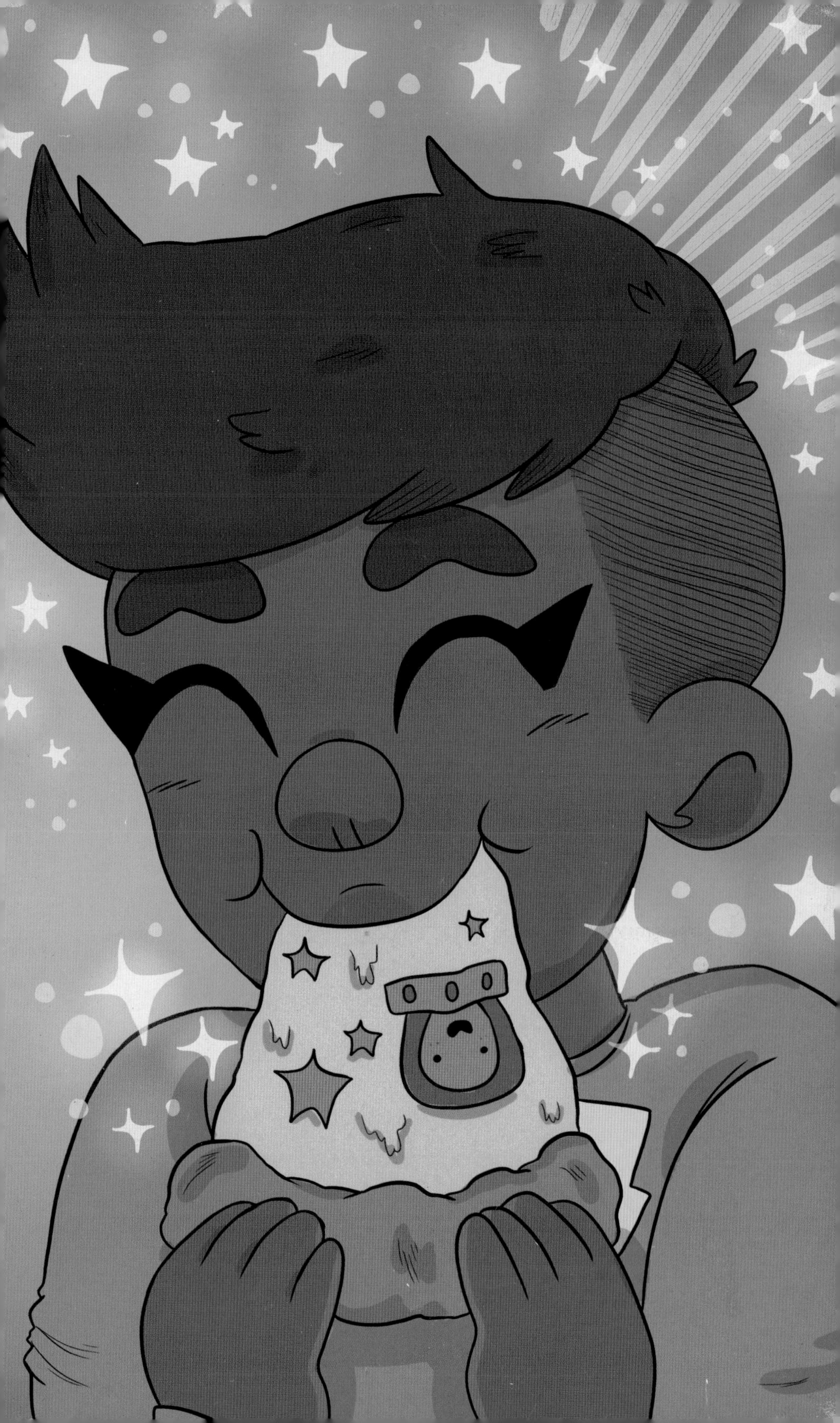

ACKNOWLEDGMENTS

I'd like to thank my parents and family for supporting me and listening to me ramble on about the video games that captured my imagination at a young age.

I'd like to thank my partner, Stef, for helping me figure out the twists and turns in the story early on and for doing a wonderful job in lettering the book, too.

Thanks to my incredible agent, Steven Salpeter, who was instrumental in getting my story out into the world, and the team at Curtis Brown who work their magic behind the scenes.

A huge thanks to Cassandra Pelham Fulton, David Saylor, Phil Falco, and everyone else at Scholastic for helping make this story into an actual real book that exists in the world. Their guidance has been indispensable.

Finally, thanks to my cats for always keeping my lap warm while making this book, and a special thanks to you, for reading this adventure!

ABOUT THE AUTHOR

Sarah Graley is a cartoonist who lives with four cats and a catlike boy in Birmingham, UK. She is the creator of *Kim Reaper*, and the writer and artist for the Rick and Morty comics miniseries *Lil' Poopy Superstar*. She was nominated for the Emerging Talent category at the 2015 British Comic Awards for her long-running diary comic *Our Super Adventure* and original titles *Pizza Witch* and *RentQuest*. Visit Sarah online at sarahgraley.com.